The Sporting Image: '

An anthology of creative writing based upon real-life events in sport

Edited by: Clive Palmer

Co-Authored by:

Clive Palmer, Iain Adams, Ray Physick,
Mitchell J. Larson, Anthony Maher, Joel Rookwood,
James Kenyon, Chris Hughes

The Sporting Image: What If?
An anthology of creative writing based upon real-life events in sport

Edited by: Clive Palmer

University of Central Lancashire

Published By:
SSTO Publications
School of Sport Tourism and The Outdoors
University of Central Lancashire
Preston, Lancashire
PR1 2HE

First published in the United Kingdom in 2010 by:
SSTO Publications
School of Sport, Tourism and The Outdoors
University of Central Lancashire
Preston
Lancashire
PR1 2HE

Produced by Action Publishing Technology Limited
132 Bristol Road Gloucester GL1 5SR

Notice:

The contents of this book as presented are creative stories stemming from interpretations of real-life events. Whilst the accounts have some factual research to underpin them, the outcomes they propose are deliberately fictitious for the purposes of entertainment achieved through developing writing skills and by the use of imagination to create a 'good tale'. They are set out in good faith for the general guidance of student supported research and the promotion of pedagogical discussion in teaching and learning contexts. No liability can be accepted by the Editor or the Co-authors (first or second named) for loss or expense incurred as a result of relying upon particular circumstances or statements made in this book.

ISBN: 978-0-9566270-0-1

SSTO Publications

Contents

See also the previous Sporting Image publication

The sporting image: sports poetry and creative writing.

Edited by Clive Palmer in 2009.

With a *Foreword* by John Lindley

Published by the Centre for Research Informed Teaching, University of Central Lancashire,
Preston,
UK.
ISBN: 978-0-9562343-2-2

Available online from Amazon.co.uk, Play.com and other good bookshops, at,
£5.99.

This book is a collection of sports related poetry and creative writing which stemmed from a university module called The Sporting Image.

Following a poetry writing workshop to help students structure their ideas and poetry writing skills an engaging degree of self-expression about sporting concepts seems to have emerged which we are proud to showcase within these pages.

Many sports are featured including boxing, cricket, football and gymnastics and many issues tackled such as teamwork, comradeship, cheating, beauty and ugliness in sport. Consequently this is a varied compilation which we hope will give the reader as much pleasure to read or even perform, as we have had in producing it.

Journal of Qualitative Research in Sports Studies
ISSN: 1754-2375 (Peer Reviewed)

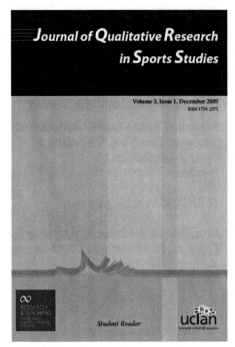

Edited by Clive Palmer

Volume 3, Issue 1, 2009.

Published by the Centre for Research Informed Teaching, University of Central Lancashire,
Preston, UK.
ISBN: 978-0-9562343-7-7

Vol. 3 Available online from:
Amazon.co.uk, Play.com and other good bookshops at £9.99.

Vol 1 and Vol 2 were limited print runs.

The Journal of Qualitative Research in Sports Studies presents a valuable opportunity for students; undergraduates and postgraduates to write mentored publications of their research activities in the sport's world.

The papers are externally reviewed by academics from institutions (UK and overseas) who have an interest in researching sport and Physical Education and who share a similar vision for raising student confidence in their academic writing and encouraging greater involvement with researching sport from a qualitative standpoint. Towards these ends the journal has three central aims which the Editorial Board hope the reader will recognise as educationally valuable in terms of academic quality and student centred support in academia:

(a) To showcase and share student research at either undergraduate or postgraduate level.

(b) Through a process of mentoring and external review, help to improve student's confidence to present their ideas formally.

(c) To create a contemporary resource of qualitative research within the sports world which is accessible to students and informs their ongoing investigations.

If you have any enquiries for a potential submission or topic research, please do not hesitate to contact the editor through the UCLAN website.

Acknowledgements

There are a number of people who I wish to thank for sharing generously their time, energy and enthusiasm to tease the *What If?* publication into existence. First and foremost are the students who embraced the *What If?* challenge so confidently at the outset and provided such a disparate range of topics that we as staff could never have envisaged. Part of the intrigue of this project has been to set imaginations free and then wait to see what comes back. If a reader's curiosity is stirred about the stories on the contents page it stems directly from what did come back from those relatively untethered imaginations. Thank you to the students for their confidence in us to set them on a path of discovery and to some degree, to experiment with an aspect of their final degree assessment - which they might regard now as being worthwhile.

Thank you also to Philip Caveney for running the workshop on creative writing from which some important lessons were learned for stylised writing. Following the workshop I know that Philip gave ongoing support to students and offered an open door for help should it be required; your interest in our project is very much appreciated, thank you.

No small debt of thanks are due to our mentoring co-authors who have shared their wisdom, time and energy with students to make the best of their work; Mitch Larson, Ray Physick, Iain Adams, Joel Rookwood, James Kenyon, Chris Hughes and Anthony Maher. I know they have faced their own challenges in the mentoring process and I thank them all for their confidence in me to guide them towards this finished product of which they should rightly be proud.

Thank you also to John Metcalf and Paul Hall for sharing their stories which are stylised accounts of their lived experiences in sport. The inclusion of these two cameo chapters helps to make a link with the sports world in almost the opposite direction to what the co-authored chapters have done by embracing the creative *What If?* Meeting somewhere between the two may be a sense of reality in sport filtered through a mesh of creative and interpretive writing which might render their accounts all the more accessible and engaging for us.

There have also been a host of proof readers who have volunteered their valuable time to cast a critical eye over drafts of chapters. Their attention to detail and support for various authors is very much appreciated; in particular thank you to Norman Seddon, Val Sellers, Katherine Jones, David Hughes and Mark Hickman, but also to the many other friends, parents and colleagues who have supported students and staff in listening to ideas and reading early drafts of their stories.

For technical and practical support thank you to our publisher; Miles Bailey and his staff at Action Publishing Technology Limited and to John Minten, Head of School for Sport, Tourism and The Outdoors for supporting the *What If?* project towards this final publication.

Lastly, but by no means least, thanks are due to my wife Rin and daughter Grace, not only for colouring in my initial ideas for the cover design but also for tolerating a longer than average distraction from family life that this publication has required for a short while.

Clive Palmer
Cheshire
11th June 2010

Foreword

It's always exciting when something unexpected happens.

When I was first approached to work on some fiction writing with a group of students, based in the Sports Department at UCLAN, I'd be lying if I said I had great expectations for the outcome. After all, so far as I was aware, none of these students had ever tried writing fiction before. And... I'm not being mean or anything, but... well, it's not just something you can have a go at. It takes years and years of dedicated practice. Doesn't it?

But then I went in to do a workshop with the students, taking along what I thought of as a brilliant example of the short story – *Mrs Packletide's Tiger* by Saki (H.H. Munro). I chose it because it so brilliantly packs an absolute wealth of information into its 1,300 words; and in the deliciously bitchy interplay of dialogue, reveals so much about the characters.

The students listened politely enough to what I had to say, and then entered into the practical side of the workshop, where they broke themselves into duos and created fictional sporting characters, around which they wrote alternating lines of dialogue; sort of mini scripts. When it came time to read back what they had written, I had a surprise in store. Every one of the participants exhibited levels of humour and invention that made the workshop an absolute delight to run. I cheered up considerably. Maybe things weren't going to be quite so grim after all.

A little time passed... and then I began to receive the short stories themselves. I started to read through them and quickly realised that it was time to put in my order for a large slice of humble pie.

Here were stories to delight and intrigue the reader... stories that thrilled and amused in equal measure, stories that explored the imagination of the writers, but remained easily accessible to all.. In most cases, the students needed only the lightest of guiding hands to hone their work to a satisfying conclusion. And here too was a valuable lesson for yours truly; that writing is not exclusively the domain of the specialist. Given a little time and encouragement, talent can blossom in the unlikeliest of places.

And now, here's the tangible proof of that success – an actual, honest-to-goodness book featuring 30 short stories to delight and entertain you. The miracle of POD publishing means that the stories can be made available to anyone who's interested in reading them and I am only too happy to recommend them to anyone who enjoys a good read. It only remains for me to thank tutor, Clive Palmer, for getting me involved in the first place and the students themselves, many of whom, should they find themselves struggling to make headway in their chosen field of expertise, might seriously consider seeking careers in literature.

All in all, it's been quite an education.

Philip Caveney
Royal Literary Fellow
University of Central Lancashire
January 2010

Notes on Contributors

First authors

The first named authors are Undergraduate students from the University of Central Lancashire, Preston (except James Kenyon who is from Liverpool Hope University). They are third year students following the Sporting Image module which is open to all those reading sport, however the majority of students opting for this module have a specialism in Sport's Journalism. For many of the students this opportunity to publish their work is valued highly as it may be their first offering for public consumption - although some have benefitted from publishing and reporting as part of work experience placements with local newspapers. In the stories within this volume they have had an opportunity to research an event and tell a story of their own making – or at least interpretation.

Mentoring Co-authors

Clive Palmer is a Senior Lecturer in the School of Sport, Tourism and the Outdoors at the University of Central Lancashire, Preston. An experienced teacher and researcher he was awarded his Ph.D. on Aesthetics in Men's Artistic Gymnastics from Liverpool John Moores University in 2003. He has since written widely in socio-cultural areas of sport, publishing for example, *The Turn to Aesthetics - An Interdisciplinary Exchange of Ideas in Applied and Philosophical Aesthetics* (2008). He is a strong advocate of research informed teaching and actively promotes opportunities to showcase student writing and student research which communicates their experiences and discoveries through the study of sport. He is the Editor in Chief of the *Journal of Qualitative Research in Sports Studies* (1754-2375) and recently edited *The Sporting Image – Sports Poetry and Creative Writing* (2009), which was the first publication stemming from the module The Sporting Image, this What If book being the second. His academic interests include gymnastics, ethnography, aesthetics and the philosophy of sport, Physical Education, sport's pedagogy and Outdoor Education.

Philip Caveney was born in North Wales in 1951 and has been a published author since 1977. His first novel, *The Sins of Rachel Ellis* was an occult mystery, but through the 1980's and 90's, he published a string of hard-hitting thrillers including *Speak No Evil* and *Skin Flicks*. In 2007, he

published his first book for children, *Sebastian Darke: Prince Of Fools*. The book spawned two sequels and has been published in 20 countries around the world. Most recently, he launched the Alec Devlin series – 1920's set tales featuring the adventures of a 15 year old archaeologist. Philip has been the facilitator of the Manchester Writers Workshop for over 25 years, helping writers at all stages of their craft to develop their skills. In 2009, Philip teamed up with the Royal Literary Fund and took over the post of RLF Fellow at University of Central Lancashire where is available to share his knowledge and expertise with students, through a series of 1 to 1 tutorials. For further information please see:
Personal website: http://www.philip-caveney.co.uk/

Anthony Maher received an undergraduate degree in Sports Development with Physical Education from Liverpool John Moores University. He has a Masters degree in the Sociology of Sport and Exercise from the University of Chester, and is currently enrolled as a part-time Ph.D. student at the University of Central Lancashire, where he also works as an Associate Lecturer in Sports Development. The inclusion of pupils with special educational needs in mainstream school physical education was the focus of both his undergraduate and masters theses and he hopes to further build on these projects for his doctorate by looking at this process from the perspective of special educational needs coordinators and learning support assistants. More generally, Anthony's academic interests include the development and structure of modern sport, sociological theory and its application to sport, equality in sport and social research methods. The *What If* volume offers his second piece of published writing, the first being an article review for the *Journal of Qualitative Research in Sports Studies* (Maher, 2009). Together with teaching, research and writing, Anthony also enjoys exercising and travelling.

Joel Rookwood studied Football Science at undergraduate level, followed by Masters degrees in Notational Analysis, Sports Sociology and Sports Management. He has a PhD in football fan culture, and lectures in football studies at Liverpool Hope University where he also runs the Sport Development degree programme. Joel has travelled to 120 countries, 30 of which have included supporting and managing practical and research-based football programmes within a developmental and/or charitable capacity. He has also watched football in many countries across the world and is a member of the English '2 Club' having watched a match in every professional ground in England and Wales. His research interests include fan culture, identity, spectator violence, subcultures, development, peace promotion, social integration and higher education learning and teaching initiatives. He has written numerous papers and book chapters and is the author of *Fan perspectives of football hooliganism: defining, analysing and responding to the British phenomenon and social development in post-conflict communities: building peace through sport in Africa and the Middle East* (2009).

James Kenyon is a recent graduate of Liverpool Hope University and is an ex-student of both Clive Palmer and Joel Rookwood. Having achieved a first class Bachelor's degree in Sport Development and Sports Studies, he is currently completing a Masters degree in Research Methods with a view to enrolling on a Sports Sociology PhD once he has completed his thesis. Despite his relatively new academic career, James has collaborated with both of his ex-lecturers on a number of peer-reviewed publications and academic conferences, and he is also Student Editorial Officer for the *Journal of Qualitative Research in Sports Studies* (1754-2375). During the course of his studies James has been the recipient of Liverpool Hope University's; Deans' List Scholarship Award, Sports Studies Prize and Senior Scholarship Award. James' research interests include; identity (particularly Scouse identity and culture), gangs and gang dynamics, race and racism, ethnography, Olympic values and Olympism and community sport. To complement his academic interest in sport, for the past nine years James has coached a number of sports to some of the most disadvantaged young people living in Liverpool and Sheffield. He is also an avid footballer and plays regularly for his local Saturday-league football team.

Chris Hughes is a recent graduate of University of Central Lancashire - class of 2010, with a Bachelor's degree in Sports Coaching. Following a career as a chef in the hotel and restaurant industry, Chris returned to full-time education in pursuit of stimulation, creativity and learning through a sporting environment. His research interests include ethnography, coaching philosophy, coach decision making and creative writing within sport. He hopes to further his education as a post graduate by studying for an MPhil and PGCE alongside mentoring and developing student led qualitative research. Chris' sporting passion is for football, however, considering his enthusiasm to give anything a go he is currently an extremely frustrated novice rock climber, trying to learn the art of "bouldering".

Iain Adams is a Principal Lecturer in the School of Sport, Tourism and the Outdoors at UCLan, Preston. He worked as a PE teacher in Dorset after gaining a BA in PE/geography from the University of Birmingham and a PGCE from Madeley College. He then won a scholarship to study for a Master's degree and went to the University of North Dakota, USA. Completing an MSc in Sport Psychology, he continued through to his PhD in Platonism and Sport funded by working as the Women's Badminton Coach. This was followed by periods of working, coaching, teaching and consulting in Los Alamos (New Mexico), Jordan, Bahrain, and Indonesia. After returning to the UK from Indonesia, he decided to become a full time pilot, a profession he had worked in part-time since his 17th birthday. Eventually realising he was missing the most important years of his children's growth; he went back into full-time education at UCLan. He developed the module *Sporting Image* to introduce others to his passion of seeking to understand how sport is portrayed in other cultural forms.

Ray Physick is a PhD student at the University of Central Lancashire, his area of study is football and fine art. Ray is also a part-time member of staff at the university. His book, *Played in Liverpool,* was published in 2007 by English Heritage and forms part of English Heritage's *Played in Britain* series (www.playedinbritain.org.uk). Most books about Liverpool sport are football focused but *Played in Liverpool* was the first book to offer an historical analysis of the development of Liverpool sport. *Played in Liverpool* was followed in 2008 by *Boxing Venues of Liverpool,* a book published by the Liverpool Echo. The book looked at the development of Liverpool boxing through three key venues: Pudsey Street, Anfield and the Liverpool Stadium. Ray has also made several contributions to the Encyclopedias of Sport and football in 2001 and 2003. He is a keen football, boxing and cricket fan and has been a Liverpool supporter all his life.

Mitchell J. Larson is Research Fellow in International Business at the University of Central Lancashire Business School. Dr. Larson received his doctorate in History at the University of Wisconsin-Madison (USA) by completing a history of the first two American-style business schools formed in the UK during the 1960s. This project familiarized him with a number of significant historical fields, including British political and economic history, the history of management in the UK and the history of Higher Education. During his post-graduate training he served as a graduate teaching assistant three times with Professor Alfred E. Senn (now emeritus); Senn's module entitled, The Political History of the Modern Olympics introduced him to the history of sport; the business elements of the Olympics and elite sport which have recently become part of his research programme. This volume represents his first entry into the field of teaching-led research.

John Metcalfe is a Senior Lecturer in the School of Sport Tourism and The Outdoors at The University of Central Lancashire, Preston. His main sporting passion is ultra-endurance mountain biking and he has competed in some of the sport's hardest races, including the IditaSport in Alaska, The Great Divide race from Canada to Mexico, and numerous 24 hour solo races. John's research is currently focussed on the physiology of long distance mountain bike racing. He has contributed to many of the country's mountain bike magazines and is the author of Mountain Bike Fitness Training.

Paul Hall is an International Gymnastics Judge and Coach, currently running the Huntingdon Gymnastics Club, Cambridgeshire, and working with the Senior Great Britain Men's Squad towards the London Olympics in 2012. With over 20 years of coaching experience, Paul has consistently produced gymnasts at Commonwealth, European, World and Olympic level. He has coached over 12 British Champions, both in Men's and Women's Artistic Gymnastics, many of whom have gone on to win medals at International level. He is Coach to twice European Champion and World Medallist, Louis Smith, who, in 2008, created history by producing a bronze medal on the Pommel Horse at the Beijing Olympic Games, and is also the Coach to Daniel Keatings, current World All Around Silver Medallist in London, 2009. Paul travels extensively with his sport and is a Lecturer with the International Gymnastics Federation, having conducted courses in Saudi Arabia, North Korea, Egypt and Europe. He has published technical papers on gymnastics as well as various accounts of extraordinary events that have enriched his life. Outside of the gym Paul enjoys climbing, writing, and exploring nature.

Introduction

"Please Read Me". Just imagine: reading, writing and researching about the lived experience in sport - what if...

Clive Palmer

This publication originates from an undergraduate module at the University of Central Lancashire called *The Sporting Image*. The module's cohort comprised in the main of third year students reading for Sports Journalism and some for Sports Studies degrees. The focus of the module being upon iconic features in sport; characters, events, artefacts and images etc. which can be discussed critically from an aesthetic and cultural point of view.

This is the second publication from the module following *"The Sporting Image, Sports Poetry and Creative Writing"* (Palmer, 2009) which was supported by a [sports] poetry writing workshop. Many of the poems transpired to be auto-biographical in nature, or biographical of other's experiences in sport as well as there being a clear aesthetic design to that kind of writing and importantly, its performance. The storytelling theme of the poems began to merge into longer narratives of the lived experience, see Adamson (2009: 51-53), Randall (2009: 56), Wilson (2009: 75-79) and Hall (2009a: 80-88) which has an increasing relevance to research in socio-cultural aspects of sport. There were over 65 poems included in the book and admittedly some were better than others. To this end, a valuable aspect of our teaching was about some aesthetic criteria for this genre of writing, thereby allowing students to make informed judgements about the quality of their own and other's work - in this case poetry (2009). The same message about making reasoned, informed aesthetic judgments of quality in the short story was true for the *What If?* project for the 2010 cohort. Sparkes (2009: 304), on the topic of "representational forms and the issue of quality", urges similarly for the importance of equipping the author/reader with some aesthetic knowledge for reasoning about how good or otherwise a stylised personal narrative or realist tale might be. Pedagogically the poetry endeavour seemed to be not only well justified but extremely valuable for student learning which positively challenged their intellectual and writing skills for later life – and therefore was worth repeating in some way.

As a development on from the poetry book, the longer research-narrative concept gave staff the idea that students might compose short stories which could become re-interpretations about an aspect of sport to demonstrate their creative writing skills. The learning of such writing skills, even at an introductory level, would be demanding and educationally worthwhile in their own right. Additionally the stories would have to be founded upon extensive background research to be plausible and hopefully, as third year students they would have the research bit honed to perfection. The idea being that for an imaginative story to be told, the ending re-written or the new thread to be plausible, the research would have to be all the more thorough, which could only be a good thing by any educator's standards. And so, *What If?* was born, or rather, it was carved!

Having formulated the idea my next step was to track down a professional novelist who would be willing to lead a writing workshop for creative short stories in the subject of Sport, alien to him as it turned out, with 50 completely novice but eager third year students... all with a view to publication - easy! After a short but critical search, critical for me that is, I was very lucky and fortunate to meet Philip Caveney, a professional novelist working on secondment in Higher Education who ran a fantastic workshop for us. This workshop became the foundation for the *What If?* publication. From that point on, ideas for chapters, potential collaborations and invited 'cameo' stories snowballed to flesh out the current table of contents.

Overview of contents

Following the acknowledgements there is a succinct but informative Foreword from Philip Caveney; conciseness being part of his criterion for quality in literature. Philip was UCLAN's Royal Literary Fellow in-residence and his brief account provides an interesting insight to his perception of the task, and of me probably, for making this unusual request of his skills, time and energy.

Introduction

The idea behind the phrase "Please Read Me" in the title, as well as being an obvious request to the reader, is adapted from Lewis Carroll's *Alice's Adventures in Wonderland* when Alice was faced with a bottle which said "Drink Me" on its label (Carroll, 1865: 29). She drank the contents of the bottle and embarked upon a wonderful adventure as the book's title suggests. It is my interest in the storytelling aspect that I mean to emphasize and draw parallels with our efforts in the *What If?* publication.

But it is also to point out that Carroll's (1865) story has a philosophical subtext and that similarly, all the stories in *What If?* have a biographical or ethnographic subtext of research writing. Carroll (1865) seems to have achieved this philosophical dimension by confronting Alice with dilemmas and decisions along her journey. 'What ought she do?' when given a choice, mulling over a few options and envisaging the what ifs... The scenarios which Carroll places Alice in may play-out some ethical, moral and aesthetic scenarios for those who wish to pick up on them. Correspondingly, many of the *What If?* stories leave 'paper trails' of thought or possibilities for broader consideration should the curious student, researcher or philosopher wish to follow their 'scent'.

The use of the imagination and storytelling to facilitate the teaching of more complex theory may be a powerful mode of educating which appeals to us as mentoring co-authors working in Higher Education. On this educative note the name "Lewis Carroll" was a pseudonym of Charles Lutwidge Dodgson who was a Don at Christ Church College in Oxford where he taught all his working life from 1849 to 1881 (born 1832; died 1898). A contrasting publication in this vein of imagination/theory/storytelling may be Jostein Gaarder's *Sophie's World* (1996) which is more of a philosophy text 'up front' with a story loosely wrapped around it. Gaarder (1996) intends to teach us philosophy from the outset, albeit as may be comprehended through the eyes of an enquiring child. *Alice's Adventures in Wonderland* seemingly did not set out to teach such things and nor really did *What If?* However, the avenues of thought are there to be explored.

Mini-autobiographies: mentors and education

As part of *What If?*'s general introduction - before the stories commence, the mentoring co-authors have been invited to tell their own stories about;

- their conceptions of the task,
- the challenges presented for them about mentoring undergraduate writing,
- and to tell something of their educational journey in life.

These mini-autobiographies are offered to help establish a context for how the chapters may have been interpreted. The idea being that their take on a student's creative account may be imbued with their life history, their view of the world, and that it might be interesting to see what that was like, even if we are only permitted a selective snippet. For example, Ray Physick is a published football and boxing historian which will inevitably have had some influence upon his work with Ashley Walker in a chapter entitled *West*

3

Ham vs Millwall – a football tragedy (Chpt. 23). A more appropriate marriage between pugilism, football and research one could not imagine for these two London-based rivals in football, their respective 'supporters' being noted for having worked out their differences with their fists in the past. This insight to the mentoring co-author's knowledge and experience may be seen very rarely in other texts and *What If?* could be all the more unusual for it. It is fair to say that a student's blue-print of life history may have been just as influential for him or her when conceiving of their story - which would be an interesting avenue of research to follow at a later date. Consequently, the section of mini-auto-biographies, which I had originally called the Learning and Teaching Mini-Chapters for want of a better phrase, creates a rich 'educational tapestry' indicating the breadth and depth of expertise which has been supportively brought to bear upon the 'raw material' to present the finished chapters. For the curious there is more pedagogical discussion on the issues of mentoring by co-authors (second named) under the section *Mentoring and collaboration – who's learning from whom?* below. What is worthy of note at this point, however, were the reports from mentors that their learning curve on this task was perhaps as steep and challenging as it may have been for the students to write the stories in the first place, but for different reasons. In many cases, deep critical reflection about the quality of product elicited from our educative efforts in Higher Education generally were provoked, whilst others found the opportunity to write in this style liberating, demanding and enjoyable – but rarely 'easy'. Personal interpretations of situations and events would shape the final chapters; "it all depends on your perspective" as they say and "what you see depends on where you stand". To begin to shed some light upon how the mentors might have seen things, the Notes on Contributors may be an interesting place to start to explore the unique and distinctive stock of experience shared with students to make the best of their work.

Dual-authored chapters

The dual authored chapters, 27 in all, form the main body of the book and range enormously in the subjects they tackle, the characters portrayed and in historical settings. Consequently there is no particular ordering of these chapters by topic or subject area which might have otherwise appeared false or contrived. Rather they appear pretty much in the order that they were sent to me as editor, so a chronological grouping of sorts does exist being indicated by clusters of chapters by mentoring co-authors.

The title of each chapter and the phrasing of its opening line is designed to give a hint of what adventures might lie within – this being a tactic learned from Philip's workshop. Within each dual-authored chapter there is a common structure that has been followed for consistency; they are basically in two sections, a Research Preface followed by a Creative Story. The Title leads directly into the Research Preface. The Research Preface is the investigatory element to set the scene for the Creative Story. Mentoring co-authors are always second named in the chapters with the originating authors first named. The order is significant as it distinguishes the pedagogical investment made by each author. The Creative Story brings the chapter to a close... posing for the reader a tantalising "what if?" References appear at the end of the Research Preface which in some cases, for example Chapters 3 and 16, take the form of a guided bibliography where the mentor has developed his research ideas to incorporate some guidance notes in the reference list. This will contain some additional information about the sources which may be considered an active part of the chapter to tell more comprehensively the development of real-life events, highlighting the relevance of occurrences, or the divergence of the imaginative story from those chronicled events.

Some stories have developed from genuine first hand accounts, for example the chapters by Paul Gorst (Chpt. 6) and Elisa Langton (Chpt. 7). Paul Gorst's story *Gerrard goes to jail* is based upon his own newspaper reports which he made as a student on work-placement during his Sports Journalism degree. He was fortunate enough to be present at Steven Gerrard's trial in Liverpool Crown Court and then later, to integrate his own reports with others from the media to re-live the development of the case hearings towards a verdict. His creative story starts as the court case closes. By contrast, Elisa Langton's chapter is a moving account of the lived experience but told through the eyes of another. Her re-telling of her Uncle Kevin's experiences at Hillsborough on the day of the stadium disaster is fast paced and seeded with potential loss. Gripping stuff. I have enjoyed reading all the chapters and as I write I am acutely aware of the editorial privilege of being the only person to have a full overview of the book – until its publication.

Single authored 'cameo' chapters

Finally there are three single authored 'cameo' chapters at the end of the book which are auto-biographical in nature. All three are stylised accounts of events in real-life which through the literary skills of their authors permit a sense of 'gritty reality', closeness and personal insight to their experiences which a purely descriptive report might fail to capture and impart. I am extremely grateful to John Metcalfe and to Paul Hall for sharing their stories with us as each account emphasizes a valuable sense of journeying, of being there and coping with social challenge in a sporting context. We have much to learn from them, and perhaps to question from these tales. They seemingly also have great relevance to us as researchers of experiences in sport, but particularly because in these cases, the authors have used creative writing skills in their reflective accounts. This tactic in writing seems to have some advantages for the reader such as promoting interest in their story, cultivating greater sympathy with the person and developing curiosity about the outcome of events. All of these may be useful strategies for the socio-cultural investigator who wishes to communicate his discoveries to others. In fact John Metcalfe mentioned having as much fun if not more, while composing his tongue-in-cheek reflection as he did during the adventure itself, such may be the motivation to articulate his experiences in an effective and engaging way. Paul Hall, a man ready for an adventure at the drop of a hat, shares in dry comedic fashion his experiences of top-level gymnastics coaching in North Korea. This may be an enviable glimpse in to an otherwise closed world that the rest of the sporting community have been deprived of until now, should they wish to look. I know it was certainly an eye-opener for Paul – read the chapter and it will open your eyes too!

The closing chapter (Chpt. 30) is about my experiences at *Bash Street School* which becomes auto-ethnographic in nature because it is linked to my first account in the following section of this Introduction entitled *Essex boys can't write*. The *Bash Street School* story is a branch line of early experiences in Physical Education which was not explored in *Essex boys can't write*. *Bash Street School* is a richer, more descriptive, and hopefully vivid account of some experiences in education which deliberately says more i.e. has greater detail about a shorter passage of time compared to the longer span of time chronicled in the preceding *Essex boys can't write*. Limitations and opportunities for gaining a fuller picture of the scene at *Bash Street School* are also discussed which may lift the passage towards one of socio-cultural research rather than pure autobiography or creative short story. I have deliberately attempted to stylise the chapter which could be described as comic/tragic/realist bound up with repetition of themes to carry the story along. For example, there are repeated references to pirates and swashbuckling seafaring types and further cross reference in pertinent places to seminal films such as Angels with Dirty Faces (1938) (in *Essex boys can't write*) and A Few Good Men (1992) (in *Bash Street School*) which may reveal more aspects about my character than if I simply tried to describe my interests.

Sonic engagement: I have also attempted to engage the senses in *Bash Street School*, reflecting upon my corporeal experiences of being on the receiving end of the Whacking Stick (self explanatory). Sparkes (2009b) explores the importance of acknowledging data from the senses (sight, sound, touch, taste and smell) for achieving a more comprehensive understanding of human experience and that this seemingly needs to be established more effectively in "good" qualitative research. As an aside, for an interesting example of storytelling using visual data in qualitative research see Rookwood and Palmer, (2009a) - a story without words - which is complemented by a critical discussion about the application of visual data and its opportunities and limitations in field research, see Rookwood and Palmer (2009b). Now, back to *Bash Street School*: a stylistic feature of repetition was used to create a sonic occurrence with many "WHACKs" appearing in the text. It was the noise of the whack that was significant to me at the time, along with the other sounds and smells which constituted this part of my PE experience. As they say, "pain is temporary!" but the memories seemed to last a lot longer for me. The WHACKings were always dispensed in an echoing corridor accompanied by varying "ouches", "shouts" and "wails", or conversely there were the aspirant-manly "whimpers" indicating a non-verbal willingness to "just take it like a man" and a complicit 'deal' with the whacker: an "I'll shut up if you'll just get on with it so we can get on with the PE lesson", kind of thing. My PE was really quite a sensual experience! More of a Physical Experience than a Physical Education one might say.

Rice (2003: 8) emphasized the importance of sound in human experience in terms of both knowledge and imagination claiming that "there was an immediate relevance of sonic meaning to ethnographic enquiry". This was developed further by Bull and Black (2003: 3) who urged for a concept of "deep listening" that could make us rethink the following in our worlds:

> The meaning, nature and significance of our social experience; our relation to community; our relational experiences; how we relate to others, ourselves and the spaces and places we inhabit; and our relationship to power.

Bull and Black's (2003) comments above appear to have summed up quite accurately what was occurring for me on the receiving end of that Whacking

Stick over 20 years before their publication. An interesting observation is that I have had the opportunity to read my chapter aloud - to 'perform' it to colleagues during which I smashed my plastic ruler to bits on the desk as a result of re-enacting the noisy WHACKS. At the start of my reading I introduced the concept of the WHACK by saying the word "WHACK" and immediately followed it with a hard, resounding slap on the desk with my ruler. With the association between the word and the noise made I dropped the verbalised "WHACK" and replaced it with the shocking noise and physical action of my right arm poised to whip. My ruler gradually disintegrated like a cartoon swordsman who gets his weapon chopped down until he's left with just a stump in his hand. The sense of loss in my story was palpable for the listeners and this seemed to be embodied by the gradual demise of my ruler. This reading performance appeared to be quite a moving experience for my two colleagues (and for me) who reported a form of deep reflective listening as I read my way through the piece. They were even anticipating the noise as I raised my right arm to thrash my desk once more. I had therefore built into my story an opportunity for sound to be heard, felt and reflected upon. Other than that, *Bash Street School* is merely a story seeking your consideration as it may have some resonance with readers about their own PE experiences. It is hoped that for those students who may aspire to teach PE that this chapter provides some pause for thought in their determined mission to become qualified teachers. I have recounted the tale verbally several times in my lectures over the years to good effect for those who cared to listen and so have taken this opportunity to commit it to paper in the hopes that it might promote a positive effect for teaching Physical Education and Sports Pedagogy.

Upon the theme of engaging the senses, dialogue features prominently in all the chapters and this may pre-dispose them to "live performance" allowing a deeper level of engagement with the experiences portrayed through visual and aural means. For example, the chapter by Robert Bartlett (Chpt 1) about Aron Ralston who cut his arm off in order to survive whilst on a trek would lend itself to reading and acting out in some way, or even Michael Glover's (Chpt 8) account of Mike Tyson having a guardian angel might be interesting forays into verbal oration and visual performance. Such an undertaking would have immediate relevance to our teaching within the Sporting Image module but could also have wider relevance for how research data of the lived experience might be acted out in the form of "ethnodrama" (Saldana, 1999; Barone, 2002; Sparkes, 2002). Ethnodrama is another representational form of telling a story more vividly by physically re-enacting it. According to Sparkes (2002) an ethnodrama evolves when data gathered in the field are transformed into theatrical scripts and performance pieces. Interestingly such a blurring of boundaries in research and engagement with a new expressive form would necessitate a further set of aesthetic criteria to be employed - theatrical criteria in this case - to make informed judgements of quality about the research undertaken and the performance itself. Could the reporting/portrayal of good research become marred by poor acting skills and vice-versa?

However, in general support of creative writing within research is Tierney (2002: 385) who suggests that qualitative researchers might broaden the narrative strategies they employ so that their texts are "built more in relation to fiction and storytelling, rather than in response to the norms of science and logical empiricism", and this may extend to reading them out aloud for an audience to contemplate.

Setting the scene:
"What's this, *What If?* all about then?" said the curious man in the pub,
"Agro"... replied the student.

"CONFLICT and DIALOGUE" were the two key messages we learned from the writing workshop which seemed to free up the student's imagination to attack their stories with gusto. Philip assured us that conflict plays a central role in the majority of good novel writing which seemed to raise the student's spirits no end. Mindful of their intended careers, perhaps the opportunity for grinding axes and dishing the dirt in sport was the only spark they needed to ignite their enthusiasm for this task.

"There has to be a sense of loss or injustice to maintain interest and develop a plot towards a good ending", Philip said.

The antithesis being that a nice story may be just a dull story to tell – why bother with that? Additionally, understanding the role of dialogue was also crucial in that the storyline and events surrounding it could be carried through characterised speech. This would help to move the story on quickly instead of having descriptive passages of "this happened" and then "that happened" etc. A useful and practical point here also for the students was "not to have too many characters in their story", in order to prevent the dialogue (and the reader) from becoming confused; the reader would not know who was saying what to whom. In the outcome, most of the stories kept to two main characters about whom a plot develops. A few other writing exercises saw the students marginally equipped as 'novelists' and brimming with confidence to re-appraise and re-write any sporting event, personality or occurrence that seemed to be fair game for their inventive imaginations. I must confess that after the workshop I was a little curious as to what might come back in response. All I could do was prepare them the best I could and set them off, like a nervous but optimistic parent setting their child 'free' to ride a bike without stabilisers for the first time. It is not without some sense of risk that we can sometimes take action; if the child fell off, failing in his or her task, the child, and probably onlookers, might blame the parent for poor judgement. Might the same fate lay-in-wait for me on the *What If?* project? It quickly transpired that the students had embraced the task with considerable enthusiasm and that an impressive range of sporting cheats, thugs, losers (and a few footballers) would be getting their comeuppances and that some pure-as-the-driven-snow sporting personalities would suddenly have skeletons in the cupboard leading to scandalous expulsion from their worlds. Their responses included pretty much everything else in-between when the "good turned bad" or the ostensibly dubious character "turns good" in the end, replete with tragedies, mysteries, real-life tales and injustices settled, all potentially served up to a media-hungry public - it was a veritable journalist's heaven.

To set the ball rolling we had an example of a potential *What If?* circumstance which was to ask, What if Jesse Owens had been white? From there the student would be required to research some aspects of Hitler's attitudes towards black and ethnic minorities, (which is not difficult if you scrape around a bit!!!) and then to construct a story centred upon the athletics events in Berlin in 1936 (eg. Mandell, 1971, *The Nazi Olympics*). There were also some published examples of work which helped to frame our intent for this project which I think were helpful for the students in our pedagogic quest.

In preparation for the module I had read Bernard Cornwell's graphic novel about the Battle of Agincourt (Cornwell, 2008) when the King's archers, although hugely outnumbered by the French won the day in an extremely bloody battle in Northern France at a place called Azincourt, a name which he adopted as the title of his book. There are three significant features about Cornwell's (2008) novel that related to us: first that the book was richly descriptive and used dialogue to lead the story; secondly that the full account is an interpretation of events from an archer's point of view; and thirdly that there is an extensive body of research included in the volume revealing Cornwell's underpinning investigation to tell the tale. Perfect,

10

apart from the fact that it was well over 500 pages long and no student would ever read that much! Whilst it was bulging with conflict it was not about sport (although it was a form of competition) but it served to indicate well what we wanted in the *What If?* project.

Significantly there has already been a book of *What If?* published, now on a second edition which features stories from historians that re-interpret events and suggest new possibilities and outcomes to high profile instances in history (Cowley, 2002). Some gems within Cowley's (2002) volume include; *Pontius Pilate Saves Jesus – Christianity without the crucifixion* (Eire, 2002) and *Enigma Uncracked – the Allies fail to break the German cipher machine* (Kahn, 2002) and many other great stories but nothing on sport (!) and no supporting body of research, however it was a useful piece in the initial jigsaw of guidance that we were piecing together.

Two further books of high adventure and daring-do were illustrative for the group. These were Heinrich Harrer's *The White Spider* (1976) which is his account of the first ascent of the north face of the Eiger in 1938 and Bob Langley's (1982) classic *Traverse of the Gods* which is a mountaineering adventure set in World War II that attributes the second ascent of the Eiger in 1945 to a Nazi Mountaineering Force. The titles of both books are taken from the names of pitches of climbing on the north face of the Eiger. Harrer, climber extraordinaire and a German military man, omits this second successful ascent from the back of his book, which has a researched chronology of all the ascents made on the north face since 1935 – perhaps he was biased? This may be because the controversial second ascent was shrouded in mystery, it being a "top-secret military mission", a behind-enemy-lines scenario which had vital implications for the development of the atomic bomb. The plot thickens! Heinrich Harrer's omission may also be because Harrer at the time was being held by the English in a prisoner of war camp in northern India where upon he escaped his captors and spent the next Seven Years in Tibet (1988). That is, he was never there (!) and perhaps crucially, the Nazi Mountaineering Force were never officially there either. A good picture of storytelling potential was developing for the students now stemming from these books of adventure, escape and survival. *The White Spider* was backed by research and a wealth of life experience, but also complemented by a very convincing novel which was probably backed by even greater research to enhance its plausibility with the original account by Harrer. Bob Langley's (1982) *Traverse of the Gods* is of course riddled with juicy conflict and even softened with a compassionate love story which lulls the reader to believe in the 'what if' that he poses. However,

11

whilst Bob Langley was a seasoned journalist and TV presenter he was not a sports journalist and whilst mountaineering may be "sporty", it's not really a Sport that was followed by any of these students. I had a little way to go yet before I was satisfied that I had done all I could to set them off on their journeys.

There were four other hopefully-useful texts to highlight to the students before the full force of their imaginations could be set free to wreak havoc in sport's literary world. This was to ensure with a reasonable level of confidence that skilfully composed, clearly reasoned and well researched drafts would appear before me six weeks later. Their opportunity to think, write, draft and re-draft was relatively short so my guidance and the students' preparation could not be left to the last minute. It was not a case of "anything goes" for the *What If?* piece. I also wanted to cement the academic relevance of the task and the standards required in terms of writing for publication, research in socio-cultural contexts and in sports journalism for them.

First, that as Editor of the *Journal of Qualitative Research in Sports Studies* I was very experienced in supporting student writing for publication and suggested that they might read this for appropriate academic presentation of their research preface. I also pointed out that every article within that journal is dual authored in a similar way that their chapters would appear and that many of the articles also come from like-undergraduates. Secondly was an edited book called *Talking Bodies* (Sparkes and Silvennionen, 1999) which contains auto-ethnographies; personal accounts of trials and tribulations in and around sport, which demonstrate a style of writing that students may not have considered in their studies before. Thirdly was a book entitled *Playgrounds of the Gods* (Stafford, 2008), which was referred to in conjunction with *Talking Bodies* (Sparkes and Silvennionen, 1999), to make new sense of the experiences which Stafford (2008) describes. The purpose of this combination was to broaden the students' horizons about what kinds of discussion and writing style might be possible in *What If?* - particularly if they visited the chapter by Peter Swan for his dry-witted observations of people in changing rooms – all scrotums and towels! (Swan, 1999). The last book was Joan Ryan's (1996) *Little Girls in Pretty Boxes* discussed below.

The book *Playgrounds of the Gods* by Ian Stafford (2008) featured a personal, real-life account of experiencing many different sports at elite levels. These included football, squash, athletics, rugby union, rowing, cricket and boxing – at last a recognisable menu of activities that these students could relate to. As a bonus, Ian Stafford is also a seasoned sports journalist which seemed to tick an important box for this discerning group. Unfortunately there is no chapter of supporting research for this book, it was therefore my pedagogical responsibility to point the students towards some. *Playgrounds of the Gods* is an engaging story about a 34 year old sports fanatic who wanted to believe that he was not too old to keep up with elite sportspeople at their own game. Totally preoccupied with his health and fitness and the concept of his former self as a strong, capable and physically literate professional, Stafford seemed to be worried at this juncture in his life that he might not be able to 'cut it' anymore as a credible sportsman. His commitment and undertaking seems to have been a case of "it's now or never". At 34, a major threshold to middle age as he saw it, he was concerned about his 'rapid onset' of aging, physically and socially. For example, he was becoming aware of his body's ability to store fat reserves whether he wanted them or not and the fact that his nine year-old daughter regarded him as "old" and "past it" frustrated him; he was clearly not ready for the pipe and slippers just yet. He committed himself to a rigorous training regime and commented that, "slowly my weight began to fall and muscles began to appear, like small animals emerging from a long and deep hibernation" (Stafford, 2008: 16). At his stage of life he seemed to appreciate that his body may be stagnating; it was not capable of all it used to accomplish with relative ease and that these challenges might restore something of his former self. However he comes to realise that the injuries and hardship endured might actually now be accelerating the aging process somewhat. But he was happy, he was living his dream and for a while at least he got to experience life as a top sports person. Interestingly, what Stafford (2008: 256) does offer by way of an appendix is an itemised list of persistent injuries sustained from each sport and lived with as he progressed from one to the next, for example,

> *Rugby:* sprained left pectoral muscle; sprained ligaments in left ring finger; new muscle tear in right calf; cut and bruised knees; sore and flaky ears.

> *Boxing:* return of sprained left pectoral muscle; cut nose, mouth and lips; concussion - dizziness nausea and headaches; sprained left thumb; suspected trapped nerve in neck causing subsequent faintness [blackouts].

This list of body-brokenness and fear/acknowledgement of the aging process that Stafford (2008) seems to have locked horns with has been explored in depth by some researchers to shed light upon the experience of "physical alteration" in relation to the social worlds they may inhabit. For example, Andrew Sparkes' *Fragile body-self* (1999a) and *When I am old I will...* [in press] are two auto-ethnographies about an aging, breaking body in mid-life trying to regain some muscular form, and perhaps credibility, at a local fitness gym. Burdened with memories of his former self, a most capable sportsman, Sparkes analyses his creaking body that now causes deep critical reflection on a social state of affairs that is perceived to reject him – or is at least one he is uncomfortable in and appears not to embrace him. This seems to create a sense of anguish for Sparkes whose 'agile persona' now occupies a body whose inadequacies, as he may see them, are revealed publicly. An aspect of critical interest to Sparkes, albeit frustrating for him, seems to be the divergence between how he perceived himself to 'fit in' to sport socially in the past and how he perceives himself to 'fit in' now – i.e. on the periphery, like a visitor. They are seemingly two different stories – telling almost of completely different lives.

Then there is Denison's (1999a) auto-ethnography which reveals how he as a young man aspired to be an international middle distance runner. He trained hard and revered the giants on the major Athletics stage; even saw himself being there alongside them. But then he describes his sombre personal torment, when he abandoned his dream upon realising that he probably did not have the ability to compete at that level. He had it all planned out in his head and there is almost a sense of bereavement for a life lost - he would have to find something else to do with his existence now. Also, Denison's (1999b) second contribution is a collection of short ethnographies which build up a picture of sporting excellence through the ages, from childhood to parenthood. The child thinks of nothing else but playing rugby for his national side, the New Zealand All Blacks, and discovers that his father did exactly that in the 1970s. The child is curious about his father's lack of encouragement to repeat the honour, whilst his father has been nursing a devastating knee injury since 1972 which forced him to retire from playing the game. This had left him barely able to walk. "Train for a career or play the game" was the question the father faced as a young man. He chose the game forsaking the career which, as things turned out for him, meant drifting from job to job in short term employment for the rest of his life. Following his knee trauma he had to reconstruct his sense of being, find a way of getting along with his injuries and think about what he might advise his son to do if the same situation ever arose. "Train for a career or play the game..." the dilemma is highlighted for us to contemplate.

A number of researchers' investigations about reconstructions of self-identity and self-worth have focused on people with more extreme injuries such as rugby players who, either through their sport or other circumstances became paraplegic (Sparkes and Smith, 1999; Kleiber and Hutchinson, 1999). These accounts reveal some of the challenges for the victims to re-build their identities when they had already established firm ideas about masculinity and what men should be able to do, which typically did not include their new appendage of a wheelchair following spinal cord injury. The studies explore the personal and social journeys of this dramatic physical alteration; the question begged of the victims was not What If? but What Now? The conflict often lay within themselves or against society – or both. (See also Smith, 2008).

[Further interesting academic references to develop this general theme may be to Henning Eichburg's work which could be described broadly as a phenomenology of human movement, energy and societal interaction. This sweeping definition is so general that it is probably inaccurate although some initial probing of Eichburg (2009a; 2009b), whose accounts of "Fitness on the Market" and the "People's Academies and Sport: Towards a Philosophy of Bodily Education" would have great relevance to the literature being discussed above - see references].

Lastly, recommended to the students was the moving biography by Joan Ryan (1996) *Little Girls in Pretty Boxes* which is about female gymnasts and ice skaters in the USA competing for places on their national team to get to the 'big prize'; the Olympics. Ryan, also a sports journalist reporting for the San Francisco Chronicle, conducted nearly 100 interviews with performers, parents, coaches and other support staff. She presents a fairly grim picture of the degrading health of the young elite performers and the actions of the coaches and parents which seemed not only to instigate the situations of abuse but maintain and promote them. A chronic deception of appearance is at work in these stories; the outward display of beauty and health conceals the actually broken and failing bodies which have been sacrificed by their owners for the greater cause – in search of Gold. These tales are disturbing to say the least. Gymnasts of 12-16 years would be training 40-60 hours a week, working through the pain of performing with hairline fractures in their bones, the result of severe long term dieting and other problems associated with malnourishment such as stunted growth. There was also the destructive psychological trauma which accompanies the deception - obsessions with weight and being picked for the team – which get out of control and sometimes lead to extreme rehab or even death. In

Ryan's (1996) eyes, Coach Bela Karolyi was at the root of many of the problems reported to her during her research. Accounts of bullying, verbal abuse, attempted suicide, sexual abuse by coaches and parents and a number of sad and avoidable deaths from bulimia occurred around his direct influence. Karolyi seemed to care only for medal success at the Olympics and would take the quickest route to get there, at whatever cost. There also is one disturbing account of parents who signed over guardianship of their daughter to an ice skating coach, thinking that he would make better decisions for her welfare and progression in life than they could - a kind of formalised abandonment. Needless to say, no creative dramatisation is necessary in this book and there is plenty of conflict to consider.

Literature? Learning? Students? – *What If?*

It was intended that all the works cited above would provide a multi-dimensional mirror for reflecting upon experiences in and around sport. Also that they may provoke a deeper and sometimes more critical (self) reflection for us to learn from about the physical and psychological milestones which may be encountered in our lives. Like looking at our reflections in a hall of distorting mirrors we may become curious about how we appear to others and what others look like to us, such is the strangeness of the new forms. Reflection, reconstruction, re-interpretation and representation are seemingly what all the chapters in *What If?* strive to do in some way. These concepts, which may be at the heart of much socio-cultural research in sport, when combined with an exercise to develop writing skills may be a valuable exercise for budding researchers, or sports journalists, as was the case with *What If?* Some notable chapters from students in *What If?* that tackle the concepts of identity and reconstruction are Alastair Turner's story about Rubin Carter (Chpt. 4) – a boxer 'trapped' in an old body, Richard Wilson's story about Dame Kelly Holmes who faces a drugs scandal (Chpt. 11) and John Kopczyk's story about Rio Ferdinand who similarly finds himself at the root of a drugs scandal (Chpt. 12)... ALLEGEDLY!

My efforts to provide what might loosely be described as a pedagogical literature review was to set students off reasonably well equipped to make their own decisions about how to write about their chosen topic. It was also to combat the inevitable questions from some students,

"Yes, that's all well and good Clive, but I still don't know what you want".

16

The "I" can often become "we" from protesting individuals for collective unity in being lost – a false sense of security and safety in numbers whilst drifting at sea. My advice to these few students about their predicament was, in so many words, that "the best way out of the darkness may be to make a decision and commit to a course of action". The beauty of this task was that I had no clear concept of exactly *what* I wanted, only how it should be presented. Some revelled in the freedom whilst others took a little time to find their way. A student stopped me in the corridor one day to say,

"Blimey Clive, I'm knackered, I had to get up at 2am in the morning and start writing for this chapter, it's all buzzing round in my head, I had to write it before I lost it... it's great though, no other piece of writing on my degree has got me out of bed like that!"

The students were branching out on a new and vulnerable limb at the end of their degrees but knew they were well supported to venture their ideas. Consequently a high level of enthusiasm about writing and research was demonstrated, the results of which we are able to share in this book. It is fair to say also that the challenges were similar for the mentoring co-authors who were stretched to engage in this kind of writing and each will have his own story to tell about the experience.

Mentoring and collaboration – who's learning from whom?

All of the mentoring co-authors and the authors of the cameo chapters are researchers in sport of one manifestation or another but are at different stages on their journey through education and life. From a mentoring point of view this presented a very interesting profile of pedagogical expertise that would influence the content of *What If?* However, due to their wide range of experience there is a limit to which general comments might be made, although there were some common experiences which are worthy of note in this introduction. A more detailed overview of where mentors may be on their educational 'safari' up to the point at which they met *What If?* being offered in the mentoring co-authors mini-autobiographies.

Mentoring in general

Becoming a second-named mentoring co-author seemed to define a pedagogical investment that was distinct from that of the first-named student author from whom the story originated. It may seem fairly obvious at first glance what help the mentoring co-author might be providing: sorting out spelling, punctuation, re-ordering sentences and generally tidying up the text. Of course they did that, where it was needed, but a lot more seemed to be going on as reports of progress and then chapters filtered back to me.

The learning curve for the mentors in taking on a mentoring role and working with stylised writing was extremely steep. Similarly the emotional and intellectual challenges presented by the task of mentoring/co-authoring work may not have been too far away from what many of the students reported for writing the stories in the first place. From my perspective, in such instances both the mentors and the students were "in the zone" educationally, – as my old lecturer used to say, "*you're not learning unless you've got brain-ache*". I had brain-ache for months working on this project, it was very satisfying! Discussions about mentoring often centred on their feelings of frustration and 'being lost' with what to do with the story ranging to enjoyment, liberation and freedom experienced from this style of writing. They reported it as being demanding, challenging and thought-provoking at many different levels for them, but most of all an enjoyable and fulfilling task to have attempted. It was clear they had gained a lot from it as mentors – and as writers in some cases.

Mentors first had to come to terms with the responsibility for altering another person's writing which they may not have done before, particularly for publication. This coupled with any confusion and frustration that they may have felt to make sense of the student's story, seemed to raise questions for them, such as, "should they get involved at all" or if they do 'interfere' would the product be "any good" and implicitly, how might that reflect upon them. Mentors would often send me final drafts of chapters with the qualifying disclaimer of,

"Here you are Clive, for what it's worth..." or, *"Yes I enjoyed that, but I don't know if it's any good, you'll have to have a look"*.

On every occasion I did have a look and on every occasion I thought that what they had done with the student's work was remarkable. The sense of 'being lost' seemed to relate to their confusion about how to judge how good the final product was, i.e. 'good' in terms of the story itself and 'good' in terms of pedagogic mentoring. The academic challenge of mentoring within this style of writing was, in many cases, so new to them that there was no benchmark in their experience for quality. It was very far removed from marking and/or correcting a 'normal' essay. So, stemming from my view of mentoring student work, a message to my mentoring colleagues (and readers) is that we stand by our original task to students and our beliefs that it was a good developmental task for them as final year students on their intended career paths as, predominantly, sports journalists. We stand by the fact that these chapters may be a reflection of our efforts to improve students' work and to share it in the public domain. Having done so, the *What If?* publication can be used to inform our teaching on the Sporting Image module in years to come and perhaps, if judged as suitable, used as reference for learning at other H.E. institutions.

With the pedagogical high ground now firmly seized, a cautionary note about the identity of student writing is required. In all cases these chapters are student's first attempts at planning short stories and integrating creative ideas in text for academic submission (in Sport). Consequently some of the stories may upon initial reflection appear simplistic; for instance, there might have been plots and sub-plots which could have been developed or characters who did other things to 'spice' the story up. I do not see these as shortcomings for the intended audience of *What If?* who are primarily undergraduate students. Rather, I hope they might feel encouraged to develop their literary skills and writing confidence in a similar vein. Underlying this is the concept of access to the text; the stories stem from student work and therefore should be accessible to students. The stories are examples of what a student's work might look like if the 'teacher' helped them to develop it further than the student did or could – that is our role as mentors.

From a teaching point of view the "access issue" seems to be a major advantage of mentored writing in this manner, given that much academic writing is not intended for undergraduate consumption. Academics write primarily for other academics, their arguments often being shared in peer reviewed journals. It is seemingly very difficult for experienced writers or academics to write at a level that is genuinely accessible for the broad spectrum of students who come into Higher Education. A glance through a research methods book or peer-reviewed journal may indicate this. The point being made is that once a writer has moved forward in their experience it is very difficult for them to 'go back' which for novelists and indeed learners may not a problem; personal improvement being their quest; but for teachers/lecturers it seemingly is a problem if they wish to stay in touch with their primary audience. An interesting test of this social development concept may be to ask an adult to paint a picture of, for example, a house or a dog, that a 3 or 4 year old had painted. Even if they were to copy it directly they would likely not get close to its child-like naivety and erratic perspective which we admire so much in children's painting. It might in fact take a very experienced artist to get close to such a product. This is not to claim that children's painting is high quality art, rather that is it difficult to undo or even ignore formative experiences. All of this seems to indicate that in academia we are moving on constantly as we develop; we teach, write and publish, and therefore we risk leaving behind the students who by dint of coming to university at 18 years old (usually) do not 'move on' with us. The new starters are always at the start line. Also mentors often felt they could do so much more with the story IF it was their own and probably felt a little frustrated that they couldn't do more, feeling inhibited by the student's planning/structure of the original story. Far from being a disadvantage this 'limitation' may in fact be a good thing to preserve the identity of student's work and to hopefully promote access to the text by for active discussions in future teaching.

A spectrum of mentoring experience

The range of mentorship/life experience shared with the students in *What If?* may be as eclectic as the range of stories presented by the students in the first instance. Please refer also to the contributor's notes and personal learning and teaching mini-autobiographies by mentoring co-authors which will shed further light upon personal reflections about their involvement in *What If?* What that section does not provide are the links between the authors in terms of the progressive overview of mentoring for *What If?* which are outlined below.

There are eight mentoring co-authors who have contributed to the book. All but two of the mentors are teaching staff in Higher Education working in the area of Sport Studies, the exceptions being James Kenyon and Chris Hughes who are both students. Chris Hughes mentored his chapter whilst he was an undergraduate on his Sports Coaching degree which established one end of the mentoring spectrum for *What If?* His involvement meant an undergraduate mentoring and publishing a fellow undergraduate's work which is a commendable achievement. Next in line is James Kenyon who is a Masters degree student from Liverpool Hope University. I invited James to the writing workshop having published three articles from him in the *Journal of Qualitative Research in Sport*. James is the only person in *What If?* to have written his own story as a first named author and then to have become a mentor of a UCLAN student. Therefore he has experienced the 'full force' of *What If?* from both 'sides of the fence' and I know he has faced similar challenges echoed by students and other mentors in this creative-writing project. The next phase of the spectrum are Ph.D. students and staff.

Anthony Maher and Ray Physick are both Ph.D. students who also work at UCLAN. Having registered for their studies at roughly the same time they may be at similar stages in their post-grad research journeys. Anthony is a younger researcher than Ray and investigating aspects of Physical Education whilst Ray is exploring the artistic qualities of football-related art. John Metcalfe, author of one of the cameo chapters is also a Ph.D. student working at UCLAN and shares his writing which is in keeping with the context of *What If?* but not particularly with his own research as an exercise physiologist. For him, his chapter represents a distinct departure from the scientific writing he is more accustomed to as a Ph. D. researcher. Lastly, academic staff including myself, Iain Adams, Mitchell Larson and Joel Rookwood establish the opposite end of the spectrum who bring with them a wealth of experience in teaching, researching and publication. Their diversity in socio-cultural research has positively affected not only the content and pedagogical direction of *What If?* but also their teaching and mentoring of students under their supervision. Their interests and investigations span; art and aesthetics in sport, to sports history, to social reconstruction of broken societies using sport as a medium for change. These staff have shared generously their knowledge and wisdom with students and grappled with the challenges of mentoring student work, in some cases for the first time. In all cases the breadth of experience in life, writing, education and applied subject knowledge from co-authoring mentors has added considerably to the richness of the learning spectrum. For the hawk-eyed peruser of contents pages a duplication appears in the list of chapters which is not the mistake it might appear to be at first glance. Emma Jones' chapter *What if Jesse Owens was white?* appears twice after being mentored simultaneously by Iain Adams (Chpt. 21) and Ray Physick (Chpt. 25). Following a conversation with both mentors it was decided to keep both chapters in, deliberately under the same titles, as it seemed to open an interesting discussion about the potential differences in how a story might be interpreted by different people, authors and readers, and by different mentors in this case. No-one is 'on trial' here except perhaps Jesse and Adolf.

A significant reflection from the staff's point of view has been for us to question the value of our requests for 'normal' academic essays as assessment in modules. Whilst these stories did originate as assessment pieces, we envisaged they would have 'life' after submission, not just 'death' upon granting a percentage grade. As an assessment the stories were judged by slightly different criteria according to set levels for passing a module with one clear limitation being of wordage, 2500 words maximum, and the demonstration of academic research skills etc. The marking process was a convenient time for initial editorial screening which as it turned out was not the most effective means for determining all the content of *What If?*. This said, it did point us in a direction towards some initial chapters for the book, the practical judgement for a mentor being the amount of work that might be required to lift a creative idea towards a finished chapter. Thus it was not always "the best" academic submissions which became book chapters.

Upon this note on mentoring and pedagogy for *What If?* there were some useful texts which I recommended to mentors and students to help them with creative writing and formulating text. These were Marion Field's books *Improve your Punctuation and Grammar* (2009a) and *Improve your Written English* (2009b) which are accessible and made plain good sense for relatively novice writers. Marion Field was head of English at a large comprehensive school and was an examiner for GCSE English – reading her books was a bit like going back to school but that was just what I needed in this new and challenging task. Then there was Ritchie Macefield's (2005) *Secrets of University Success* with great tips for writing clearly and succinctly. Again, very accessible in terms of level and to the eye; all three of these books setting out their text with generous line spacing and font sizing in order not to overload and deter the curious reader. There were also two very good publications which were focused more at students on creative writing courses. These nevertheless, made good reference for planning ideas and developing storylines and could also help social researchers to make connections with creative writing skills and the effective presentation of their data or research idea. The edited volumes were by Harper (2006) *Teaching creative writing* and Singleton and Luckhurst (2000) *The creative writing handbook, techniques for new writers* (see guidance notes in reference list).

The aesthetic of *What If?* - presentation and production

There are some aesthetic features in the design of *What If?* which may, even at the surface, point to the storytelling nature of this book. Upon this premise I have designed the appearance of *What If?* not only to echo vestiges of the cultural act of passing down wisdom through stories but also to reinforce some aspects of what we have learned through this creative writing project, for example, the central role of conflict in novel writing. It has been my aim that the appearance of the book might tell the reader something of its *intent* if not its actual *content* before the stories are read.

Less obvious to the reader will be that I always had a fairly clear idea of what *What If?* might look like as a finished product. This was achieved by working to a known format, a working model, which was Alan Tomlinson's (2007) excellent book *The Sports Studies Reader*. Tomlinson's (2007) book contains 450 pages of abbreviated short essays and pertinent discussions for the Sports Studies student. Accessibility seems to have been a watchword for Tomlinson (2007) in the 72 chapters he compiled. A generous use of spacing on opening pages to chapters and the use of small capitals in the first line of text are repeated in *What If?* for eye-catching effect. He also opted for a very simple cover design which given the range of topics within his book was seemingly a wise and uncomplicated choice.

Working from the outside in, then, the cover design of *What If?* is also simple and uncomplicated, its contents being too eclectic to be represented pictorially in a reasonable way on the cover. The design on Tomlinson's (2007) book is an attractive swirl of red and black; a basic combination of colours and forms which help to define it from others on the shelf. By contrast Cowley (2002) has attempted a mixed pictorial representation of the contents in his book, *More What If?* which appears confusing and thus helped me to decide that that was not what I wanted for *What If?* The *What If?* publication would be a 400 page tome-like collection of stories which question, pose possibilities and cast doubt. There seemed to be an interesting juxtaposition between assuredness and scepticism which I wanted to emphasize in the aesthetic of the book. Consequently, *What If?* became the book of "solid doubt" – unswervingly confident in our utter scepticism. This is hopefully represented by the cover design concept of the book as a metal ingot; a 'casting' of solid doubt, which features a raised and polished question mark to affirm the questioning intent of the authors.

Within the text a large capital letter is used at the start of each Research Preface and Creative Story. This is an echo from the tradition of storytelling down the ages, when the dressed capital letter was used by the "Scop" in Anglo-Saxon poetry. The Scop (pronounced "shop") would not only read but 'perform' epic accounts of battle, conflict, death and glory for an audience, who may typically have been illiterate. For the story to be recounted effectively, the Scop was aided by the illuminated or dressed capital which was itself surrounded by pictures which acted like a visual auto-cue for the correct ordering of events. This feature in the text of *What If?* seemed to doff a cap appropriately to the traditions of storytelling - not only the reading but also the performing of the stories for others to learn from and question.

The fonts used in type-setting also have their inferences towards conflict and make a contribution to the aesthetic of the book. Many publishers use a mixture of Sans Serif and Times Roman fonts for clarity and spacing effect which is also strived for in *What If?* The title fonts are in "Trebuchet". The Trebuchet was the most lethal siege weapon of the middle ages (1300-1500s), a massive catapult for firing deadly missiles over the high walls of castles (Biesty, 1994). The Trebuchet was used by the English to attack the French at Harfleur, prior to Agincourt (Cornwell, 2008) under Henry V (1415) firing boulders, burning logs, burning skulls and even dead cows to spread disease amongst the castle's inhabitants. The font used in the main text is "Georgia" about which there is also no shortage of conflict-inference. Georgia is a country which borders the Black Sea and Azerbaijan; a satellite country to Europe sitting between East and West which has been fought over for hundreds of years on social, political and geographical grounds. Georgia has suffered two bloody civil wars and a military coup and is currently the centre of increasing economic conflict over oil, the lifeblood of the world economy. It is hoped that the idea of using these fonts to deliberately represent conflict will help to reinforce the sense of doubt and 'what if?' which might arise from reading these tales. With regards to spacing and layout: depending upon the story, if the reader got a sense that they were 'racing' through the pages then that may be facilitated in part by the type-setting. A generous line space is used in the main text with the aim of being easier on the eye to read which might in turn permit 'space' to think by not overcrowding the senses – this seems to have been a strategy in the textual layout of the study skills books mentioned above which may be one aspect of their design that makes them appealing for the learner.

In closing I have enjoyed the challenge of editing this volume and it has been a pleasure to mentor students' initial stories towards final chapters. I am confident that this sentiment is echoed by all the mentors who have contributed to the book and that all authors may have gained something that is positive and worth sharing in our educational arena.

Clive Palmer
Cheshire
2010

References

Adamson, J. (2009) No time like the present (pp. 51-53). In, Palmer, C. (Ed.) *The sporting image: sports poetry and creative writing.* Published by the Centre for Research Informed Teaching, University of Central Lancashire, Preston, UK.

Barone, T. (2002) From genre blurring to audience blending: reflections on the field emanating from an ethnodrama. *Anthropology and Education Quarterly*, 33, 2, 255-267.

Biesty, S. (1994) *Castle cross-sections*. Dorling Kindersley, London.

Bull, M. and Black, L. (2003) Introduction: Into sound (pp. 1-18). In, Bull, M. and Black, L. (Eds.) *The auditory cultural reader*. Berg Publishers, Oxford.

Carroll, L. (1865) *Alice's adventures in wonderland*. Puffin Books Ltd., London (Republished in 1962: reprinted in 1988).

Cornwell, B. (2008) *Azincourt*. Harper Collins Publishers, London.

Cowley, R. (Ed.) (2002) *More What If? – eminent historians imagine what might have been* (second edition). Pan Books, Pan McMillan, London.

Denison, J. (1999a) Boxed in (pp. 29-36). In, Sparkes, A.C. and Silvennoinen, M. (Eds.) *Talking bodies – men's narratives of the body and sport*. Jyvaskyla University Printing House, SoPhi, Finland.

Denison, J. (1999b) Men's selves and sport (pp. 156-162). In, Sparkes, A.C. and Silvennoinen, M. (Eds.) *Talking bodies – men's narratives of the body and sport*. Jyvaskyla University Printing House, SoPhi, Finland.

Eichburg, H. (2009a) People's academies and sport: towards a philosophy of bodily education. *Sport, Ethics and Philosophy*, 3, 2,139-158.

Eichburg, H. (2009b) Fitness on the market: forget 'the single individual'! *Sport, Ethics and Philosophy*, 3, 2, 171-192.

Eire, C.M.N. (2002) *Pontius Pilate saves Jesus – Christianity without the crucifixion* (Chpt. 3, pp. 48-68). In, Cowley, R. (Ed.) *More What If? – eminent historians imagine what might have been* (second edition). Pan Books, Pan McMillan, London.

Field, M. (2009a) *Improve your punctuation and grammar*. How To Books Ltd., Oxford.

Field, M. (2009b) *Improve your written English*. How To Books Ltd., Oxford.

Gaarder, J. (1996) *Sophie's World*. Phoenix, London

Hall, P. (2009) *CASUALSKI* , hospitalisation Moscow style (pp. 80-88). In, Palmer, C. (Ed.) *The sporting image: sports poetry and creative writing*. Published by the Centre for Research Informed Teaching, University of Central Lancashire, Preston, UK.

Harper, G. (Ed.) (2006) *Teaching creative writing*. Continuum, London.

Note: This is an edited book with an interesting selection of chapters which may be particularly relevant to developing writing skills across a range of study areas. For example, in addition to the chapter on Poetry there are chapters on Creative Non-fiction and Research in Creative Writing which would be useful reference for qualitative researchers who are describing "the lived experience".

Harrer, H. (1976) *The white spider*. Granada Publishing Ltd., London.

Harrer, H. (1988) *Seven years in Tibet*. Paladin-Grafton Books, London.

Kahn, D. (2002) *Enigma Uncracked – the Allies fail to break the German cipher machine* (Chpt.18, pp. 305-317). In, Cowley, R. (Ed.) *More What If? – eminent historians imagine what might have been* (second edition). Pan Books, Pan McMillan, London.

Kleiber, D.A. and Hutchinson, S.M. (1999) Heroic masculinity in the recovery from spinal chord injury (pp. 135-155). In, Sparkes, A.C. and Silvennoinen, M. (Eds.) *Talking bodies – men's narratives of the body and sport*. Jyvaskyla University Printing House, SoPhi, Finland.

Langley, B. (1982) *Traverse of the Gods*. Sphere Books Limited, London.

Macefield, R. (2005) *Secrets of university success*. Mind Shift International, UK.

Mandell, R.D. (1971) *The Nazi Olympics*. Souvenir Press, London.

Palmer, C. (Ed.) (2009) *The sporting image: sports poetry and creative writing*. Published by the Centre for Research Informed Teaching, University of Central Lancashire, Preston, UK.

Palmer, C. (2007/8/9) Editor in Chief, Volumes 1,2,3: *Journal of Qualitative Research in Sports Studies*. University of Central Lancashire, UK.

Randall, N. (2009) My dream, my memory (p. 56). In, Palmer, C. (Ed.) *The sporting image: sports poetry and creative writing*. Published by the Centre for Research Informed Teaching, University of Central Lancashire, Preston, UK.

Rice, T. (2003) Soundselves: an acoustemology of sound and self in the Edinburgh Royal Infirmary. *Anthropology Today*, 19, 4, 4-9.

Rookwood, J. and Palmer, C. (2009a). A photo-ethnography, a picture-story-board of experiences at an NGO football project in Liberia (part 1). *Journal of Qualitative Research in Sports Studies*. 3, 1, 161-186.

Rookwood, J. and Palmer, C. (2009b). A photo-ethnography, a picture-story-board of experiences at an NGO football project in Liberia (part 2). *Journal of Qualitative Research in Sports Studies*. 3, 1, 187-210.

Ryan, J. (1996) *Little girls in pretty boxes: the making and breaking of elite gymnasts and figure skaters*. Women's Press Ltd., London.

Note: See also - Wikipedia search for "Little Girls in Pretty Boxes [online]. Available at: http://en.wikipedia.org/wiki/Little_Girls_in_Pretty_Boxes for a brief overview of the book and informative hyper-links with many of the aspects covered in Ryan's account. (Accessed 26th May 2010).

Saladana, J. (1999) Playwriting with data: ethnographic performance texts. *Youth Theatre Journal*, 13, 60-71.

Singleton, J. and Luckhurst, M. (Eds.) (2000) *The creative writing handbook, techniques for new writers* (second edition). Palgrave, Hampshire, UK.

Note: An edited book with some excellent chapters to stimulate and guide the thoughts of writers. A chapter entitled Words Words Words explores meaning and interpretation of phrasing and provides some useful exercises to become more creative within our written language. The Writing Self focuses upon the experiences of the writer as being central to the writing process and adds useful dimensions to what could become aspects of ethnographic research. Their final chapter on Editing and Rewriting would also be helpful to those who wish to communicate clearly their ideas in a written form.

Smith, B. (2008) Imagining being disabled through playing sport: the body and alterity as limits to imagining others' lives. *Sport, Ethics and Philosophy*, 2, 2, 142-157.

Sparkes, A.C. and Silvennoinen, M. (Eds.) (1999) *Talking bodies – men's narratives of the body and sport.* Jyvaskyla University Printing House, SoPhi, Finland.

Sparkes, A.C. (1999a) The fragile body-self (pp. 51-74). In, Sparkes, A.C. and Silvennoinen, M. (Eds.) *Talking bodies – men's narratives of the body and sport.* Jyvaskyla University Printing House, SoPhi, Finland.

Sparkes, A.C. and Smith, B. (1999) Disrupted selves and narrative reconstructions (pp. 76-92). In, Sparkes, A.C. and Silvennoinen, M. (Eds.) *Talking bodies – men's narratives of the body and sport.* Jyvaskyla University Printing House, SoPhi, Finland.

Sparkes, A.C. (2002) *Telling tales in sport and physical activity: a qualitative journey.* Human Kinetics Press, Champaign, IL.

Sparkes, A.C. (2009a) Novel ethnographic representations and the dilemmas of judgement. *Ethnography and Education*, 4, 3, 301-319.

Sparkes, A.C. (2009b) Ethnography and the senses, challenges and possibilities. *Qualitative Research in Sport and Exercise*, 1, 1, 21-35.

Sparkes, A.C. [in press] 'When I am old I will...!' In, Humberstone, B. (Ed.) [in-press] *Third age and leisure research: principles and practice.* LSA Publication no. 108. Leisure Studies Association, Eastbourne.

Stafford, I. (2008) *Playgrounds of the Gods - A year of sporting fantasy.* Mainstream Publishing, London.

Swan, P. (1999) Three ages of changing (pp. 37-47). In, Sparkes, A.C. and Silvennoinen, M. (Eds.) *Talking bodies – men's narratives of the body and sport.* Jyvaskyla University Printing House, SoPhi, Finland.

Tierney, W. (2002) Get real: representing reality. *International Journal of Qualitative Studies in Education*, 15, 4, 385-398.

Tomlinson, A. (2007) *The sports studies reader.* Routledge, London.

Wilson, B. (2009) Financial security (pp. 75-79). In, Palmer, C. (Ed.) *The sporting image: sports poetry and creative writing.* Published by the Centre for Research Informed Teaching, University of Central Lancashire, Preston, UK.

Supporting creative writing for teaching and learning about sports culture - personal reflections from mentoring co-authors.

An aspect which has made this book so eclectic and interesting is the stock of knowledge and experience of the mentoring co-authors which has guided the editing of each creative story. The diversity of their experience across personal training, formal education and in life has shaped the conception of the original academic task, through to the mentoring and 'polishing' of these final chapters. Consequently, the purpose of this section is to shed some light upon that guiding experience which may in turn permit the reader a glimpse into the co-authors' values and intrinsic interests about learning and teaching in Higher Education.

Note: whilst the following short chapters are essentially personal and auto-biographical they may be written stylistically to suit the mentoring co-author and the nature of the information they wish to share.

Essex boys can't rite, wright, right, write... I got there in the end

Clive Palmer

Born in 1966, the 1970s and 1980s were my formative years in compulsory education. I grew up on Canvey Island which is at the most southerly tip of Essex on the Thames Estuary. Not particularly known for being a Seat of Learning, Canvey Island was more associated with the Del Boy image, dodgy builders, mods and rockers and as a rather scruffy seaside resort for Londoners to visit. In time, some of these 'seeds' would lay more permanent roots and visit London instead – such was their desire to become a "commuter". Curiously enough, however, sport featured quite highly on the agenda of my childhood experiences. I started performing Olympic Gymnastics at 8 years old and continue my involvement with that sport to this day. In the late 1970s and early 1980s I was at Furtherwick Park Secondary School where many life-opportunities presented themselves, for better or for worse. Similar to the boys in the film, Angels with Dirty Faces (1938) many young pupils' lives might have followed a different path from this school but luckily, I never got caught or even beaten up too much. (See also the chapter by Glover/Palmer – "a dirty

29

face with an angel"). It was the kind of school where the boys did 'engineering' - woodwork and metalwork and the girls did 'food technology' – cooking. Some of the more popular girls would leave school early to have their babies – advanced biology perhaps? Some of the boys would leave school early having found seemingly lucrative careers which required no qualifications at all! Lucky them. Furtherwick Park is a school that on paper will always appear to be struggling which, in my experience may not be a full account of the valuable social experience of *being there*. A recent OFSTED report (2004), 20 or so years after I left, placed the school on "special measures" and explained how some thoughtful pupils, no doubt keen to impress the inspectors during their visit, vandalised the toilets beyond use whilst some others went for a spot of shop-lifting at lunch time in the high street. Things did not appear to have changed too much since my day which was strangely reassuring. This said, I had a great time at school and I wouldn't change a minute of it.

Sport was a major feature in the make-up of Furtherwick Park. For some it defined what the school was about, an early kind of Sports College in effect. Sport masqueraded under the guise of Physical Education. Whilst it was very physical it was never very educative. In retrospect I learned nothing about PE in my time there but a lot about competing in sport. The long con was on and I, the mark, went for it with gusto, I knew no better. After all, Physical Education had nothing to do with learning, that all went on in the classrooms, supposedly. The 'PE' 'teachers' were totally focused on winning at competitions at local, county and national levels. It is fair to say that they weren't too bothered with local spoils, in the sense that a neighbouring school team would likely get bull-dozed by a Furtherwick team anyway. It was county and national recognition which the PE staff hankered after and I was part of the merry little gang who would realise it for them.

The school's spectrum of sports and leagues included in the main, rugby (a lot of rugby) and athletics (a lot of athletics) and cricket (for *a rest*, or for *the rest* who were no good at rugby or athletics). At one point, nearly the whole of the Essex County rugby team came from Furtherwick Park School. I chose not to play rugby after school. There is only so much you do. However, I did become very good at Pole Vaulting which sealed my fate for the next five years in those so called 'PE lessons'. I trained for pretty much nothing else in every PE lesson and during before-and-after school sports training. As Essex County Champion in pole vaulting for 4 years running and County record holder I achieved a place in the top ten national rankings at age 15 and was rewarded with chronic back pain for the rest of my life.

Thanks. I was also training in gymnastics every week and competing at County and Regional level in that sport when I discovered canoeing. I took up kayak slalom (K1) and started competing in that as well. All these sports seemed to complement each other and I didn't appear to be getting any worse at them, so I carried on – with all of them! It also occurred to me that I wasn't sat on the school gate during day where the early leaver's contingent would gather and look in on what they opted out of. "You gotta be in it to win it" I thought. There had to be a reason for me to be in school and them to be out of it. So I chose, somewhat ignorantly, to work hard on examined subjects, gambling that they might come in useful at some point in the future. Curiously, I always enjoyed the bigger projects to investigate stuff. My woodwork folder and geography project were items to behold. In athletics the school became National Champions for three years on the run and I was in the first team to achieve this for the school. Close behind me were some great performers; Mathew Simpson (a national level shot putter), Rob Denmark (GB international middle distance runner) and Dean Macey (World Champion, Olympian and Commonwealth Gold medallist at Decathlon) all of whom came from Furtherwick Park school on Canvey Island. There is also my neighbour on Canvey and fellow gymnast at the time, Paul Hall, who is now the National Olympic Men's Gymnastics coach achieving the highest accolades the sport has ever seen in Britain (see his chapter in this book and his contributors note: Hall and Palmer, 2008; Hall, 2009). Why was so much sporting talent bursting from such a mediocre educational establishment? How would we get on in life? I can only describe it personally as my being resourceful and determined to succeed at something when the odds appeared to be against me to succeed at anything. I am sure my teachers may have judged things differently from their side of the educational fence. I thank them all sincerely for their efforts to teach me.

"Get a job son, get a trade behind you" was the popular advice from family and school. Higher Education was never on the horizon for me when I was at school. I was curious though, what kind of person might go there? Who ever it was, it didn't seem to be someone like me, I thought. Surely someone would have said something if it was? I headed to South East Essex Sixth Form College (SEEVIC) with my seven O Levels (GCSEs equivalent) from Furtherwick Park and the academic advice given to me there was that I should sign up for more O Levels. "You don't have the right combination of subjects to study at A Level" I was informed. Anyway, I was following my gymnastics friend Paul Hall to college who was only a year ahead of me. He was doing some A levels, whatever they were. All I knew was that they were much longer qualifications and seemed to get in the way of training so I followed the college's advice (what I now know to have been utterly appalling advice) and studied metalwork, geology and electronics - at O Level. I already had an O Level in woodwork and enjoyed that at school (I had rather been put off metal work at school) so the metalwork now seemed like a convenient distraction to the other subjects now being followed. Sure enough I passed them and won another County championship in the pole vault. Paul got into dispatch riding in London and was earning "mega bucks" on his second-hand motor bike which he'd bought after saving enough money from his paper round - and saving to pass his motorbike test. A formal "test" and qualification by the way, which had nothing to do with college - I was not totally clear where his A levels fitted into his career plan. A levels seemed pretty pointless to me – just 2 year long schooly-type O levels. There were quite a few folk at college doing them and I couldn't fathom why, I had no idea they might lead somewhere. The options seemed to be after school; work or college; after college, work. Was there anywhere else to go? I kept my head down and didn't ask too many questions. At least we were having fun at college.

SEEVIC was probably famous for a few things. One good thing that I discovered years later when I started teaching was that a key text book for PE and Sports Studies had been written there, Sport Examined (Beashel and Taylor, 1992). It featured the sports staff Reg and Margaret Simmons and pictured the sports hall where I trained in gymnastics. "Ere look, I was there" I would point out to my teaching colleagues, who weren't overly impressed for some reason. One not so good thing but absolutely hilarious at the time was the legendary food fighting which used to take place in the Common Room. Upon a warning shout "foodfight" the air would be thick with ham, bread, tomatoes and other edible missiles flying around with some not inconsiderable momentum. Bottles of drink and flimsy plastic cups of tea were also mutually sanctioned ammunition sources. Tables upturned for protection like cowboys in a bar room shoot-out it was quite a raucous scene. When some 'cluster bombs' – a snowball of cheese, crisps, lettuce and bread - found their targets it was immensely satisfying. Eventually these regular events were reported in the local press with disgust, "students' disgraceful behaviour contravenes public hygiene standards" the common room was locked for the rest of my time at SEEVIC.

So, equipped with more O Levels than any man could eat I joined the Royal Air Force at 18yrs. However, a pattern of (un) professional advice and (mis) fortunes was beginning to emerge. I applied to the RAF to become a Physical Training Instructor (PTI). A logical choice given my sporting interests, it was a sure thing? My gymnastics and athletics were as strong as ever and my K1 slalom canoeing had expanded on the 'outdoors' front to include sea kayaking, rock climbing and mountaineering. I had an impressive pile of governing body badges to qualify me in these sports and a growing list of titles and medals from competitions. I went for a three day assessment at RAF Cosford and ran circles round the other applicants only to be told that my racket skills weren't very good and my knowledge on cricket was poor. "Not today thank you" seemed to be the message. I am not quite sure if it was my PE experiences which were at fault here or if they had perhaps missed something in my portfolio of skills. Not to be deterred, I joined the Airforce as a sheet metal worker! I knew that metal work O Level would come in handy for something. In fact I was more interested in the Carpenter trade in the RAF but the metalwork option paid more. I followed the money. However, whilst in the Services, stationed in Oxfordshire, I represented the RAF and the Combined Services for 5 years in athletics at National level and competed in Slalom, White-water Racing and Surfing disciplines of canoeing for the RAF and also led expeditions in rock climbing and canoeing in the UK and throughout Europe. If my one O Level in metalwork had opened all these doors what on earth were A Levels all about?

There had to be more to life than banging hammers to repair aircraft, and then the aircraft used to kill people. A cunning vicious circle, it was certainly killing me. As an eternal pacifist and with the Gulf War looming I left the RAF in 1990. I remembered from Furtherwick Park the College address of my Outdoor Pursuits teacher written inside the lid of his rucksack. I.M. Marsh College, Barkhill Road, Aigburth, Liverpool. I wrote to them and asked if I could do their course in Outdoor Education. With the National Curriculum going public in the same year that I had entered Higher Education as a mature student, two 'new' chapters in education were opening. At Liverpool Polytechnic, later to become John Moores University, I trained as a Science teacher with Outdoor Education. In truth it was my Maths, English, Physics, Woodwork and Metalwork O Levels that got me there given that my outdoor pursuits skills were pretty much honed.

A four year Masters degree in Physical Education followed my four year B.Ed (Hons). I was now a teacher but keen to learn more. The MA experience introduced me to philosophy and aesthetics which I was able to apply to the sport of gymnastics through an in-depth ethnographic study of artistic quality in Men's Artistic Gymnastics – which developed into my Ph.D.

And the rest they say is history.

Having been utterly deprived of my Physical Education at secondary school - to some degree cheated out of it probably through ignorance, I am fairly clear in my mind about what good quality PE might constitute now. In this respect I thank my PE teachers for being perfect role models of how not to teach PE. As for sport; competing and coaching I continue to gather experience and devise tenacious means of getting on. I feel my journey through education has equipped me well to motivate students at all levels to make the best of their opportunities here and now and for their future.

Like sport, education is a challenge, it is there to be enjoyed, so choose your challenges carefully and commit to them 100 percent.

Clive Palmer

NB: This short auto-biography is linked to the final chapter in this book which is entitled, *Rose tinted torture and the tale of Wayne Lacey - Physical Education, a force for good at Bash Street School*. The chapter above, *Essex boys can't write*, provides a potted overview of part of my journey through education and life. The closing chapter, which is a progression within this tale, provides a more detailed 'richer' descriptive account of one of the episodes discussed above, i.e. some experiences of Physical Education. It is a reflective account which may stimulate some thoughts for future research in the area.

References

Beashel, P. and Taylor, J. (1992) *Sport examined* (second edition). Thomas Nelson and Sons Ltd. Walton-on-Thames, Surrey.

Hall, P. and Palmer, C. (2008) Unfolding events at the Beijing Olympics 2008 – public diary of a gymnastics coach. *Journal of Qualitative Research in Sports Studies*, 2, 1, 143-160 .

Hall, P. (2009) *CASUALSKI* , Hospitalisation Moscow Style (pp. 80-88). In, Palmer, C. (Ed.) *The sporting image: sports poetry and creative writing.* Published by the Centre for Research Informed Teaching, University of Central Lancashire, Preston, UK.

Ofsted Report (2004) *Inspection Report at Furtherwick Park School, Canvey Island Essex. Inspection: 24th -27th November 2003* [online]. Available at: http://www.ofsted.gov.uk/oxedu_reports/download/(id)/51331/(as)/115333_259202.pdf (Accessed on: 3rd February 2010).

Education, research and writing: a student perspective

Anthony Maher

Since many of the chapters within this book originated from the work by third year (Level Three) university students, I thought it useful to focus some of this personal chapter on my time as an undergraduate student. By adopting this approach, I hope to help the reader to gain a student-eye-view insight into Higher Education generally, and research and writing in particular, from a learner's "purview"; their 'we-perspective' to use a term coined by the sociologist Norbert Elias (Elias, 1978). Only three years have elapsed since I, myself, was a Level Three student. Therefore, perhaps unlike some of the more 'senior' contributors to this book, I vividly remember what it was like to be an undergraduate student. Before continuing on that tack, however, a few words on my life pre-university may provide a useful backcloth for understanding this chapter.

It would be much more than an exaggeration of the truth to say that I knew from an early age that I wanted to teach. Much of the time I spent at secondary school involved one thing; playing a lot of sport, football in particular. The remainder of my time was spent dreaming of the day I'd finally be old enough – although, admittedly, by no means wise enough – to leave compulsory schooling to join the 'real world'. Not that I had the vaguest idea what the real world entailed. I was adamant, nonetheless, that the real world couldn't be as boring or tedious as the day-to-day monotony of school. "Your school days are the best days of your life" my parents, sister, aunty and uncle would often say, a claim I would vehemently oppose. If only I knew.

Supported by little in the way of academic qualifications or job experience – I hadn't bothered to partake in the compulsory work-placement at school, opting, instead, to play computer games at home for two weeks – I found it very difficult to gain employment when I left school. Eventually, after much searching, I found a job as a labourer/apprentice joiner. It didn't take me long, however, to conclude that manual work wasn't for me. Despite having no qualifications I was under the – slightly deluded, perhaps – impression that I could do more with my life. I knew I was fairly intelligent; not 'stupid', at least. The problem, I realise now, was that I didn't have any drive or ambition; I didn't apply myself at school or in any other context unless it involved sport. After moving between various meaningless short-term jobs, I decided that I needed some stability in my life. The answer, according to my sister and girlfriend, was to go to college. Immediately, I was very sceptical. It had been three years or so since I'd last written more than two sentences. Notwithstanding my initial scepticism, I decided – or, at least, others did for me – to enrol as a mature student on an access course at Liverpool Community College (LCC) to study sport, what else! It was all that I was remotely interested in. It was during my time at LCC that I set my first long-term goal; I wanted to become a PE teacher. After all, I still really enjoyed playing and watching sport, and that's all PE is, isn't it; sport? The long holidays were another aspect that made teaching so appealing.

Upon graduating from college I applied to and was subsequently accepted by Liverpool John Moores University (LJMU) to study Sport Development with PE. My first choice was to study for a secondary school PE teaching degree but much to my disappointment then, my relief now, my application was unsuccessful. It was during my time at LJMU that my interest to teach at Higher Education first emerged. Through various modules, I became increasingly interested in the theoretical, rather than the more practical, side of sport. Facilitating social inclusion through sport, sports policy and developing grassroots sport were topics that I studied with much enthusiasm. In fact, it was a Level Two social inclusion module that introduced me to an area of research that would become the focus my undergraduate, Masters and Ph.D. research projects; namely, the inclusion of pupils with special educational needs (SEN) in mainstream school PE lessons. A four-week placement at a large secondary school in Liverpool, the identity of which I shall not disclose here, ended any lingering ambitions I had of teaching secondary school PE. All my efforts from this point onwards were geared towards gaining employment as a university lecturer in a sport-related discipline.

I first began to read academic textbooks and journal articles while studying at LJMU. I'd always enjoyed reading, Charles Dickens and George Orwell were and still are among my favourite authors, but I had never really bothered to do much 'wider reading' during college. Perhaps unsurprisingly, then, I didn't have the slightest inkling of how to reference sources. Endeavouring to learn the often ambiguous 'rules' to Harvard referencing is something I remember quite vividly. Once I had become fairly comfortable reading and referencing these sources, however, I then began to study how they were written; how academics structure their chapters, paragraphs, sentences, etc. In turn, I compiled my own dictionary of words and phrases that I found useful, a process amongst others that I believe helped me to expand my academic vocabulary and articulate my ideas much more coherently and succinctly – I hope. In fact, 'Anthony's Dictionary', which is now much larger than the first edition, is a resource that I still use on a regularly basis.

I was first introduced to research methods as a Level Two (second year) undergraduate student. Thankfully, perhaps, the module didn't embrace the theoretical complexities of ontology, epistemology, positivism, phenomenology, realism, inductive, deductive and so on; it was more a superficial exploration of research design and methods. Nevertheless, I was instantly hooked. It wasn't long after I decided that, together with teaching at Higher Education, I wanted to be "research active". The development of my research and writing skills continued at University of Chester, where I studied for a Masters degree in the Sociology of Sport and Exercise. Unfortunately, space does not permit an examination of the time I spent at Chester, nor the time I have spent as both an Associate Lecturer and now Ph.D. student at University of Central Lancashire. What it does allow, however, in the light of these career developments, is a brief reflection on the mentoring process I undertook for this book.

I was initially hesitant when asked to mentor the students, mainly because of the creative writing dimension of each chapter. For the last eight years or so, I've been taught to write in a quite regimented, systematic and insipid style; a style that could be considered the polar opposite of a creative style. It still feels quite surreal to use an apostrophe to juxtapose two words! The last time I wrote anything remotely creative was while at secondary school. In a similar vein to the premise of this book, my English teacher charged me with the task of writing an alternative ending to John Steinbeck's *Of Mice and Men*; I still maintain that my ending was more innovative than Steinbeck's! Nonetheless, despite my initial reluctance I can honestly say that I feel extremely privileged to have been part of this unique project. For me, there is nothing more fulfilling than contributing, in whatever way possible, to the social and academic development of students. In my opinion, the role of university educators is to endeavour to ensure that students become more independent thinkers, researchers and writers; in short, educators should attempt to make their services redundant.

Anthony Maher

References

Elias, N. (1978) *What is Sociology?* Columbia University Press, New York.

Learning, travelling, writing, communicating - a central quest in academia

Joel Rookwood

C.S. Lewis once said, "I believe in Christianity as I believe that the sun has risen. Not only because I see it, but by it I see everything else". My approach to university life – engaging, teaching, learning, researching and writing, reflects my underpinning faith. I do not always succeed in this regard, but this is always my objective. In my current role as a lecturer I have combined my abilities and passions for teaching, researching, learning, writing and helping others to broaden their understanding of the social world and their place therein. Consequently, my interest in social constructs such as identity, behaviour and development has been afforded a fertile environment for rigorous critical examination.

The journey and evolution of status from undergraduate to post-graduate to post doctorate represents a fascinating voyage of discovery and the range of sporting topics in this volume seems to capture something special about that development. On my journey it has been a privilege to learn from engaging educators who presented challenging experiences for me both in education and in sport – football predominantly. I have seen this sport used as a tool to promote as well as mitigate violence. In my own research I have gained a more holistic understanding through an examination of the former, but my interests are firmly centred on the latter.

As a relatively young researcher and lecturer I have been blessed with an educational career short in years yet punctuated by a multitude of rich experiences. My interests led me first to facilitating football camps overseas in the USA for example and then to deeper involvement with NGO (Non Governmental Organisations) projects which use sport for humanitarian reasons in fractured and divided communities. These have typically been with post-war communities or areas of serious social conflict such as Israel, Bosnia, Liberia and Columbia. I firmly believe that every opportunity has an expiration date and that challenges are to be sought after. With this in mind I have grasped many opportunities to engage with, represent and serve the inter-subjective lived reality of people who may be misunderstood, misrepresented and mistreated. Employing social tools such as those relating to sport to promote international social development, build peace and to foster Christian involvement is a rewarding and challenging process, fraught with limitations and possibilities. Critical academic questions are now being raised in the hope of rendering practitioners better prepared and increasingly conscious of their work; and this is what I consider a key function of academia and a primary responsibility of scholars.

I have enjoyed the process of working with Clive Palmer, whose editorial engagements have extended well beyond the content of this book. His efforts and the motivations that inspire them are to be commended and his impact on my own development is difficult to fully express in words. Working with a promising student in Jamie Kenyon is also proving an enlightening experience for me. I first met Jamie when delivering a Sport Development lecture at Liverpool Hope University. He was and remains unswervingly Scouse, appropriately critical and thoughtfully engaged, characteristics I always admire. I later supervised his outstanding undergraduate dissertation, which would have more aptly suited a Masters level submission. I am currently overseeing his MSc thesis, which explores issues central to contemporary Liverpool framed within a consideration of their wider contextual significance.

I was recently invited to facilitate a sport development project in a Tibetan refugee camp in India and I accepted the offer on the proviso that I could select the participants. Jamie's name topped that list and the initiative proved an incredible experience for us both, filled with blessings and lessons. We have also started to collaborate and disseminate work, focusing on both the local and the global issues and this creative offering is our latest collective offering.

For his chapter I have provided technical support aimed at developing Jamie's writing. This has posed fresh questions for me in respect to my role and approach to supervision. I have also helped to shape the historical and socio-political framework of the piece surrounding the 1972 Munich terrorist attacks at the Olympics. This was informed by my experiences of working with and more importantly learning from Palestinians and Israelis, who in my opinion are amongst the warmest people to inhabit this planet (along with the citizens of the Wavertree district of Liverpool that Jamie and I both call home).

I enjoyed the process of mentoring Jamie and I am certain that this creative resource will inspire future work.

Joel Rookwood

Mentoring: a process of personal development

James Kenyon

I t was a freezing Saturday afternoon in November 2009 at Walton Hall Park (or Wally Hall Park as it's known locally) and the football team I play for, Vegas F.C., were two-one up in a Liverpool local men's league match against Everton Deaf F.C. – a team of footballers, which as the name suggests, is entirely made up of young people with varying degrees of hearing impairment. With the referee having been asked at the beginning of the game to wave a red towel each time there was a need to blow his whistle, the game was midway into the first half before he decided that this complex level of multi-tasking was well beyond his capabilities. Blowing his whistle *and* waving his red towel *and* keeping up with the game, all at the same time, were proving too much for the middle-aged referee that afternoon. But what made the situation worse was how he went about letting his feelings be known to the Everton players using an impassioned repetition of the "F" word. He spared his criticism for few shouting at the players on my team, both the managers, all the spectators, some of the spectators from games on other pitches, the token policeman who was based off to one side on his quad bike, and pretty much anyone that was within an earshot of him:

> *"Oh for **** sake! It's not my fault they can't ****ing hear! They shouldn't be playing in this ****ing league! I can't be ****ing expected to remember to do this all the ****ing time!"*

Predictably, such an outburst was met with a sizeable degree of hostility from most of those watching and playing the game; indeed, I spent the following ten minutes trying to stop one Everton player's dad from assaulting the referee (while the policeman sat by and did nothing). But when the mêlée had finally subsided and the football resumed, I couldn't concentrate properly on the game, my mind was now consumed by ideas. All I could think about was how good a research project the Everton team's story would make, who I could approach to co-author it with me, how it could be structured, which methodological approaches would be useful, what the potential outcomes could be, etc. Quite simply, in sports management terms the Everton Deaf F.C. team is an example of *best practice*: a team of *athletes with disabilities* competing and succeeding in an "able-bodied" league. And so I decided right there on the pitch, in the middle of the first half of the game, that people needed to know how such an undertaking can be achieved so it might be emulated elsewhere. But no sooner had I had that thought that another much more powerful one hit me: "perhaps, thinking like this, I'm a sports sociologist, a young aspiring academic yes, and maybe this 'field' is where I'm going to stay for a while (no pun intended).

I've been to university twice now. The first time was in 2001 when I enrolled on a Sports Development and Coaching degree at Sheffield Hallam University straight after completing my A-Levels at 18. But I wasn't ready for studying back then. Although I'd shown some early promise, I was naïve and going through personal problems, I was no longer concerned with the education process, my marks were comparatively poor and I was generally more interested in drinking it up with the lads from the hockey team than reading Hylton's *Sports Development: Policy, Process and Practice*. So for a number of reasons I ended up leaving Hallam before the beginning of my third year and returning home to Liverpool. Upon returning to my hometown, I initially volunteered as a sports coach at a local inner-city primary school. But when the time came for me to find paid employment, the job that I'd wanted to do and the reason I'd gone to university – to be a sports development officer – was by then, an occupation in which only someone with a degree would be considered. So I had to find something else to do as well as coaching football and hockey voluntarily. At first, I started training as a chef but didn't appreciate being bawled at by a Gordon Ramsey wannabe, who in turn didn't appreciate my reply on the day I finally snapped. I started working nights as an auditor in the Liverpool Moat House Hotel, a "four-star" establishment which has since been demolished to make way for the city's new Liverpool ONE complex. Then I was hired by a global investment bank to settle stocks and shares trades between financial institutions throughout the world, and although I didn't particularly like the job, I excelled at it. I ended up training new members of staff, writing an expanse of training literature and policy documents, and developing and delivering training workshops, things which I found to be the most fulfilling parts of a job I hated being in. Luckily for me though, as I was beginning to cement my reputation as somewhat of a 'rising star' in the company I didn't want to work for, the directors decided to outsource the whole department to India in order to save money and handed my team our notices. This left me with a choice to make. On the one hand, an associate in Amsterdam had hinted that his company were keen to hire me to do the job that I had been doing in Liverpool, ... and for much more money. Or alternatively, I could use my redundancy package to pay off some debts and go back and finish university. Perhaps then I could compete

41

for employment as a Sports Development Officer. After discussing my options with a close friend I decided on the latter and reasoned that I'd regret not having finished university in the future, and that it would open a few more doors in terms of career options. So I applied and was accepted at Liverpool Hope University to study BSc (Hons) Sports Development and Sport Studies.

This time was different though: I applied myself to my studies, I read numerous books and journal articles and listened to the odd podcast and watched the odd documentary. I engaged in the educational process by volunteering as a student-staff liaison representative and participated as much as possible in every seminar discussion. At the end of my first year, although I'd achieved some excellent grades, when Clive first asked me if I would be interested in submitting my main essay that year to the *Journal for Qualitative Research in Sports Studies* (JQRSS), my first thought was that he'd got it mixed up someone else's. At the time, the idea of being published in an academic journal was unthinkable to me. While my standard of writing had clearly improved since attending Hallam, never did I think that what I'd written was something that others might be interested in reading. Nevertheless, I was encouraged by Clive's enthusiasm for the project, and more so, by his enthusiasm for my '*Can we have our ball back please?*' essay. That first article, unsurprisingly, required extensive mentoring and rewriting, and the academic writing process did not come as naturally to me as I'd first hoped. I had a tendency to 'waffle' and use colloquial words and expressions, which the review process helped me to resolve: I was beginning to learn how to write more formally and more succinctly. Although perhaps more importantly at that stage, I was walking a very fine line between critical thinking and outright cynicism, and it was Clive who made sure that I stayed on the right side of the line. Writing and then re-writing the paper was hard work, but a challenge that I relished and one in which the outcome inspired me to want to write another. The second article (written toward the end my second year), *Funding and Sponsorship*, did not stem from any assessed piece of undergraduate work but from my own interest in commercialisation in sport and Olympic social legacies. The aim of this piece was to highlight some of the issues regarding the funding of the London 2012 Olympics and the use of National Lottery money. When I approached Clive to ask whether he would be interested in mentoring such an article, he replied positively, and so work began on an essay which, when completed, was much bigger than anything that I'd been required to write in my first and second years as an undergraduate. Although this paper still needed a fair degree of mentoring and re-writing, my ability to argue points critically and to identify where my writing could stimulate discussion had improved substantially since the first article. Additionally, as a result of this mentoring process (and the one previous), there had also been a marked increase in the quality of my degree assessments and I was clearly benefitting from the growth in confidence that comes from having work published.

About halfway through my second year, I took my newfound confidence and writing ability and applied for a job at Liverpool Hope University's *Centre for Widening Participation and Outreach* as Peer and Academic Writing Mentor. The underpinning agenda of this role was to raise the aspirations of those students who might not have considered university as a viable option because of specific social or economic circumstances, and through this employment I was able to develop my own mentoring skills and instil confidence in the young people I was working with, like Clive had done with me. Then at the beginning of my final year as an undergraduate I was invited to travel to the Tibetan Homes Foundation in northern India to take part in the Liverpool Hope University's *Global Hope* education initiative. The aims of this project were to make grass-roots interventions into the Tibetan Homes Foundation's sporting culture and provide their staff with a platform to engage in an in-depth discussion concerning sport development, coaching, sport psychology and physiology. It was this project that provided the inspiration for my third article for the JQRSS, *Sporting education – a Global Hope?* co-authored with the project's leader Joel Rookwood. From the moment I was invited to take part, Joel's support and was invaluable. Through his mentoring I learned to appreciate a number of important things about writing at this point in my development; how my coaching skills and knowledge can be applied to a world wider than the streets of Liverpool; how to research hard-to-reach environments; and, how to remove the journalistic slant from my academic writing. Joel also helped me to refine some of the ideas that I wanted to present in the article and offered some of his own. There was a lot more collaboration in the writing process on this article which I enjoyed – stemming from the fact that we were both on the project - I learned a lot from Joel's knowledge of international issues related to sport development. By the time the article was complete, I had graduated with a first class degree and had started my current postgraduate course, an MSc in Research Methods. I felt secure in the knowledge that I already had two academic publications, with a third on the way which chronicled some of my more formative experiences in HE to date. When the Tibet article was finished, Clive informed that he had yet to receive a journal article review submission for the JQRSS and asked if I'd be interested in writing one as my first solo publication. I of course jumped at the chance; for it was now time for me to show what I'd learned from the mentoring process and in doing so, discuss with my target audience something which was very close to my heart – sports coaching. Writing the review was a very satisfying experience and one which, I think, successfully demonstrated how far my writing had come in the three and a half years since my first essay was published.

Which brings us to this book: *The Sporting Image – What If?* When Clive contacted me about a taking up a role in this project, naturally, I was pretty excited. Interestingly enough, at the time I had not long finished reading *More What If?*: *Eminent Historians Imagine What Might Have Been* edited by the American military historian, Robert Cowley. Like *The Sporting Image – What If?*, Cowley's book also consists of a collection of essays and creative writing stories based around plausible alternatives to defining moments in history. So to get the chance to be involved in what is essentially a sport version of Cowley's book was an exciting prospect. My choice of topic was an easy decision: the Munich Olympics was something that I'd always wanted to write about. Before now, with all the publications, films and documentaries about the Munich Massacre, it looked unlikely that I would ever get the chance; the subject seemed to have reached saturation point. But with *The Sporting Image – What If?* I could tell this story from a different viewpoint and offer a counterfactual version of what actually took place. Joel was the obvious choice of mentor given his multitude of experiences in working with and writing about Palestinians and Israelis in sport's initiatives. Together, what we offer is a potential answer to the question of whether a successful rescue of the hostages was possible and how history might have played out had a successful rescue actually taken place.

Having the opportunity to fulfil the role of mentor on a second chapter was a much more challenging task than I'd initially anticipated. For Claire Burgess's story about the Carlisle United goalkeeper, Jimmy Glass, I had to draw on my collective experiences of being a mentee to Clive and Joel, and of being a Peer and Academic Writing Mentor at Hope's *Centre for Widening Participation and Outreach*. For her chapter I initially provided the type of support that Clive provided for me during my first couple of publication experiences: I helped Claire find clarity in her ideas and demonstrated how to present these more succinctly. I later suggested ways in which the chapter could be amended in order that that the research preface was more reflective of the excitement of the events that actually took place and also that the creative writing story seemed more realistic. I thoroughly enjoyed the process of mentoring Claire's account, picking up the threads of what is a great story in football and hopefully, making Claire's version of it entertaining for others. A great deal has been learned from the experience by Claire as author but particularly by me as her mentor.

James Kenyon

The learning journey - from classrooms to kitchens and back again

Chris Hughes

From writing menus to writing assignments and stories: It's all the same to me. Baby vegetables, Jersey Royals, delicate herbs and the Great British spring lamb provide the disgruntled chef with much needed light at the end of winter's tunnel. There was nothing more satisfying. However long in duration, a typical day would pass with what seemed to be the blink of an eye. My feet barely touching the floor all day with more blood, sweat and tears than I care to remember.

So, it's Tuesday morning and two baby lambs are carried through the back kitchen door by the butcher. How do we prepare them? and more importantly how do I teach a young *commis chef* to do it? Do I tell him to refer to the book he uses when he goes on his day release to college? No. "See him, the bloke who just brought them in, well he's what we call a butcher, ask him, you stupid little…" No. Having being on the receiving end of countless verbal violations and spending 2 years ducking out of the way of flying spoons and ladles, its simple. We treat them with utmost respect, we know exactly where they have come from, what they have eaten, we stroke them (yes, I know they are dead), smell them; discuss what bits we're going to use for this that and the other. We lay them down at different angles so we can see its true proportion and map out our desired point of entry with a sharp knife. I guide the young lad around the animal; together we break it down, trim fat, remove sinew, we scrape bones, never wasting a single ounce. It's a journey from the back door to chopping board, to stove, to plate. The single most important component within the journey is the fact that we totally engage, we touch, see, taste, smell, we listen to the skin crisping in the pan and we care for and take responsibility for every single piece. At the end of the day, that's what it deserves.

My philosophy on teaching and learning has been constructed from several positive and negative experiences within formal education however, nothing has had more impact than my contrasting previous career.

The journey I speak of, in my view, is a journey we take everyday, sometimes without even becoming conscious of it. I believe education and learning to be intertwined, a tactile ever evolving system that when effectively engaged can form a coherent lasting structure; a balanced view on life, an escape from the mundane, an opportunity to be challenged.

Creative writing in a sporting sense makes total sense. We ask players, coaches and even ourselves within a sporting environment to be creative; don't be afraid of trying different combinations, is there an alternative way of attacking that left wing? However, we must not fall into the trap of simply being creative just for the sake of it. We must be doing it for the good of the team, there needs to be a successful outcome, our creative writing must be written academically, in other words form a coherent structure.

Faced with the task of mentoring a piece of creative writing on Brian Clough, I quickly encountered the occasional problem of, where do I start? Initially, great stuff, books, documentaries, newspaper articles, interviews, autobiographies and even films. This was going to be easy, writing creatively about such a charismatic football figure who loved to play creative football. What I found myself doing was listening to interviews, watching his teams play whilst reading material about the man and his players. I wanted to see the man for who he was, what he believed in and ultimately what he would have been like in charge of England. In an email to Clive I wrote "I feel like Robert DeNiro or some famous actor when they attempt to almost become the character they will be playing". I tried to absorb so much that it felt as though I knew Brian Clough; he was sat right next to me helping me writing it.

Creative writing, the Sporting Image module and this book all attempt to interpret sport for what it actually is – a creative pastime. What does sport really mean to us? How do we feel when we watch our side play beautiful football? and What if? What if? What if? The beauty of this particular project is the fact that students and mentors alike are free to express their writing skills within correct academic protocol. The resulting stories can provide the reader with an alternative insight into a particular sport, situation or person and even portray a given person in their true light as opposed to their falsely documented nature. Much to the contrary of several biographies and even a feature film, such stories in the case of Brian Clough enable the reader to digest the literature and question for themselves What if?

Chris Hughes

Going around: I don't want to land yet; I'm having too much fun

Iain Adams

1 4th March 1990, Goodwood Aerodrome. Alex Corner gently banked the mocca and white Cessna 152 into approximate alignment with Runway 24. With flaps at 20 and the speed at 65kts he lined up on the centre line and transmitted "Kilo Victor, final, touch and go". The tower responded immediately "Kilo Victor cleared touch and go". He lowered full flap and as the aircraft reached about 6' above the runway, slowly eased into level flight and closed the throttle. As she sank, Alex eased the stick back and about 3" above the runway the stall warner chirruped and the main wheels sank onto the runway. Three beaut's in a row. The weather's great, wind down the runway, visibility at least ten miles, traffic light. It's solo time.

Sitting alongside I watched him set take-off flap, take-off trim, carburettor heat cold and scan the engine temperatures and pressures as his hand moved back to the throttle to select full power. I briskly tapped his wrist out of the way and stated "My aircraft". "Your aircraft" responded Alex. "Kilo Victor staying down, student going first solo" I informed the air traffic controller.

I had been steadily moving my seat back as the lesson progressed; now I was all the way back, out of Alex's peripheral vision, subconsciously he was used to not seeing his instructor in the plane. I taxied to the tower, hopped out, secured my straps and instructed Alex to call for taxi for one circuit, go enjoy himself and remember to pick me up. Up in the tower, I watched my cygnet become a swan. A nice landing and a jaunty taxi back to the flying school. The plane was safe. To the controller's amusement, forgotten I trudged back across the airfield, my first 'first solo', my first trudge across the airfield, but not the last.

Most instructors, teachers, coaches, gurus, professors, lecturers, educators, trainers, tutors, whatever we call them, are in it for intrinsic reasons; the rewards are not financial. One of the delights in teaching is seeing people achieve. You suffer their failures and rejoice in their victories. Who can ever forget the sight of a small child surfacing and vigorously shaking their head and looking around to suddenly realise they have moved across the pool, maybe only one yard, but moved. "I CAN SWIM!" The joys of watching the small primary school football team win all of their games against much

48

bigger schools and finally win the cup at the end of the season. Every junior boy, and some girls, had to play because we didn't have enough otherwise; at a bigger school most would never have played sport for the school. With the season over, one or two parents actually thank you for the hundreds of hours you have put in with their kids; some of course simply moan "I hope you will be more considerate with your practice times next year". You're not paid, you race back from university to get there, and give up your Saturdays, fortunately the pleasures are in the achievements of the kids themselves.

I stumbled into teaching accidently; a scholarship had seen me qualify as a commercial pilot and contracted to Midland Counties Dairies as one of their executive pilots for five years. Then they went bust, I took a part-time job flying an executive jet and went to Birmingham University to do a PE degree to fill in the time, I was an enthusiastic footballer and kayaker. Less enthusiasm and more skill used to intone my instructors. To help build up my flying hours to obtain the coveted Airline Transport Pilot's Licence I began instructing – and found my niche in life. Sit back and let others scare me to death rather than doing it myself.

I can still hear the shrieks of joy from Dave, a totally blind undergraduate, on a ten day canoe trip into the wilderness of the Boundary Water Canoe area, no roads, houses, or telephones for days in any direction. He had developed sufficient confidence in himself, and me, to paddle down Grade 3 rapids in the front of a Canadian canoe, climb 100 foot cliffs, jump from the cliffs into the lakes and torrents below, guided by my instructions. In the evening around the campfire, he wouldn't shut up about the sounds, feelings, vibrations, and scents of his experiences; a totally different perspective, priceless.

I have been fortunate in being able to spend my adult life flying aeroplanes and teaching/coaching sport. This has included teaching prospective PE teachers in America, Jordan, Bahrain, Indonesia and Britain. The motto "do no harm" is not good enough. Our students must positively add to their own and other people's lives.

Assessor, examiner, auditor, inspector, appraiser, evaluator, judge and jury; the more stressful side of my life. "Dr Iain, just three marks, please give me three more marks and I can graduate and go out and teach". No way, I would not want you teaching my son, so why would I let you teach anybody's children? A bad PE teacher can impact negatively on well over 5,000 children over a teaching career, nobody gave me the right to please one individual and do that much damage. But it still stresses me to fail students, especially third years; I may be forcing them to spend another year at university, more thousands of pounds on fees, beer and curry.

Jasper X complained bitterly when I first failed him on his General Flight Test which would have given him his Private Pilot's Licence and allowed him to take passengers; "I was safe enough for most of the flight and I have promised my wife a flight for her birthday". "I wouldn't let my wife fly with you, so why would I let you fly yours? You would have damaged my plane in that simulated forced landing, go do more of those with your instructor and re-book a flight test when he is happy".

Sadly, higher education is, arguably, the least rewarding educational assessment regime, often measured through hours of reading scripts with tortuous syntax, a plethora of spelling errors and a dearth of original ideas. The instantaneous feedback of a physical skill accomplished denied. At least 'What If...' has actually brought forth some enjoyable reading.

Wendy, Alex's beautiful girlfriend, has already covered him with kisses when I get back to the flying school; Alex is drunk with pride, deep satisfaction and champagne. I had tipped Wendy off that given the right conditions, he could solo any lesson now. Obviously Wendy is driving home; I'm flying again, no champagne for me. "Wow, I get to sleep with a pilot tonight" says Wendy. "Why wait 'til tonight" laughs Alex and they exit the Flying School. I could have sent Alex solo last week but he was not quite relaxed and confident enough. It would have been safe but stressful. Now he's enjoyed the flight, been to heaven once today, and is on his way again. I've made three people happy, but that includes me, how selfish. Teach and make people happy, teach and be happy.

Iain Adams

Rewriting history to get at the truth

Ray Physick

I n everyday life we often pose the question 'what if...' "If only I had done this instead of that", life would be easier. Likewise when looking at historical events people often consider what life would have been like had the outcome of history been different. What would Britain be like if Hitler's Germany had been victorious or would the Civil Rights Movement in America have achieved greater success had Kennedy not been assassinated? Such hypothetical approaches to history are flawed in that they do not have knowledge of people's responses to such hypothetical outcomes. Nevertheless, such scenarios are interesting in the sense that it requires the writer of counterfactual history to at least have an in-depth knowledge of the actual historical events. Moreover, re-reading history before going on to write a 'what if' version of history does help to clarify what such people as Hitler and Kennedy actually stood for.

Sport, perhaps, has the greatest potential when it comes to 'what if' scenarios. What if such and such a striker had not missed that penalty we would have won the European Cup. Such debates are what keeps sports fans going when faced with seeing their team lose a crucial match. In a way it is all part of the build-up to the next sporting event that might see your team, your favourite tennis player or golfer succeed next time.

The 'what if' stories I edited all contained the elements outlined above. All the stories are introduced by a research preface that required the student to do some background reading before writing their creative story. This process was a way of students refining their knowledge about actual events. Moreover, it forced students to deal with issues that face sport in the modern day. Issues of class, racism, nationality and how a country uses sport for its own national interest; all were revealed in the research prefaces and in the creative stories.

Emma Jones' research preface showed the depths of the white supremacist views of Nazi Germany; it also revealed that Jesse Owens was never fully accepted by white America during his life time. Despite the election of a black president overt and covert racism is still apparent in America, forty years after the Civil Rights Movement. The Bourgeois Blues side of life as detailed in Leadbelly's song was clearly apparent in the USA during Jesse Owens' lifetime. Emma's story reminds us of this while at the same showing how horrendous the Nazi regime was. Hitler's befriending of the 'white'

51

Owens reveals splits in the Nazi party, splits that actually existed in Germany, especially before the Night of the Long Knives in 1934. The story also serves to show that Jews, both in Germany and around the world, were not compliant victims but did attempt to resist the horrors that faced them during the Nazi years.

Ashley Walker's story about football hooliganism was also well researched. Her preface showed that the problems of football hooliganism are deep-rooted and date back to the nineteenth century. Hooligans are usually portrayed by the press as some kind of sub-human species, but Ashley's preface serves to show that such behaviour does reflect wider societal problems. Moreover, she demonstrates that such behaviour is often exaggerated by the press, a press that duly ignores the fact that most fans are well-behaved and would never get involved in hooliganism. The story generates an atmosphere and gets across the enthusiasm for cup football among fans. The fact that a father and son are at the heart of the story serves to remind us, that as football gets more expensive for ordinary fans, the ability of families to get to a match is becoming ever more restrictive. The conclusion of the story is very powerful, it demonstrates how events can get out of control and how a violent situation can lead to tragic consequences. However, the twist at the end also serves as a reminder to us all that the press and media can often distort events, and give false impressions about the actual course of events, false impressions that can lead to false conclusions. As the story implies such reporting often leads to people being wrongly accused. Ashley clearly shows that there are wider societal issues implicit both in the story and the research preface.

David Hurst's story about a sporting scandal also reveals a lot about modern sport. The sporting celebrity is a major factor in selling modern day sport. David Beckham, for example, is touted around the world by the Football Association in the cause of the England World Cup bid. Values such as football tradition, what a World Cup hosted by England could offer to the world, get lost in the midst of the money culture that dominates world sport.

David focused upon Michael Vick the American footballer who got wrapped up in drug taking and dog fighting scandals. The celebrity culture that abounds in sport, and wider culture, often places talented people such as sports men and women in a parallel world: a world that is removed from the reality of the everyday sports fan. Sport heroes have been lauded by sports fans since time immemorial. However, the mass media and modern technology have placed sports celebrities in a fantasy world far removed from the fans who idolise such heroes. The research preface to David's story shows that Vick went to gaol for his misdeeds. Unlike many other people leaving gaol Vick was able to join another football club upon release. His talent as a footballer made him a prized commodity hence he was able to command a multimillion dollar contract. The modern day celebrity is a product of the commercialisation of sport, sport that competes in a globalised world. As the creative story shows even though Vick had a dubious past the fans of the club will forgive such misdeeds as long as the team is successful. In modern day sport, apparently, success is not possible without the sporting star.

All three stories, as well as the research prefaces, demonstrate that despite its ability to appeal to a wide range of people, sport, today and historically, still has to contend with issues such as class divide and racial prejudice. Such issues are rooted in a world that values financial gain above everything else. William Morris wrote in *News from Nowhere* (1890) (a classic work combining utopian socialism and soft science fiction - his play on media is interesting even today), about a society that valued people's abilities in a more equitable way; a place where leisure and culture practices were incorporated into the mores of society. A society that abhorred the commodity culture that was developing in Morris' time and one that now dominates the world at the expense of cultural development. To a modern day observer such a society would seem utopian: but a world based on common values where different skills have equal value because they make a contribution to society as a whole is a utopia worth striving for.

A world based on William Morris' values? Seems like there is another collection of 'what if' stories in making here.

Ray Physick

References

Morris, W. (1890) *News from nowhere and other writings*. Penguin Classics – (reprinted in 1994) London.

Mea Culpa (my fault)

Mitchell J. Larson

I write this essay with no small sense of accomplishment, for if my colleagues were completely honest, they would justifiably blame me for coming up with the initially questionable idea of a student essay based on the concept of 'counterfactual history'. For his first volume of student-staff collaboration, Clive had asked the students to compose poetry reflecting on the work they had undertaken in the module. Doing another book of poetry seemed repetitive and we were keen for a new challenge and development. So during the summer of 2009 Clive, Iain, Ray and I met over coffee to talk about an adequately challenging assignment for the students' second written piece of assessed work. The module was "The Sporting Image," and so many of the twentieth century's sports figures were, literally, iconic: boxer Muhammad Ali and Jesse Owens, the black American sprinter in Hitler's 1936 Olympics, immediately sprang into my head. The others soon chimed in with their own sporting heroes and villains and the idea gained momentum: the *What-If* book was born.

Counterfactual history remains controversial within the historical profession and only a handful of scholars have endeavoured to give it a philosophical justification worthy of the name. This is not the place to rehearse that debate. What the concept did offer us in the context of teaching a university module was that the assignment would challenge students to use a combination of writing skills, historical research, and conceptual creativity to complete the assignment. We allowed them to select their own sports personality or historical event to transform in their essay because this would enhance their level of commitment to the work and provide a sense of 'ownership'. Students in their final year of university education are (ideally) more than capable of writing a predetermined number of words to answer an essay topic selected for them by their tutors. The problem is that they approach the task rather mechanically and without the spark of passion that lies behind really lively and enjoyable prose. In the worst cases student essays are copied or bought from vendors on the internet with no student thought involved whatever. What we sought was a way to remove them from the comfortable cocoon which such mechanical and predictable work allows and force them into some original and creative thinking without giving them complete *carte blanche* to invent whatever entirely fictional story suited their taste (that is also very challenging but in a different way). Judging from the essays in this volume, we succeeded more often than not with this exercise.

Where the blame comes in was after the term finished and the marked student essays came back to the tutors for additional 'tweaking' for publication in the book. I feel slightly guilty for helping to come up with the original idea but subsequently editing only two student essays myself! None of us knew how much work it might be to turn some of these creative stories into tolerable-enough prose to put our names on while still sleeping at night. The joy of it – yes, there was a good bit of fun here – came in considering the implications and the 'big issues' touched on by the students, often consciously but sometimes unconsciously. Space limitations for the students' work as well as for the finished product necessarily curtailed some of the discussions that might have arisen had we been granted more space. In one of the essays I edited, entitled *World Cup 1986: what if Fashanu had eclipsed Maradona?*, the student broached a major issue in sport at all levels and one that transcends sport by reaching into human society at large. The student's implicit dream of a world without (or with substantially less) bigotry against homosexuals might be viewed in a variety of ways. When I read the original draft I realized the possible depth of the ideas that students could explore through this type of assignment and the potential layers of the underlying question, 'what if?'. As the tutor, one always wonders about the degree to which students are cognizant of their own insights when they are writing something like this. More than likely the student did not have the time to reflect on the experience fully. The fact that it was there, though, gave me hope that the spirit of the assignment had been fulfilled and that the student, whether he knew it or not, had probably embarked on a train of thought that may have important ramifications for him in later life.

What else, as tutors, can we ask for?

Yes, I know – we tutors could be greedy and demand things like proper grammar and spelling and all the things that make the written expression of ideas so challenging to us all, and no less so for today's students, whose patience too often seems entirely expended waiting for a friend to return the latest text message in the nearly incomprehensible texting language – or 'tanglish', as I like to call it. Repairing the technical parts of the writing without losing its flavour or the tone imparted by the student was difficult – I am not sure how well, if at all, I achieved this in the essays I edited.

On the other hand, almost by definition I could not have written the essays the students composed as they are tales told from a certain perspective, written at a certain age, and so on. What is important to me as a key sporting moment will not be the same for them and vice-versa, nor will the lessons learned from particular events or individuals necessarily be the same. This is as it should be. But at a basic level our students need to learn how to transmit their most important or valued ideas (not always the same thing) to the next generation just as we are doing now. It is important for them and for future generations that they learn to think for themselves and to write down their ideas well, for this is how our species grows: we create, develop, and share our ideas....I hope for the benefit of all.

Mitchell J. Larson

Chapter 1

The tragedy of Aron Ralston

Robert Bartlett and Clive Palmer

Research Preface

THIS IS A THIRD PERSON ACCOUNT of how American climber Aron Ralston went out one day to Blue John Canyon (Canyonlands National Park, Utah) to climb solo on the rock faces and in the canyons. Before he left, Ralston told nobody of his whereabouts or what he was planning to do. It was a seemingly spur of the moment climb, something which he would later go on to regret.

The fact that he went to the wilderness on his own meant that this story could be written well in two ways; a first person account of his experiences or third person account, there being no-one else there to write it from their point of view. When considering whether to write in the first or third person, Boehmer (2001: 154) states that, "it is one of the central decisions a writer must make, as it affects the angling, the force, the atmosphere and the shape of the story – especially if it's fiction". The particular nature of Aron's account would be challenging to impart in first person, although the conflict between man and mind was an interesting tussle to consider. However, the problem with first person perspective in this story is that, in truth, Aron's experiences were such a gruesome, traumatising and disturbing event that they deserved to be discussed with sincerity and not overly dramatised. The unfolding events were sufficiently dramatic without embellishing them further. For the writer, it would be immensely difficult to imagine what pain would have been felt by Aron throughout this ordeal and the psychological boundaries which appeared to have been crossed on this journey of suffering. It seemed as if writing in the first person risked not doing justice to his experiences and perhaps diverting attention to immediate difficulties rather than long term consequences for Aron.

Boran (2005: 120) explores the idea of incorporating more than one character into a story; "*whose* story you tell determines what *kind* of story you tell". Again, this was an interesting concept to consider in this context, as there could be more *characters* than just Aron himself – although he was alone he did a lot of talking during his ordeal. Whilst climbing in the canyon, a very large loose boulder fell down and crushed Aron's arm. He was in a narrow gulley at this point and the boulder trapped him in this lonely and hidden position. He was trapped and injured with nobody actually knowing where he was. Ralston was stuck there for six days in total, in which time he battled various forms of psychological problems, including depression, exacerbated by the effect of severe dehydration on his body and mind. During this period he had come to terms with death, made peace with the world and had even recorded a video tape with his free hand, stating his last will and testament. After the fifth day of hanging there, Ralston's trapped hand and lower arm had died from lack of blood circulation. Taking Boran's (2005) thoughts into account, it could be important to have a second voice as well as Ralston's own in the story; to display the nature of the truly awful state that Ralston himself was in. For this reason a sole voice was included, representing the voice of his conscience in the piece. The conscience utters the same phrase of warning which repeats throughout which alters in emphasis and poignancy as events unfold for Aron.

Not only was it the mental struggle that Ralston had to cope with, it was also the physical struggle. For six days, Ralston had just been trapped there trying to force the boulder up and off of his hand and arm. At the end of the six days, when the hand and arm had "died", Ralston reasoned that to self-amputate his hand and arm was the only way to free himself. It took him one hour to operate fully, using a blunt knife to saw through the muscle, veins and sinew and then using his own body weight to hang and snap the bones. He was now free of the boulder. Although not trapped, Aron was still miles away from his truck and without any means of communication he could not raise the alarm. He proceeded to abseil on his rope, one handed, down a 65 foot cliff face and then hiked, dehydrated, through hot sun whereupon he was rewarded for his efforts and saved after he came across several hikers. Ralston was finally air-lifted to hospital to safety, where a life saving operation meant that he can now carry on with his life. He is actually back to his rock climbing and lives an otherwise full and normal life. However, he has found a new and very successful dimension from his arduous experiences as a public speaker and publisher. A truly life – changing event?, arguably for the better with 20:20 hindsight? Possibly.

Boran (2005: 149) also states that the creative writer needs to find a way to appeal to the reader's senses through scenes. This is a very important factor to consider in how the horror of the situation that Aron finds himself in is conveyed to the reader. The most obvious solution is to make the amputation scene more grotesque in its descriptive nature and to constantly refer to the state that Ralston is in both physically and mentally. However, as mentioned above it seemed that the events as they unfolded were sufficiently dramatic in real life and did not warrant being overplayed.

Evans (2000: 178) explores how the use of background information can add bite to a story. Although Evans (2000) is referring to journalistic writing, it is an appropriate concept to consider when writing a short story. To add in any background of Ralston's climbing experience could be important, but would also allow room to manoeuvre when considering the subsequent editing. Similarly, background information was equally important to add context to the story. A simple description of Ralston's situation and how he got there would add a simple but useful context to the story, whilst also providing some factual background to the piece.

Hicks (1999: 131) posts an interesting idea of how even news stories, in the current climate, are written to tease, intrigue and entertain, as well as inform – just as short stories are. It applies to creative writing, just with a little more freedom, but the main objectives of this story are to express the morality of the situation that Ralston finds himself in and to convey his ultimate courageousness in order to survive as well as to inform the reader of his background and why he chose to go through with his actions. An entertainment factor for this tragedy comes through by the use of description, writing style and most importantly the ending.

In conclusion, reading the background information and Aron Ralston's account of the situation (2005) has provided some interesting angles to provoke thoughts for twists and turns within the creative piece. The research for this has focused upon how Ralston coped whilst going through his most life-threatening experience and why he decided to take matters into his own hands to extricate himself. The key difference in reading a journalistic piece about the event is that they would ideally be time-lined and factual. Within this story, even though it is fictionalised, the feasibility of how events transpire are realistic, which may been seen to add to the quality of the tragedy as told.

References

Benoist, M. (2004) Climber who cut off hand looks back. *National Geographic News* [online]. Available at: http://news.nationalgeographic.com/news/2004/08/0830 040830 aronralston. html (Accessed on 18th January 2010).

Boehmor, E. (2001) *Writing in the first person*. In Bell, J. and Magrs, P. (Eds.) *The creative writing coursebook*. Macmillan, London.

Blogspot (2008) *Aron Ralston, trapped, the rock climber who amputated his own arm* [online]. Available at: http://aronralston.blogspot.com/ (Accessed on 18th January 2010).

Boran, P. (2005) *The portable creative writing workshop*. New Island, Dublin.

Evans, H. (2000) *Essential English for journalists, editors and writers*. Pimlico, London.

Hicks, W. (1999) *Writing for journalists*. Routledge, Oxon.

Ralston, A. (2005) *Between a rock and a hard place*. Atria Books, USA.

Creative Story

The tragedy of Aron Ralston

Robert Bartlett and Clive Palmer

SLOWLY BURNING IN THE MIDDAY HEAT, trapped alone with nothing but his thoughts for company, Aron was trapped in a deep canyon. The boulder, roughly two feet across had fallen and jammed in the narrowing space where Aron was climbing. As the boulder wedged itself in under the force of gravity it trapped his lower right arm pinning him against the wall. His right hand, crushed to smithereens under the weight of a loose boulder, was now nothing more than a death certificate waiting to be served.

Struggling, Aron felt his hopes crushed as another attempt at pushing the boulder upwards failed.

"You shouldn't have come here alone" his conscience was echoing through his empty, forlorn mind.

"SHUT UP! ARRRRRRRRRGH! PLEASE, HELP! FOR GOD'S SAKE HELP ME!" Aron screamed, but he knew nobody was there.

"You shouldn't have come here alone..."

It was the sixth day. Aron Ralston had come, alone, to climb this canyon. Stranded under a tonne of immovable pressure, he was now regretting his decision not to tell someone, anyone, of his whereabouts.

With his free hand, Aron wiped the dust from his mousy hair. The remote walls of the canyon seemed somewhat comforting now; Aron was at a claustrophobic peace. Just two days ago, he estimated, as he made his last will and testament to a small video camera. Staring up towards the boulder, Aron glanced upon his etchings in the side of the rock.

61

RIP Aron Ralston.

A wry smile formed across his weather-beaten face. Maybe it was the heat, or the lack of water, but Aron knew that this was his grave.

He hissed in pain as dust covered the messy stab wound on his arm. On the ledge above him lay the blunt knife of the micro-tool that he had used to sever the fleshy bits of his right arm. The steel shone scarlet in sunshine.

"Cheap crap" he cursed. The blade was too blunt to cut through bone. He now hung in a bloody, exhausted state, drifting in and out of consciousness as the hours passed by.

With one last effort, he contorted his body upwards and pushed all the remaining strength he had into the boulder. It didn't budge an inch. Tears began to carve through Aron's grimy cheeks and before he knew it, he was sobbing against his wounded arm.

Dejected, he watched as a small piece of rock crumbled and fell from the face and smashed on the canyon floor some two hundred feet below him. Nothing left but a pile of smoking dust – and then it hit him. The divine inspiration.

Bones don't have to be sawn, they can be broken. Why hadn't he thought of this before?

Reaching over to the ledge, Aron steadied himself, making a vice out of some spare climbing karabiners. Arranging his position to drop his body weight with maximum efficiency against the resistance, he braced and took two deep breaths before snapping the first bone. A crack, followed by a horrendous scream of agony which filled the canyon to its brim.

"No-one can hear you scream".

"Long full life", he gasped. Thoughts of his future raced around his head, thoughts that had slowly diminished over the past week. His wife, a young son and a dog running joyfully around the back garden kept playing on repeat in his mind. Even the simple things like meeting friends for a coffee, or reading the paper, seemed like such a luxury at this moment in time.

For six days, SIX DAYS, Aron had been hanging in utmost agony, slowly going at his dead arm with a blunt blade. The solution had been there all along; so simple, so costly.

Aron began sawing away at the remaining fleshy tissue, blood splurging across his face as he severed through his own artery. Another bone break, another unforgiving scream of anguish.

"Long full life, long full life" Aron spurred himself on, slicing through yet more muscle. He was now covered in crimson; noticing how much blood he was beginning to lose, Aron finally cut through the last bits of skin on the underside of his arm. Finally free from the rocky tomb, Aron lay back against the rock face and looked up to the heavens. A single bead of nauseating sweat dripped off his forehead in the baking sun.

Head spinning and delirious, Aron was struggling to focus on the task before him. He swore he could hear the faint sound of a rotary blade in the distance, but with the tremendous loss of blood and lack of fluid over the past week, he began to put it down to hallucination. Nevertheless, if it was somehow real, it meant that he had less than half an hour to get himself rescued. 'Birds' like those don't stay in the sky long, he reasoned, they need refuelling.

"Come on, man!" He grunted and hauled himself into action.

"You should never have come here alone."

"COME ON! SHUT UP!" he screamed, kicking away dust in frustration. Spreading his weight across his feet, Aron slowly began to rise from the tomb that encased him. He heaved his way up the side of the canyon, the muscles in his remaining arm straining to keep him alive. Aron had to climb to the top of the canyon and then abseil off the cliff edge to lower ground, and then get back on the trail to civilisation.

The weight of the rope wrapped around his shoulder began to tear through his skin as he climbed, he really couldn't afford to lose more blood. With one last forceful push, he dragged himself to the top and lay there for a moment, exhausted, before breaking into a fit of hysterical and tearful laughter. He was free.

"Come on, come on, please, come on..." he whispered into the afternoon sun.

Dazed from the heat, Aron picked himself up and clutched at the bloody stump where his forearm used to be. Wrapped in his once white shirt, it was now a deep shade of red and dripping profusely onto the rocky bed below.

He began to stumble the two hundred feet or so towards the cliff edge. Every step was getting heavier, and his eyes were beginning to fade. The sand in his boot was beginning to wear away the skin on the underside of his feet. Each step felt like standing in fire.

"You shouldn't have come here alone"

"No, come on, just a bit further..." Aron begged his swollen body to carry on. Confused, he began pleading with himself to make it to the cliff edge.

"A...bit...further..."

Finally, after what seemed like hours, Aron broke down on the Cliffside. His head thumped, his mind heavy and he was struggling to breathe. But he'd made it.

"Almost there... almost safe", he choked.

This time, he definitely heard the comforting roar of rotary blades in the distance. Rescue was on the cards, surely.

"God rewards those who work hard and boy I've worked hard here, come on, just a bit further" he muttered to himself.

Not knowing how, a rush of warmth circulated through Aron's body – somewhere, somehow, they'd come for him. The rope began to slide slowly off his raw shoulder, but battered and bruised, he didn't care. He wouldn't need it now. He could taste water, food, bed.

"You shouldn't have come here alone."

The noise of engines and whooshing of chopper blades seemed to get louder. On full alert now, Aron stumbled up and mustered enough energy to scream across the deep valleys and into the sky. Laughing, he started to leap up and down, adrenaline pumping through his veins like electricity. Jumping again, he fell backwards awkwardly onto his ankle.

"Bloody rocks" he cursed, but he was too tired to care. Help was finally at hand.

Suddenly, Aron noticed a hissing noise gradually getting louder around him. Like interference on a radio struggling to find its station, it was quite a distraction. He looked again to the skies, nothing there. Strange. The sun pierced through him still. Was it the helicopter?

"You shouldn't have come here alone." Hiss. HISSSSS.

And then, silence. Aron looked at his feet in shock. The rope was gone. Scarpering towards the cliff edge, he peered over the side to the horror below. Falling softly through the air, the rope twirled like yellow ribbon. As it fell twisting through the air as Aron stood there, motionless. He sank to his knees in defeat, sobbing into the hot dust and smacking his remaining fist into the earth. It was over.

"PLEASE, HELP ME!" he screamed, his voice cutting out in tears half way through. Shattered, he lay there, weeping. Thoughts of his future began to fade from memory again, the sun slowly frying away his self belief.

He could feel the blood escaping rapidly from his wounds now, he was getting weak. The effort summoned to fight every instinct in his body when amputating his arm had begun to catch up with him. He coughed, spluttering up more crimson as he gasped for breath.

"You shouldn't have come here alone".

Aron rolled over onto his back, fighting for his own body to stay awake. Visions were racing through his mind; the first climb, the canyon in the distance, a loose boulder falling, crushing, a blood curdling scream, bones shattering. Light, oh the piercing light!

His heart beating furiously against his chest, the pounding seemed to echo throughout the whole canyon. Aron was shaking uncontrollably now; the weight of the light crushed him down into the dirt. Two hundred feet below him, deep into the canyon, laid his trusty rope, still warm with his blood. He lay there, trying to contain the shaking. The sky seemed whiter than normal, a peaceful palate of nothingness.

Slowly, Aron closed his eyes and listened to the faint sound of the rotary blades fly off into the distance.

"You shouldn't have come here alone".

And with that, the world stopped turning for Aron Ralston.

Chapter 2

What if Muhammad Ali did not conscientiously object the Vietnam War?

Jon Cockrill and Clive Palmer

Research Preface

MUHAMMAD ALI WAS BORN CASSIUS CLAY on January 17th 1942 in Louisville Kentucky. He took up boxing at the age of 12, six years later he was winning light-heavyweight gold at the Rome Olympics in 1960 (Hauser, 2004: 190). Shortly after his Olympic success Clay turned pro, quickly amassing a 19 fight unbeaten record in just under three years. The run included technical knockouts against Archie Moore and Henry Cooper, and earned him a world title shot against Sonny Liston, his twentieth opponent (Boxrec.com, 2009).

Clay went on to defeat Sonny Liston in Miami in February 1964, when the champion did not return from his corner at the beginning of the seventh round. It was after this fight that Clay announced he was a member of the Nation of Islam and changed his name to Muhammad Ali. The Nation of Islam at the time was also called The Black Muslims which was a sect of the Islamic faith. It is claimed by Ali that he had been attending Nation of Islam meetings in secret for three years previous, in fear that he would not have got a shot at the world title if it were common knowledge that he was a member. This was seemingly not a good move for him to make at the time with regard to his relations with 'White America', as Hauser, (2004: 81) points out, "Before 1964, it seemed as though almost everything Cassius

Clay did, fitted within the context of establishment white values. He wasn't white, but he was the next best thing".

Hauser (2004) points out that it is widely claimed that the Nation of Islam used Ali as a public relations tool, despite at the time Ali being treated with suspicion from many sectors of American society because of his religious stance. Ali was influential because he seemed to be able to reach out and connect with a wider demographic of American society because of his sporting achievements and status. Elijah Muhammad, the Nation of Islam's leader, claimed Ali's win over Sonny Liston as "a victory for Islam" – [interestingly] having refused to support him publicly before the fight, believing that Ali would lose (Telegraph.co.uk, 1999).

In the early 60s, the United States found themselves becoming more involved in the Vietnam War. In 1964 Ali was not eligible for the armed forces as his reading and writing skills were sub-standard. However in 1966, with the Americans increasing troop levels in Vietnam at an alarming rate towards their peak in 1968, the bar for academic ability was lowered, meaning Ali was suitable for draft. Between the years 1964 and 1968, General William Westmoreland was the commanding officer of all American troops in Vietnam. In these four years he saw his troop numbers rise from 16,000 to their peak 535,000, under the presidency of Lyndon Johnson (Hickman, 2001).

Ali declared himself a conscientious objector to the Vietnam War when he was notified of his status to be called up for draft. He claimed that the war was against the teachings of the Qur'an, and that as a Muslim he was not obliged to take part in Christian wars or any war that has not been declared by Allah. It was also in 1966 that Ali famously said, "I ain't got a quarrel with the Viet Cong. No Vietnamese ever called me a nigger". The statement became the unofficial motto of Ali's objection, with him claiming that he had stronger enemies amongst the racist white Americans, as opposed to the communist North Vietnamese soldiers. In April 1967 Ali refused to step forward from the line in a recruitment parade to join the U.S. Armed forces. Three times he was requested to step forward at this induction in Houston. Three times he refused. The attending officers reminded him that should he refuse the draft he could face a $10,000 fine and five years imprisonment. Once again he refused to step forward and as a result he was arrested and stripped of his title and suspended by the New York State Athletic Commission.

Ali was found guilty of being a conscientious objector a few months later, although it was upheld through the Court of Appeals and then passed on to the Supreme Court where the case was eventually heard in June 1971, and the conviction was reversed. Ali had been somewhat lucky that in the four years between his arrest and final hearing, the public opinion of the war in Vietnam had dipped a great deal. He was not permitted to fight and spent much of his time speaking at colleges and rallies, gaining back the popularity he enjoyed in the early stages of his career. He said at a college campus, "I'm expected to go overseas to help free people in South Vietnam, and at the same time my people are being brutalized and mistreated" (Hauser, 2004: 187).

The 'angle for the creative story is drawn from the experiences of Bob Hope (1903-2003) who is the most famous figure from American show business that had an effect on the military. Despite never actually being a member of the armed forces, Hope was named an Honorary Veteran by US congress for his stage performances for the United Services Organizations that saw him entertain troops during World War Two, the Korean War, the Vietnam War and more recently the Gulf War. His Christmas specials that he filmed in Vietnam in 1970 and '71 remain in the top 30 highest viewed prime time telecasts in U.S. history (Anton, 2008).

Had Muhammad Ali reversed his objection to fight in Vietnam and joined the U.S. Armed Forces, it is doubtful his role would have been solely that of a soldier on the front line. At the time, in the 1960s, the heavyweight champion of the world was the most important man in sport and the fact he was fighting against communism in the Vietnam War would have been used as a propaganda tool. Similarly, Joe Louis was used to the same effect during the Second World War. Joe enlisted in the U.S. Armed forces and fought exhibition bouts throughout his service to strengthen the morale and fighting spirit of the troops. This would have probably been the case for Ali, As Lemert (2003: 113) points out, "Ali would have had an 'easy' life in the army compared to the other servicemen. He would have been able to box during the years of his finest athletic skills".

References

Anton, B. (2008) *Bob Hope: his classic television performance,* Articlesbase.com [online]. Available at: http://www.articlesbase.com/art-and-entertainment-articles/bob-hope-his-classic-television-performances-466164.html (Accessed on 20th January 2010).

Boxrec.com (2009) *Boxer: Muhammad Ali – Biography* [online]. Available at: http://boxrec.com/list_bouts.php?human_id=000180&cat=boxer (Accessed on, 20th January 2010).

Hauser, T. (2004) *Muhammad Ali, his life and times* (second edition). Robson Books Ltd., London.

Hickman, K. (2001) *Vietnam war: General William Westmoreland* About.com: Military History [online]. Available at: http://militaryhistory.about.com/od/1900s/p/westmoreland.htm (Accessed on 7th December, 2009).

Lemert, C. (2003) *Muhammad Ali: trickster in the culture of irony.* Blackwell, Oxford.

Telegraph.co.uk (1999) *At once a pawn, and the King of the World* - a comprehensive but sometimes flawed life of the greatest [online]. Available at: http://www.telegraph.co.uk/culture/4718179/At-once-a-pawn-and-the-King-of-the-World.html (Accessed on 20th January, 2010).

Creative Story

What if Muhammad Ali had not conscientiously objected the Vietnam War?

Jon Cockrill and Clive Palmer

THE CHAMP WAS BEING USHERED ALONG a lengthy hollow corridor. The slender nature of the passage and the size of his frame meant the two Lieutenants either side of him were struggling to remain in control. They reached the end of the corridor and the smaller of the two junior officers anxiously manoeuvred his forearm around the Champ's midriff and opened the door to his right before hastily taking a step back, letting the door open on its own.

General William Westmoreland sat in a green leather chair behind a sturdy looking mahogany desk. As he raised his head to acknowledge his visitors, a somewhat starstruck look adorned his face. He quickly rectified his lapse in authority and stared somewhat harshly at the man in front of him, who was blocking what little light the corridor behind him had to offer. "General, Sir," the small Lieutenant announced loudly in a typical US militaristic fashion, "Mr Ali, as you requested". He dropped his salute from his temple with the speed and precision of a Samurai Warrior and stared through his General, awaiting recognition and further instructions. "That will be all, Lieutenant," Westmoreland said calmly, slightly tired of the noisy protocol which the Army seems to think reasonable for personnel entering and exiting an office. Barely acknowledging the Lieutenant's presence as he dismissed him, he turned his admiring gaze on the champ, "Step inside Mr Ali, take a seat".

The Champ stepped further into the room, he inhaled deeply through his nose as he sat opposite Westmoreland, his mouth closed, his eyes fixed on his opponent. The General tried to maintain his stare back, but to no avail.

71

He looked towards a corner table. On it was a crystal decanter and several matching tumblers.

"Would you care for a scotch, Mr Ali?" Westmoreland said as he stood from his chair and began walking towards the table.

The Champ's glare turned into a look of amused disbelief, "Now Willy, why would you be so dumb to ask me a thing like that?" he said as he turned to the General who by now had began pouring a fair sized measure into his glass, "I don't drink, I don't gamble, and I sure as hell don't ride no helicopter in the jungle for you, Willy".

The General looked down at his glass and took a good mouthful of Blue Label. He hadn't been called "Willy" since basic training, when he had no-one under him and everyone on top, it was different now. There were the best part of half a million men in Vietnam and he sat on top of them all. Despite this however he was struggling to gain any mental control over the man that sat before him. "You ain't going to be in no chopper, Mr Ali" the General said, changing the tone of his voice to a friendly, persuasive, reassuring tone, "hell, you ain't going to be on no battlefield".

"You're right I'm not, thank you for your understanding Willy," interrupted the Champ as he rose to his feet and turned to the door.

"God damn it, Mr Ali, get the hell back in that chair" the General shouted, immediately regretting his aggressive response, he breathed in and calmly continued, "if you walk out of this room, you will be arrested as fast as Sonny Liston hits the deck these days. You'll be detained by the Houston District Attorney's Office, who will see that you never fight again *and* see you good for a five year stretch in the can". Westmoreland had moved back behind his desk, leaning over with his fists supporting his straight arms. He nodded towards the chair, "Now sit back down, Mr Ali. I guarantee you it is in your interest".

The Champ turned back towards Westmoreland, standing behind his chair mirroring his opponent's stance, "I'm all ears, Willy," as he moved his outstretched arms from the back of the chair, the furniture almost seemed to breathe a sigh of relief from the strain it had been put under, the Champ moved round and parked himself back in the seat, "Come on Willy, let's hear it".

Westmoreland had sat down, he looked nervous, uncomfortable, his hands were clasped together with each index finger elongated and pressed against his lips, his forehead creased with a concentrated frown, pondering his opening line. He began, "You're at the top of your game, Mr Ali. Why in God's name would you want this ride that you're on come to an end?" Westmoreland's uncomfortable look had developed into a grimace, "I know the Nation of Islam have got you in their pocket".

"I ain't in the pocket of nobody" the Champ interrupted sharply, looking up to the framed photograph of President Johnson on the wall behind Westmoreland. He continued, "if one of us is in the pocket of anyone, I'd say it's you, Willy".

Westmoreland leaned forward, the irritation of being called Willy was starting to grate and it showed on his face, "Well you're welcome to your opinion Mr Ali, let us say for argument's sake that we're both inside pockets, because Elijah Muhammad's pretty god-damn insignificant when compared to that of the god-damn president"! Westmoreland banged his fist on the leather lined desk with a thud.

"You may believe that to be the case, but I am not fighting no war for no white boy, in his White House, and if he's got any sense, his white flag." The Champ felt antagonised by Westmoreland's behaviour, waving his finger before saying, "I've said it once before, aint no Viet Cong........"

"........ever called me nigger." Westmoreland interrupted, and sat back in his chair weighing up whether stopping the Champ mid sentence in such a way, and using such a word when he was in such a mood, was a good move. "It's a good line Mr Ali, got people talking, and thinking. But it sure as hell ain't good enough to keep you here. I've got several hundred thousand Negroes in Vietnam, all fighting for the cause of the United States".

"And what if I don't *care* for the *cause* of the United States, Willy?" the Champ responded quickly.

"Well what if the United States didn't care for the cause of the Nation of Islam, Mr Ali?" Replied Westmoreland, as he lent back anticipating the Champ's next move.

"I think that it's pretty clear that you already don't, so don't you threaten me, Willy". A sneer had adorned the face of the Champ, he pointed towards Westmoreland, whose anxiety had faded into a sense of arrogant comfort.

"Oh no, we don't. We don't care for your practices, your views or beliefs, or the shit you spill out to pothead hippies in Colleges around the country. The Nation of Islam just isn't enough of a worry to us to give a damn about". Westmoreland leaned further forward across the desk, his stare was uninterrupted, looking up towards the Champ's eyes, "The thing is Mr Ali, we can nip this Nation of Islam thing in the bud, we can take away *your* voice and with it, *its* voice, you got to remember who has got the bigger pockets, Mr Ali". Westmoreland reached to his tumbler of Blue Label, as he drank he glared towards the Champ, his insides bustling with adrenaline.

"You can't shut us down, Willy."

"Oh I can shut you down and unless you go to Vietnam I will. I have enough pull in the Senate. Hell, I play golf with half the members of Congress. Mr Ali you have to go to Vietnam, and if you don't, well I'll see to it that the Nation of Islam is no more". At last Westmoreland felt empowered, he had the Champ where he wanted him and could feel the cogs ticking and the engine whirring beneath his scalp.

The Champ raised his head, his mood was evidently lower than it had been at any point during this meeting with Westmoreland. "Willy," he said, "if I get on a plane to Vietnam, I will mean nothing to the Nation of Islam for getting involved in your crazy war".

"Yeah, yeah... but you could be a martyr and your people love a martyr don't they. You go to Vietnam, you save the Nation of Islam from a great deal of hardship from the American government. Can you see the deal? We're fighting god-damn communism here. When all this is over you can come clean. You publish memoirs. This doesn't mean you lose, Mr Ali."

"I don't lose? You're absolutely right I don't lose." The Champ rose to his feet, inhaling as he stretched to his full height and, whilst sneering across at Westmoreland he pointed and said, "I'll let the people know one day, Willy. I'm going to be around for a long time, Willy. When all this is over with them Viet Cong I'll be sure that everyone knows.

Westmoreland held his palms aloft in gracious acceptance of the Champ's intentions, "Alright then Mr Ali, we have a deal then. You'll begin basic training and look to complete an 18 month stint with the U.S. Armed Forces" he leaned forward to reason with the Champ, "you ain't going to be shooting no Viet Cong and they ain't going to get close to you either. You're America's most valuable sporting asset. With you out there the troops will feel like the Heavyweight Champ of the World is there fighting alongside them. A show of strength in the enemy's back yard will help the boys be brave, just like you are in the ring Champ. Your only responsibility is to put on a couple of shows, just like Joe Louis did, damn I'm not asking you to be Bob Hope."

"You play golf with Bob Hope too, Willy?" The Champ asked, mocking Westmoreland's self righteous sense of importance.

"Oh of course," replied Westmoreland accentuating his answer to play along with the Champ's accusation, he placed his index and thumb together on the side of his trouser and sarcastically said, "Me, you, Bob Hope and half a million Americans, we're all in the same pocket now, Mr Ali."

The Champ on his feet, had a defeated look on his face, an unusual feeling for Ali. Westmoreland stood and called in his Lieutenant, "Take Private Ali to Staff Sergeant Miller, Lieutenant". He said before pouring the remains of his Blue Label into his mouth.

Chapter 3

What if Sir Edmund Hillary and Sherpa Tensing were not the first to reach the summit of Mount Everest in 1953?

Adam Sharples and Clive Palmer

Research Preface

ATTEMPTING TO REWRITE THE HISTORY BOOKS about such a famous event in British mountaineering may have been counter-productive for this exercise. Precisely because a great deal has been published about the first ascent of Everest there seemed little point in changing the story directly if nothing else, for familiarity and perhaps credibility for those who may know the story well. Rather, more detail was added to create an element of deviance and moral corruption between the climbers and doubt about this historical event. The genre of the creative story may be best described as action and mystery with a historical perspective to inform the reader about this event and entertain them with a new twist upon ethical behaviour. Consequently, by creating a sub-genre of mystery and 'what if' possibilities, it leaves the reader feeling 'out of the know' wanting to discover more. It was important, however, not to use too much specialist jargon to avoid creating a niche audience, by which only people with specialist subject knowledge might understand.

The 1953 expedition on Everest was led by English Brigadier Sir John Hunt, who had a total of 400 men on the team, mainly made up of Sherpas who were there to carry supplies – this may indicate the grandeur of the task which began in March 1953. The Times newspaper reported (1953: 6) that "the first attempt on Everest was made in 1921", in which George Mallory featured, who would later die on the mountain with his companion Sandy Irvine in 1924. It was considered that the 1953 expedition was the last attempt the British would have to be the first to conquer Everest after seven failed attempts. The fictitious part within the creative story is the location of a satchel in which Mallory's camera was located. In Sir John Hunt's book, *The Ascent of Everest,* Edmund Hillary (1953: 206) memoires from the summit records, "We had looked briefly for any signs of Mallory and Irvine but had seen nothing". Hillary and Tensing took a different route to their predecessors, approaching from the southern side rather than from the North Col so it would have been extremely unlikely that anything could have been found. The controversial theory, from where the creative story idea stems, began in 1999 when the body of Mallory was found, however some of his belongings were missing including the Kodak camera he had been given for the expedition. Likewise the location of his body and other irregularities such as not having an ice axe has led to claims that George Mallory may have got to the top of Everest in 1924. Andrew Irvine's body is still missing (Hahn, 1999).

In planning to write this creative piece Branston and Stafford, (2003: 36) point out that Tsvetan Todorov, a leading Bulgarian structural linguist, argued that "stories begin in a state of equilibrium before an occurrence causes unrest, disturbing the equilibrium before finally the status quo is restored". This could be classed as a run of the mill "story arch" which seems sufficient in this case to tell the story clearly. That is, it is not too complicated thereby not distracting from the ethical dilemma which the climbers are faced with, in fact it may intensify it. The initial equilibrium is created by setting the scene for Hillary and Tensing inside the tent just before their summit push. Then the discovery of Mallory's camera causes a state of unrest. Finally the two decide how they are going to proceed which restores the status quo.

Propp's (1969) character model was also useful for shaping the conflict between the characters and the situation they found themselves in. Although Propp's (1969) model contained eight roles, the short story contains three of them; the hero, the villain and the helper. According to Smith (2000: 187) "from a sociological point of view, [the characterisation permitted by Propp's (1969) model] offers potential evidence for understanding narratives as social facts" which may allow us in turn to "affirm the autonomy of culture". Smith's (2000) reference to culture is also relevant to the hierarchy / social order of the characters in this story. For example, the hero in the story is Edmund Hillary who has Western values, seen as being a member of the Commonwealth and representing British interests in exploration. Whereas Tenzing is classed as the helper to the hero which may be interpreted as an inferior position, underpinning his status as being subservient and coming from the far East – this is known as binary opposition of characters. According to Edgar and Sedgwick (2002: 43) binary opposites are a "culturally specific interpretation which reflects elements from the ambient world". The term used by Edgar and Sedgwick (2002: 43) "culturally specific" seems also to highlight the social and economic divide between the East and the West at the time of the expedition 1950s. Although New Zealand wasn't geographically Western, New Zealanders shared Western social values as Rosen (2003: 89) points out, "as a result of the National Act 1948, Commonwealth countries had the right to enter Britain and even bring over their families". It is interesting to note the current twists and turns of the British Government with regard to Commonwealth and National allegiances over repatriation of Nepalese Ghurkas to the UK, the rights of whom were successfully championed recently, by the actress Joanna Lumley (Tomforde, 2008). The social divide between Hilary and Tensing emphasizes the binary connotations for this tale, of Hillary being the 'stronger', 'bigger', 'hero' as opposed to Tensing who was the 'weaker', 'smaller', 'helper'. In reality these connotations could not be further from the truth, apart from the fact that Hillary was a physically bigger person

Despite giving a brief account of the two characters' background and upbringing, the main differentiation between the two in the text was created through certain linguistic choices/tones to identify them. This is evident for example in,

"Oi, Norgay! Get your ass over here you're gonna wanna see this" and Tenzing responding, *"Tenzing no understand Sir? If this ever found out ... we get killed"*.

The main difference highlighted by such speech are the character's nationalities and adeptness with the English language. In the first example the author has adopted some common lexical choices such as the guttural "Oi" to mimic speech and the informal contractions "gonna" and "wanna" which indicate the characters fluency in English. These latter features help lower the tenor of the piece and create a colloquial register. The second example, of a non-English speaker, contrasts by using ellipsis to miss out "does not" in the interrogative and "would" in the declarative. The use of lexical choices helps distinguish who the main character is in a passage whereby due to the second character not being able to speak full-English it gives out potentially pejorative connotations of subordination and weakness.

The link between the story and modern day sport can best be exemplified when studying deviance in sport. The story indicates how far one might be prepared to go in order to achieve their aim having worked so hard to obtain it in the first place. This can be linked to corruption in sport – the manipulation of a sporting event to determine the outcome. According to Cashmore (2000: 422) "as soon as money became involved [in sport], corruption followed". However, in the story, instead of money there was life-long fame at stake on a national and international stage of always being remembered for completing the first successful ascent of Everest. Maening (2005: 189) seems to agree with Cashmore's (2000) argument indicating that the "deviant behaviour of some athletes to corrupt sport prevents others from winning on a fair stage". Therefore, what Hillary and Tenzing did, by keeping the camera secret, may be at variance with the objectives and moral values of society at large. A society who may wish to compete fairly themselves or celebrate the honest success of others who compete and represent peoples and nations without having to discover after the event, that there was scandal or cheating. To live the lie or make a timely confession and suffer the consequences seems to have been one of the dilemmas created for these characters in this creative story.

References (and guided bibliography with notes)

Branston, G. and R. Stafford (2003) *The media students book* (third edition). Routledge, London.

Cashmore, E. (2000) *Making sense of sport,* (third edition). Routledge, London.

Edger, A. and Sedgwick, P. R. (2002) *Cultural theory: the key concepts*. Routledge, London.

Hahn, D. (1999) Everest north side, Mallory and Irvine expedition, *Mountain Zone.com* [online]. Available at: http://classic.mountainzone.com/everest/99/north/disp5-4dave.html (Accessed on 23rd January 2010).

Hillary, E. (1956) *High adventure*. The Companion Book Club published courtesy of Hodder and Stoughton, London.

Note: This publication is Edmund Hillary's own account of what occurred on that expedition which is a useful contrast to how the expedition was reported in the press (Times,

1953) and how the expedition was portrayed in John Hunts book(s). Of particular relevance to this creative story may be Hillary's comments about the importance of photographic evidence of their achievements on the mountain, for example, "I realised how important these summit photographs were" (Hillary, 1956: 243). This seems to introduce an interesting element of doubt that What If this creative interpretation of the ethical dilemma faced by these two climbers, or part of it, was true?

Hunt, J. (1953) *The ascent of Everest*. Hodder and Stoughton, London.

Hunt, J. (1954) *The ascent of Everest* (second edition). The Companion Book Club published courtesy of Hodder and Stoughton, London.

Note: The first edition of John Hunt's book was issued in 1953, the year of the expedition, which revised and updated in 1954 and perhaps after this. This begs a question of reliability about many of these books which claim to offer a truthful account of what actually went on. If it was truthful in the first instance why alter it? Perhaps there was a need for reinterpretation or retelling of instances in a manner which may have been deemed more acceptable at the time, less offensive perhaps. Either way the writing skills of John Hunt seem to be the focus of attention here, rather than his climbing skills, which may indicate the importance of interpretive writing about real-life events.

Irving, R.L.G. (1942) *Ten great mountains* (second edition). The Travel Book Club, London.

Note: Irving (1942) provides his reflections about famous mountains which he has visited and climbed upon and tells something of their history in mountaineering terms. Consequently, this is a firsthand account from a British mountaineer who was on Everest long before the summit was reached, but long after the 1924 and 1933 expeditions from Britain. Might he have seen evidence of Mallory and Irvine, or even been searching for it? What if he'd found some telling evidence? Interesting accounts are given of the 1924 expedition and 1933 expedition when an ice axe was found at the First Step – a high point on Everest, which surely could only have been left by George Mallory and Sandy Irvine.

Maening, W. (2005) Corruption in international sports and sports management. *European Sport Management Quarterly* (June 5/2).

Propp, V.I.A. (1969) *Morphology of the folk tale*. University of Texas Press, Texas.

Note: A useful range of character theories, such as those posed by Vladimir Propp (1969), Jonathan Bishop (2008), John Campbell, Gorden Fletcher and Anita Greenhill (2002, 2009) and Erving Goffman (1959) are available online: (Accessed 27th January 2010). http://en.wikipedia.org/wiki/Character_theory_(Media)#Propp.27s_Character_theory

Rosen, A. (2003) *The transformation of British life 1950-2000; a social history*. Manchester University Press, Manchester.

Sommervell, T.H. (1938) *After Everest, the experiences of a mountaineer and medical missionary* (second edition). Hodder and Stoughton, London.

Note: Howard Sommervell was a member of the 1924 British expedition to Everest during which George Mallory and Sandy Irvine. This is an interesting and sincere first-hand account of climbing of the day which underplays the arduousness of their task generally and in particular, downplays the major accomplishment of the author to establish a high camp with Edward Norton, which was the key to permitting Mallory and Irvine to make a summit bid.

Smith, P. D. (2001) *Cultural theory: an introduction*. Blackwell, Oxford.

Stobart, T. (1977) *Herbs, spices and flavourings* (second edition). Penguin Books Ltd., London.

Note: Tom Stobart was a widely travelled man who was responsible for filming the climbing of Everest in 1953 - he was the camera expedition man. Stobart's (1977) Introduction (pp.13-33) illustrates his depth of interest in travelling and filming in challenging situations. Once again the desire for photographic evidence of the climb is compounded by this independent writing.

Stobart, T. (1960) *Adventurer's eye* (second edition). The Popular Book Club, London.

Note: In this text Tom Stobart offers a firsthand account of climbing and filming the 1953 Everest expedition from his perspective. Once again it emphasizes the importance of gathering evidence on film. Chapter 28 (pp. 229-238) *To he top of the roof of the world* discusses how the expedition was filmed and the difficulties he faced in this role. Chapter 29 (pp. 238-248) *We find ourselves famous* is particularly revealing and relevant to the context of this creative account. Dealing with and coping with the fortunes of fame he paints a picture of being distinctly uncomfortable with the fame and attention that is drawn to himself through his mountaineering accomplishments. There is also the permanent legacy of his film which is always there to haunt him.

The Times (June 02 1953) *Everest conquered; Hillary and Tensing reach the summit*. Available at: http://www.timesonline.co.uk/tol/news/world/article3175412.ece (Accessed on 8th December 2009).

Note: see also The Times Everest Colour Supplement, 1953: To the summit, the story of the British Everest expedition, 1953. By the *Times Special Correspondent* [online]. Available at: http://extras.timesonline.co.uk/pdfs/everest.pdf (Accessed on 25th January 2010).

Tomforde, A. (2008) Britain's retired Gurkha soldiers win final victory *Monsters and Critics. Com* [online]. Available at: http://www.monstersandcritics.com/news/uk/features/article_1434056.php/Britain_s_retired_Gurkha_soldiers_win_final_victory_News_Feature#ixzz0dcxoXy7D (Accessed on 25th January 2010).

Ullman, J.R. (1956) *Man of Everest the autobiography of Tenzing* (second edition). The Reprint Society, by arrangement with George G. Harrup and Co. Ltd. London.

Note: The book by James Ramsey Ullman presents a biography of Sherpa Tenzing which traces his climbing exploits in Nepal before 1953 and explains how he got to the point of being selected to accompany Edmund Hillary to the summit of Everest. Ullman describes a quiet man, full of humility and respect whose life was changed dramatically, probably for the worse, by the fortunes of fame bestowed upon him as a result of his climb. Interestingly there will have been a high degree of interpretation by Ullman in this text as there is no written form of the *Sherpa* language (Ullman, 1956: 29), everything being converted first by an interpreter and then by Ullman to produce this most readable account. (Sherpa is the name of a tribe of people originally from Tibet, it seems to be a Western reduction of the term to mean porter or guide, i.e. that Sherpas have performed such a function for Western expeditions).

Creative Story

What if Sir Edmund Hillary and Sherpa Tensing were not the first to reach the summit of Mount Everest in 1953?

Adam Sharples and Clive Palmer

MANY PEOPLE BELIEVE THAT THEIR DESTINY is written in the stars. Others, however, believe that their destiny can be changed depending on the paths they choose to take in life. The journeys along these paths may be accompanied with passion and determination, a raw hunger to succeed in following one's dream. In other words, no matter how hard the challenge along that path, even if dealt the cruel hand of fate, any obstacle can be overcome in pursuit of an ultimate goal.

May 29th 1953, Mount Everest, Nepal.

A flame glimmered from the match providing just enough light to see the figures through the blackness of their tent. Edmund directed the flame towards the thermometer which was placed handily between the ration packs and oxygen canisters which their lives depended upon, it read -25°C. The wind outside blew ferociously, hitting their tent like a battering ram hammering against an un-relenting door. It was Edmund's state of unrest which woke his partner who miraculously, after being subject to the worst weather that 28,250ft above sea level can provide, had remained entangled in a deep sleep for the best part of four hours. His partner's name was Tenzing Norgay, a native Nepalese climber who was classed as one of the world's best two mountaineers. The other was Edmund.

The reason for Edmund's unrest was about to be revealed to his loyal companion. Tenzing wasn't going to take the news kindly, mainly because everything they'd worked for their entire life now hung in the balance. Their frosty and claustrophobic temporary home was now fully lit thanks to an oil lamp which illuminated their tent like a fiery warning beacon atop a hill.

Ed removed his face mask supplying oxygen from the canister that sat beside him. Both men were in the 'death zone' and needed a regular supply of oxygen to live at this altitude – they were currently being fed two litres per minute but may need five litres with what Ed about to uncover.

"Oi, Norgay! Get your ass over here you're gonna wanna see this", exclaimed Edmund in a state of panic.

"Mr Tenzing, coming – you New Zealand people are hard for Tenzing understand," replied the Sherpa in a more relaxed tone, scraping together his best English.

Edmund Hillary grew up with his parents in Auckland, New Zealand. Throughout his childhood he was obsessed with travel and adventure and by his early 20s he had already climbed all the mountains his country had to offer. Taking over his family business, Ed went on to be a successful bee-keeper and one day intended to return to his profession after scaling the world's largest peaks. Now, at the age of 33, he found himself just 750ft from his ultimate aim in mountaineering, the top of Everest!

Norgay made his way over and stared at what Ed was holding in his hand. The object they had discovered was half buried in the cold snow, encased in ice and quite unrecognisable; they had moved it to pitch their tent the night before. Now, somewhat thawed, they could see that the mysterious object was in fact a sheep skin satchel and it was at this precise moment that its significance dawned upon them.

"You thinking what I'm thinking Tenz, nobody ain't ever been this high up Everest before so how on gods sweet earth is there a bag just lying there over 28,000ft above sea level?" ranted a confused Hillary. "And you're not gonna to like this either my friend". Edmund opened the bag and removed a 1912 Kodak pocket camera, the type popular amongst soldiers in World War One. The rest of the sack was filled with maps and other items which they gave no more attention to. They seem to have discovered enough for one day. It was the camera which was of great significance. How could such a small object like this be so significant in the bigger picture? Evidence...

"The camera is God damn Mallory's, he's been missing for the best part of 30 years. He can't have got to the top! We've gotta be the first to get there!" Tenzing gazed at Hillary in a state of shocked silence, unsure what to think about the future of their expedition. A million and one questions flooded through Edmund's head, do they go and look for more evidence? Do they continue their struggle to the top? Who do they tell? Do they even tell anybody?

The camera belonged to an English mountaineer named George Mallory. Mallory, along with his climbing partner Andrew (also known as Sandy on account of his blonde hair) Irvine mysteriously disappeared on route to the top of Everest in 1924. It was Mallory's third assault on the mountain and up-until-now nobody was sure whether or not the pair made it to the top. The two were last seen by their expedition colleague Noel Odell, an English geologist and climber on the expedition, who claimed to have seen them approaching the final push for the summit.

The camera Edmund grasped tightly could answer secrets that had been dormant for over a quarter of a century (1924-53). Now they had to decide what to do with the news.

"So what we do now Mr Hillary?" asked Tenzing looking for inspiration from his 'leader'. Hillary's response was quick and to the point, "Nothing. We do nothing. I ain't wasting my whole life wanting to be second best to two Englishmen who got to the damn top 29 years before us!"

Tenzing was astonished at what he'd just heard. The Sherpa was a man of principle, a devout Buddhist who wanted what was best for everyone. However what he also wanted was to be someone his people could look up to, to be a role model of success to help his people rise above the hardships of everyday life in the Himalayas.

The Sherpa broke the silence. "Tenzing no understand Sir? If this ever found out we get killed".

Irvine and Mallory were both considered legends back in England and since this was a British led expedition, under the command of Brigadier John Hunt, the consequences of betraying the British in any way could indeed be 'life threatening'.

"And you tell me who's gonna find out Tensing because I'm sure not gonna tell anyone."

Tenzing, looking in dismay was reluctant to acknowledge but in the back of his mind knew Hillary was right, a lifetime's endeavour for recognition could be taken away from them in the blink of an eye.

"Man cannot go through life without having to make sacrifices for the greater good", Ed reasoned. Their chance to go in the record books was too good to miss. The fame and the fortune of how life might be different (for the better) played over and over in their minds. But could their conscience cope with living the lie, leading a life of constant, unrelenting lies and deceit?

By 11:30am on May 29th 1953 four flags fluttered from the snow capped summit of Mount Everest. Two flags represented the birth places of the men, Tenzing's Nepalese flag and Edmund's flag of the United Nations was present. The other two were that of Great Britain (founders of the expedition) which fluttered proudly in their presence along with that of India. Hilly and Tenz had made it, unsure in the knowledge of whether or not they were second best – but did that matter? The two had made their decision and they were going to stick to it.

"It time Mr Hillary" said Tenzing in a rather reluctant fashion.

Without delay Edmund removed a small silver cartridge from the pocket of his coat. The object glistened in the morning sun firing off a ray of light strong enough to transmit an S.O.S signal. The Sherpa knew what they were doing was wrong in all so many ways but both men had worked their entire life in pursuit of their dream – to be the first men to successfully climb the world's third pole – Mount Everest.

What Edmund had removed from his pocket was the three inch black and white film reel from Mallory's 'vest pocket model B' camera. And without thinking twice about it Edmund exposed the black ribbon of film and threw the cartridge and film over the unforgiving slopes that lay before them, hoping it would never be seen again.

June 2nd 1953, London, England

Thousands of people lined the streets of London in celebration of Queen Elizabeth *II*'s coronation as ruler of Great Britain. An estimated 20 million people watched on their cumbersome 14 inch' black and white televisions whilst others tuned in on their wireless sets, determined not to miss out on the news events. Two BBC correspondents gave a live running commentary on the royal pageant in London describing proceedings as the most important occasion since the end of World War Two. Earlier that morning the London Times newspaper had reported the achievements of Ed Hillary and Tenzing Norgay's journey about which the BBC also went on to broadcast:

"It is with great satisfaction that I have the privilege to announce that the British Expeditionary Team, under the command of Brigadier John Hunt, have made a successful ascent of Everest. A special commendation should go out to our Commonwealth compatriot Edmund Hillary of New Zealand, who along with Tenzing Norgay, have become the first people to conquer the world's greatest summit. On a down-note we understand there was no evidence of Irvine or Mallory whose tragic disappearance in 1924 still remains a mystery. We conclude by speaking on behalf of the Nation when we say 'thank you' for your efforts".

The boys who dreamed of becoming adventurers had their dream come true. However, fate was to intervene in finding their destiny. Despite overcoming the biggest obstacle the physical world can provide in the shape of Mount Everest the pride that they should have been feeling was one of deviance, deceit and 'what if'. What if they had been lucky enough to remain ignorant of the satchel by not seeing it, what if Mallory and Irvine had made it, what if anyone found out... what if... what if. The façade put on show to the public was one to last a lifetime – only Hillary and Tenzing knew the truth about what really happened that day. Maybe Edmund's destiny lies elsewhere, whether it's enduring the Antarctic or scaling the River Ganges which were some of his adventures after 1953. The truth about their discovery on Everest will never be revealed and now lies securely with them in their graves.

RIP
Sir Edmund Percival Hillary, KG, ONZ, KBE
(20th July 1919 – 11th January 2008)

Tenzing Norgay, GM (George Medal)
(late May 1914 — 9th May 1986)

See also:
Academy of Achievement (2008) *From bee keeper to world explorer*[online]. Available at: http://www.achievement.org/autodoc/page/hiloint-2 (Accessed on 27th January 2010).

BBC (2005) *On this day 1950 – 2005* [online] Available at: http://news.bbc.co.uk/onthisday/hi/dates/stories/may/29/newsid_2492000/2492683.stm (Accessed on 27th January 2010).

Chapter 4

Rubin Carter - how much can a man lose?

Alastair Turner and Clive Palmer

Research Preface

RUBIN 'HURRICANE' CARTER WAS BORN on the 6th May 1937, in Clifton, New Jersey. In 1966, at the height of his boxing career, Carter was wrongly convicted, twice, of a triple murder and imprisoned for nearly two decades. During the mid-1970s, his case became a cause celébrè for a number of civil rights leaders, politicians, and entertainers. The most famous of these being Muhammad Ali and then Bob Dylan, who wrote the song 'Hurricane' in honour of Carter in 1975. He was ultimately exonerated in 1985, after a United States district court judge declared the convictions to be based on racial prejudice.

Carter grew up in Paterson, New Jersey and certainly had a troubled life. He was arrested and sent to the Jamesburg State Home for Boys at age 12 after he attacked a man with a Boy Scout knife. He claimed the man was a paedophile who had been attempting to molest one of his friends.

Carter escaped before his six-year term was up and in 1954 joined the Army, where he served in a segregated corps which is where he developed a love for boxing and took up the sport with some considerable success. In his first ever boxing match he knocked out the All Army heavyweight champion Nelson Glenn. Then still within the US Army but serving in Britain he won two [Army based] European light-welterweight championships and in 1956 returned to Paterson with the intention of becoming a professional boxer (Biography.com, 2010). Hirsch (2000: 73) describes Carter as a powerful boxer with speed and skill, "Carter bobbed, feinted, ducked, then lashed out with his first punch of the fight – a whizzing left hook that caught Glenn flush on his chin, spilling him to the canvas". Soon after his return to Paterson, the police arrested Carter and forced him to serve the remaining 10 months of his sentence in a state reformatory. Carter was again arrested in 1957, this time for purse snatching; he spent four years in Trenton State, a maximum-security prison, for that crime.

After his release, he channelled his considerable anger towards his situation and the plight of Paterson's African-American community, into his boxing— he turned pro in 1961 and began a startling four-fight winning streak, including two knockouts. For his lightning-fast fists, Carter soon earned the nickname "Hurricane" and became one of the top contenders for the world middleweight crown. In December 1963, in a non-title bout, he beat then-welterweight world champion Emile Griffith in a first round KO. Although he lost his one shot at the title, in a 15-round split decision to reigning champion Joey Giardello in December 1964, he was widely regarded as a good bet to win his next title bout.

As one of the most famous citizens of Paterson, Carter made no friends with the police, especially during the summer of 1964, when he was quoted in *The Saturday Evening Post* as expressing anger towards the pre-occupations of the police towards the black neighbourhoods. His flamboyant lifestyle (Carter frequented the city's nightclubs and bars) and juvenile record rankled with the police, as did the vehement statements he had allegedly made advocating violence in the pursuit of racial justice.

Carter was training for his next shot at the world middleweight title (against champion Dick Tiger) in October 1966 when he was arrested on June 17th for the triple murder of three patrons at the Lafayette Bar & Grill in Paterson. Carter and John Artis had been arrested on the night of the crime because they fitted an eyewitness description of the killers ("two Negroes in a white car"), but they had been cleared by a grand jury when the one surviving victim failed to identify them as the gunmen. Now, the state produced two more eyewitnesses, Alfred Bello and Arthur D. Bradley, who had made positive identifications. During the trial that followed, the prosecution produced little to no evidence linking Carter and Artis to the crime, a shaky motive (racially-motivated retaliation for the murder of a black tavern owner by a white man in Paterson hours before), and the only two eyewitnesses were petty criminals involved in a burglary (who were later revealed to have received money and reduced sentences in exchange for their testimony). Nevertheless, on June 29, 1967, Carter and Artis were convicted of triple murder and sentenced to three life prison terms.

Carter and his supporters continued to fight the conviction, accusing the Paterson police of a racist conspiracy against Carter. The most famous of these supporters was Lesra Martin, a teenager from a Brooklyn ghetto and a group of Canadians who were helping Lesra with his studies. The subsequent trials were rife with inaccuracies as Leslie Maitland (1976) wrote in the New York Times,

> Alfred P. Bello who identified Rubin (Hurricane) Carter and John Artis as the gunmen in a triple murder here during the two men's first trial nine years ago, then recanted and then renounced his recantation depicted himself on the stand today as a man who had lied consistently to almost everyone involved in this long and complicated legal battle.

Lewis Steel was one of the lawyers representing Carter who went to print years later about the racism case – prompted by a feature film about Carter's life, The Hurricane in 1997. He points out that,

> During years of appeals through the New Jersey state court system in the late 1970s and 1980s, not one of the more than 20 state court judges who reviewed the case was willing to confront the racism behind the unproven accusation that Carter and Artis murdered three randomly chosen whites to avenge an earlier killing of a black man by a white man. Nor were the state court judges willing to expose the police for their racist acts (Steel, 2000: 4).

Lewis M. Steel was a Civil Rights attorney practicing in New York City. He was part of the Carter-Artis defence team from 1975 to 1988. Steel was the lead attorney for John Artis.

Finally, in 1985, Carter was freed when an appellate judge ruled that he had not received a fair trial. This time, prosecutors chose not to try Carter a third time and he has been free ever since. There have been many objections to the freeing of Carter. John Artis had already been on parole, but even to this day Carter has not been found innocent and no new suspects have been named. There are many conspiracy websites on the internet that still try and prove Carter's guilt, such as; Top ten myths about Rubin Carter and the Lafayette Grill murders.

In 1997, a movie about Carter's life, The Hurricane, was made starring Denzel Washington as Carter. The movie has become almost as controversial as the man himself, beginning with its opening scene where

91

Carter's loss to Giardello is portrayed as a racist robbery, some people have criticized it for taking liberties with the true facts of Ruben Carter's life.

References

Biography.com (2010) Rubin "Hurricane" Carter Biography - born 1937 [online]. Available at: http://www.biography.com/articles/Rubin-Hurricane-Carter-9542248?part=0 (Accessed on 1st March 2010).

Carole, D. and Bos, J.D. (2009) *Rubin 'Hurricane' Carter* [online]. Available at: http://www.awesomestories.com/famous-trials/hurricane (Accessed on 8th December, 2009).

Carter, R. (1991) *The sixteenth round: from number 1 contender To #45472*. Viking Press, New York .

Chaiton, S. and Swinton, T. (2000) *Lazarus and the Hurricane: the freeing of Rubin "Hurricane" Carter*. St. Martin's, Griffin, USA.

Flatter, R. (2007) *Hurricane found peace at storm's centre* [online]. Available at: http://espn.go.com/classic/biography/s/Carter_Hurricane.html (Accessed on 8th December, 2009).

Hirsch, J. (2000) *Hurricane: the miraculous journey of Rubin Carter*. Mariner Books, New York.

Maitland, L. (1976) *Witness at Rubin Carter trial tells hearing he lied often during case* [online]. Available at: http://select.nytimes.com/gst/abstract.html?res=F50C10FD3F59157493C5A8178AD95F428785F9 (Accessed on 9th December, 2009).

Manning, L. (2000) *Top ten myths about Rubin Carter and the Lafayette Grill murders* [online]. Available at: http://www.members.shaw.ca/cartermyths/index.htm (Accessed on 9th December 2009).

Martin, L. (2009) *The Hurricane* [online]. Available at: http://www.lesra.com/ (Accessed on 9th December 2009).

Steel, L. (2000) First person; history's on the ropes in 'Hurricane', *Los Angeles Times Archives* [online]. Available at: http://pqasb.pqarchiver.com/latimes/access/48269118.html?dids=48269118:48269118&FMT=ABS&FMTS=ABS:FT&type=current&date=Jan+24%2C+2000&author=LEWIS+M.+STEEL&pub=Los+Angeles+Times&desc=First+Person%3B+History%27s+on+the+Ropes+in+%27Hurricane%27&pqatl=google (Accessed on 9th December 2009).

Feature Film:
The Hurricane (1997) Starring Denzel Washington and Dan Hedaya. Inspired by the book "The Sixteenth Round: From Number 1 Contender To #45472" by Rubin Carter [online].Available at http://www.chasingthefrog.com/reelfaces/thehurricane.php (Accessed on 27th January 2010).

Creative Story

Rubin Carter - how much can a man lose?

Alastair Turner and Clive Palmer

TOMMY PICKED HIMSELF UP OFF THE FLOOR and wiped the trail of blood away from his face. This was the second time this week that he had been met after school by the group of older boys. The first time they had just called him names but this time the biggest of the group had punched him and kicked him while the others cheered him on. Tommy had no idea why they were doing this but thought it must be because he was new at school, some sort of initiation ritual. As he walked down the street towards his new home he wished he was still in New York City and not stuck here in the backwaters of Paterson, New Jersey.

Tommy had been forced to come and live with his Grandfather after his parents were killed in a car crash. He had only been here a week when he was forced to enrol in John F. Kennedy High School. Tommy had lots of friends back in New York but he felt like and outsider - he was an outsider to Paterson and his new school. When Tommy reached the front porch of his Grandfather's house, which would not feel like his home for some time, he checked his reflection in the window to make sure there was no sign of blood and the fight and he walked inside.

His Grandfather, as usual, was asleep in front of the TV with yet another baseball game winding to a close. Tommy had only met his Grandfather for the first time the previous week at his parent's funeral and had taken an instant dislike to the old man. Tommy was used to a much more liberal life with his Mom and Dad but as soon as he got 'home' he was made to sweep up leaves, clean the garage and several other jobs he never had to do in New York.

"Hey I was watching that" bellowed the old man as Tommy turned over the TV station.

"Sorry Grandpa, I thought you were asleep" Tommy replied.

"Well I wasn't, and anyway don't you have chores to do?"

Tommy got up and walked through to the back yard where a fresh pile of leaves had fallen. As he stood there rake in hand he began to cry, he had done a lot of that in the past ten days but he remembered the words his Grandfather had said on the day of the funeral, "It's no use crying over it".

Then there was a shout from inside the house, 'those leaves aren't going to sweep themselves boy, get on with it and then fix us some tea, I'm starvin". *You never know,* Tommy dreamt, *maybe they will?*

The next day, when the bell rang to signal the end of the school day Tommy's stomach was in knots. *Please don't let them be there again* he thought. But sure enough the same four boys were stood just outside the school gates waiting. Tommy managed to block the first blow but the second caught him square in the gut knocking the wind out of him and dropping him to his knees. Just as Tommy caught his breath the boot of the biggest boy smashed into his face. For the second time in two days Tommy felt the sensation of blood on his face. This however was much different, where the previous day he felt a sting and trickle like a rain drop on his cheek this was like a stream. "Hey, you've got blood on my boot you little prick" shouted the boy "Wipe it off". Tommy went to clean the boot but as he did the boy stamped on his hand.

Tommy cried out in pain and then shrieked "Why are you doing this to me?"

"Go ask your Grandfather" the boy replied as he walked off down the street laughing "and tell him De Simone says hi"

Tommy was still crying when he reached the house, there was no point in trying to cover up the fight, the blood was still coming out of his nose and his lip was swollen and bruised. As he walked through the door his Grandfather shot out of his chair and raced across the room. He moved surprisingly well for a man of his age.

"What the hell happened to you?" he shouted at Tommy "Are you alright, who did this to you?" Tommy had never seen the look of anger that he now saw in his Grandfather's eyes, he had changed from the old guy sitting by the fire to an angry and determined man. It seemed to have taken years off him and Tommy struggled to recognise him. Tommy told his Grandfather what had happened during his first week at school. How the same boys had been waiting for him the past three days.

"Why didn't you tell me? We could have done something about this", questioned his Grandfather.

"What could 'we' have done?" Tommy sobbed "This never happened in New York, people never hit me and laughed about it".

"Why did they do this? What did you do to them? Who were they?" asked the old man, now with a fire burning behind his eyes.

"I don't know" replied Tommy "I don't know their names, they are just older boys from the school". But then he remembered what the biggest of them had said. "Grandpa" he said sheepishly, "who's De Simone?"

"De Simone" roared his Grandfather "how do you know that name?"

Tommy was scared by just how angry his Grandfather was now. He stood there fists clenched and physically shaking with an anger that Tommy had never seen in his life.

"One of the boys said it", he replied "he said tell your Grandfather De Simone says hi" whatever that is supposed to mean?

A second later his Grandfather grabbed Tommy by the wrist and dragged him to his feet, then led Tommy out of the house and towards the garage.

"Get in" his Grandfather said.

"Why?" replied Tommy

"Because" said his Grandfather "We're going to sort this once and for all"

The car screamed down the road and through the centre of Paterson. Tommy had never been driven at such speed and winced every time his Grandfather threw the car into a corner or overtook another vehicle. Then suddenly the car screeched to a halt and his Grandfather jumped out and ran up to a house. He then banged furiously on the door.

"De Simone, get out here you piece of crap" the old man yelled, "Get your ass out here right now, how dare you bring my Grandson into this?"

All of a sudden the door opened and a man who looked in his early forties appeared. Tommy looked on in amazement. This was all so new to him, the fight, the car ride and now his Grandfather racing up to a huge house to be met by some guy in smart suit. As soon as the door was fully open his Grandfather punched the man. Fast and hard. This, however, was not the punch of an old man but that of someone skilled and used to fighting. His Grandfather moved so quick that the man never saw the blow coming and was lifted clean off his feet and sent crashing to the ground.

"You stay away from my family and tell that no good son of yours to keep his hands to himself or I will be back round again," his Grandfather roared at the fallen man, who was clutching his face and had a look of both shock and fear on his face.

His Grandfather walked back to the car got in and set off back down the street. Tommy did not know what to say, he could not believe what he had just seen. When they finally got home, a trip that took twice as long as the journey there, Tommy ran straight from the car and up into his room. He still could not believe what he had happened. As soon as he mentioned the name De Simone his Grandfather had changed into the Incredible Hulk, full of rage. Tommy was startled by a knock at the door.

"Can I come in" his Grandfather said.

"Yes" Tommy replied

When the door opened his Grandfather was carrying a tray with a mug of hot chocolate, a bag of ice and a big book placed precariously on it.

"That's for you, and that's for your face" his Grandfather said placing the drink on the bedside table and the ice bag in Tommy's hand. "I suppose you want to know what that was all about?"

Tommy looked at his Grandfather and did not know what to say. His head was still spinning from the day's events, not only his fight, if you could call it that, but the image of his Grandfather punching a man to the ground with astonishing efficiency and without hesitation.

"Well, here goes then" his Grandfather started "you know me as Grandpa but to the rest of the world, or at least people from these parts, I am Rubin 'Hurricane' Carter". He opened the book and put it on Tommy's lap. Tommy stared down at the pages of photographs that showed action shots from boxing matches and press photographs of a menacing looking man with a shaved head and a goatee beard holding championship belts.

"Is this you?" asked Tommy.

"Yes" replied his Grandfather "I was the Middleweight champion, the best boxer in the world. Unfortunately that brought a lot of attention on me and some bad things happened". He flipped the book through a few pages onto a startlingly different photograph, one of a man sat in a courtroom with his head in his hands. "This is also me, the man you saw earlier was Paul De Simone, and his father tried to frame me for murder. And from the sound of it you've had a run in with his no good son. I'm sorry you were dragged into this, it had nothing to do with you and that's why your Mother moved you all away to New York, so you could start a life far away from all these problems".

Rubin got up and started to walk towards the door, "I miss my Mom" Tommy said.

"So do I" Rubin replied. He walked over and kissed Tommy on the forehead, "so do I".

97

Thierry Henry "Handball" - Ireland vs France 2009, football world cup spoils or was the world cup just spoiled?

Thomas Leydon and Clive Palmer

Research Preface

WHILST PLAYING FOR FRANCE ON NATIONAL DUTIES Thierry Henry's controversial handball against the Republic of Ireland on Wednesday 18th November 2009 caused a media storm of heated debate. The ethics of this game were firmly in the spotlight for its on-pitch illegalities and the kangaroo court of justice seemed to be presided over by anyone who might have a vested interest in the verdict either way of the ruling. Was it handball? Maybe, perhaps, possibly... it depends. Within the rules of football it may only be handball if the referee sees it and even then such a decision may be subject to further interpretation. Was it accidental for instance? Only Thierry Henry may know this. Even if the referee did see something which appeared to be *like* handball, each match official and each player from both teams could have seen the event from different angles (or not at all in some cases) possibly leading to as many different interpretations of reality as there were people on the pitch. Then there are the media and public 'judges' watching feverishly on television sets all over the world all making their own decisions on whatever they think they saw, based upon whatever the cameraman chose to show them. The majority of viewers relying upon this second order broadcast of the event, i.e. those not spectating at the match itself, would have been served up immediate repeats from numerous angles and in slow motion replay which may have merely reinforced their prejudices and/or allegiances towards their teams, the match officials and the players and particularly towards Thierry Henry himself. May be, he just played the game well, as any other player might do in such an instance? France were the victors in the first leg, winning 1-0 at Croke Park in Dublin. Ireland were 1-0 up in Paris, in the return leg after 103 minutes. The game had gone to extra time due to the tie being all square at 1-1 on aggregate. Robbie Keane playing for Ireland, had scored the goal that night which had upset many a passionate Frenchman who probably expected France to progress comfortably qualifying for the world cup finals in South Africa in 2010. After their first leg victory over Ireland, it seemed like the world cup spoils would be for France, and the world cup plans of Ireland would just be spoiled.

Back at Stade de France it looked like the tie was heading for penalties, until the 104th minute when the ball fell to Thierry Henry (FRA) in the Ireland penalty area. He controlled the ball twice with his hand before squaring the ball to William Gallas (FRA) who headed home. This sparked a massive celebration from the French players but even bigger protestations from the Irish. Their protests were to no avail and the goal stood. The referee had made his decision based upon what he saw. There was no way back for Ireland and the game ended up 1-1, with the French winning 2-1 on aggregate and earning their place in the world cup finals. The Irish were left devastated by the result. That seemed to be the end of the world cup for them. But arguing about the incident was just beginning and would gather pace in the following weeks. A simple search on the internet for "Thierry Henry handball" will reveal the high degree of attention this [now] historic moment in football has received, with many impassioned memories stirred from Diego Maradona's (Argentina) Hand of God incident against England in the World Cup quarter finals in 1986.

After the France Ireland game there were seemingly not unreasonable calls for the game to be replayed. Ireland appealed to FIFA (world governing body for football: Fédération Internationale de Football Association) for the game to be replayed as they felt they had been cheated out of a place in South Africa. FIFA rejected Ireland's appeal and there was a huge amount of frustration in the Ireland campaign over the affair. However, the Football Association of Ireland didn't stop there. They once again appealed to FIFA but this time it was to request that they (FIFA) gave them a place in the world cup finals by extending the number of teams in the competition from thirty two to thirty three. This was once again rejected out of hand by FIFA and this signalled the end of Ireland's world cup hopes. FIFA then went on to announce that they were going to award Ireland with a special fair play plaque for what happened on that Paris night. This decision was met with disgust from Irish players, fans and officials alike. They felt that it was no consolation for missing out on the finals and that it was an insult rather than an award for being fair and honourable contestants (Hytner, 2009, James, 2009). In addition there have been numerous personal attacks on Thierry Henry that he was a blatant cheat (Cascarino, 2009) which may be unfair when one considers the wider range of implications that are possible to envisage. For example, might Thierry Henry have cheated on behalf of a nation making the national team of France the cheats?; might have the referee cheated for some reason?; might have Thierry Henry *played well* within the rules and even if he did cheat on the field of play, which is debatable, it may not make him a cheat in life. His actions that day may not make him a bad role model to follow in the circumstances – sporting or otherwise (see for relevant discussions about the philosophical stance towards the playing of games and the possibility for moral development from them see: Suits, 1972, 1995; D'Agostino, 1982; Reid, 1999; Jones and McNamee, 2003; Wellman, 2003; McFee, 2004; McNamee, 2008). The emotive language and the strength of the allegations in the media made against Thierry Henry and about his character "as a man", seemed to constitute a vicious personal attack, for example, "Thierry Henry is an insincere cheat who has tarnished his reputation for good" (Cascarino, 2009). This would appear to be very upsetting for any person to bear least of all perhaps for one who has dedicated his life to playing his sport *well*, particularly when representing his country. If one accepts that playing football may not be a full account living one's life then the character assassinations in the press may be doing more harm than good for the "handball" situation, for football in general and in particular, for Thierry Henry.

The What If element in this story is what if Henry's handball was spotted? It was interesting to consider what could have happened if an official had spotted the infringement and pulled the player up for it. I felt intrigued to consider what could have happened differently as a result. I decided to go with the idea that things would have happened very differently if the goal had been disallowed. This strategy seemed to have the potential to make my story as interesting as possible and more entertaining for the reader. I think the idea that things in life could be very different had it not been for one tiny event is very interesting and one that appeals to me. It goes to show how small margins can cause huge differences and had that goal by France not counted then Ireland could possibly have qualified for the world cup finals. As an Englishmen watching the game, I was rooting for Ireland as I was curious to see how they would do in the finals. I, along with many others was disappointed when they failed to qualify, especially in the circumstances that it happened. Therefore, I saw this as an opportunity to explore the curiosity I felt and perhaps develop a sense of curiosity which a reader might feel about this story.

One layman's theory in football is that the stronger nations may be favoured by FIFA. For example, that FIFA rejected Ireland's appeals for a replay of the match or a place in the finals because they are a smaller footballing nation and were perhaps unlikely to do very well in the finals anyway. One conspiracy theory is that 'what if' it had happened the other way round? Would FIFA's decision have been in favour of Ireland? The belief seems to be that if it had been an Ireland player who had handled the ball in the run up to the goal then they might have been more understanding towards the French's pleas. Some common conjecture amongst 'public experts' is that the French have a lot of power in FIFA, that they influence FIFA's decisions and are favoured by FIFA generally. Anglo-French relations over football have never been so 'cordial'!

In researching for this creative story the incident was watched back time and time again in order to visualise how the "what if" story might fit around the actual events. The incident was on all news stations and all over the internet by the next day so there was a good deal of information on the topic to supplement the writing and give a sense of being there. *The Portable Creative Writing Workshop* book by Pat Boran (2005) was used to develop a writing style which helped to identify characters and to communicate the outcome of the story with a sense of drama. Reading this book really helped me to understand a way in which I could tell my story but in an attractive way for the reader. I also spoke to a number of very passionate Irish football fans to get their views and thoughts on the whole incident. This in itself was an interesting experience and helped to stimulate the sense for conflict and injustice which seemingly, any good story might need.

References

Boran,P. (2005) *The portable creative writing workshop*. New Island, Dublin.

Cascarino, T. (2009) Thierry Henry is an insincere cheat who has tarnished his reputation for good November 19th 2009. *The Times* [online]. Available at: http://www.timesonline.co.uk/tol/sport/football/article6922619.ece (Accessed on 27th January, 2010).

D'Agostino, F. (1982) The ethos of games (pp. 42-49). In, Morgan, W.J. and Klaus, V.M. (Eds.) *Philosophical inquiry in sport* (second edition). Human Kinetics, Champaign, Ill. USA.

Hytner, D. (2009) Irish hopes crushed as Thierry Henry hands victory to France *The Guardian* [online]. Available at: http://www.guardian.co.uk/football/2009/nov/18/world-cup-france-republic-of-ireland (Accessed on 31st January 2010).

Jones, C. and McNamee, M. (2003) Moral development and sport – character and cognitive development contrasted (pp. 40-52). In, Boxhill, J. (Ed.) *Sports ethics, an anthology*. Blackwell Publishing, Malden, MA, USA.

James, S. (2009) Richard Dunne wants none of Sepp Blatter's 'moral compensation' Saturday 5 December 2009 *The Guardian* [online]. Available at: http://www.guardian.co.uk/football/2009/dec/05/richard-dunne-republic-of-ireland-blatter (Accessed on 31st January 2010).

McFee, G. (2004) *Sport, rules and values, philosophical investigations into the nature of sport*. Routledge, London.

McNamee, M. (2008) *Sports, virtues and vices, morality plays*. Routledge London.

Reid, H. (1999) *Sport, education and the meaning of victory* [online]. Available at: http://www.bu.edu/wcp/Papers/Spor/SporReid.htm (Accessed: 14th January 2010).

Suits, B. (1972) What is a game? (pp. 16-22). In, Gerber, E.W. (Ed.) *Sport and the body, a philosophical symposium*. Lea and Febiger, Philadelphia, USA.

Suits, B. (1995) The elements of sport (pp. 8-15). In, Morgan, W.J. and Klaus, V.M. (Eds.) *Philosophical inquiry in sport* (second edition). Human Kinetics, Champaign, Ill. USA.

Wellman, C. (2003) Do celebrated athletes have special responsibilities to be good role models? An imagined dialogue between Charles Barkley and Karl Malone (pp. 333-336). In, Boxhill, J. (Ed.) *Sports ethics, an anthology*. Blackwell Publishing, Malden, MA, USA.

Creative Story

Thierry Henry "Handball" - Ireland vs France 2009, football world cup spoils or was the world cup just spoiled?

Thomas Leydon and Clive Palmer

I T ALL STARTED FOR THE REPUBLIC OF IRELAND'S National football team on the 6th September 2008 in Mainz, Georgia. For the Manager of Ireland, Giovanni Trapattoni, it was his first competitive match in charge and he was hell bent on getting off to a winning start.

"OK lads, this is our first step on the road to South Africa. Let's make it a winning start shall we?" said Giovanni.

A collective roar went up from the Irish players huddled in the away changing room. Most of them were used to the modern facilities provided by the English Premier League clubs, so these rather grubby surroundings in post-Soviet Georgia were a slight culture shock to them. The players then bustled their way through the tunnel and out into the cold night air which seemed to shock them into a new level of consciousness. Captain Robbie Keane gave some words of encouragement to his team mates shortly before kick-off. The World Cup in South Africa in 2010 was the aim of everyone in the Ireland camp. Two hours on and the players returned to the changing room tired, muddy but in good spirits.

"Great performance! This is a tough place to come to, and to win 2-1 is just brilliant, well done, it probably could've been more but let's not dwell on that" said Giovanni. He could always see an angle for more goals but felt it best not to focus on opportunities missed, particularly as it was time for the boys to be jubilant. He appreciated their success as much as anybody.

"Top game that lads, we should be proud. Bring on Italy", said Robbie.

Giovanni hardly had time to enjoy the victory as he was whisked away to face the media.

"Giovanni, do you feel it will be yourselves, Italy and Bulgaria fighting it out for the top two places in your group?" asked one of the savage journalists.

"I feel we have a great chance of qualifying. Of course, we have the World Champions, Italy in our group and Bulgaria will be very tough. But let's not rule out Cyprus, Macedonia and the Georgians, they'll be tough also. And there are the French? I honestly believe there will be no easy games for us in this campaign" Giovanni replied.

It was a cold night in November in the Stade De France in Paris. The Irish turned up in hope rather than with the expectation that they might win. They were the underdogs.

"It's been a long fourteen months since the first qualifier against Georgia, it will be a shame if it ends here tonight". Giovanni said.

"We overcame the odds to finish second in the group behind Italy and we can overcome the odds tonight". Republic boss, Liam Brady replied.

"It was so hard to take, losing the first leg play off to France, we deserved better, we can do better", Giovanni said.

The teams play out the first half of the match...

"It was only 1-0, it's still...." Liam said, before being interrupted by the door to the manager's office swinging open, "five minutes till kick off" Coach Marco Tardelli announced to Giovanni.

Giovanni and Liam looked at each other and with no further words uttered; they walked into the changing room where they are greeted by a strangely quiet and tense Irish changing room. Giovanni knew his team needed him right now, this is what he gets paid for, what he had to say now could make or break a team's morale. With the second half about to start his team had a mountain to climb if they were going to get to South Africa.

"Its half time boys, we're one down but there's a long way to go. Think about the people back home. Your friends and families, their hopes are in your hands. You can do this. Go out and make them proud". Giovanni said.

"COME ON BOYS!" was the collective cry from the Irish players. They hurriedly stormed their way out of the changing room; each one of them was preparing to declare war on the French.

The cold Paris evening was not dampening the travelling Irish fans. The Irish team weren't disappointing the fans either. Half an hour gone and the Irish have been on top, creating chances and the French seem shell-shocked. Giovanni is constantly screaming hurried messages at his players. Robbie was relishing his role as the Captain, he was leading from the front and dragging the Irish team forward.

The mood of the crowd reflected what was happening on the pitch. The Irish following was clearly up for the game whereas the mood amongst the French fans was quiet and sombre. It was hard to tell whether they were nervous or so arrogant that they didn't see the need to whip up an intimidating atmosphere to help their side.

There was thirty two minutes on the clock when Kevin Kilbane (IRE) picked up the ball on the left hand side of the Irish midfield. Kevin was already beginning to feel the graft he had put in during the first half but this didn't stop him playing a neat ball to Damian Duff (IRE). With the ball fast approaching the byline Damian heard a familiar cry.

"Damo! Pull it back, I'm here", cried the ever demanding Robbie...

Damian sent an inch perfect pass into his team-mate's path and he fired the ball past a static French keeper. The equaliser was in. The roar that went up was deafening. There were 81,000 spectators in the ground with only 3,000 of these being Irish fans and the amount of noise generated by them after that goal could easily get passers-by thinking the home side had scored.

"You beauty!" Keith Andrews (IRE) screamed as all the other jubilant Irish players piled on top of a heroic Robbie.

Pleased but still concentrating on the job in hand, Robbie interrupted the celebrations.

"Back in positions now lads, that's just the equaliser".

The Irish weren't going to rest on their laurels and they kept the attack coming, looking to find the goal that would put them ahead. The French, shocked by the battle they were being faced with were forced into life and were forced to stand up to the Irish onslaught.

There was 103 minutes on the clock.

Giovanni was talking nervously to Liam, their eyes locked on the on action.

"We've done well to get to extra time, all we need is one final push..."

Giovanni paused immediately at the sight of Thierry receiving the ball in the Irish box, he controlled it and knocked the ball across the face of goal where his team mate William Gallas (FRA) was waiting gratefully to nod the ball home.

"HAND BALL!" the Irish players screamed as the opposition ran off celebrating. The protests were as frantic as the French celebrations were jubilant. The entire Irish contingent surrounded the dumbfounded referee who had pointed to the centre circle.

"The Linesman's flag's up". An Irish player cried.

Seeing this, the referee raced over to converse and in quick time the referee called Thierry over and issued him a swift booking for handball and proceeded to give Ireland a free-kick. The tables were turned, suddenly it was the green shirts that were celebrating while the blues were in disbelief at what had just happened. Champagne was flying all around the visitors changing room. South Africa here we come.

"We're there" exclaimed Keith, as the singing and dancing around him was becoming more raucous, in a manner which only Irishman who are going to the World Cup finals in South Africa might know how to. They all came to an echoed hush as they realised what was on the over-sized television screens provided for France's visitors. The streets of Irish cities were lined with jubilant fans celebrating their team's victory.

The Johannesburg sun was burning down on the pale skins of the thousands of Irish fans who were congregated in the Soccer City stadium. The day was the 11th July and the final of the World Cup was why they were all there. The Irish faithful surely still had the dramatic 3-2 victory over England in the semi finals on their minds. Today, it was business. Underdogs for the whole campaign, they have continued to defy the odds and have one hurdle left to overcome and they will be world champions. This obstacle was Brazil.

The dressing room was less boisterous than in previous matches. The Irish had gone into every game as 'odds on to lose' and approached each game feeling no pressure. This time it was different. They would step into the South African sun with all eyes on them and an expectant audience. This was their time. This was their chance.

The Brazilians began the match with the expected flair and imagination that is associated with them, they were running circles round the Irish. The usual effort and determination was still clearly there from the eleven Irishmen but they couldn't get to grips with the samba flair of their world class opponents.

Desperate cries could be heard from the underdog's warriors, trying to spur their teammates on.

"We're better than this Ireland, extra ten per cent from each of you" Robbie screamed in desperation after another close shave by the Brazilians. Wave after wave of attack right until ninety minutes was played with no score, but almost remarkably there was no way through for Dunga's side.

Damian cleverly wins a corner in stoppage time, a chance for the Irish to kill a bit of time before extra time.

The ball is bouncing around the box, it's flicked goal-wards and bounces of the post and precariously across the goal line. Robbie is battling to get himself to the ball first.

Commentators around the world go crazy at the dramatic circumstances unfolding before their eyes.

"It must be, surely, just a touch needed from Keane!"

Robbie battles and stretches to get to the ball. One touch is all he needs, poised and squaring himself to aim at the goal, it's a sure thing. If he can just make contact with the ball, any part of his body will do then Ireland are the World Champions...

The ball hits his hand...

"Gerrard goes to Jail" what if Steven Gerrard was found guilty of assault and affray in July 2009.

Paul Gorst and Clive Palmer

Research Preface

THIS STORY IS AN ALTERED HISTORICAL TIME-SCAPE of Steven Gerrard's five-day trial in the summer of 2009. Gerrard was on trial with a charge of assault and affray dating back to 29th December 2008, when he was involved in an altercation at a Southport bar. He was eventually found not guilty and cleared of any wrongdoing. However this story begins at the point when the real-life trial ended - at the summing up and verdict by the judge. I have altered the outcome to find Gerrard guilty on two counts of assault and affray and the story tells of his journey from the courtroom to the prison.

I have assumed the position of Gerrard himself and the story lets the reader in on his feelings, thoughts and emotions that may have been going through his mind at the time. Although the story is primarily an altered historical piece it is written in a dramatic style with a surprise ending that hopefully leaves the reader in suspense.

I chose this as my creative story because I was there in court during the actual trial, working for Mercury Press Agency during my undergraduate studies in Sport's Journalism. This gave me a very good insight to the details of his accusation and his defence and the atmosphere in the courtroom. All of which helped to develop a good creative story grounded from a real life event.

The remainder of the research preface (below) is structured as a news reel which charts, at least in part, the unfolding events surrounding the trial through news coverage at a local level and a national level. The news trail leads to the point where the jury arrive at their verdict for Gerrard.

Background to the story – real life events.
29th December 2008:

Steven Gerrard was arrested on suspicion of assault in a Southport bar.

Earlier that day Gerrard had lead Liverpool to a 5-1 victory over Newcastle United and Liverpool went to the top of the Premier League.

Gerrard and friends celebrated the win with a night out in Southport.

As the night progressed Steven Gerrard got into an altercation with local businessman Marcus McGee. The pair argued and a brawl erupted with Gerrard's friends also getting involved.

Gerrard was one of six men arrested for assault and affray in the incident, and he was eventually released at 11:30pm.

Mr. McGee suffered various injuries in the fracas including a head wound, a black eye, a lost tooth as well as needing four stitches.

A statement for Merseyside Police said:

> "Merseyside Police is investigating an assault that took place in the early hours of Monday December 29 on Bold Street in Southport. At around 2.30am this morning officers attended a disturbance at a licensed premises on Bold Street. Six men were arrested on suspicion of section 20 assault, on Lord Street".

The news-trail reported:

1. LOCAL HEADLINE:
"Nation's media swarm Southport streets after Steven Gerrard arrest"

The Southport Visitor
Report by Mark Johnson and Jo Kelly
Monday 29th December 2008

See the news at:
http://www.southportvisiter.co.uk/southport-news/southport-southport-news/2008/12/29/nation-s-media-swarm-southport-streets-after-steven-gerrard-arrest-101022-22567137/ (Accessed on 1st February 2010).

2. NATIONAL HEADLINE:
"Gerrard arrested in assault probe - England and Liverpool footballer Steven Gerrard is under arrest following an assault at a nightclub".

BBC News

BBC News sport's desk
Monday 29th December 2008

See the news at:
http://news.bbc.co.uk/1/hi/england/merseyside/7802932.stm (Accessed on 1st February 2010).

Monday 20th July 2009:
The trial's opening day was quickly adjourned overnight after discussions between the two legal teams which took up the majority of the day. This meant the trial actually began on Tuesday 21st July 2009.

3. LOCAL HEADLINE:
> "Steven Gerrard case adjourned overnight"

Liverpool Click
Report by Angela Johnson
Monday 20th July 2009

See the news at:
http://www.clickliverpool.com/news/local-news/125322-steven-gerrard-case-adjourned-overnight.html (Accessed 1st February 2010).

Tuesday 21st July 2009:
Steven Gerrard arrives at court for day two of his trial.

The court hears the opening statements from the prosecution who claim Gerrard punched McGee, "with the speed and skill of a professional boxer". They add that, "On that night, Gerrard let his fist and not his feet do the talking".

Prosecution also claim that Gerrard is not a violent man and is a hero to the people of Liverpool, but on that night he let himself down.

"Whatever [Cristiano] Ronaldo is worth, Stevie G is worth £20m more". Adds Mr. David Turner, QC.

"Never in one hundred years was this self defence. He acted like a professional boxer and not a professional footballer".

The court is also shown the CCTV footage from The Lounge Inn in Southport on the night of the incident. The five other defendants admitted the charge of affray.

4. LOCAL HEADLINE:
> "Steven Gerrard trial enters day 2"

Liverpool Click
Report by Martin Thomas
Tuesday 21st July 2009

See the news at:
http://www.clickliverpool.com/news/national-news/125325-steven-gerrard-trial-enters-day-2.html (Accessed 1st February 2010).

5. NATIONAL HEADLINE:

"England and Liverpool star 'punched man like a boxer' in bar row court told"

Mail News Online
Sportsmail reporter
Tuesday 21st July 2009

See the news at:
http://www.dailymail.co.uk/sport/football/article-1201134/England-Liverpool-star-Steven-Gerrard-punched-man-like-boxer-bar-row.html
(Accessed on 1st February 2010).

Wednesday 22nd July 2009:

The court hears evidence from Marcus McGee.

Both prosecution and defence barristers question Mr McGee. They asked if he swore at Gerrard, McGee replied, "one hundred percent and categorically not".

McGee also said he could not recall how long into the exchange of words between the pair, that he was struck, "I don't recall how soon after the exchange I was hit. It is quite clear that Steven Gerrard hit me a couple of times".

The court also heard evidence from Nathaniel Lockie who was working at the bar on the night of the incident and Gina Lond who is the girlfriend of Marcus McGee.

6. LOCAL HEADLINE:

"Gerrard trial hears further evidence from Marcus McGee"

Liverpool Click
Report by Paul Gorst
22nd July 2009

See the news at:
http://www.clickliverpool.com/news/national-news/125353-gerrard-trial-hears-further-evidence-from-marcus-mcgee.html (Accessed on 1st February 2010).

7. LOCAL HEADLINE:

"Steven Gerrard mobbed by well-wishers outside court"

Liverpool Click

Report by Paul Gorst
Wednesday 22nd July 2009

See the news at:
http://www.clickliverpool.com/news/national-news/125359-steven-gerrard-mobbed-by-well-wishers-outside-court.html (Accessed on 1st February 2010).

8. NATIONAL HEADLINE:
"Steven Gerrard trial: Alleged victim claims he faced 'barrage' of blows
Footballer had bad attitude and was being aggressive,
Marcus McGee tells court"

Guardian.co.uk
Press Association
Wednesday 22nd July 2009

See the news at:
http://www.guardian.co.uk/football/2009/jul/22/steven-gerrard-trial-victim
(Accessed on 1st February 2010).

Thursday 23rd July 2009:
Today is the turn of Steven Gerrard to give his evidence.

The court heard a transcript of the interview between PC Tynan and Steven Gerrard on the night of the arrest. Gerrard had been asked, on a scale of one to ten how drunk he was. He answered with "a seven". He also told the arresting officer how he'd been drinking Budweiser as well as a strong alcoholic cocktail called a Jammy Donut.

Gerrard claimed he was acting in self-defence when he approached Marcus McGee,

> "I just wanted a chat but he was quite aggressive and I thought he was going to give me a smack. That is when I threw the punches. I thought he was going to hit me, so I hit him. There was like a melee of punches being thrown by both of us".

The court also heard a character witness statement from Ex-Liverpool player and manager Kenny Dalglish, saying that this incident was dramatically out of character for Gerrard.

The day ended by both prosecution and defence giving their closing statements to the jury.

9. LOCAL HEADLINE:
"Jury set to return Gerrard verdict tomorrow"

Liverpool Click
Report by Angela Johnson

Thursday 23rd July 2009

See the news at:
http://www.clickliverpool.com/news/national-news/125387-jury-set-to-return-gerrard-verdict-tomorrow.html (Accessed on 1st February 2010).

10. NATIONAL HEADLINE:
"Gerrard: I threw three punches and I was seven out of ten drunk"

Mail News Online
Report by James Tozer
Thursday 23rd July 2009

See the news at:
http://www.dailymail.co.uk/sport/football/article-1201420/Liverpool-star-Steven-Gerrard-I-threw-punches-I-seven-drunk.html (Accessed on 1st February 2010).

Friday 24th July 2009:
The jury was sent out by Judge Henry Globe to reach their verdict who said Gerrard should only be found guilty, "only if you are sure he used unlawful force and necessary violence".

The jury were sent out around half past eleven am and returned less than two hours later with a verdict of "not guilty".

"You walk away with your reputation in tact Mr. Gerrard. The verdict is a credible verdict for this case" said Judge Henry Globe.

Meeting the assembled media outside the court, Gerrard thanked his legal team and his family for their support and said he couldn't wait to get back playing football.

11. LOCAL HEADLINE:
"Steven Gerrard "Not Guilty" jury"

Liverpool Click
Report by Paul Gorst
Friday 24th July 2009

See the news at:
http://www.clickliverpool.com/news/national-news/125426-steven-gerrard-not-guilty-jury.html (Accessed on 1st February 2010).

12. LOCAL HEADLINE:
"Steven Gerrard trial: Jury out at Liverpool Crown Court"

Liverpool Daily Post.co.uk
Report by Andy Kelly
Friday 24th July 2009

114

See the news at:

http://www.liverpooldailypost.co.uk/liverpool-news/regional-news/2009/07/24/steven-gerrard-trial-jury-out-at-liverpool-crown-court-92534-24231657/ (Accessed on 1st February 2010).

13. LOCAL HEADLINE:
> *"Liverpool FC captain Steven Gerrard not guilty verdict*
> *in Liverpool crown court trial"*

Liverpool Echo.co.uk
Liverpool Echo sport's desk
Friday 24th July 2009

See the news at:

http://www.liverpoolecho.co.uk/liverpool-news/local-news/2009/07/24/liverpool-fc-captain-steven-gerrard-not-guilty-verdict-in-liverpool-crown-court-trial-100252-24231891/ (Accessed on 1st February 2010).

14. NATIONAL HEADLINE:
> *"Rafael Benítez pleased Steven Gerrard can*
> *now focus on football again"*

Guardian.co.uk
The Guardian sport's desk,
Saturday 25th July 2009

See the news at:

http://www.guardian.co.uk/football/2009/jul/24/rafael-benitez-steven-gerrard-cleared (Accessed on 1st February 2010).

References (listed/numbered in order of appearance)

1. Johnson, M. and Kelly, J. (2008) Nation's media swarm Southport streets after Steven Gerrard arrest (Monday 29th December 2008) *The Southport Visitor* [online]. Available at: http://www.southportvisiter.co.uk/southport-news/southport-southport-news/2008/12/29/nation-s-media-swarm-southport-streets-after-steven-gerrard-arrest-101022-22567137/ (Accessed on 1st February 2010).

2. BBC News sort's desk (2008) Gerrard arrested in assault probe (Monday 29th December 2008) *BBC News* [online]. Available at: http://news.bbc.co.uk/1/hi/england/merseyside/7802932.stm (Accessed on 1st February 2010).

3. Johnson, A. (2009) Steven Gerrard case adjourned overnight (Monday 20th July 2009) *Liverpool Click* [online]. Available at:

http://www.clickliverpool.com/news/local-news/125322-steven-gerrard-case-adjourned-overnight.html (Accessed 1st February 2010).

4. Thomas, M. (2009) Steven Gerrard trial enters day 2 (Monday 21st July 2009) *Liverpool Click* [online]. Available at: http://www.clickliverpool.com/news/national-news/125325-steven-gerrard-trial-enters-day-2.html (Accessed 1st February 2010).

5. Sportsmail Reporter (2009) England and Liverpool star 'punched man like a boxer' in bar row court told (Tuesday 21st July 2009) *Mail* [online]. Available at: http://www.dailymail.co.uk/sport/football/article-1201134/England-Liverpool-star-Steven-Gerrard-punched-man-like-boxer-bar-row.html (Accessed on 1st February 2010).

6. Gorst, P. (2009) Gerrard trial hears further evidence from Marcus McGee (Wednesday 22nd July 2009) *Liverpool Click* [online]. Available at: http://www.clickliverpool.com/news/national-news/125353-gerrard-trial-hears-further-evidence-from-marcus-mcgee.html (Accessed on 1st February 2010).

7. Gorst, P. (2009) Steven Gerrard mobbed by well-wishers outside court (Wednesday 22nd July 2009) *Liverpool Click* [online]. Available at: http://www.clickliverpool.com/news/national-news/125359-steven-gerrard-mobbed-by-well-wishers-outside-court.html (Accessed on 1st February 2010).

8. Guardian Press Association (2009) Steven Gerrard trial: Alleged victim claims he faced 'barrage' of blows Footballer had bad attitude and was being aggressive Marcus McGee tells court (Wednesday 22nd July 2009) *Guardian.co.uk* [online]. Available at: http://www.guardian.co.uk/football/2009/jul/22/steven-gerrard-trial-victim (Accessed on 1st February 2010).

9. Johnson, A. (2009) Jury set to return Gerrard verdict tomorrow (Thursday 23rd July 2009) *Liverpool Click* [online]. Available at: http://www.clickliverpool.com/news/national-news/125387-jury-set-to-return-gerrard-verdict-tomorrow.html (Accessed on 1st February 2010).

10. Tozer, J. (2009) Gerrard: I threw three punches and I was seven out of ten drunk (Thursday 23rd July 2009) *Mail News* [online]. Available at: http://www.dailymail.co.uk/sport/football/article-1201420/Liverpool-star-Steven-Gerrard-I-threw-punches-I-seven-drunk.html (Accessed on 1st February 2010).

11. Gorst, P. (2009) Steven Gerrard "Not Guilty" jury (Friday 24th July 2009) *Liverpool Click* [online]. Available at: http://www.clickliverpool.com/news/national-news/125426-steven-gerrard-not-guilty-jury.html (Accessed on 1st February 2010).

12. Kelly, A. (2009) Steven Gerrard trial: Jury out at Liverpool Crown Court (Friday 24th July 2009) *Liverpool Daily Post.co.uk* [online]. Available at: http://www.liverpooldailypost.co.uk/liverpool-news/regional-news/2009/07/24/steven-gerrard-trial-jury-out-at-liverpool-crown-court-92534-24231657/ (Accessed on 1st February 2010).

13. Liverpool Echo Sport's desk (2009) Liverpool FC captain Steven Gerrard not guilty verdict in Liverpool crown court trial (Friday 24th July 2009) *Liverpool Echo.co.uk* [online]. Available at: http://www.liverpoolecho.co.uk/liverpool-news/local-news/2009/07/24/liverpool-fc-captain-steven-gerrard-not-guilty-verdict-in-liverpool-crown-court-trial-100252-24231891/ (Accessed on 1st February 2010).

14. Guardian sport's desk (2009) Rafael Benítez pleased Steven Gerrard can now focus on football again (Saturday 25th July 2009) *Guardian.co.uk* [online]. Available at: http://www.guardian.co.uk/football/2009/jul/24/rafael-benitez-steven-gerrard-cleared (Accessed on 1st February 2010).

Creative Story

"Gerrard goes to Jail" - a journalistic journey - what if Steven Gerrard was found guilty of assault and affray in July 2009.

Paul Gorst and Clive Palmer

WE THE JURY FIND THE DEFENDANT Steven Gerrard GUILTY on two counts of assault and affray.

With that one sweeping sentence, my life as Steven Gerrard, Liverpool FC captain, England international, was dead in the water, or rather drowned in the cesspools of scandal and scrutiny.

"Steven Gerrard, you have been found guilty of assault and affray, you must spend two years in Walton correctional facility", said Judge Henry Globe. Globe – a fitting name, because at that very moment, like an omnipotent 'world' dictator, he held total control over everything in mine. I had two daughters, a wife, family, friends, everything, and he took it away with contemptuous ease.

My world dulled. The once exciting, colourful vision that had illuminated my existence was replaced in the blink of an eye. The forecast for my future now looked bleak with long dour days of dreary darkness and un-diluted repetitiveness. My liberty curtailed I now had a new master, a new form of discipline. I steeled myself for life as Steven Gerrard: Prison Inmate.

I trudged down the steps of the Crown Court, cuffed like a common thug. I was mobbed by what seemed like thousands. The number of them posing and posturing as wellwisher's had dwindled however. I've so often been a source of inspiration to the people of the city, not any more. I felt as though I'd let them down. I didn't so much as fall as willingly dive off a lofty height of 'grace' without a head-guard to protect from the impact.

I felt a forceful hand on my back as I neared a police car.

"Come on you Gerrard! In you get son..." called a voice from behind me. It was PC Tyrant whose pleasure at my detainment was plain for all to see. Perhaps he is a Blue? It was clear he relished the chance to send me down. Like a comically over-sized feather plumped neatly into the top of his police helmet, this was his chance to say "I sent Gerrard down!" The police car pulled away from a cluster of flashes and shouting, frenzied and hungry they seemed to be circling like scandal starved vultures feasting on a mass cull. The press will be satisfied.

"Right Steven, what's going to happen is you're going to Walton to meet the Warden and he'll ease you into your new surroundings," said Tyrant's assistant, PC Goody.

New surroundings? He made it sound like I was moving furniture to a new home. I could appreciate his way of handling the situation however.

"Look, the idea of 'prison' isn't how it's perceived on the telly you know Stevie, it's full of people who just want to keep quiet and do their time" said PC Goody.

I'd always thought the good cop/bad cop dichotomy was a worn-out, decrepit cliché, but seeing Tyrant and Goody in tandem made me realise it was still a fit and healthy concept.

"Listen you, all your goals an' medals for the Reds, won't cut any ice with us, so just keep your head down an' shut up." Said Tyrant, clearly revelling in his role as 'Bad Cop'.

He seemed to take perverse pleasure in enforcing the law. Their job must be done, but Tyrant seemed to take an overly joyous view of sending people to jail. Suddenly the uneasy atmosphere was broken with what sounded like the beginning of a post-match interview.

"So Stevie, what about that header against Milan in Istanbul? That was something else that!" said Goody.

"Er... yes I just got into position and flicked it on and luckily it went in at the far post", as I tried to answer but the apprehension in my voice was easily detectable.

"What was it like lifting the European Cup?" asked Goody, turning round to hear my answer as I sat in cuffs behind a Perspex shield. His definition of 'appropriate' time and place may have been a little wayward here, but his intentions were in the right place I suppose.

"It was just a memory that will stay with me for life, just amazing." I offered. Perhaps I should have given this man more detail, but my thoughts were unsurprisingly elsewhere.

"Well you'll have to use these memories when you're all on your own Gerrard, it'll be a while before you see a football pitch again!" barked Tyrant.

As we approached the gates of the prison, there seemed to be twice as many unscrupulous and scurrilous snappers, scurrying to find the juiciest bait they could to feed to the ravenous rags they represented.

"Are you sure you don't want to strike a pose Gerrard?" taunted Tyrant, who was now sporting a wide grin. He was the personification of glee. Sickening.

"Just get me in there will you, tell them all to do one!"

"Come on, they're just trying to do their job. Like you used to when you scored all them goals". His particular emphasis on the words 'used to' made every sinew in me sear with un-repentant rage that I had to wrap, bind and confine deep within the core of my being.

"I just want to get on with things, I don't want to be looked at like an animal on display".

"You never wanted them to stop snapping before. All them times when you were happy to steal the limelight, take the front page and the back. What's different now?" His condescending tone riled up the most dormant feelings of hate amidst a stomach pit that was holding a plethora of contrasting emotions. Tyrant's remarks were becoming like bile squirting up to visit a tired and sickly throat. I was shocked, upset, tired, confused but at this moment I was furious, and I had bitten my tongue to the point of splitting. Enough was enough.

"I think you're loving this aren't you? Sending me down, so you can tell all your friends in the pub tomorrow. It's sickening."

"Sickening is it? I'm not going to take this kind of abuse off a convicted criminal. I'm just doing my job. I can make life very difficult for you for the next two years sonny. I'm very friendly with a powerful man you're about to meet. You'll be soon regretting opening that big mouth of yours". His threat was clear as a bell. It was a threat alright and he wanted me to know it.

"Alright! Alright! Get back, all of you, now!" fumed Goody, who seemed to hold a similar disdain towards me for this particular band of travelling wayward souls known as "the press".

The prison was a giant slab of a building, devoid of any creativity, imagination or flair. The architecture of the building seemed to be based upon a block of cheddar cheese and the lack of flamboyance lent the building all the appeal of a common slug. There was no colour and the decoration was in short supply. It was grey, cold and heartless. A fitting place to correct the wrongs that society breeds. My home for the next two years.

"Right Steven we're going to introduce you to the warden of this particular facility. His name's Jonathan Stern, he'll take you on from here."

No sooner had Goody informed me of what would happen, than Tyrant hijacked the conversation and assumed the position of master of ceremonies. "He's seen plenty of so-called superstars like you as well Gerrard, so you better not think he's going to be awe-struck! There's going to be plenty of people who may not like what you do for a living as well, so you better get used to that!"

"Now. Who do we have there then Mr Tyrant?" came the voice from behind me. An eerie silence fell over the corridor. All that was audible was the sound of shoe heels getting louder after each tap on the cold hard floor.

"This is Steven Gerrard of Huyton, Liverpool. Two years for assault and affray, Sir".

"I know who he is Tyrant, now leave us be. I want to introduce Mr. Gerrard to his new abode".

Stern's baritone was subtle and soothing. A far cry from the gruff bark that strangled the air wherever Tyrant went, and a world away from the timid tones that were pushed forcefully from the larynx of Goody.

The warden sounded like he'd seen it all before. "So another big-time-Charlie gets a little too big for his boots and ends up behind bars, is that about the sum of it Gerrard?"

"No, Mr Stern, it was just one of them things that…"

"Save it son, the jury has spoken and it doesn't matter what I think and it certainly doesn't matter what you think".

I felt his controlling manner had been chiselled and refined through years of dealing with the under-class that frequent these places. His body language stamped 'I'm in control' presumably to create the right first impressions upon his normal visitors. "I run this place, so you either make my job easy or I make your entire existence difficult, understood?"

"Yes Sir".

I felt contrite. It was like being back at school being reminded of how to behave. "Don't run in the corridors Mr Brown my old Head Teacher used to shout. But I loved running. I didn't like the rules one bit, but I was prepared to keep my council – at school and here, if there is a difference? 'When you walk through a storm, hold your head up high' goes the legendary anthem of the Kop, but here was different. I knew I would be a target.

 "Your status holds no weight in this place, you'll just be another number to me. I won't have it any other way, understood?"

"Yes Sir".

Stern was different to Tyrant. Tyrant's brand of enforcement was too forced and unnatural. In truth, he was quite comical. Stern however, he knew he was the boss, and everyone else knew it too. "So Steven, this is your 5-star accommodation for the remainder of your stay".

He led me into the pitch black cell and slammed the door shut as though to accentuate the depths of despair to which I had plummeted. The noise of the door confirming the state of my liberty.

Shrouded under the cloak of the night, silent, I stood there staring from the window at the black mist that encapsulated the scene. I heard the metalic scratch of a blade on metal, like new chalk on a blackboard, piercing the silence. Suddenly from the shadows, a whispered…

"Oi Gerrard, welcome to the cell, I'm an Everton fan. And so is my mate Stanley… Stanley Knife."

Uncle Kevin's tragic tale of being there, an eyewitness account of the 1989 Hillsborough disaster

Elisa Langton and Clive Palmer

Research Preface

IN ORDER TO SHARE THIS MOVING STORY, Elisa Langton's uncle Kevin has recounted his memories of being in the crowd at the Hillsborough disaster in 1989. To generate a close up sense of *being there* the story is told in first person by Elisa who 'assumes' the role of her Uncle. This has necessitated a good deal of research about the incident to be combined with a personal writing style to impart something of the atmosphere and feelings in the stands that day. The racing sentences with good punctuation seem to carry the reader on with confidence but at a pace which is intended to mirror the speed of the unfolding tragic events at the Hillsborough stadium. In fact Elisa, currently a third year undergraduate in 2010, may have only just been born at the time of the disaster 21 years ago. Therefore this story may be a good example of ethnographic research writing to interpret someone's first-hand experiences which might then be reflected back as an authentic account which others might learn from or relate to. This kind of 'data' may seemingly complement other forms of information about the event helping to provide a more comprehensive understanding of its impact upon people. Information such as statistics about policing, numbers injured, timescales and other management shortcomings may fail to give a clear account of the insider's experiences. Both views are valid with the latter statistical information perhaps being useful for apportioning blame and compensation whilst the former qualitative account may help to give an insight to the effects of the tragedy at a personal level.

The 1989 Hillsborough Disaster

The 15th of April 1989 is a date that will be remembered as one of the worst days in football history. 96 Liverpool fans died as they were crushed into a pen inside the Hillsborough football ground. Due to the police opening the gates five minutes before kickoff, it led to a surge of fans pushing their way into the already full stand.

Liverpool fan Rob White spoke about his entry to the ground, "I only recall seeing one steward at the start of the tunnel and he was merely observing those people passing through the tunnel. No check was made of my ticket or, to my knowledge of anyone else's ticket" (Taylor, Andrew and Newburn, 1995: 41).

The crush from the fans behind meant people struggled for breath at the front of the stand. Peter Wells, Divisional Superintendent of the St John's Ambulance said, "People were just pressing down on each other and suffocating but there was no way we could get in there. They were vomiting and could not get the vomit out of their mouths" (Taylor *et al* 1995: 67).

But it was the question of who was to blame for this horrific disaster that was to cause the most controversy. Newburn (1993: 30) has stated that, "In all, some 730 people complained of being injured inside the ground and 36 outside it. Out of the 730, 30% are thought to have entered through gate C after 2.52pm". It was the opening of the gates that lead to the unsupervised entry of football fans. From such figures, parties at fault might be identified.

To this day justice has not been done for the families of the 96 who died. Reports in newspapers days after the disaster began to blame the Liverpool fans. Harrison (1999: 143) stated that The Sun printed "The Truth. Some fans picked pockets of victims. Some fans urinated on the brave cops. Some fans beat up PC giving kiss of life". This caused the City of Liverpool to erupt, they were being blamed for the death of their own fans. Scraton (2009: 116) adds his observation that, "The Sunday Mirror reported between 3,000 and 4,000 Liverpool fans 'seemingly uncontrolled' tried to force through the turnstiles". Liverpool fans were being targeted as football hooligans and it was The Sun's editor, Kelvin Mackenzie who seemed to be at fault for such irresponsible reporting.

It is to the police where we look for help in matters like this. But in this situation it was the apparent failure of the Police to tell the truth about goings on that day which meant they were unreliable as a source for honest accounting and investigation about their part in the tragedy. It was not only the reputation of the police seemed which to be at stake but also their credibility with the people they aimed to serve - all in order that they might protect their reputation?

Chief Superintendent David Duckenfield, who was in charge of the policing at Hillsborough, lied in his statement and said that the gate was not opened by a police officer and he somehow came up with an explanation that could back up his interpretation of what happened. Armstrong (1998: 79) stated that, "this checkpoint system helped reinforce the police pronouncements and constructs that the Hillsborough disaster was an organised attempt by ticketless fans to storm the gates to gain entry".

McArdle (2000: 90) added, "some police officers, who are trained to regard football fans as a threat to public order mistook fans desperate attempts to escape by scaling the fence for an attempted pitch invasion and used their truncheons to beat them back into the pen". It is this stereotype of football fans that seemingly caused the police to act in the way they did. Maybe their dubious past experiences with Liverpool fans and football hooliganism could have derived from the Heysel disaster where the Red's fans gained forced entry to a stand containing Juventus fans, causing a wall to fall down where 39 Juventus fans were killed. "While Liverpool fans were not among the most dangerous in the UK they did have a fiery reputation that had been fuelled by a number of recent incidents" Bodin (2005: 37). So maybe it was a result of Liverpool's history which explained why the police decided to take it as an act of hooliganism.

Factors often cited in the theory of spectator violence and hooliganism are day time drinking, post-event riots and protest riots. Stemming from his research, Young, (2000: 385) defined football violence in Britain as being class-derived, "Soccer crowd disorder was thus viewed as a unique cultural adaptation to the lower working-class environment". However, the class issue seems of little consequence or consolation for the losses at Hillsborough. It is true that some supporters do drink alcohol before and after matches, but the police seem to have linked the stereotype of the drunken football fan to account for their uncontrollable actions whilst trying to get into the ground before the match. This may not have been the case! Shockingly, following the accusation by Duckenfield that fans were drunk on arrival to the ground Scraton (2009: 115) points out that the following tests were administered on the corpses, "The Coroner's unprecedented decision to take blood alcohol levels of all who died was plainly influenced by allegations of excessive drinking" These investigative actions stemmed from Duckenfield's allegations.

Liverpool fans were outraged by this statement and quickly formed a Hillsborough Families and Support Group (HFSG). This group was for all the families of the bereaved fans. At first survivors were not allowed to join the group because of the guilt they felt for being alive. The disaster left many fans with long term health problems and many were filled with guilt and shame because they couldn't save the other people. Many survivors suffered with Post Traumatic Stress Disorder, with common symptoms such as "anxiousness, hyper-vigilance, loss of appetite, disturbed sleep and nightmares" (Schein, Spitz, Burlingame and Muskin, 2006: 67). Whether it is because justice does not seem to have been carried out for the fans, or whether it is the personal tragedies which grind deep into a person's psychological state which need constant counselling - some of these symptoms still affect those affected by the disaster today.

Lord Justice Taylor was asked to lead an inquiry following the disaster. He produced two reports; one outlined what had happened and the second outlined future safety recommendations for football grounds. In the second report Taylor staged an argument for a ban on standing in terraces, which if it were in place at the time could have prevented the Hillsborough disaster. On page 12 of the report Taylor stated that, "When a spectator is seated he has his own small piece of territory in which he can feel reasonably secure. He will not be jostled about by swaying or surging" (Taylor, 1989: 12). The majority of football stadiums are now "all seater".

The HFSG have set up a campaign called Justice for the 96. It was formed as part of the 20th anniversary of the Hillsborough disaster. Reports from the police of what really happened have still not been released and no one has yet been found accountable to blame for the disaster. On this anniversary the HFSG asked the people to visit their website, "On the twentieth anniversary of the deaths of 96 people, please take time to read and digest the *true facts* surrounding Hillsborough" (Hillsborough Campaign for Justice, 2009). The HFSG website also contains accounts of what really happened at Hillsborough, personal; for the fans on the pitch and logistical; the actions of the police to manage the situation. The site also features the group's ardent efforts since 1989 to call some authority figures to account for the safety and well being of thousands of people in a public place.

This is my uncle Kevin's story.

References

Armstrong, G. (1998) *Football hooligans: knowing the score.* Berg Publications, Oxford.

Bodin, D., Robene, L. and Heas, S. (2005) *Sport and violence in Europe.* Europe. Council of Europe Publishing.

Harrison, S. (1999) *Disasters and the media.* Macmillan Press. London

Hillsborough Justice Campaign (2009) *20th anniversary of the Hillsborough disaster* [online]. Available at: http://www.contrast.org/hillsborough/home.shtm (Accessed on: 1st December 2009).

HFSG, (2010) *Hillsborough Families Support Group* [online]. Available at: http://www.hfsg.net/ (Accessed on: 2nd February 2010).

Lord Justice Taylor (1989) *The Hillsborough stadium disaster report.* [Online] available at: http://www.fsf.org.uk/uploaded/publications/pdfs/hillsborough%20stadium%20disaster%20final%20report.pdf (Accessed on: 1st December 2009

McArdle, D. (2000) *Football, society and the law.* Cavendish Publishing Limited, London.

Newburn, T. (1993) *Making a difference?* National Institute for Social Work, London.

Schein, L., Spitz, H., Burlingame, G. and Muskin, P. (2006) *Psychological effects of catastrophic disasters: group approaches to treatment.* Hathworth Press Inc. USA.

Scraton, P. (2009) *The truth* second edition. Mainstream Publishing Company, Edinburgh.

Taylor, R., Andrew, W. and Newburn, T. (1995) *The day of the Hillsborough disaster.* Liverpool University Press, Liverpool.

Young, K. (2000) Sport and violence. In, Coakley, J. and Dunning, E. (Eds.) *Handbook of sports studies.* London. Sage.

Creative Story

Uncle Kevin's tragic tale of being there, an eyewitness account of the 1989 Hillsborough Disaster

Elisa Langton and Clive Palmer

IT WAS A BEAUTIFUL SPRING MORNING as I, Kevin Melia began the pleasant drive down to Sheffield along with my cousin Steven Woods. For a 21 year old going to watch your football team, in our case it was Liverpool, playing away in the FA Cup the excitement is unbearable. We left with plenty of time so we could go for the religious pint before the game. We had made the same journey a year ago for the same tie, but there was something about this day, it felt special. As we drew closer we met some (Nottingham) Forest fans passing by in cars, the friendly banter had started as the opposition's flags were waving out the window and chants were being sung from the cars speeding past.

I left the car with my ticket clenched tight in my hand there was no way I was losing this. Heavy traffic from the motorway meant we had arrived with only ten minutes before kickoff, no time for that pint. From listening to passers-by, it seemed that many other fans had had the same experience. There was this noise I could hear from a distance, it sounded like what I'd imagine a war to sound like, minus the gun shots and bombs, but men shouting, some sounding distressed. There were thousands of fans piled back pushing and jostling and shouting at police outside the Leppings Lane end, where the Liverpool fans were situated. As we drew closer, we could see that the traffic had caused problems for thousands of Liverpool fans, there was a pile up outside the turnstiles, I could just make out policemen sitting on horses trying to control the situation, but it didn't seem to be working.

We had managed to push our way through and found ourselves in the middle of the pack of fans, it was hot, and there was no room to move. Stephen was starting to panic, he had very bad asthma and the pressure of people around him was starting to strain his breathing, I knew we needed to get out. A few minutes later I felt a gust of fresh air, the pressure was lifted as a policeman had opened the gate to the turnstiles, I didn't need my ticket now, as thousands of fans surged through the gates towards the stands.

But the situation got worse, we were through the turnstiles and into the outskirts of the ground, stewards were shouting, "go to the side blocks there's seats free". However the quickest way into the ground was down the tunnel, we had no choice we were in the tunnel. Orderly queuing was impossible as we were thrown into a bottleneck and the only direction to move was forward, I could feel the breath of the person behind me speed up as it became more difficult to breath. As I turned round to grab Stephen's arm it dawned on me that I had lost him, I was on my own.

I had somehow managed to reach the other side of the tunnel and it was then that I realised what I was entering. It was a death pit, too many people had been let into the already full stand, fans were suffocating. I heard screams from people surrounding me, screams that sent shivers down my spine, terrifying screams that will live with me forever. There was no room for me to move, as I jumped up to see what was going on in front of me, I found myself stuck, I was crushed between two people, my feet didn't touch the floor again. I felt like I was being slotted into a compressor from the sheer force of the people behind me. I could feel the heartbeat of what felt like three people through my clothes. Some were climbing over the terrace fences to safety; I wished that I could be in their position.

But where was Stephen? After being squashed with my feet lifted off the ground I was half a metre above everyone else so I began looking for him. My mind began to work overtime, where was he? Had he had an attack? Was he ok? I had no luck, everyone looked the same, all I could see what an ocean of hands waving for help. I felt a tug at my leg, as I looked down I saw a middle aged man. His lips moved but no words came out, he needed help so I shouted over to a policeman who was perched on the fence at the side of the pen. "Help" I said, "this man is dying and we need help". I shouted until my throat was dry and no matter how loud I shouted and swore at the policeman for help, he just looked straight through me as if I wasn't there. I tried to drag the man to the same level as me, but I could only reach him with one hand, as I attempted to lift him by his red coat I saw his head drop towards his chest, I couldn't save him, the lack of air and the crush of fans had killed this man in front of my eyes. I felt sick but I didn't have time to think, I had to get out and find Stephen.

I didn't think it could get any worse. Just as I thought that, it did. The pain became so intense on the bottom half of my body it felt as though the 'blood streams' had been cut from the tops of my legs. I presumed the game has been stopped as I looked over at the spill of fans on the pitch. As I looked up at the stand above I could see people waving down their hands offering help, although as I tried to stretch my arms up to them, I couldn't reach. I said to the man in front "we've got help, we need to get up there, and they will pull us up". But there was no reply. As I touched the face of the man, it was cold, lifeless and turning blue, the life had been crushed out of him. If I was going to save myself I had to use this man as my ladder, it was terrible, as I hoisted myself onto his limp shoulders I whispered "I'm so sorry". As I remember, two fans above grabbed my hands and pulled me to safety, I don't know what made me do it but I looked back down to the crowd of weak, vulnerable people. Maybe in hope to see Stephen or maybe it was the guilt of using a dead man as my lift to safety.

There was a sense of coldness around the ground, nobody knew what to do. As I looked from the higher tier, I wanted to go and rip down the fences that were surrounding the helpless fans and give them some air, some space to breathe. Then I thought, *where was Stephen?* I ran down the steps, my legs felt like jelly as I took each step, the blood had not had time to re-circulate again, making them feel boneless. As I reached the pitch I could not believe what I was seeing, it was like a scene from a war movie. The stadium had been transformed into a disaster area, fans were improvising and making DIY stretchers by ripping down advertising boards to carry the hundreds who need medical treatment. The atmosphere was strange, some were filled with tears of joy as they survived as they found their loved ones, whereas others cried tears of sadness and heartbreak as they towered over the bodies of relatives. There was however a sense of togetherness between the fans, both Liverpool and Nottingham Forest, people were coming forward to see what they could do to help the injured.

There were two ambulances on the scene, priority was given to those who could be saved. The rest were left to die in the dry mudded goal mouth. My heart was in my throat as I began to look through the bodies, I prayed I wouldn't find Stephen lying on the grass. As I walked along the pitch I could see the bodies of fans from all ages, from children to middle aged men, but still no Stephen. As my eyes began to fill with tears at the prospect of finding him lying on the floor, it hit me. I looked up and saw a short dark haired, stocky figure about ten metres away. My heartbeat sounded like the rhythm of a drum, as my feet started moving quickly, almost tripping I could see the figure walking towards me, he was dazed and upset, I wiped the tears from my eyes and I saw standing there, red faced with his inhaler in hand, Stephen.

My emotions were indescribable, I grabbed him in my arms and cried. We didn't speak for the next five minutes, as we looked back at the stand, there were no words to say. The drive home was very much the same, I don't know whether it was the shock or relief that we had got out alive but we didn't want to speak about the events that had occurred. As we arrived home to the tears of my parents, I had time to reflect on the day and what could have been. We had got lucky but my heart remains with families and friends of the 96 who didn't.

Chapter 8

Mike Tyson – 'a dirty face with an angel'

Michael Glover and Clive Palmer

Research Preface

THE STORY BEHIND MIKE TYSON is one of incredible highs and lows. His record in the ring involves both high profile wins and losses, while his record outside it conveys a number of crimes and misdemeanours the pinnacle of which is the ten year prison sentence for the rape of Desiree Washington in 1991. There is, however, a sequence of events in the years leading up to Washington's rape which moulded Tyson's behaviour both inside and outside of the ring which culminated in this most heinous of crimes.

Torres (1989) reveals how Tyson began a career in crime at the tender age of seven when he broke into the shop below the flat he lived in. He entered through the floor boards. In a particularly insightful story into Tyson's future behaviour involving sexual violence, Torres (1989) tells of when Mike accidentally broke a toy gun he was given as a present along with a doll. In an act of aggression Tyson violently snapped the head off the doll and in an interview with Torres years later said, "I felt an immense thrill when I ripped the head off the doll. It was like an orgasm" (Torres 1989: 17).

Tyson's aggression and violence developed as he increased in age and size. After he was picked on in his early school years, however the future heavyweight champion of the world one day decided it was time to fight back and discovered he had a talent for inflicting injury. Torres (1989) describes how this was the beginning of a close relationship between Tyson and violence. After retaliating against his bullies "Mike did not wait to be provoked. Now it was he who started things" (Torres 1989: 27).

Torres (1989) also reveals how Tyson was introduced to, participated in and saved from a life of stealing, mugging, gun crime and drug taking. Sugden (1996) states how Tyson's behaviour saw him arrested 40 times by the time he was 12 years old. It was at this age when Tyson began living in Elwood Cottages, a special wing of the Tryon School and Youth Correctional Facility for the deeply troubled. It was here that Tyson first began boxing with Bobby Stewart, a counsellor at the school and former boxer. Spotting his potential, Stewart referred Tyson to boxing trainer Cus D'Amato who took the young boy under his wing, teaching him the art of boxing and turning him into the wrecking machine of the late 1980s. His criminal past, however, seemed to have left its mark on Tyson and would never entirely leave him. "Mike's demons were pulling on him and he never seemed to try to free himself from their grasp. Still he dreamed big dreams" (Torres 1989: 74).

Tyson's professional career began in 1985 and the following year, according to Sugden (1996), he became the youngest ever world heavyweight champion at the age of just 20. He went on to be the first undisputed world heavyweight champion, holding all three major belts at the same time. However, Sugden (1996: 184) states that "after the deaths of his guardian and mentor Cus d'Amato and his manager Jim Jacobs, Tyson appeared to lose the ability to distinguish between himself as predator in the ring and his persona outside it". Tyson was left to deal with a mixture of incredible wealth, fame and popularity, and without D'Amato and Jacobs to control him a return to his childhood behaviour was inevitable. For example, Sugden (1996: 184) explains that, "Tyson's physical development was matched only by the size of his ego, which was inversely proportional to the underdeveloped state of his super-ego (social conscience)". Tyson lost the undisputed crown in 1990 to James Douglas, who himself relinquished it at his first defence to Evander Holyfield (Bellfield, 2006).

In July 1991, Mike Tyson's criminal background and, as Sugden (1996) claims, his lack of social conscience found a new depth of depravity when he raped beauty queen Desiree Washington in an Indianapolis hotel room. Piper (1995: 77) talks of Tyson's sexuality, saying that it "hinged on violence and a disregard for consent". On the witness stand, Washington, according to the Washington Post (1992), told of how Tyson "lured her to his hotel room on a date and forced her to have sex as she tried to fight him off". In

February 1992, an Indianapolis jury convicted Mike Tyson of raping Desiree Washington and he was sentenced to ten years in prison with the final four years suspended (New York Times 1992).

Tyson was released in March 1995 and chalked up three more knock out victories within a year, one of which regained him the WBC heavyweight title from Frank Bruno (ESPN, 2002). In late 1996, Tyson would fight who many thought would be his first genuine test since release from prison when he faced Evander Holyfield. Originally, the fight was due to take place in autumn 1991 for the undisputed crown, which by now belonged to Holyfield, but did not occur due to Tyson's rape conviction (Bellfield 2005). As stated on ESPN (2002), Holyfield won via technical knock-out and took Tyson's WBA heavyweight title in the process. It was the rematch the following year, however, which plunged Tyson into controversy once again. As reported on Slam!Boxing (1997), Tyson was disqualified and later banned for biting a chunk out of Holyfield's ear in retaliation to repeated head butting by his opponent.

Following this event, it was a general view that Tyson's once awesome boxing ability had diminished as a result of his time in prison, although it did not stop him going back to prison in 1999 for nine months on an assault conviction. Another comeback fight came in 2002, when Tyson eventually faced Lennox Lewis after being banned once again following, according to Anderson (2007: 74), "Tyson's threatening demeanour at a pre-fight press conference in New York, which ended in a fracas". Tyson, by now somewhat a washed up and past it fighter, was knocked out in the eighth round. The following year, Tyson sunk to his lowest position when he declared himself bankrupt (Biography.com, 2010).

NB: The title of this chapter is a play on words from the title of a famous film called Angels with Dirty Faces (1938) starring James Cagney, Pat O'Brien and Humphrey Bogart. It was a story of children growing up to be gangsters, learning to live by 'street rules' but presided over by a 'higher force' looking after them. The parallels with Tyson's life history are striking – even to the use of boxing for the young disadvantaged boys in their society.

Reference List

Anderson, J. (2007) *The legality of boxing: A punch drunk love?* Birbeck Law Press, Oxon.

Bellfield, L. (2005) *This month in boxing history* March 1991-Mike Tyson vs. Razor Ruddock [online]. Available at: http://www.saddoboxing.com/939-boxing-history-mike-tyson -ruddock.html (Accessed on: 9th December 2009).

Bellfield, L. (2006) *This month in boxing history:* Buster Douglas – Mike Tyson 1990 [online]. Available at: http://www.saddoboxing.com/2811-month-boxing-history-buster-dougl as-mike-tyson-1990.html (Accessed on: 9th December 2009).

Biography.com (2009) *Mike Tyson biography* [online]. Available at: http://www.biography.com/articles/Mike-Tyson-9512980?part=4 (Accessed on: 3rd December 2009).

ESPN (2002) *Mike Tyson timeline* [online]. Available at: http://static.espn.go.com/boxing/new s/2002/0129/1319772.html (Accessed on: 3rd December 2009).

New York Times (1992) Tyson gets 6-year prison term for rape conviction in Indiana, *New York Times* [online]. Available at: http://www.nytimes.com/1992/03/27/sports/tyson-gets-6-year-prison-ter m-for-rape-conviction-in-indiana.html (Accessed on: 2nd December 2009).

Piper, K. (1995) Four corners, a contest of opposites (pp. 71-79). In, Chandler, D., Gill, J., Guha, T. and Tawadros, G. (Eds.) *Boxer: An anthology of writings on boxing and visual culture.* Institute of International Visual Arts, London.

Slam!Boxing (1997) Tyson banned for life *Slam!Boxing* [online]. Available at http://www.canoe.ca/BoxingTysonHolyfield/jul9 banned.html (Accessed on: 3rd December 2009).

Sugden, J. (1996) *Boxing and society: An international analysis.* Manchester University Press, Manchester.

Torres, J. (1989) *Fire and fear: the inside story of Mike Tyson.* Cox and Wyman Publishing Ltd, Reading.

Washington Post (1992) Tyson found guilty of rape, two other charges *Washington Post* [online]. Available at: http://tech.mit.edu/V112/N4/tyson.04w.html (Accessed on: 2nd December 2009).

Creative Story

Mike Tyson -'a dirty face with an angel'

Michael Glover and Clive Palmer

MIKE TYSON STOOD AT THE FOOT OF A KING-SIZE BED inside his penthouse hotel suite. He stared for a moment at the woman sitting on top of the dark, silk sheets. Her ample backside placed perfectly on the edge of the mattress as she glanced around the room waiting for her host to make conversation.

Nothing could be further from Tyson's mind than conversation. He continued his role as voyeur from the foot of the bed, his target seemingly confused by the silence on their 'date'. Dressed all in black in designer track pants and t-shirt, Tyson could feel his muscles tense as he contemplated what he could do once he overpowered the girl. His biceps stretched the t-shirt a size too small and he could feel the adrenaline pumping through his veins. His immediate needs would soon be met, but never fully satisfied.

"So, when's your next fight?" Desiree Washington asked from her position on the bed in an attempt to get the conversation ball rolling. Her voice was cocooned in unawareness of what Tyson was planning to do with her.

There was no response. It was as if Tyson had seen her lips move but not heard the sound coming out. He simply stared sadistically at the movement of her full lips, painted a vibrant red.

Desiree could now sense something was wrong. Still she waited for a reply from her 'date' but still none came. She prayed he was just shy and did not know what to say to her, that his stationary pose and eerie silence was just a nervous reaction while he searched his brain for small talk.

"I think I'd better leave," Desiree said as she began to get up from the bed, worried by what the plan all along had been for her since Tyson persuaded her to meet him here on a date. As Desiree edged towards the door, unsure

137

of what her 'date' would do next, she felt a solid grip on her wrist and an overpowering force against her desired direction of movement.

"I want you to stay," Tyson demanded in his high-pitched and lisp-packed speech. With his hand still surrounding her wrist, he gave her a tug towards him and her inferior in weight body duly obeyed as she stumbled back towards the king-sized bed. He was a heavyweight champ, and he was not about to let this lightweight, let alone female lightweight, dictate what was going to happen.

Tyson could feel his body heat begin to rise in anticipation of what was about to take place, what he had wanted to happen since he first lay eyes on this woman just a few hours ago. He took a step towards Desiree and she fell back onto the bed. The gap between the two bodies was narrowed as Tyson took another step towards her, ignoring her plea to let her go.

A bang on the door pulled Tyson from his concentration. Another bang and this time a voice followed. "Are you okay in there? Mr Tyson, what's going on?" The voice seemed calm and in control but Desiree's fear still concentrated her stare at the giant heavyweight standing over her.

The door again was shaken by a resounding bang. Tyson, now disturbed from his plan, strode over to the door with violent intentions and looked through the peep hole. It was a man he did not know, yet, oddly, a man who still looked familiar. Something told Tyson, something entangled in all his violent and abusive nature, to trust this man.

Opening the door, he saw the man's face clearly; a weathered complexion with dark skin and a clean shaven jaw. He stood just over six foot tall and wore a navy pinstripe suit with a dazzling red tie as well as a trusting look and spoke in a deep voice. "Mr Tyson, I think you should stop and think about what you're doing," he bellowed, looking him square in the eye.

Tyson turned to look at the frightened looking girl on the bed. For some reason the words spoken by the mystery man at the door stuck inside Tyson's head. The heavyweight walked over to one of the big sofas in his penthouse suite and sat down, wondering if he would actually have gone through with any of the sadistic thoughts in his head. Out of the corner of his eye Tyson saw Desiree Washington seize her opportunity and dash out of the open door to freedom. He didn't care; the man in the pinstripe suit and dazzling red tie had got inside his head.

"Who are you, anyway?" Tyson said in his high-pitched voice. But the man in the pinstripe suit had already disappeared down the corridor.

Mike Tyson stood in the corner of the ring, his trainer shouting boxing buzz words at him as he stared at Evander Holyfield, his opponent, in the opposite corner. This was it, fight night; the chance to win back the undisputed heavyweight crown. But in the few seconds before the first round bell Tyson couldn't help but think back three months to when he was in his hotel room with Desiree Washington. What if he'd raped her? He wondered if he would be stood in this ring right now if he had not been disturbed by the man in the pinstripe suit and had gone through with his plans to self gratify?

The ring of the bell for the first round suddenly brought Tyson back to reality and drained his body of the nostalgic feelings. Tyson went at Holyfield in his usual attacking style, trying to knock his opponent out in the first few minutes as he had done so many times in the past. Holyfield, though, was a much higher class of fighter.

Tyson would swing his sledgehammer punches into the body and head of Holyfield, but his opponent would just take them as if they were nothing. At every opportunity, knowing it would frustrate his opponent, Holyfield would grapple with Tyson; hugging him close to stem the flow of sledgehammer blows.

"You can't touch me, boy," Holyfield whispered into the ear of Tyson while in one of their close quarter tussles. His taunts filled Tyson with rage. He was desperate to knock that stupid smile from Holyfield's face.

The bell for the second round sounded and Tyson went at Holyfield again with an onslaught of flying fists. But again his opponent just grappled him and held his head close, whispering insults as he boxed in Tyson's mind. "Can't throw your punches now can you, Mikey?" he would say. "What's wrong with your gloves, Mike?"

Both warriors continued; each landing a few blows but spending most of their time wrestling with their sweaty heads clashing side by side. Holyfield continued his insulting jibes but by now was adding something else to his plan. As the two fighters' heads locked together Holyfield began to move his head in towards Tyson's, butting him above the eye. Tyson felt the anger within himself begin to rise.

The third round began and the two fighters' heads were again locked together. Holyfield forced his head into the spot above Tyson's eye, which was now beginning to swell badly. Tyson's blood was now at boiling point with anger burning through his body. As their heads came together in another clash and grapple, Tyson noticed his mouth placed next to his opponent's ear. He thought of the pain he could cause Holyfield, of the regret he would have for ever daring to head butt him in such a disrespectful manner. "Just bite his ear, hard" Tyson thought to himself. It would be so easy. Bite it, pull it, rip it off".

As he stared at the ear of his opponent with his jaw tense and teeth at the ready, the focus of Tyson's gaze switched to the crowd in the background. A man in the front row craved his attention, Tyson could not help but notice him; he was wearing a pinstripe suit with a dazzling red tie. The two men stared at each other for a few seconds and, projecting his voice above the roar of the crowd, the man in the pinstripe suit spoke to Tyson.

"Mr Tyson, don't do what I think you're going to do", the man in the pinstripe suit bellowed in his deep voice. "You can win this fight, Mr Tyson. You can knock him out."

"But I can't do it", Tyson said in hope of a reassuring reply. "He keeps head butting me".

"Win the fight", the man said abruptly.

Just as they did three months ago, the man in the pinstripe suit's words got into his head. Tyson didn't know who this guy was, or where he came from, but he felt the need do what he said. The words spurred Tyson on, there was to be no more dallying about the task in hand. Mike Tyson was going to regain the undisputed heavyweight crown here, now, tonight.

Surprising Holyfield with a burst of energy, Tyson broke free from their latest bought of head and chest clashing and caught him with two of his sledgehammer blows, one on each side of his head. The punches were hard and bursting with intent.

Holyfield knew he was in trouble. Another punch came, and another, fast, a left hook this time that connected with the side of his head, causing him to wobble. A huge right fist came pile-driving into the face of Holyfield and he found himself on the canvas. Before he knew what was happening, the referee had counted to ten and he had been beaten. Mike Tyson was the new undisputed heavyweight champion of the world.

Tyson was overjoyed. He had done it. As the referee raised the new champ's arm, Tyson turned towards the crowd where he had seen the man in the pinstripe suit just seconds before. But, just as he had in the hotel three months earlier, the man had disappeared without a trace. Tyson, though, somehow knew and inwardly hoped this would not be the last he saw of the man in the pinstripe suit.

Taxi for Agent Alan, to Rio and the French Connection

Sean Dean and Clive Palmer

Research Preface

THE CREATIVE STORY IN THIS CHAPTER is a spoof comedic account of Alan Shearer playing the part of a CIA Agent. In order to spin such a yarn it is seemingly helpful to know some context as to how such a story might come about. The tale starts when Alan retires from playing football after an illustrious career in the game. To all intents and purposes his stature and reputation within football as a player and now as an ambassador for the game may be a perfect cover to mask his secret agent activities for the USA!

Alan Shearer was born in, Gosforth, Newcastle in 1970 to working-class parents Alan and Anne Shearer (Wikipedia, 2009). His father wanted him to take up football as a youngster. His football career started when he was a teenager playing for Wallsend Boys Club and from here he was scouted to trial at Southampton. He was offered a contract to play for Southampton in April 1986 (Wikipedia, 2009). Alan played for the Southampton first team in 1988 and was already starting to show his goal scoring prowess when he, "became the first man to score 30 Premier League goals in three successive seasons" (Newcastle United Football Club, 2008).

After spending four years at the club he went on to play for Blackburn Rovers Football Club. At Blackburn FC, who paid at the time "a British record £3.6m fee in 1992" (NUFC, 2008), he would have his best years of football success in the Premiership. Blackburn managed to win the

143

Premiership in the 1994-95 season with Alan Shearer scoring a league record of 34 goals and take the title against Manchester United on the last day of the season (Wikipedia, 2009). The following year Blackburn FC could not defend their title even though Alan was the Premiership's top goal scorer again and this would attract two clubs to bid for Shearers talents in the process.

Manchester United wanted to sign Alan Shearer in 1996 but this was not to be, as Newcastle United signed him again at what was at the time "a world-record fee of £15m" (BBC, 2006). He spent his final years as a player at Newcastle United FC, which was the team he always wanted to play for since he was a teenager at Wallsend Boys. At Newcastle however, he would never emulate the success he had at Blackburn Rovers, the best they achieved in his time there being runners up in the Premiership and the FA cup.

A number of prestigious accolades were awarded to Alan; he won PFA (Professional Footballer's Association) player's player of the year award in 1995 and 1997, for Blackburn and then Newcastle. He also became Newcastle United's top goal scorer with 206 goals to his name, overtaking Jackie Milburn's record of 200 (BBC, 2006). He was also the Premiership's top goal scorer of all time with "260 goals in 441 games" (BBC, 2006). He was also named as Overall Player of the Decade, Domestic Player of the Decade, Outstanding Contribution to the Premier League and Top Goal Scorer (Talkfootball, 2008). Alan also received an OBE in 2001 (Order of the British Empire medal) for his services to football and was entered into the football hall of fame in 2004 for his contribution to both Club and Country (Talkfootball, 2008).

Alan Shearer worked with many charities during his playing career and carried on his generous work when he retired. Perhaps his most significant fundraising effort was the 1.6 million pounds he generated for charities in the North East of England (Mail Online, 2006). His testimonial match for Newcastle United against Celtic on the 11th May 2006 was also dedicated to raise money for charity as well as being a farewell game paying tribute his football career (NUFC, 2008). There were many charities that benefited from the generous dedication from this part of the football world, for example,

> Among the organizations to benefit were the Nordoff Robbins Music Therapy charity, which received £608,000, the NSPCC, who received £347,000 and Newcastle General Hospital A & E and the Freeman

Hospital were given £95,000 each. Wallsend Boys Club, where Shearer began his illustrious footballing career also received £15,000" (Mail Online, 2006).

Helping out these charities meant a great deal to Alan because he wanted to help others to benefit from his successful football player, not just himself. He considers himself very lucky to play football at the highest level and to have the opportunity to give something back seemed the right thing to do (Mail Online, 2006).

His England career started in 1992, when he was a regular in the Southampton team and proving to be a prolific goal scorer for them. One of the best years in Alan Shearer's history was in1996 when he claimed a first team spot in the England squad and England were going to play in the 1996 European Championships (Soccer-fans-info, 2007). Even though England did not make the final of that tournament Alan achieved his own success by winning the Golden Boot with five goals scored in the tournament. During the lead up to qualifying for the European's in 2000, Shearer struggled to score goals for England, in fact, "he had failed to score in eight games" (BBC, 2000). He did manage to score a hat-trick against Luxembourg (Talkfootball, 2008; BBC, 2000), which allowed England to qualify for the Euro 2000 competition. Due to injuries throughout his career, he retired from International football after the Europeans in 2000 as it, "was becoming a challenge too far" (BBC, 2000). As a result of his injuries he struggled to regain that extra speed to beat defenders and found it harder to score. However, his goal scoring record for England was impressive scoring thirty times in sixty three games, making it almost a goal every other game (BBC, 2000).

Having retired he now works for the BBC on the television show Match of the Day. Alan Shearer said he wanted to have time to do other things before becoming a manager too soon. However, after completing his UEFA pro license, Alan was able to manage a premier league team and was asked to manage Newcastle United for the remainder of the 2008-09 season. He took up the challenge, as he was ready, the BBC gave him eight weeks off and saw him appointed at the start of April for the remaining eight games. The task was to try and save Newcastle United from regulation from the Premiership to the Championship (Telegraph, 2009), which ended up them being regulated. He is still a pundit for BBC's Match of the Day, alongside Gary Lineker and Alan Hanson.

References

BBC (2000) *Sad farewell for Shearer,* BBC Sport [online]. Available at: http://news.bbc.co.uk/1/hi/euro2000/teams/england/799370.stm (Accessed 4th December, 2009).

BBC (2006) *Injury forces Shearer retirement* BBC Sport [online]. Available at: http://news.bbc.co.uk/sport1/hi/football/teams/n/newcastle_united/4929358.stm (Accessed 3rd December, 2009).

Mail Online (2006) *Shearer gives £1.6million testimonial money to charity*, Mail Online [online]. Available at: http://www.dailymail.co.uk/tvshowbiz/article-412938/Shearer-gives-1-6million-testimonial-money-charity.html (Accessed 4th December, 2009).

Newcastle United Football Club (2008) *Managers: Alan Shearer (2009),* NUFC [online]. Available at: http://www.nufc.premiumtv.co.uk/articles/alan-shearer-2009-20090402_2241256_1643848 (Accessed 3rd December, 2009).

Soccer-Fans-Info (2007) *Alan Shearer Biography*, [online]. Available at: http://www.soccer-fans-info.com/alan-shearer-biography.html (Accessed 3rd December, 2009).

Talkfootball (2008) *Alan Shearer*, [online]. Available at: http://www.talkfootball.co.uk/guides/football_legends_alan_shearer.html (Accessed 4th December, 2009).

Telegraph (2009) *Alan Shearer to be Newcastle United manager until end of season*, Telegraph Sport's Desk[online], available at: http://www.telegraph.co.uk/sport/football/leagues/championship/newcastleunited/5086053/Alan-Shearer-to-be-Newcastle-United-manager-until-end-of-season.html (Accessed 4th December, 2009).

Wikipedia (2009) *Alan Shearer* Wikipedia [online]. Available at: http://en.wikipedia.org/wiki/Alan_Shearer (Accessed 3rd December, 2009).

Creative Story

Taxi for Agent Alan - Rio and the French Connection

Sean Dean and Clive Palmer

HIS PHONE BLEEPED IN AN UNUSUAL WAY, "oh no, not now", he knew what it meant and his heart started racing. But right now he was on set at the BBC commentating on a live broadcast following a match that saw Newcastle lose to Sunderland in an exciting 3-1 derby victory. Alan was magnanimous in the defeat of his former club and generous with his comments about Sunderland, even charitable one might say. But realizing what was going on in the real world his eyes shifted furtively. He was in a rush now... and it was official...

"Excuse me Gary, excuse me Alan", he said, as he stood up impatiently and pushed past the pair of panicking pundits (NB: and that's not easy to say on any day of the week, well done reader). In doing so he stood on Alan's toe, unintentionally of course, you could call it a professional foul amongst friends, "oww you Makem baffoon" Hanson bawled in his subtle Glaswegian tone, not known as a person for mincing his words.

"Oh sorry mate, and it was your left as well, shame, well, you were crap with that one anyway, and Liverpool never missed you, bloody jocks always gettin in the way" he muttered and made for the nearest exit. Gary offered some crisps to Alan Hanson by way of consolation and called to Alan Shearer helpfully as he scurried away, "you can put your travel expenses in anytime if you're in a rush mate, perhaps see you in the week for a pint yeh?" SLAM went the studio door. He was gone in a flash. He was a spook now. Expenses and social niceties would have to wait.

Following a *code red* text message from Washington, Alan Shearer CIA agent, was assigned to a secret mission to track down Jean "Silvio" Motsonelli, who is at the top of the ten most wanted list by Interpol and now the CIA for drug dealing and match fixing. A notorious criminal, Motsonelli is the head figure of a number of European match fixing cartels.

147

His illegal gambling on the international football scene is fuelled by drug money, compounded by drug taking and features million dollar bribes on an almost weekly basis to influence parliamentary figures and football club owners. In his home country of Italy these people are sometimes one and the same. Having originally been arrested in Colombia whilst 'on holiday', Motsonelli had escaped from a high security mountain top prison called Gwan Tanamo Heights in the USA. He had managed somehow to flee the American continent and get himself to France to complete some unfinished business. Unfinished business would inevitably involve some extreme discomfort for a few of Motsonelli's 'associates'. Typically, a trail of dripping red bodies and snowdrifts of cocaine were usually strong indicators that "Moti" had been in town. Agent Alan, now on his way to Heathrow Airport near London was, therefore, ideally placed to be first on the scene for the CIA. Unknown to Motsonelli however was the miniature surveillance tag which had been implanted under the skin in his right leg. It was a sensitive tracking device. There was no escape for him worldwide, he was committed to a life of being hunted. Motsonelli would have to cut off his leg to have half a chance at running away this time. However, a desperate man in desperate times may come to rely upon desperate measures, nothing could be left to chance and Agent Alan had to act quickly. Agent Alan's mission was to find Motsonelli and take him to a CIA safe-house in Marseilles in the south of France. From there he would be immediately transported in an unmarked plane on an unregistered flight to somewhere 'nice' in the USA.

Agent Alan landed at the Charles de Gaulle Airport in Paris, where Motsonelli was reported to be hiding in the crowds. The airport was busy, people were running to catch their flights and others were engaged in contemplative people-watching, when to his surprise, he saw Motsonelli walking casually down the escalators. He obviously thought he was invisible in his chic Italian sheepskin coat amongst the throngs of cosmopolitan travellers at Charles de Gaulle. And he might have been considered chic if were not for the fact that it was July and the temperature was a scorching 35 degrees Celsius. Alan started sprinting after Motsonelli, pushing everyone out of his way.

"Motsonelli where do you think you are going?" Alan called out to the man in the sheepskin coat.

Motsonelli looked round and glared at Agent Alan realizing that he wanted more than a friendly chat.

"I am a free man I tell you," replied Motsonelli, "no-one can stop me now, I am invincible".

Motsonelli took off like a shot, knocking people down as he dashed towards the airport doors. Alan was huffing and puffing as he tried to keep up with him, trying to catch him. Agent Alan had to admit that he had let himself go a little since he retired and was now pretty much out of shape. He spared a thought for the heady glory days at Blackburn Rovers when he could run all day. But now, his knees were hurting and he had a niggling groin injury which seemed to be plaguing his current performance. He wondered what Gary and Alan might say about him now...

At an impressive speed Motsonelli burst through the airport doors onto the taxi rank and lay-by. He opened the taxi door and threw the driver out and drove off like a maniac. Agent Alan stopped at the entrance doors gasping for air like a man on sixty fags a day. Not having a chance to catch Motsonelli by tackling him to the ground rugby-style was frustrating. "Never mind" an old lady said as she passed by, as Agent Alan sat down on the curb having run out of steam. "Never mind what?" he thought. The fact that I am half this old lady's age but twice as decrepit, or the fact that Motsonelli out ran him wearing a sheepskin coat in the height of summer. At that moment Alan received a phone call from the head office of the CIA, a welcome distraction in any fast moving chase story. Head office wanted an update on how he was getting on with his assigned task. While he was speaking on the phone he was trying to recover from nearly having a heart attack from chasing down his fugitive. Agent Alan, as honest as the day is long, let them know how difficult things were for him right now and that he was having no luck in his attempt to detain Mr. Motsonelli. It was a good thing that Motsonelli was wearing the tracking device otherwise it would take days or even weeks to capture him. Alan wanted to know where he was heading next so that he could make his next move to try and take him down now he had the element of surprise (again?). Agent Alan was frustrated at Motsonelli for making him look like an idiot when chasing him at the airport. The CIA head of office were tracking Motsonelli's every move by satellite and they reported that he was heading towards the Eiffel tower, which was an hours drive from the Charles De Gaulle Airport. Agent Alan reported in the affirmative and resumed his mission, "Roger Wilco, the mark is mine". Inwardly he thought, "oh no blimey, I haven't got t run up there now have I?" These were exactly the kind of thoughts he had on the playing field towards the end of his football career, like a racing driver revving on the grid who says, "Hey guys, what's the rush anyway?", it was time to stop. However, now an international criminal was at large who would never know where the end of the race or the game was, and Agent Alan bolstered his resolve to catch him.

While Alan was on the phone to the Head Office of the CIA, someone was overhearing the conversation and Alan could see him. After finishing the phone call he quickly turned round to see who the gentlemen was. Dressed up in a suit and not looking like an ordinary citizen waiting for their flight to be called, Alan put his phone back in his jacket pocket and proceeded further down the taxi rank. As he approached the door of a taxi the gentlemen introduced himself saying to Agent Alan he was Agent Fudgeland from the CIA. Agent Rio Fudgeland in fact. He was sent by the CIA to keep tabs on Agent Alan and to make sure he brought Jean "Silvio" Motsonelli to the French safe-house. Agent Alan let Agent Rio know that he did not need spying on to catch Motsonelli and that his presence was not appreciated. He told Rio Fudgeland that he was wasting his time, coming all this way for nothing. Agent Rio insisted that he was going to do more than just sit back and let Alan take all the glory for catching Motsonelli and reaping the rewards.

"Do you think I am going to let you take all the glory" said Agent Rio.

"You told me that you were assigned to spy on me to make sure I brought Motsonelli back?"

"Yes, that's about the size of it, Head Office said you were a bit washed up on this job and that you'd probably screw it up, too easily distracted they said, and besides, France is my patch, bozo".

"No chance, I am going to catch him myself", said Agent Alan.

"We will see about that, you don't even know where he is?"

"Oh yes I do"

"Oh no you don't"

"Oh yes I do, do, do oo oo" he sung waving a finger and skipped a few steps to the taxi door.

"I have been reliably informed" Agent Alan said smugly, "that he is heading towards the Eiffel Tower as we speak".

Agent Alan's mission seemed to have been usurped by the CIA Head Office and re-assigned to Agent Rio to bring back Motsonelli. It was now a race between Alan and Rio (just like old times perhaps?), Motsonelli now just a pawn in a personal battle for recognition at CIA Head Office. A promotion could be at stake here, either way it could mean less running around for the winner. Agent Rio Fudgeland had decided that he was going to capture the dangerous criminal. Both Agents were now desperate to outdo each other to catch their guy. Alan shows his CIA identity badge to the taxi driver and the taxi driver steps out and Alan races off, wheels screeching to find Mitchell. Agent Rio does the same to the next taxi driver in the queue and is right behind him in seconds, wheels spinning on the hot tarmac, determined not to let Agent Alan out of his sight.

Agent Alan is driving at 40mph, weaving in and out cars on his way to the motorway. At this point he is thirty minutes from the Eiffel Tower, with Agent Rio Fudgeland right behind him. Agent Rio tries his best to overtake Agent Alan, which he fails to do as there is too much traffic on the road. "Holiday makers in hire cars, the bane of any agent's life when they need to be doin' a car chase", Agent Rio shouts at his windscreen. They both get to the motorway swerving and skidding into various lanes. Rio bides his time and maintains a steady speed of around 55mph allowing him to drive without being reckless. It also seems to get better economy that way he reasoned and wished he had cruise control. Agent Alan pushes on doing 60mph, but is a little more aggressive n the fuel pedal to get a great miles-per-gallon return. He tries to steady but Agent Rio is always there, a constant presence which frustrates Alan further. Alan ponders...

"My carbon footprint must be huge in this job, I wish I'd nicked a hybrid-fuel taxi, I wonder if Sting is a CIA Agent as well, he was at the Christmas do, it must weigh awfully on his conscience".

Agent Alan was one hundred meters in front of Agent Rio and at this point they are both fifteen minutes away from the Eiffel Tower. The traffic on the motorway clears for a while and there is more space for Agent Rio to catch up to Agent Alan and overtake him. Agent Rio throws caution to the wind and really hoofs it. He hits 70mph, catching up to Alan side by side. Rio already has nine points on his licence and he's not risking a ban for anyone, even the CIA. Alan decides to increase his speed a little more and puts his foot down. Rio follows suit and puts his foot down as there are no speed cameras on this stretch. Agent Rio, then, in a moment of madness having recently watched re-runs of the Dukes of Hazard, decides to ram Agent

Alan's taxi into a line of queuing cars to his left. Agent Alan just manages to keep control of the taxi while swerving and narrowly missing two family hatchback cars. They were only cheap Citroens although he did manage to smash a wing mirror off both cars as he passed them. In truth the drivers were probably quite grateful for Alan making their cars look more authentic for the Paris streets. Agent Alan considered himself lucky to not have crashed completely and then caught Agent Rio up again by accelerating along the hard shoulder and re-entering the main carriageway with due care and attention for other road users, but he was on the brink of losing such respect. Agent Rio had slowed to rubber-neck at the accident he was hoping to cause. Agent Alan decides to ram into Rio Fudgeland in pure anger "I'll show him". Full-on road rage had gripped Alan now. The impact causes Rio's taxi to career into a sky-blue Ford Mondeo Estate, Zeetec CDTi with 6 speed but only cloth seats, with air con and cruise control (as redeeming features) causing him to look on helplessly while Agent Alan drove on by towards the Eiffel Tower. Agent Alan thinks that he is not going to see Rio Fudgeland again following such a horrendous collision. He thought Agent Rio might be too injured to move or might even be trapped in the mess of tangled metal that was once a taxi.

Agent Alan slowed his driving, feeling a little less stressed as he was only a few minutes away from meeting up with Motsonelli. He needed to gather his thoughts. Fortunately for Agent Rio Fudgeland who was indeed out of the race now, the air bag had gone off and saved his life. However he was left stranded in taxi he stole from the airport trying to exchange addresses and insurance details with an irate Frenchman whose Ford Mondeo had just been smashed into. He'll probably lose his no-claims for that one. Alan drives straight to Eiffel Tower entrance and pulls up leaving the taxi running.

Agent Alan phoned the CIA Head Office again to make sure that Motsonelli was still at the Eiffel Tower. The call gave him a chance to sit down for a bit and catch his breath. The CIA reported that the arch criminal had seemingly been most obliging by waiting for his pursuer. In actual fact Motsonelli had been distracted. With such a good view from the tower Motsonelli had been watching a dreadful road accident on the motorway! He was indeed at the famous location and as Agent Alan was walking towards the entrance building, an attractive young blonde woman ran out and was telling everyone that a man was at the top of the Eiffel Tower ready to jump. Agent Alan quickened his pace and passing close to the lady, close enough to appreciate the scent of the Channel No. 9 perfume she was wearing, he felt that niggling groin injury again, certainly niggling but curiously not causing so much pain this time. As a secret agent he thought it his prerogative to ask this lady to dinner when this drama had been concluded. A secret agent's life just seems to be one conquest after another. Somewhat frustrated he thrust his right hand deep into his trouser pocket and searched frantically for some loose change to pay for his entrance ticket. Straight away Agent Alan took the lift to catch Motsonelli. Clearly there was the option to take the stairs and the Work-Life balance policy at the CIA would have indicated that he take the time to ascend via the "healthy option". But the company was paying, or would at least reimburse 75% of it if he kept the receipt and anyway, time was of the essence. There's always an excuse for not doing exercise, and he knew it. The decision about how to ascend the Eiffel Tower was not as straightforward for Agent Alan as one might think. He was making steady progress in the lift but he was petrified. Gripping one side of the lift with his eyes closed his worst nightmare had come to haunt him. After all his years of playing football he never had to reveal his severe claustrophobia and dreaded fear of heights. Even CIA agents can have their foibles and weaknesses. Women, driving and being stuck in lifts were Alan's. Every second could not come quickly enough for Alan, he was trying to keep it together, even though he was going higher and higher up the Tower.

Finally arriving at the top of the tower, Alan could see Motsonelli ready to jump. Alan was looking panicky and his heart was racing from being so high above the ground. He talked to Motsonelli insisting that he come down from the edge of the Tower and give himself up.

"Come down now and stop being silly Motsonelli, you don't know what kind of grief I have gone through to get here".

"I told you, no one can stop me, not even you *Agent Alan*... and I am going to jump".

"Surely we can talk about this, just step down onto the platform".

"I can't step down now, there's too much a stake, million dollar bribes are in with the Mafia and the professional football leagues will crumble, parliaments will fall and the price of cocaine on the street will go sky high, and besides, I jumped the barrier in front of that woman down at the kiosk, it would be so embarrassing to go back down in the lift now... no my friend there's only one way down for me and that's the quick way". Motsonelli pointed over the edge.

With some urgency in his voice Agent Alan replied, "Don't be silly man, look, I can smooth things over with the lady downstairs I am sure of it, and don't worry about all that other stuff, everything will be ok, you mark my word".

With such a perfect excuse to introduce himself Agent Alan's mind was already contemplating the menu at the Chinese restaurant that he was going to take Bridgette to. He had noticed her name on her badge pinned to her white translucent blouse causing the delicate material to gape suggestively in the warm Parisian breeze. The rising heat of the afternoon causing her to perspire gently on her fleshy white... (ok reader, I think we all know where that one's going – let's get back to the situation). However, for Alan there seemed to be so much to live for at this moment.

Motsonelli came to his senses and said that he would go back to Gwan Tanamo Heights in the USA and live out the rest of his life behind bars.

"There is no way I will leave prison, I will die an old man in there" Motsonelli suddenly wanting pity from Agent Alan, a strong sign that he was not going to jump and perhaps the crispy duck and pancakes was on?

"Yeh that's what you said last time you were at Gwan Tanamo, mind you, they'll watch you a little more closely now. I can make your sentence reduced if you come with me now", Alan said with hope in his voice for a quick resolution. They had plenty of time, the *Dragon Jaune Chinoise* didn't open until seven o clock and they served until 11pm. It was 5.15pm now.

After talking for twenty minutes, Motsonelli decided to give himself up. As they were going down in the lift again Alan was closing his eyes with fright and holding his breath whilst Motsonelli looked on at him with laughter. "Agent Alan is not so tough after all", he said. In the distress of his immediate travel sickness Alan permitted the cheeky indulgence of a man who would not see the free light of day again. After experiencing the torture of the Eiffel Tower, Alan led Motsonelli towards the taxi that was still running. Then, out from nowhere came Agent Rio Fudgeland who had made it to the Eiffel Tower on foot. With Alan's back turned Agent Rio Fudgeland pulled out his gun and shot Alan three times in the back.

"I told you I was taking Motsonelli back"

"You didn't think you saw the last of me did you? get real"

Agent Alan fell to the ground with blood covering his back and finding it hard to breath, strangely, he wondered if things had finally caught up with him. Rio Fudgeland got a hold of Motsonelli and threw him in the taxi ready to go straight to the safe-house in Marseilles. Agent Rio would claim the glory for capturing the fugitive, and, saving football leagues from corruption worldwide, preserving the status quo of the Italian parliamentary system and for keeping the price of cocaine at an accessible level for regular users.

Also, for leaving Alan die on the ground where he fell.

Poor Bridgette.

Chapter 10

Dame doped to doom

Richard Wilson and Clive Palmer

Research Preface

HEALTH WARNING (OURS PROBABLY) AND DISCLAIMER: It is **not** our claim or inference that Kelly Holmes has used illegal substances at any time for unfair advantage in her athletics career. She was a fine and honourable athlete who is now, as Dame Kelly Holmes, a valued ambassador for sport and Physical Education. The background to her races and the double gold medal victories for 800m and 1500m in Athens 2004 presents a good opportunity for a dramatised story which has the potential to promote some relevant educational discussion on the drugs in sport issue in the context of this book.

CONFLICT AND CONSEQUENCES SURROUNDING main characters in a novel or creative essay play a key role for generating interest. Part of the assignment brief that was the basis for this chapter was to select a sporting occasion or icon and then to consider an alternative course of events for him or her. The alternative course of events to become the twist; the "what if" of the creative tale. Part of the planning process was to think who might have furthest to fall in a social and sporting sense. There were several candidates in this sporting social elite including, "Lord" Sebastian Coe, "Sir" Steve Redgrave, "Sir" Chris Hoy and now "Dame" Kelly Holmes. Dame Kelly Holmes was selected mainly because of her long battles with injury which seemed to make her Olympic victory all the more sweet, which in a creative and dramatic sense we could turn so sour! This is not because of any malice or ill-feeling towards Kelly, rather that by entertaining a negative possibility that there could be some productive educational discussion about the wider issue of drugs in sport and their consequences in later life. For example, if Kelly Holmes was found guilty of using illegal substances would she be stripped of her medals and her Peerage? Dougie Walker, a Scottish sprinter who was competing at the same time/era as Kelly Holmes was accused of abusing the steroid Nadrolone (wrongly it may seem, see Panter and Palmer, 2009; Maclean, 2000), which wrecked his sporting career and life chances - compared to Kelly Holmes that is (see McGinty, 2000 "Dougie Walker: How I drowned my drug ban torment with drink and pizzas").

Before Kelly Holmes had her Olympic success in 2004, Athens, her early career was blighted with injury, which she reflected upon during an interview with The Independent newspaper, "Injury problems troubled her again later that year and she admitted that they sometimes caused her to lose heart. Kelly said, "when your body falls apart it gets to you and there are only so many setbacks you can take and only so many things you can come through" (Randall, Barnes, Thompson and Townsend, 2004). Kelly's ongoing and troubled relationship with a half-broken body which seemed to have so much potential to win at competition but rarely did, could leave her with a frustrated alter-ego that might persuade her to take a quick fix when people weren't looking. It is easy to imagine a voice inside her head urging her to take the help offered by some steroids, just to get through the winter training perhaps, which might have been very tempting. Kelly could have been a prime candidate in her slightly torn physical state and slightly fractured psychological state and helped by the fact that she trained in South Africa, out of prying eyes for many seasons.

In a long athletics career, Kelly Holmes always seemed to struggle to get into perfect shape to show her real potential in top-class competition (BBC Sport, 2004). Kelly Holmes *the nearly there girl* was hankering for that illusive Olympic Gold medal for over ten years, which came at the end of her career, within a year she had retired at 32 years old. A potted history reveals a litany of bronze and silver 'success' which for a person who may only live for gold could have become quite frustrating:

> **Silver medal** – 1994 European Championships, Helsinki for 1500m.
>
> **Gold medal** - 1994 Commonwealth Games, Victoria for 1500m.
>
> **Silver medal** - 1994 World Championships, Gothenburg for 1500m and
>
> **Bronze medal** for 800m.
>
> **Silver medal** – 1995 Commonwealth Games, Kuala Lumpur for 1500m.
>
> **Bronze medal** – 1998 Olympic Games, Sydney for 800m.
>
> **Gold medal** - 2000 Commonwealth Games, Manchester for 1500m.

Bronze medal – 2002 European Championships, Munich for 800m.

Silver medal - 2002 World Indoor Championships for 1500m.

Silver medal - 2003 World Championships for 800m.

Gold medals – 2004 Olympic Games, Athens for 800m and 1500m.

Until 2004 at the Athens Olympics that is, when she took Gold in the 800m and then Gold in the 1500m. The chosen event for the creative story is the 1500m final which is written as if the first author, Richard, is there in person spectating at the race. In the 1500m final Kelly would come up against world champion Tatyana Tomashova. Tomashova was moving down from her preferred 5000m and Holmes was moving up from her recent win at 800m. The final was on the 28th of August 2004 and saw Kelly Holmes repeat her strategy of favouring to stay at the back of the running group until breaking on the final lap and taking the lead on the final bend to finish in a winning time of 3 minutes 57.90 seconds. Kelly Holmes was determined to run in both events at the Olympics but following her success in 800m she told the Guardian newspaper that she was an "emotional wreck". Yet with her winning of both events, "she became the first Briton in 84 years to achieve the Olympic middle-distance double" (Routledge, 2009).

The creative story attempts to highlight a major issue found in sport which is deviance and the illegal use of drugs in an attempt to prevail at competition. With the perfect performance from Kelly in both of her races and the fact she achieved a personal best time in the 800m, the decision was made to change Kelly in to a deviant athlete who took illegal substances to push her body to a new level of performance that she had previously failed to produce in competition. Deviance in sport is not, unfortunately, an unfamiliar occurrence although fewer cases of drug abuse seem to reach the press at the time of the event, with cases being dealt with before or after. This may be a deliberate tactic between the mass media and the organisers of major events, such as the IOC (International Olympic Committee) to avoid the negative press of cheating and doping being associated with their competition. For example, the Ben Johnson affair was a sordid distraction from an otherwise most entertaining Olympics in Seoul 1988 (Francis and Coplon, 1990, "Speed Trap"). Coakley (2007: 155) believes that, "deviance occurs when an athlete rejects the goal of improving skills or the expectation that the means to achieve goals is to work harder than others". To protect sport against cheating through drug taking, competitors are constantly being monitored by home nations on a system, called

Whereabouts, introduced by WADA (World Anti-Doping Agency) which requires the sports person to make known their whereabouts and availability for drug testing on a daily basis for one hour a day, 365 days a year all plotted out on a calendar one year in advance. This is only one strategy, albeit a fairly intrusive one, to catch the drug-cheats. However their efforts in some circumstances may be thwarted by the ever improving drugs themselves, the strategies for using them such as micro-dosing and the masking agents which strive to render traces of the drugs as undetectable by the usual examinations. Today WADA remains the leading body for keeping drugs out of sport at an international level. They state that, "WADA works towards a vision of the world that values and fosters a doping-free culture in sport." (WADA, 2010). In striving towards this aim they create many rules, policies and sanctions for competitors. However, for some driven competitors who just like a challenge may just see the officious activities of WADA as being another thing to be beaten, on their long list of things to be beaten. This may represent a loss of creativity on WADA's behalf to recognise the root of the problem whose reactive rules may restrict the freedoms of all competitors in order to catch the few. After all, most athletes may like being chased, it may be in their competitive nature and for some it might give them a sense of being ahead of the game, whatever 'game' (cheating or not) they might be playing.

Major success at the Olympics may be a pathway to receiving national adoration, to become the pride of a nation, which was seemingly the outcome for Kelly who was also rewarded with a Peerage in 2005 to become Dame Kelly Holmes. Success can be a life changing experience from which athletes can be rewarded with not just a gold medal but looked up to as a role model that others could want to emulate (Wellman, 2003) whether they wanted to be a public role model or not. For some athletes, this additional pressure and burden of social expectation could be a strong enough persuasion for them to take performance enhancing substances, assuming that they are confident in their ability to hide their actions at the time and have the personal resolve to keep up the deception for years afterwards – living the lie as it were. As Prendergast, Bannen, Erickson and Honore (2003) point out, "as athletic pressures and financial gains of the Olympic Games heighten, more toxicities are likely to occur despite attempts at restricting performance-enhancing drugs".

The creative story hopes to highlight to the reader that although the temptation for taking drugs may be high and the reward might seem significant, if it goes wrong then the consequence could be national disgust and constant international suspicion that they might still be cheating. And their hope of returning back to that event or sport on the Olympic stage all but obliterated. One example of this may be Dwain Chambers, the UK 100m sprinter whose plea to compete once again in the Olympics was rejected by the British Olympic Association after he became banned for drug abuse. He was barred from the 2008 Beijing Olympics (Randhawa, 2008) and now from competing at London 2012 Olympics (Cottrell, 2009) despite the fact that Dwain still represents Britain on the international stage and is the current European sprint champion (60m indoors). There seem to be consequences all round for cheating through illegal drugs with the athletes typically losing out whilst others seem to plod on or even gain from the situation. There may be lessons here, assuming that the drug testers, the media and the policy makers are playing on a level playing field? (Francis and Coplon, 1990; Panter and Palmer 2009).

A reflective comment to conclude upon is that throughout this assignment it has been difficult to impart a message to readers which highlights anything but the obvious moral code - that if the athlete is willing to cheat then the athlete must be willing to receive the punishment if it goes wrong. However there seems to be many more layers of education to be considered which might benefit a wide range of people who may be adversely affected by the cheating/drugs in sport issue. These groups may include current 'top' athletes who may be "world class" to the young players in schools who may be grappling with notion of "fair play" from their experiences on the playgrounds to the class room to the sports field. Sitting slightly less comfortably against the people who wish to play fairly or educate others to play fairly may be a contrasting group who seemingly make their livings from the fact that cheating in sport using drugs exists. Claret (2010) recognises some of these 'interested parties' and terms them as the "athlete's entourage" which have been added below to highlight the breadth of the 'industry'. This is an industry which has been on a long-term cycle of trial and error learning since the 1980s where there are many perils and consequences for the athletes, who seem typically to lose out, whilst the others, typically, seem to gain.

There seems to have been a lot of experimenting with using drugs and experimenting with dealing with those who have been caught leading to the general inference that many parties except the athlete appear benefit from cheating in this manner. Quite a gamble for the person who commits to taking drugs, the effects of which will remain with them for the rest of their lives.

An athlete's entourage may include:
- Drugs suppliers
- Drugs traffickers
- Drug takers (Athletes/sports performers, but there may be others?)
- Drugs testers
- Policy makers (Governmental)
- Coaches
- Family members
- Press/media
- Impact on leagues; promotions, relegations, points, following bans
- Lawyers
- Agents
- Governing bodies (National and International)
- WADA (World Anti-Doping Agency)
- Researchers
- Sponsors
- IOC (International Olympic Committee)

Investigating the story and writing the story has offered an insight into how athletes taking drugs may be condemned by the public who as a whole seem to remain collective in their disapproval of cheating. For Dwain Chambers, to have won in Olympic competition and to have beaten the drugs testers in so doing may actually be a bitter sweet pill for him to live with for the rest of his life. The story hopes to entertain the reader and describe in as much detail the spectacle of an Olympic games, and highlight to the reader that drug taking in sport is wrong, harmful and uncomfortable for all who may be affected by it.

Reference list

BBC Sport (2004) *Olympics 2004, Holmes keeps on running*. BBC Sport [online]. 29th August 2004 [online]. Available at: http://news.bbc.co.uk/sport1/hi/olympics 2004/athletics/3609426.stm (Accessed on 23rd February 2010).

Claret, L. (2010) *The role of WADA in developing anti-doping education*. Presentation at the Research Seminar Series: Anti-Doping Policy. Seminar Four, Understanding athletes' attitudes towards doping, the implications for policy, particularly education policy. UK Sport, London, 24th February 2010.

Coakley, J. (2007) *Sports in society, issues and controversies* (9th edition). McGraw Hill, New York.

Cottrell, C. (2009) Dwain Chambers admits defeat in London 2012 quest. *More than games.com*, posted Wednesday 11th November 2009. [online]. Available at: http://www.morethanthegames.co.uk/athletics/117160-dwain-chambers-admits-defeat-london-2012-quest (Accessed on 23rd February 2010).

Francis, C. and Coplon, J. (1990) *Speed Trap, Inside the biggest scandal in Olympic History*. Grafton Books, London.

Maclean, R. (2000) Olympic Challenge: transcript Tuesday, 28th March, 2000 *BBC News, Scotland* [online]. Available at: http://news.bbc.co.uk/1/hi/scotland/692155.stm (Accessed 3rd November, 2009).

McGinty, B. (2000) Dougie Walker: How I drowned my drug ban torment with drink and pizzas, *Sunday Mirror* article posted 17th September 2000 [online]. Available at: http://findarticles.com/p/articles/mi_qn4161/is_20000917/ai_n14509557/ (Accessed on 27th February 2010).

Panter, S. and Palmer, C. (2009) Who are you calling a liar? Questioning the levels of Integrity in modern elite sport through an ethical and political agenda. *Journal of Qualitative Research in Sports Studies*, 3, 1, 79-90.

Prendergast, H.M., Bannen, T., Erickson, T.B. and Honore, K.R. (2003) The toxic torch of the modern Olympic Games. *Veterinary and Human Toxicology*, 45, 2, 97-102.

Randall, D., Barnes, A., Thompson, J. and Townsend, K. (2004) *Kelly Holmes: The extraordinary story of the army girl plagued by injury who never gave up on her dream*. The Independent Sunday, 29th August 2004 [online]. Available at: http://www.independent.co.uk/news/people/profiles/kelly-holmes-the-extraordinary-story-of-the-army-girl-plagued-by-injury-who-never-gave-up-on-her-dream-558206.html (Accessed on 23rd February 2010).

Randhawa, K. (2008) Drugs cheat Dwain Chambers banned from Beijing Olympics. *London Evening Standard.co.uk* 18.07.08 [online]. Available at: http://www.thisislondon.co.uk/standard-sport/article-23517730-drugs-cheat-dwain-chambers-banned-from-beijing-olympics.do (Accessed on 23rd February 2010).

Routledge, C. (2009) Biography – Kelly Holmes, *Answers.com* [online]. Available at: http://www.answers.com/topic/kelly-holmes-1 (Accessed on 23rd February 2010).

WADA (2010) About WADA – *World Anti-Doping Agency* [online]. Available at: http://www.wada-ama.org/en/About-WADA/ (Accessed on 23rd February 2010).

Wellman, C. (2003) Do celebrated athletes have special responsibilities to be good role models? An imagined dialogue between Charles Barkley and Karl Malone (pp. 333-336). In, Boxhill, J. (Ed.) *Sports ethics, an anthology*. Blackwell Publishing, Malden, MA, USA.

Creative Story

Dame doped to doom

Richard Wilson and Clive Palmer

I WAS THERE WHEN IT HAPPENED. I was there to scream at the top of my voice as Britain's most prized athlete stepped on top of the gold medal podium to receive her second gold medal of the Olympics. It seemed that fans from all over Britain embraced each other that day, like two lost lovers reunited after many years apart. In hindsight I believed Kelly Holmes had finally been rewarded at the end of a traumatic injury plagued career and I was proud to watch that amazing feat.

I had arrived in Athens on the 26th of August, 2004, welcomed by unbearable heat and a glaring sun which by now I can imagine has given athletes from around the world sleepless nights. Fans like me scurried out of the moist uncomfortable airport like rats in a maze desperately searching for the quickest way to fresh air. It was two days before the 1500 metres final and the optimism of a second gold medal from Kelly Holmes was beginning to rise. Having triumphed in the 800 metres final she reported to BBC Sport that, "I feel I am stronger than ever". For me, well, I was still so excited that I had managed to get a ticket for this prestigious event. Wouldn't it be fantastic if she could do it. A nation's pride was bound as tightly to Kelly now as her running spikes were tied to her feet. I wonder how she's coping?

The day of the 1500 metre final had arrived and the Athens arena seat 390D was beckoning for me. In a way I felt nervous for Kelly Holmes, a potential disaster was on the horizon. A woman who had been plagued by injury for her entire sporting life could once again be brought in to the public's judgemental eye via the media with another infamous strain or tear from an injury prone body. "Ahh Kelly Holmes just misses again" seems to have been an all too familiar comment from the TV commentators over the years. Then there's "Yes there's always Beijing in 2008" which also seems to have been the all too familiar comment from those failing athletes who get immediate trackside attention for losing their race. I got a feeling that this was not going to be one of those days.

I watched in awe as a gathering of streamlined physiques positioned themselves in the "starting position". Striking a pose ready for action, petrified momentarily it was as if there were a line-up of Greek Gods, bodies rippled with muscle only covered by the colours of their countries, minds focused as they stared ominously into the distance. Not a blink from their eyes, almost hypnotised by this moment in their lives. Kelly stood a hardened chiselled figure of a woman, one almost as if Zeus himself had carved her out of marble. Each athlete leant forward ready to launch into action waiting for the shot which signalled the start of the race. The gun was fired and the athletes sprung into action, stride after stride each athlete tried to place themselves in the pack as may be determined by their race strategy. Kelly, to my amazement was left at the back.

"Oh no, here we go again", I muttered, not another disastrous failure after a fantastic win in the 800m. The newspapers I had read described how she waited at the back in that race only to hurtle forward like a rocket overtaking everyone during the last lap of the race. I was apprehensive and desperate for Kelly to make her move as the American Jearl Miles Clark stormed into a dominating lead. The race drew near to its conclusion and I remember the British fans around were silent and still, almost shocked at what they were seeing, the flash of cameras all around captured the moment. When you look back it is easy to understand why so many thousands of people had been silenced by the actions of one person. Kelly Holmes had exploded into action, picking off other athletes like they were standing still in the final lap. She was doing exactly the same thing from the 800m. The bell rang and saw her go from 8th position, to first. Jaws were on the floor with possibility. The finish line was in sight and the screams from me and other fans were deafening, willing her to cross the line in first position. If there was ever a moment that left me speechless that was it. I'd become intertwined in a sea of bodies, hugging in an almost passionate way. Screams from ecstatic, overjoyed fans showing their feelings at the fact that a GB athlete had won two gold medals in Athens, the birthplace of the Olympics; we couldn't quite believe it. The smiles across every person's face could not come close to that of Kelly herself though, as she paraded around the stadium cloaked in the flag of our homeland. Russian resilience and American athleticism came nowhere near to the Great Britain master class of strategy and stamina, the super powers of the world were shown how to do it on the race track.

The crowd's noise had died down for a short while, saving their voices for when Kelly would stand on the podium and be crowned in the ivy leaves of success to receiving her gold medal. I had remained in shock for the entire event, not just that I was there at the Olympic Games, but to see a display of such determination and courage to have won the race and reached her overall goal in life, to become an Olympic champion. There she stood on the top of the podium, motionless, with a stare into the distance to watch the Union flag being raised. The echoing sound of singing in the arena I remember as more and more fans joined in the national anthem. Rousing and patriotic we stood proud to be British. In fact it felt as if all of the spectators in the stadium were British fans at that moment. Kelly was truly the diamond in Britain's crown, or so we all thought at that time.

With the day's athletics ending, British celebrations coasted on into the early hours, Athens didn't sleep and the streets and buildings became embellished in the colours of Great Britain almost as if the country had succumbed to the might of a British invasion; flags were paraded and the alcohol flowed like water.

The day after I woke up alone in my hotel, head splitting and an airport check-in time to make. The heat in Athens remained intense and uncomfortable as buses upon buses flocked to the already over populated airport, most fans subdued by the hangover they where nursing yet still a few partying their way back to Britain.

It wasn't till after the ceremony that the real drama began and the Athens Olympics got its most memorable story. It was known already by the authorities but withheld from the public for three days after Kelly claimed her Gold medal. The G.B.s *national treasure* was no more than a *national disgrace* - reduced to a cheat, reputation tarnished and career ruined when found guilty of taking EPO boost, a substance which can seriously improve training and endurance levels. It seemed that every news paper in the world had Kelly's face splashed over their front pages, labelling her as the biggest disappointment Britain had ever produced. The Olympic medals were stripped away and were replaced with disgust and embarrassment from her fellow countrymen and women. An immediate ban and a life-long sentence in more ways than one. She was abandoned and alone with only what she knew how to do well, being a competitive runner and she had come to the end of that road too. She had no other career to turn to and her options seemed to be diminishing by the day. How would she get by? For the media, the Olympics via Kelly Holmes had once again provided valuable, profit worthy front page news. A fantastic scandal to be reported upon, just the sort of coverage that they craved, but it was not a positive outlook. Just when we were beginning to think we had a paragon of clean sport and someone we could look up to the world of drugs had taken the limelight away from sporting excellence.

It is now 2005, a full a year since "the event" and people in Britain are trying to forget the pain of Kelly Holmes cheating in 2004 and are looking forward to regaining some national pride by performing in the 2006 IAAF World Cup (International Association of Athletics Federations). However the ramifications of Kelly's selfish actions went much further with greater consequences for the country. At this time Great Britain had invested millions into their bid to host the 2012 Olympics in London – headed up by "Lord" Coe. This Olympic dream had too gone by the wayside through Kelly's grimy, drug ridden hands as the IOC refused to entertain appeals that Kelly was a one-off cheat in the camp. The IOC wished not to have their prestigious 4 year spectacle of sport associated with a country that seemingly housed drugs cheats and the 2012 Games went to Paris.

When I try to ask people about the Olympics they seem to verbally wallpaper over the cracks in Britain's attendance at the Olympics. One of my work colleagues I remember him saying, "you went to that Olympics didn't you, god I bet Athens is a real nice place to go to", the shame of Kelly being socially erased, it was more pleasant to talk about Athens as a tourist venue. In a way I believe that Kelly's scandal has hurt the heart of Britain more than Maradona's Hand of God, so much so, that Britain wants to forget that it ever happened. As for Kelly Holmes, the hatred and disgust she received became too much for her and in six months of her return to Britain, she decided to emigrate to Australia. Not many know what she is doing out there and even less care, out of sight out of mind, but some say she is living on the Gold coast. She had tried to find work as a PE teacher but no-one would employ her; a poor role model to have around impressionable young people whose country aspires to greatness through sport. So she changed her name and now drifts between jobs, last spotted working for Thrifty Car Hire company in a sunny provincial town. It is quite ironic really, being on the Gold coast of Australia is probably the only gold that remains in her grasp.

In a way I feel sorry for her, a girl who had been through so much pain and anguish, constantly failing to live up to expectations purely because of her injury plagued body, when all she wanted was to make her country feel proud of her. I believe it is a risk that many sports performers could be tempted into and they seem to have some serious *lifestyle* decisions to make.

And over the finish line... what if Kelly had "done it clean?"

1. She could have been a role model for sport and physical education and taken up a public role in sport's promotion. It's a career that is not quite what she trained for but certainly a pleasant by-product of successfully carrying and fulfilling the hopes of a nation.

2. Who knows, she could have been a Dame.

Some options and consequences for "competitors" and "dopers" (although these terms may not be mutually exclusive for some people in the sport's world):

- **Take a drug** and get caught and then get banned from competing, possibly for life – that'll teach you. Get used to public suspicion.

- **Take a drug** and win - money, fame and glory. Ill-gotten gains, live the lie and get comfortable with the deception, it could be with you for life.

- **Take a drug** and lose – a lot ventured and nothing gained.

- **Don't take a drug** and win - that's the way to do it.

- **Don't take a drug** and lose - keep trying.

- **Don't take a drug** and keep losing - consider doing something else if its Gold you want.

Chapter 11

Corruption, bribery and 'The Arsenal'

Debbie Smaje and Anthony Maher

Research Preface

HENRY NORRIS' FINAL LEGACY AS CHAIRMAN OF 'THE ARSENAL' was to appoint Yorkshireman Herbert Chapman as manager in 1925 (Arsenal FC, 2009a). Chapman had enjoyed success with Huddersfield Town, winning two consecutive league titles in England, the team would also win a third title in 1926 after Chapman's departure to Highbury. Norris subsequently left The Arsenal in 1927 after the Football League, following a Daily Mail report alleging that Norris was culpable of several illegal practices, found him guilty of breaking league rules and banned him from football for life. Before dying of a heart attack in 1934, however, Norris' dream of seeing The Arsenal win the Division One title was realised when Chapman led the team first to the FA Cup in 1930, and then to the league title in 1931. Chapman constructed a side that would win three consecutive Division One titles, from 1933-1935, before he died of pneumonia in 1934. Norris and Chapman's legacy also encompassed, amongst other things, Highbury Stadium and the iconic red shirts with white sleeves, a design chosen by Chapman to replace the plain red shirts previously worn (Historical Kits, 2009). Elsewhere, in 1934, Barnsley FC, who had been relegated from Division Two in 1932 were also champions, Division Three North Champions, a title they would win again in 1939 and 1955. After a turn in fortune, however, Barnsley were relegated to Division Four for the first time in 1965, they were back there again in 1972, a year after Arsenal won their first League and FA Cup double.

On 26th April 1997 Clint Marcelle dribbled through the Bradford City defence with two minutes remaining to fire home the second goal. Oakwell, Barnsley's home ground, erupted, Barnsley won 2-0, thus ensuring their promotion to the Premier League. Seventy eight years too late, some may say, Barnsley made it to football's top flight. Almost one year later, Barnsley played Arsenal at Oakwell. One outcome of the Gunners' 2-0 victory was that Barnsley were all but relegated back from whence they came. Their relegation to Division One, the old Division Two, was confirmed by defeat at Leicester City the following week. Conversely, a 4-0 league win over Everton at Highbury two weeks later, together with victory over Newcastle United at Wembley, meant that Arsenal had another league and cup double to add to their already impressive haul of ten league titles, six FA Cups, two League Cups, one UEFA Cup and one European Cup Winners Cup.

In the years that followed 1998, Barnsley lost the 2000 Division One play-off Final at Wembley and were subsequently relegated to the third tier of English football two years later. They have since played in an FA Cup semi-final, but now find themselves as perennial strugglers at the wrong end of the Championship. Arsenal would go on to win the league and FA Cup double again in 2002, go a whole league season unbeaten as they won the title in 2004, win three FA Cups, lose in the Final of the UEFA Cup and Champions League, and move to a 61,000 all-seated stadium just a stone's throw from Highbury. Arsenal, it is worth noting, have spent an English Football League record of eighty five seasons in the top flight, whereas Barnsley have spent just one of the 102 seasons since their inception in the top flight of league football.

The creative writing section of this chapter relates to one of football's great mysteries. In 1919 The Football League met to discuss the possibility of expanding the First Division from 20 to 22 clubs. Previously, the top two in Division Two had replaced the bottom two in Division One. This time it was proposed that only the bottom club in Division One, Tottenham Hotspur, would be relegated, and that the top three in Division Two would be promoted. This meant that Barnsley FC, who had finished the previous season in third place, would play in the top-flight of English football for the first time. This proposal, however, never came to fruition, instead, it was The Arsenal who, much to the surprise of many managers, fans and journalists were promoted to Division One. The details of how The Arsenal managed to secure promotion despite the fact that they finished the previous season in fifth place remain largely unclear. Nevertheless, the official histories of both Arsenal FC and Barnsley FC (Arsenal FC, 2009b,

Barnsley FC, 2009) agree that something underhand involving The Arsenal chairman Henry Norris led to the unexpected promotion, allegations of corruption and bribery in particular have been made. Norris, unfortunately, went to his grave without revealing what actually happened (Arsenal FC, 2009b). Therefore, a fictitious account of this mystery, which is loosely based on actual events, is offered below. Before undertaking this task, however, it is expedient to provide a brief analysis of corruption in sport in order to provide a backcloth for the creative writing section.

Maennig (2005) highlights two key forms of corruption, competition corruption, which usually involves bribing of athletes, officials or other influential non-participants, and management corruption, which is more concerned with allocation of television rights, host venues for events and so on. Corruption usually takes place for one of two reasons, for personal greed or gain, or for political reasons or gain. Possibly the most interesting aspect of Arsenal's alleged corrupt behaviour is the effect this allegation has had, or, perhaps more appropriately, has not had on their reputation. Indeed, despite their murky past, Arsenal are still perceived by many as a grand old institution of English football, which may point towards an acceptance of corrupt behaviour in sport (Cashmore, 2000). At present, there are very few proven cases of corruption within English football, however, many fans accept that players are 'tapped up' – that is, approached by a rival club without the permission of their employers – by other clubs. One of the most high profile examples of tapping up a player involves Arsenal's former employee, Ashley Cole, who joined Chelsea in 2005. Cole, together with Chelsea and their manager, Jose Mourinho, all received fines for their part in the illegal approach, which breached Football Association (FA) rules (BBC, 2005). Two years earlier, there was widespread suspicion that Chelsea were tapping up England manager Sven Goran Eriksson to replace Claudio Ranieri as boss (The Telegraph, 2003). Tottenham Hotspur were also alleged to have tapped up Sevilla manager Juande Ramos in 2007 (The Times, 2007). Yet, despite so much suspicion and, in some cases, evidence that corruption is prevalent in professional football, when anyone in a position of power does speak out, such as the Luton Town manager Mike Newell (BBC, 2006), or Portsmouth Chief Executive Peter Storrie (The Telegraph, 2009), they received very little public backing from others in football. Rather, they are often ostracised for their revelations.

References

Arsenal FC (2009a) *Herbert Chapman – Overview* [online]. Available at: http://www.arsenal.com/history/herbert-chapman/herbert-chapman-overview (Accessed 8th December 2009).

Arsenal FC (2009b) *Norris Negotiates Top-Flight Return* [online]. Available at: http://www.arsenal.com/history/laying-the-foundations/norris-negotiates-top-flight-return (Accessed 8th December 2009).

Barnsley FC (2009) *1914-1939 – The Wars* [online]. Available at: http://www.barnsleyfc.co.uk/page/History/0,,10309~925081,00.html (Accessed 8th December 2009).

BBC (2005) *Chelsea, Mourinho and Cole Fined* [online]. Available at: http://news.bbc.co.uk/sport1/hi/football/eng_prem/4596209.stm (Accessed December 8th 2009).

BBC (2006) *FA to Meet Newell Over Bung Claim* [online]. Available at: http://news.bbc.co.uk/sport1/hi/football/teams/l/luton_town/4605184.stm (Accessed 8th December 2009).

Cashmore, E. (2000) *Making Sense of Sport (3rd Ed.)*, London: Routledge.

Historical Kits (2009) *Arsenal* [online]. Available at: http://www.historicalkits.co.uk/Arsenal/Arsenal.htm (Accessed 8th December 2009).

Maennig, W. (2005) 'Corruption in International Sports and Sports Management: Forms, Tendencies, Extent and Countermeasures', *European Sport Management Quarterly*, 5 (2), pp. 187-225.

The Times (2007) *Martin Jol Loses Job After Juande Ramos Says Yes to Tottenham* [online] Available at: http://www.timesonline.co.uk/tol/sport/football/premier_league/tottenham/article2741595.ece (Accessed 8th December 2009).

The Telegraph (2003) *Eriksson linked with Chelsea job* [online]. Available at: http://www.telegraph.co.uk/sport/football/world-cup-2010/teams/england/2407393/Eriksson-linked-with-Chelsea-job.html (Accessed 8th December 2009).

The Telegraph (2009) *Portsmouth Peter Storrie Says illegal Tapping Up of Players is Rife* [online]. Available at: http://www.telegraph.co.uk/sport/football/leagues/premierleague/6035804/Portsmouth-Peter-Storrie-says-illegal-tapping-up-of-players-is-rife.html (Accessed 8th December 2009).

Creative Story

Corruption, bribery and 'The Arsenal'

Debbie Smaje and Anthony Maher

IT IS 1913 AND LEICESTER FOSSE, now Leicester City FC, face the newly renamed 'The Arsenal' in the first game at The Arsenal's brand new stadium, Highbury. Originally from south of the River Thames, the previously named Woolwich Arsenal faced crippling debts and possible extinction until Sir Henry Norris took over the club, becoming chairman in 1910. Norris was also a director of Fulham FC, and had plans to form a London 'superclub' by merging Fulham and Woolwich Arsenal. These plans, however, were later blocked, leaving Norris with no choice but to settle for moving The Arsenal to a new, purpose-built stadium in North London despite huge opposition from local residents and other North London clubs such as Tottenham Hotspur and Clapton Orient. The Arsenal began life at their new home by beating Leicester Fosse 2-1 and, subsequently, finishing third in Division Two. Nevertheless, this wasn't good enough for Norris because only the top two teams in Division Two were promoted to Division One, Norris craved with all his heart to see The Arsenal playing in the top flight of English football. Although very rich and powerful, the one thing Norris couldn't influence was how The Arsenal performed on the pitch.

A year later, in 1914, the world was a very different place. World War One had begun on the eve of the new football season and the whole world was in turmoil. For one season, at least, the Football League tried to provide some normality and escape for fans by allowing the 1914-1915 season to be played out to its conclusion. The Arsenal, again, fell well short of promotion by finishing in fifth place. By 1915, the war effort had become all consuming. The league was suspended and it was four long years before it would return in 1919. By this time, however, football was changing. The Football League met to discuss the possibility of expanding the First Division from 20 to 22 clubs. Previously, the top two in Division Two had replaced the bottom two in Division One. This time, it was decided that only the bottom club in

Division One would be relegated, and the top three in Division Two would be promoted. Tottenham Hotspur were the unfortunate ones to be relegated, while in third place in Division Two was a little South Yorkshire club called Barnsley.

On hearing the news, the town rejoiced. Barnsley had been in the Football League since 1898, but they had never yet tasted the top flight, all of those associated with the club couldn't wait. Barnsley had won the FA Cup in 1912 making them hungrier for the big time. Finally, that time had come, or so they thought. Barnsley chairman John Rose and manager Percy Lewis toasted their success and began to look forward to welcoming giants of the day such as Aston Villa, Everton and Sunderland to their modest Oakwell home.

"Congratulations Percy old boy, I knew you could do it. I had complete faith in you" said Mr Rose.

"Thank you Mr Rose. It was touch and go for a while there, but the lads held their nerve, it's them you should be thanking" replied Percy, rather modestly.

"Yes, quite right. But you must not underestimate the part you played, Percy, you deserve a lot of credit".

"Thank you Mr Rose".

"Now, Percy, be a good chap and fetch that bottle of Brandy over there, I've been saving it for a special occasion".

At the same time, elsewhere, Henry Norris was seething.

"Who the hell do Barnsley think they are?" Mr Norris roared at the top of his voice while pacing backwards and forward in his lavish office.

"What right do they have to be playing in the top flight when my mighty Arsenal are stuck in Division Two, fighting it out with the likes of South Shields, Clapton Orient and Stockport County? This is not right, it's not on" he reasoned angrily to himself.

Putting his head on the desk, Mr Norris' brain was scheming, searching for ways to change the situation. Finally, the answer came to him. He smiled, and then began to laugh. His laugh pervaded and echoed in the empty hallways of Highbury.

"Ha, ha, ha... How stupid of me, it's so simple" he assured himself. "It's a bit of a gamble but old McKenna needs the money. Anyway, we're old friends, and he owes me".

After taking a minute to compose himself, Mr Norris picked up the phone and called his driver.

"Fred?"

"Yes sir?" Fred replied from the other end.

"I want you to go to Anfield, it's urgent" stressed Mr Norris.

"Of course, sir, on what business?" Fred enquired.

"It's actually urgent *and* confidential, so I think it would be best if you came to my office, we can speak in private here," said Mr Norris in a hushed voice.

"Yes sir, good idea. I'm on my way".

Later that day, Fred drove from London to Anfield, the home of Liverpool FC. He had been to Liverpool on many occasions in the past, all on business with Mr Norris. This time was no different. Parking in a space sign-posted 'visitor', Fred locked his car and walked very purposively towards the club's reception.

"Good morning sir, how may I be of service?" the receptionist queried very chirpily.

"Hello, my name is Fred James, I've got an appointment with Mr McKenna".

"Yes, Mr James, Mr McKenna is expecting you. I'll escort you to his office" replied the receptionist.

While walking through the hallways of Anfield, which were adorned with pictures of Liverpool legends, the enormity of Fred's task began to consume his thoughts. He is going to bribe Liverpool FC and Football League chairman John McKenna. He cannot believe what he is about to do. Fred's palms begin to sweat, what he is doing is illegal.

"You're only here to deliver the money" Fred reassured himself. "Mr Norris has already negotiated the price, so all you have to do is hand over the money".

"Here we are, Mr McKenna's office" said the receptionist, breaking Fred's concentration. "Please take a seat over there, Mr McKenna will be with you shortly".

"Thank you" Fred replied, in a barely audible voice.

Fred sat down. He looked around the office, it was a lot more modest than Mr Norris', much to Fred's surprise. There were a few trophies from Mr McKenna's playing day, he was a rugby player, Fred recalled. However, there was nothing to suggest that Mr McKenna held the prestigious position of chairman of the Football League.

"He *must* be skint" thought Fred.

Just then, the office door swung open and Mr McKenna entered the room. Closing the door behind him, he walked towards Fred.

"Hello Mr McKenna, my name is Fred James" said Fred, as he nervously stood and extended his hand to greet Mr McKenna.

Mr McKenna, however, did not shake Fred's outstretched hand, he did not even say hello. Instead, he walked straight past Fred and sat at his desk. Feeling even more nervous, and now slightly awkward, Fred slowly sat back down.

"Do you have the money?" asked Mr McKenna, breaking the awkward silence.

"Yes sir" replied Fred, before placing a black briefcase on the desk.

"Open it then" demanded Mr McKenna. Fred complied.

"Very good, you can go now".

"Yes sir".

"Oh, before you go, tell Henry that I want the other half as soon as the job is done".

"Of course sir, I won't forget" replied Fred while exiting the room as quickly as possible. "Phew, I'm glad that's over" Fred said to himself, instantly feeling like a huge burden had been lifted from his shoulders.

A few days later the Football League held their annual general meeting to discuss the expansion of Division One. All forty Football League chairmen were in attendance, including a smiling John Rose, who expected to hear official confirmation that Barnsley are to play in Division One in the forthcoming season for the first time in their history.

"This is it, we've finally done it. After all these years we are finally getting the opportunity to play top flight football" Mr Rose beamed to himself.

While immersed in his own fantasy, which was soon to become a reality, Mr Rose glanced to his left. Sitting a few seats away, he saw The Arsenal chairman, Henry Norris, who also appeared to be grinning.

"Don't know why he's so happy" Mr Rose pondered briefly, before returning to his own thoughts.

His thoughts, however, were soon interrupted by the chairman of the Football League, John McKenna, who called for order before beginning his announcement.

"We, the Football League, have agreed that there needs to be some changes made to the structure and format of league football in England" he began.

"This is it, this is it" Mr Rose repeated ecstatically to himself. "I will go down in history as the first chairman to take Barnsley to Division One".

"Change number one: instead of the top three clubs in Division Two being promoted, the top two will be promoted as usual, and the third team will be decided by a vote between Tottenham Hotspur and The Arsenal".

"What!" Mr Rose erupted. "What do you mean? When and why was this decided?"

"Mr Rose, please sit down. That kind of behaviour is not acceptable here" Mr McKenna rebuked.

"But I don't understand. Why have you changed your mind?" Mr Rose replied in utter amazement.

"When we proposed that the top three teams from Division Two be promoted, that is all it was, a proposal. Subsequent discussions amongst Football League members, and a couple of your fellow chairmen, have resulted in this new proposal" Mr McKenna stated.

Without saying another word, Mr Rose slumped into his chair. He did not know what to say. All his dreams, all the promises he made to the fans, players and club staff had all gone in an instant. He was totally flabbergasted.

Once the fracas had died down, and order was restored, Mr McKenna continued his address. Mr McKenna spoke of The Arsenal's history and standing in the game, how they had joined the Football League fifteen years before Tottenham Hotspur. Norris stood up and applauded loudly, together with a smattering of others in the room. Mr Rose began to protest, but the noise and activity drowned him out. Eventually, it went to the vote. The Arsenal won by ten votes to win promotion back to the top flight, Tottenham Hotspur were relegated, and Barnsley were stuck in Division Two. Norris mingled among the crowd, smiling graciously and shaking hands. Rose, at this point, had already broken down in tears, the dream was over.

Chapter 12

Rio Ferdinand - A done deal, it's in the bag...

John Kopczyk and Anthony Maher

Research Preface

RIO FERDINAND IS A PROFESSIONAL FOOTBALL PLAYER who was born in Peckham, London, on the 7th November 1978. He started his football career at West Ham United, where he progressed through the youth system before making his professional debut against Sheffield Wednesday on the 5th of May 1996. Rio subsequently made 127 first team appearances for West Ham before moving to Leeds United in 2000 for a then British record transfer fee of £18 million. It was also, at the time, a world record fee for a defender. This move, however, was fairly brief, after only two seasons with Leeds, Rio joined Manchester United for a British record fee that was reportedly in the region of £30 million. Over the 7 years or so since this move, he has established himself as an integral part of a very successful Manchester United team, and a key player for the English national football team. Rio's physical abilities and mental capacity have led some fans, journalists and fellow professionals to label him as one of the best central defenders in the world.

Rio's time at Manchester United, however, has not been without incident. On Tuesday 23rd September 2003, at the start of his second season for the club, he failed to take a drugs test at United's training ground, Carrington, claiming that he had simply forgotten about it because he was moving house (Cross, 2008). As a result, it was decided at the end of a two day hearing that Rio Ferdinand would serve an eight month ban from football, starting on January 20th 2004, and receive a £50,000 fine. This ban meant that he would miss the rest of the 2003/2004 English Premier League season and, perhaps more importantly, the 2004 European Championships in Portugal with the England national team (BBC, 2003). This ban was imposed despite the fact that Rio had attended a second drugs test two days later, where he provided a negative sample because the Football Association (FA) argued that missing a drugs test, or refusing to be tested, is the equivalent to testing positive (Keating, 2009).

Some academics, journalists and ex-professionals, in this regard, have argued against the use of drug testing because the tests have led to some athletes using more dangerous drugs in order to 'mask' performance-enhancing substances (Coakley, 1998, Waddington, 2000). Some drug testing, moreover, can be highly inaccurate and misleading. For example, in 1998 the British sprinter Dougie walker, together with an additional 350 athletes in 1999, was banned for several years after testing positive for a performance-enhancing substance called Nandrolone. Subsequently, however, it was discovered that during intense exercise an athlete's body produces small amounts of the substance naturally (Panter and Palmer, 2009). This discovery, obviously, questions the reliability of all those positive samples. Despite calls for the International Olympic Committee (IOC) to intervene, they refused to investigate the reasons for the increased levels of Nandrolone in athletes. The test results of Dougie Walker revealed that he had 12 nanograms of Nandrolone, which is over the IOC's permitted 2 nanograms limit (Panter and Palmer, 2009). To compare, a bodybuilder who injects Nandrolone directly into their muscle can have around 500 nanograms in their system (Panter and Palmer, 2009). Dougie Walker's Nandrolone levels, therefore, were comparatively very small, perhaps suggesting that he may not have taken performance-enhancing drugs. If this does turn out to be the case, then, changes need to be made to what would be a 'bad science' and failure of testing (Panter and Palmer, 2009).

Nevertheless, despite questions regarding the accuracy of drug testing methods, the fictitious element of this chapter focuses, in particular, on the view held by many that taking drugs is unacceptable in sport and, indeed, society in general. Drug taking is viewed, often, as cheating and a form of deviant behaviour, that is to say, an activity that does not "conform to the norms and expectations of members of a particular society" (Haralambos and Holborn, 1995: 386). There are those that argue that the taking of performance-enhancing drugs is unethical and can damage the health of athletes. This view, however, is perhaps paradoxical in a society where many people use pain-killers, 'mood controllers' and recreational drugs on a regular and ad-hoc basis (Voy, 1991). The story presented in this chapter, focuses on corruption in sport which is, according to Cashmore (2000: 361), "a form of deception or fraud which is present in all sports, where people are willing to do anything to determine, manipulate and have control of a certain outcome". More specific to the creative story, but without giving too much away at this stage, Rio Ferdinand offers John, the drug tester, money to cover up his positive test, in short, he attempts to use his wealth to pressure John to change the outcome of the drug test.

Although the series of events offered in the What If account are indeed fictional, it must also be noted that, according to Cashmore (2000), corruption and deviance have actually been a part of sport for many years. For example, in 2003, the same year that Rio Ferdinand failed to turn up for the drugs test, The Portuguese football club Porto were banned from participating in the 2003/04 Champions League due to corruption and bribery. They were found guilty of allegedly bribing referees in domestic matches in order to influence the outcome of games (Bugge, 2008). Seemingly in football and in many other sports there may be scandal waiting like a time-bomb to become public to the embarrassment of the few and delectation of the mass media. Whilst there may rarely be smoke without fire, we make no claim here that Rio Ferdinand is anything but a "clean", honest and honourable competitor. However in the interests of a good story we ignore the facts for the purposes of entertainment and for the purposes of education about issues of drugs in sport which may be seen usefully to be arising from this account.

References

BBC. (2003) *Ferdinand banned for eight months* [online]. Available at: http//www.news.bbc.co.uk/sport1/hi/football/3333091.stm (Accessed on 7th December 2009).

Bugge, A. (2008) *'Bribery' put Porto out of the champions league* [online]. Available at: http://www.independent.co.uk/sport/football/european/bribery-puts-porto-out-of-champions-league-840364.html (Accessed on 10th December 2009).

Cashmore, E. (2000) *Making sense of sports* (3rd edition). Routledge, London.

Cross, J. (2008) *Rio Ferdinand: past mistakes will make me a better England captain* [online]. Available at: http://www.mirror.co.uk/sport-old/football/2008/03/26/rio-ferdinand-past-mistakes-will-make-me-a-better-england-captain-115875-20363259 (Accessed on 7th February 2010).

Haralambos, M. and Holborn, M. (1995) *Sociology: themes and perspectives* (4th edition). Collins, London.

Keating, S. (2009) *High profile drug cheats exposed by WADA* [online]. Available at: http://www.independent.co.uk/sport/general/others/highprofile-drug-cheats-exposed-by-wada-1818060.html?action=Popup&ino=5 (Accessed on 9th December 2009).

Panter, S. and Palmer, C. (2009) Who are you calling a liar? Questioning the levels of integrity in modern elite sport through an ethical and political agenda. *Journal of Qualitative Research in Sport Studies*, 3, 1, 79-90.

Voy, R. (1991) *Drugs, sport and politics*. Human Kinetics, Champagne, Il. USA.

Waddington, I. (2000) *Sport, drugs and health*. E & FN SPON, London.

Creative Story

Rio Ferdinand - A done deal, it's in the bag...

John Kopczyk and Anthony Maher

I<small>T'S</small> T<small>UESDAY</small> 23<small>RD</small> S<small>EPTEMBER</small> **2003**, I glance at the clock and notice that it's 7:45am. I'm running late. I need to hurry up if I want to arrive at United's training ground, Carrington, on time. I don't want to be late for my first day on the job, carrying out drug tests on the players. I must make a good impression. So I quickly finish my breakfast, two cold pieces of toast and a hot coffee, I've been drinking a lot of coffee recently, and I gather the equipment I need for the day. I step outside and take a fleeting look at the sky, it's a bluish colour, similar to the colour of Manchester City's kit but, of course, much nicer. There is barely a cloud in sight and the sun is glowing like a huge fireball in the sky. I put the testing equipment into the boot of my shiny new Astra sports car and then set off to Carrington.

On the way to Carrington I start to get anxious and nervous. I can feel my throat swelling up, it hurts when I swallow.

"Take a deep breath, John" I tell myself. "Everything will run smoothly".

I notice a hold up of cars ahead of me. Oh no, a traffic jam. I ring my colleague, Max. Ring, ring, ring, ring rin...

"Alright John, you ok?" Max answers in a very chirpy voice.

"Hello" I reply. "Listen, Max, I'm going to be late. There's been an accident on the motorway so I won't get to Carrington till about 11ish".

"No worries mate, there's been a change of plan anyway".

"Oh right, what change?" I ask, feeling puzzled but very relieved. Thank God for that, I think to myself.

"Well, the drug testing has been split into two groups, the first at 10am and the second at 12pm. You can take the second group".

"Yeah, that's fine with me. Speak to you later Max, bye".

"No worries, chat to you soon. Have a safe journey, bye".

I finally arrive at Carrington at 11:50 am. I drive down the long, winding road toward the main gate. There are trees on either side of the road. They appear to bend over the road, much the same as an arch, blocking the blue sky and sunlight, making it dark and grim. I feel quite claustrophobic. Approaching the gate, I wind down my car window.

"Manchester United training ground, how may I help?" enquires a female's voice from the intercom system.

"Hi, it's John Kopczyk, I'm here for the drug testing this afternoon".

"Oh yes, come on in Mr. Kopczyk" the soft, calm voice replies.

"Thank you".

The enormous, elaborately decorated gates open very slowly. 'Welcome to Carrington – Training Facility of Manchester United' the sign reads that is pitched just inside the gates. I drive through the gates, down another long and winding path, until I reach the car park. I park up in a visitor's space. Wayne Rooney's Mercedes is four cars away from my car, I feel like I am in the presence of royalty. Taking the drug testing equipment out of the boot, I head to the reception wondering what it would be like to be a professional football player for Manchester United. I always wanted to be a professional footballer but, then again, who didn't? "Life would be so much easier with all that money and fame" I tell myself, somewhat naively, perhaps. Suddenly, a gush of cold air hits me in the face and I snap out of my daydream. The weather appears to have changed dramatically. I can actually see my breath when I exhale.

I reach the reception and collect my ID card. The receptionist then directs me to the room in which I will conduct the tests. Walking along the corridors, I see pictures of all of United's greatest players, Bobby Charlton, Duncan Edwards, George Best, Eric Cantona, Bryan Robson, Roy Keane, to name but a few. However, the person that I am most interested to see is my favourite player, Rio Ferdinand. I can't explain the joy I felt when I first discovered that I would be drug testing Rio. Not the best circumstances to meet your hero, I know, but a great opportunity nevertheless. It's a good job that during my interview I said that I supported Manchester United otherwise I may never have got the chance to meet Rio.

I enter the test room and set up the equipment. I put on my long, white coat. It is folded and creased as I pull it out from the packet. It fits ok and is as new as to me as I am to the job. I actually feel quite professional despite the fact that I am now even more nervous, but also excited. I've got butterflies in my stomach. I looked at my watch, it's just after 12pm. Then, at that very moment, the door opens and a rough, deep Scottish voice says:

"I'm here for the drug test".

I look up and see Darren Fletcher, Manchester United and Scotland's central midfielder.

"Yes, Darren, come in. Sign this form and fill this beaker with a sample please" I reply in a professional manner, trying with great difficulty to hide my excitement.

Throughout the visit, I see 4 other players. They all provide negative samples, much to my relief. My excitement intensifies with each meeting. The moment I have been waiting for soon arrives, it's 12:50pm and time to meet Rio Ferdinand. Rio, however, appears to be running late. No matter, he will be here soon enough. 12:50pm quickly turns into 1:20pm and I start to become worried. It's rather unusual for a player to be this late. They know the consequences. Just as I am about to pick up the phone to call the reception, someone bursts through the door.

"Alright, sorry I'm late" the person says in a broad southern cockney accent. It's Rio Ferdinand.

"Afternoon", I reply. "You're half an hour late, where have you been? I was going to pack up and leave" I explain in a firm but polite manner. I don't want to upset Rio Ferdinand.

Sounding rather nervous and anxious, he says: "Oh, training overran, and I had to sort some stuff out because I am moving house".

"Well, you're here now, so if you can sign the form over there I will be with you in a second".

As I turned round to pick up a fresh beaker, I notice that Rio has got a bag over his shoulder. Probably his training kit and boots, I tell myself, and think nothing more of it. I give him the beaker.

"Here, provide a sample in that please".

Rio, very hesitantly, takes the beaker. He seems quite tense. He looks like he is about to take the deciding penalty in a cup final with a stadium full of opposition fans jeering and booing him, praying that he misses. He goes behind the dressing screen, fills the beaker, and then hands it back to me.

"Thanks for that, you're free to go now".

"No problem" he replies nervously, leaving the room.

That wasn't as exciting as I was expecting, I say to myself. He seemed like a nice guy, though, I quickly reassure myself.

I turn round and place the beaker on the table in front of me. Taking a sample of the urine, I put it very carefully into the testing machine for analysis. About a minute later the results come through. I make my way to the printer and pick up the results sheet. "I can't believe this, it must be some kind of mistake" I say aloud. I take a second sample and undertake the same procedure. The result is the same, I am absolutely gobsmacked. I feel like I have just been punched in the stomach. Rio Ferdinand has just tested positive for performance-enhancing drugs. Before I have time to clear my thoughts, the door flies open. I turn round quickly, still in a mild state of shock. Rio is standing in the doorway, he quickly closes the door and walks over to a table. He takes the bag off his shoulder and empties the content onto the table. The table is heaped with crisp fifty pound notes.

"What's this?" I say, very surprised and somewhat shocked.

"It's yours".

"What do you mean, it's mine?"

He steps close to me. We are now face-to-face, noise-to-noise nearly, like at the start of a boxing match but, in this case, there is no referee. I can feel his breath on my face.

"We both know that I have just tested positive for performance-enhancing drugs. If anyone finds out about this my career is over, do you understand?

186

I am offering you this money to cover this up, no one can know about this" he says passionately, but very apprehensively.

"I can't take that, you know I can't. It's also my career on the line here too" I reply in a fierce tone. I can't believe he is asking me to do this, my head is swimming.

"Look, there's £40,000"...

"£40,000!" I interrupt immediately.

"Keep your voice down" he retorts. "Yeah, £40,000, I bet that's way more than what you earn in a whole year".

He pauses for a moment and then whispers:

"Take it and change the result of that test, it will benefit us both".

We are still standing face-to-face, I can feel my heart beating rapidly. I am starting to burn up, and I am sweating profusely. It feels as though I'm in the crater of a volcano, which is filled with bubbling hot lava. Rio steps even closer and pushes me up against the wall. The walls appear to close in around me, I feel claustrophobic again. I start to panic.

"No!" I say angrily. This is my first day on the job, I can't do this. I won't let you intimidate me".

By this time I am perspiring so much that beads of sweat are dripping down my face.

"Yeah, you can. Just think what you could get with all that money, or is it not enough? Do you want more? Let's make it £60,000".

I do not know what to do. On the one hand, I am thinking "no, don't take the money. It's his fault for taking drugs, why should I cover it up? It could cost me my job. He should face the consequences". On the other hand, however, I can't stop thinking about what I could do with all that money. I could pay off some of my mortgage, get a new car, even take all of my family on holiday – it's been a while since we've been able to afford a family holiday. There is also the debt I have accumulated to consider. Before getting this job I was unemployed for some time, during which I had to borrow money to get by. Anyway, Rio is one of the players I most admire..... Well, he was. Do I really want to end his career? The internal turmoil is overwhelming. All I keep thinking is: what will happen if people find out? I know I should say no but the offer is just too tempting. So I push Rio away, loosen my tie and the top button of my shirt, and, after taking a deep breath and a moment to compose myself, I say:

"Ok, I will take the money and sort things out for you, but what's happened here stays between you and me".

"Good man" he says in a very smug, cocky voice.

"You're doing the right thing for both of us, don't you think?" he adds.

"Yeah, if you say so" I reply in a barely audible voice.

"Right, I'm going to go now, I've got other things to do" he says, before heading towards the door, leaving the bag of money on the table.

What have I done, I'm so stupid I say to myself, whilst holding two bundles of cash.

At that very moment my colleague, Max, walks in and sees me with all the money. Looking shocked and slightly puzzled, Max says:

"What's that? What's going on, John?"

Chapter 13

The 1972 Munich massacre, or was it rescue?

James Kenyon and Joel Rookwood

Research Preface

THE 1972 OLYMPIC GAMES IN MUNICH should have been a peaceful and very joyous occasion. For the Federal Republic of Germany it was considered to be the ideal opportunity to demonstrate to the world how the country had changed since the atrocities committed during The Holocaust and the events of the Second World War. Significant also, is the fact that it was first time the Olympics had been held in the country since the 1936 Berlin Games, when what is often considered to be the 'Most Controversial Olympics' were unashamedly exploited for the promotion of Nazi ideologies (Guttmann, 2002: 53 - 72). Hence, the opening ceremony of the Munich Games was a landmark event in world affairs and a tremendously emotional occasion (Alon, 2006 cited in Salzmann, 2006; Lalkin, 1972 cited in OCGXXO, 1974; Macdonald, 1999). In the country that was responsible for the deaths of over five million European Jews between 1933 and 1945 (Niewyk, 2000), an all-Jewish Israeli team marched through Munich's Olympiastadion holding the Star of David flag. The significance of this Israeli representation was commemorated by the West German NOC who chose to hold a special Olympic Memorial Service in Dachau at the location of the first Nazi concentration camp (Macdonald, 1999; OCGXXO, 1974).

At the Munich Olympic site the architecture and the visual configuration and organisation were all designed to convey an image of peace, friendship and harmony (OCGXXO, 1974). Accordingly, security of the event was purposefully lax (Surtees, 2006). Prior to the Munich Games the Olympic Village had been a relatively open area and never completely enclosed, which at the these Olympics was no different – only a two-metre high fence separated the Olympic Village from the outside world (Surtees, 2006). Furthermore, the team of people responsible for the security of the Munich Olympics was composed entirely of volunteers from the local police (OCGXXO, 1974; Macdonald, 1999). In order to preserve the impression required by the host nation – i.e. that of a peaceful and friendly Olympic atmosphere – this civil security team wore non-threatening powder blue uniforms and carried weapons only on the night shift (Hohensinn, 2006; Troger, 2006 both cited in Surtees, 2006). For the most part, security was not a source of worry for those responsible for the Munich Games. Of the few security concerns that there were, the majority of these related to the Olympics most high-profile guests that year: the Israeli athletes and coaches. To alleviate these concerns, on three separate occasions, prior to and during the Munich Olympics, inspections were conducted by Olympic officials who, in conjunction with Mossad, established no obvious indications of a planned attack against the Israeli Olympic team (OCGXXO, 1974). As what happened next proves, however, they were both very very wrong.

On the 5th September 1972, the world awoke to news of a hostage situation taking place in the Olympic Village. Initially, very little was known about the attackers, how many there were, who they were, what they wanted, etc. The hostages, on the other hand, were quickly identified as athletes and coaches from the Israeli Olympic team, two of whom had already been killed by the time that Games organisers were aware of what was going on. What wasn't known about the remaining hostages, however, was how many of them there were in total. After presenting the Games organisers with a document entitled *Communiqué from the Revolutionary Sources* (Macdonald, 1999) the kidnappers identified themselves as members of the Black September Organisation; a militant group of Palestinian *Fedayeen* (see note 1) who according to Calahan represented 'the results of the culmination of tensions between the Fatah (see note 2) and the Jordanian government' (1995: 13). The ongoing conflict between Israelis and Palestinians is 'deeply rooted in history' (Rookwood, 2009: 35). That is,

190

when the modern-day state of Israel was formed in 1948 as a new national home for the Jewish race, the territory that was chosen was already internationally recognised as Palestinian (Rookwood, 2009). The Black September Organisation's name for the Munich operation, Ikrit and Biram, symbolizes a legacy of the Arab-Israeli conflict in that these were the names of two Palestinian villages whose residents were murdered and expelled from their homes in 1948 by Jewish paramilitaries (Chacour, 2003).

Black September's *Communiqué from the Revolutionary Sources* was a list of demands which included the immediate release of 234 Palestinian and non-Arab 'revolutionaries' imprisoned in Israel and Germany (Macdonald, 1999; OCGXXO, 1974; Surtees, 2006). The person in charge of the negotiations was the Munich Police Commissioner and chief of the Olympic Security Forces, Manfred Schreiber. His team of police negotiators successfully extended three deadlines imposed by the terrorists in which they had threatened to start killing the hostages if the demands of their *Communiqué* were not met. According to Calahan (1995), Manfred Schreiber concluded that his only option was to attempt to rescue the hostages. The first rescue attempt was focused on the building in which the hostages were being held: Connollystraße 31. As the volunteer and undertrained police squad prepared for the rescue – an event which was being broadcast by the world's media – the Black September commandos seemed to anticipate the imminent attack by assuming defensive positions. Having then been informed that the athletes living quarters had all been installed with television sets, which the commandos were most likely watching, the Germans decided to call off their ill-advised first attempt at a rescue (Macdonald, 1999; Surtees, 2006).

Schreiber decided next that his option was to relocate the incident away from the media spotlight and isolate the terrorists at a small airport northwest of Munich whereby police snipers could attempt another rescue operation (Bolz, 1990; Surtees, 2006). Five police snipers were deployed at Furstenfeldbruck airport who, along with a volunteer team of under-cover police officers situated in a dummy Boeing 727 parked on the airport runway, would attempt to overpower the Black September commandos and initiate the rescue of the hostages. Of all of the police officers involved in the rescue, not one was in radio contact with another (Surtees, 2006). In an interview featured in the 1999 documentary film *One Day in September* one of the under-cover police officers describes how the team on the dummy Boeing 727, feeling that they were massively undertrained for such an undertaking, decided to abandon their role in the rescue attempt only minutes before the helicopters carrying the hostages and kidnappers arrived (Hohensinn, 1999 cited in Macdonald, 1999). By this time, the authorities had also worked out that there were, in fact, eight Black September commandos, but failed to add reinforcements to, or even inform the five-man sniper team responsible for the rescue attempt (Surtees, 2006). During the fierce gun battle that ensued between the Black September commandos and the police, one of the commandos threw a hand grenade into one of the helicopters killing all of its Israeli occupants. Shortly after, another commando opened fire on the second helicopter and killed the remaining Israeli hostages. Including the two Israeli athletes who had been shot during the original attack at the Olympic Village, a total of eleven hostages were killed by the Black September Organisation. Of the eight *Fedayeen* commandos that were directly responsible for what has come to be known as the Munich Massacre, five were killed after the lengthy gun battle at Furstenfeldbruck and three surrendered to the German police.

There is a considerable amount of literature and media-output based around the Munich Massacre and its repercussions. There has also been a recent resurgence in interest following the release of the 2006 DreamWorks production *Munich*; a Steven Spielberg film loosely based on the 1984 book *Vengeance* by George Jonas. Within the majority of this literature and media base are criticisms of both the International Olympic Committee (IOC) and the German police. In the case of the former, the IOC were, at first, forced to concede to international pressure and suspend the Olympics – when they had initially chosen to carry on – until the events at Connollystraße 31 had concluded (Macdonald, 1999; OCGXXO, 1974; Surtees, 2006). After all the hostages were killed and the remaining Palestinians arrested at Furstenfeldbruck airport, there was also pressure from various quarters to cancel the remainder of the Olympics in respect of the dead Israelis (Macdonald, 1999; OCGXXO, 1974; Surtees, 2006). However, a resolute Avery Brundage, the IOC President at the time, insisted:

> I am convinced that world opinion agrees with me that we cannot allow a handful of terrorists to destroy this core of international cooperation and good will which the Olympic Games represent. The Games must go on! (1972 cited in OCGXXO, 1974: 38)

The criticisms of the German police, and more so of the man-in-charge, Manfred Schreiber, are however are much more resonant. In the 2006 National Geographic Channel's *Seconds From Disaster* documentary, an Olympic security consultant and counter-terrorism expert, critically discussed, in detail, the series of resounding errors made by German Police; errors which stemmed from three key issues: insufficient intelligence, a lack of communication and a lack of adequate training, experience and equipment (Reeve, 2000; Thompson, 2006 cited in Surtees, 2006). However, even more significant was the fact that Manfred Schreiber had already had already experienced a hostage situation a year before the Munich Games. During a bank robbery in Munich in 1971 an innocent woman was killed as a result of Schreiber's actions. He was even charged with involuntary manslaughter, although he was later cleared (Surtees, 2006). It could be argued, therefore, that the outcome of this incident would have had an adverse effect on a person's judgment and ability to make difficult decisions.

The Israeli government were in consultation with the German authorities in various forms from the beginning of the hostage crisis. Chief of Mossad Zvi Zamir was immediately dispatched to Munich by Israel's Prime Minister, Golda Meir, to discuss the idea of Israeli commandos, the Sayeret, attempting a rescue (Calahan, 1995; Macdonald, 1999). Calahan states that the Sayeret are 'elite trained reconnaissance forces drawn from the ranks of the Israeli Special Forces and experienced in hostage rescue techniques' (1995: 11 - 12). However, local state officials continually refused this offer of assistance. Following on from the Munich Massacre, it is well-publicised that the Israeli Government formed numerous assassination squads to take revenge on those they believed were responsible for planning the Olympic attack, i.e. the plot for the film *Munich*. What if, however, the Israeli Government had deployed a Sayeret team to Munich anyway during the Olympics, regardless of German resistance to the idea? What if this team had succeeded in rescuing the hostages? These are two questions that form the basis of the creative writing part of this chapter.

Had the Munich Massacre ended with the hostages being successfully rescued, there are a number of historical events that may have occurred quite differently. For example, nearly two months after the events of the Munich Olympics, a German Lufthansa passenger jet was hijacked, with the only demand of the hijackers being the immediate release of the three

James Kenyon and Joel Rookwood

surviving Black September commandos who were being held in Germany awaiting trial. The German authorities quickly released the three prisoners. In the Sony Pictures documentary *One Day in September,* Macdonald (1999) offers convincing evidence to suggest that the Lufthansa hijacking was formulated by the German authorities and the Black September Organisation. It was thought that the Germans were concerned that had the surviving Black September commandos ever stood trial that their mishandling of the situation would be exposed to the world. Therefore, it can be argued that had the rescue of the hostages been successful, like in the case of the creative writing part of this chapter, this 'hijacking' might never have occurred since the German authorities would have had nothing to be fearful of; in fact, quite the opposite would have probably been true.

Another event that might have occurred differently, had either of the Munich rescue attempts been successful, relates to the formation of the German anti-terrorist unit GSG 9. The *GSG 9 der Bundespolizei* was set-up in 1973, six months after the events of the Munich Massacre, as an elite-operations arm of the German Federal Police. Such an organisation was deemed necessary largely because of the fact that post-war constitutional restrictions prohibited the Germany's army from operating in German territory. This therefore meant – as was the case in Munich – that specially trained operatives were unable to intervene during terrorist engagements (Wegener 1999, cited in Macdonald, 1999). Had events happened like they do in the supporting creative story, the Germans might not have thought it necessary to set-up such an organisation given the perceived success of its regular police force. This idea of 'perceived success' will become clearer to the reader having read the story.

References

Bolz Jr., F., Dudonis, K. J. & Schulz, D. P. (1990). *The Counter-Terrorism Handbook.* New York, Elsevier Science Publishing Co.

Calahan, A. B. (1995). *Countering Terrorism, The Israeli Response to the 1972 Munich Olympic Massacre and the development of independent covert action teams.* Unpublished Master's Thesis. Quantico, United States Marine Corps University.

Chacour, E. (2003). *Blood Brothers* 2nd Ed. London, Christian Art Books.

194

El-Nawawy, M. (2002). *The Israeli-Egyptian Peace Process in the Reporting of Western Journalists*. Westport, Greenwood Publishing Group.

Guttmann, A. (2002). *The Olympics, A History of the Modern Games*. 2nd Ed. Champaign, University of Illinois Press.

Jonas, G. (1984). *Vengeance*. New York, Simon and Schuster

Macdonald, K. (1999). *One Day in September* [Documentary Film]. London, Sony Pictures.

Niewyk, D. L. (2000). *The Columbia Guide to the Holocaust*. New York, Columbia University Press.

Organising Committee for the Games of the XX Olympiad (1974). *Die Spiele. The Official Report of the Organising Committee for the Games of the XXth Olympiad, Munich 1972. Volume 1, The Organization*. Munich, ProSport GmbH & Co. KG.

Reeve, S. (2000). *One Day in September*. New York, Arcade Publishing.

Rookwood, J. (2009). Promoting, building and sustaining peace through sporting interaction in Israel. *Peace Forum*. 24, 34, p. 29 - 44.

Rubner, M. (2006). Massacre in Munich, The Manhunt for the Killers Behind the 1972 Olympics Massacre (Book Review). *Middle East Policy*, 13, 2, p. 176.

Spielberg, S. (2006). *Munich* [Feature Film]. London, DreamWorks Ltd.

Surtees, C. (2006). *Seconds from Disaster, Munich Massacre* [Documentary Serial]. National Geographic Channel, broadcast on September 13th 2006.

Notes

[1] Fedayeen (Arabic: فدائيون) – meaning 'men of sacrifice' (Jonas, 1984) or 'freedom fighters' (El-Nawawy, 2002) - are a group of military-trained volunteers who are not officially associated with any form of structured government.

[2] Fatah (Arabic: فتح) is the largest faction of the Palestine Liberation Organization (PLO) and is generally believed to have had a strong historical association with a number of militant and terrorist groups; for example, the Black September Organisation.

Creative Story

The 1972 Munich massacre, or was it rescue?

James Kenyon and Joel Rookwood

I **FELT THE MUD GIVE WAY SLIGHTLY AS MY FEET HIT THE FLOOR.** The air all around me was being whipped up violently by the propellers of the helicopter we'd just touched down in. I checked the map and confirmed with the helicopter pilot that we'd landed in the agreed location approximately six kilometres north of Furstenfeldbruck airport. It was 9.07 pm and there was very little light, but we *were* ahead of schedule. Good start. I made sure the pilot understood his orders that if radio contact was lost for longer than forty-five minutes he was to return without the commando team. He confirmed that he understood. We checked our equipment and our weapons and then started jogging out over the open farmland in the direction of the airport. As we moved further away from the helicopter I felt the air become calmer.

Much earlier in the day, Prime Minister Golda Meir had announced live on international television that Israel would not be negotiating with the Black September Organisation. "Blackmail of the worst kind" is how she had described the kidnapping of our Olympic athletes in Munich. I agree. From first thing this morning, Israeli assistance was repeatedly offered to the Germans from Mossad. Meir felt that only we, the elite Sayeret Commandos, had the necessary expertise and experience to bring the events to a favourable conclusion. Every time, however, this assistance was publicly, but gratefully turned down. The Germans, it seemed, weren't interested in turning their Olympic spectacle into both a political and literal warzone, and the International Olympic Committee primarily saw the kidnappings as an irritation outside of their control; a secondary priority to the ultimate celebration of sporting endeavour. However Meir did send my boss, the Head of the Mossad, out to Munich this morning to offer his support and advice to the people who were leading the hostage negotiations. Unfortunately Zvi Zamir's support and advice was largely ignored.

We weren't far away now. I stopped running and everyone else followed suit. The five other members of the team automatically assumed a defensive formation and surveyed the farmland terrain while I checked my map and compass to ensure that we were headed in the right direction. Everybody was breathing harder than when we'd disembarked from the helicopter. Whether this was because we had been running, because of nerves, adrenalin, or because of a combination of the three, I was unsure, but I was very aware of the clouds of white mist that each member of the team was producing; ghost-like shapes surrounded the head each commando – shapes that could have easily been mistaken as the souls of each of us. I quickly snapped out of it, secured my map and compass, checked in with the pilot and then resumed our journey to the airport.

"We've decided that we're going to send a team anyway."

Golda Meir not only looked angry, but it was clear in her voice. In fact every other Committee-X member sitting around the table looked irritated. Some of these people I had met previously and others I recognised from the media. I knew who everyone was and I was conscious that before now I had never been in the company of such a gathering of political power. The majority were smoking, which along with the low ceiling and their collective mood, made the air in the room seem almost oppressive.

The Prime Minister continued, "Avner, these Germans are under the impression that our problems in Munich can be solved by conversing politely with these Fedayeen dogs. They are naive and inexperienced. Zvi has informed us that the German police force has no counter-terrorism unit and no proficient snipers, the Olympic security team is made up entirely of volunteers, the German army cannot intervene because of political injunctions, and the senior officer in charge of the situation in the Olympic village, Manfred Schreiber, is not only incompetent but he failed miserably in his last attempt to bring a hostage situation to a satisfactory conclusion. Additionally, the world's media are aware of anything that the Germans are planning, and therefore these Fedayeen dogs are equally aware of anything that the Germans are planning. We find this... unacceptable."

Every syllable of the word 'Fedayeen' was heavily emphasised and almost spat through gritted teeth.

"What are my orders Prime Minister?"

"Assemble a team now. Get to Munich as quickly as possible. Await your orders. Zvi will have to determine the most ideal opportunity to proceed."

"Yes Prime Minister."

I turned to leave the committee room but before I made it to the door the Prime Minister called out, "And Avner... ensure that we are not implicated. It is very important that the Germans are seen to have accomplished this by themselves. Do you understand what the repercussions would be if we were caught interfering without authority? The enormity of this situation? We will need to be in a position to say that we weren't involved. Especially for what we have planned when this is all over."

"I understand."

Our aim was to approach Furstenfeldbruck airport from the west. From this point, the control tower was at the opposite end of the runway and our approach to it would be hidden by the decoy Boeing 727 that the Germans had positioned on the runway, side on to the west of the airport control tower. Also, the media circus that had been following the events throughout the day, we had been informed, would most likely be setting up their stations on the east side of the airport and away from our entry-exit point.

Just as we arrived at the barbed-wire fence surrounding the airport the radio on my webbing quietly came to life.

"Sayeret One come in."

"Sayeret One here."

"We have received an intelligence cable from our connection in Munich. He confirmed that there are eight Fedayeen and nine hostages in total travelling via two helicopters to the airport. The Germans are going to have a team of volunteer police officers on the plane who will attempt to overpower the leader and his deputy when they climb on board to inspect it. These officers have very little training or experience and it is worth noting that the leader is still holding a live hand grenade with the pin removed.
198

The Germans are positioning three snipers on the airport control tower and two more in their direct line-of-fire in the field behind where the helicopters will land. I repeat, Snipers Four and Five in the field will be positioned directly in the line-of-fire of Snipers One, Two and Three on the control tower. These officers have very little training, experience, or even adequate equipment. Not a single one of the officers has any means of communicating with the others. End of the report."

"Understood. Over and out."

I nodded at Commando Four and he began clipping through the fence with a set of bolt cutters. I checked in with the helicopter pilot. When Commando Four had finished we crawled through the gap and all looked down the runway toward the yellow light emanating from the control tower in the distance. Although it was eerily quiet now I knew that this silence wouldn't last for very much longer.

"O.k., let's go", I ordered.

It had taken a total of five hours to mobilise my Sayeret team and then for us travel to Munich from Tel-Aviv, initially by helicopter and then by car and finally by train. As I dumped my kit on the bed of the hotel we had just checked into, located on Goesthestraße and around the corner from Munich Hauptbahnhof, the news on the T.V. indicated that the revised five o' clock deadline set by the Black September Organisation was about to lapse. I stood staring at the T.V. for what seemed a very long time. The seconds just prior to five p.m. seemed to stretch out and defy reason, five seconds felt like five minutes. Come on... I waited, still standing. Five o' clock passed. There was no mention of any gun shots on the news. I sat down on the edge of the bed and stared at the carpet and fell into daze. I thought about how much I *really* wanted to get these bastards. *Really*. I was playing out the possible ways in which a successful rescue could be achieved in my head. I'm not sure how many minutes had passed when I was startled by the shrill ringing of the hotel telephone on the desk next to the T.V.. I answered it and listened carefully. As instructed, I headed for the nearest payphone in the street and dialled the number that I had just been given. Once again I listened carefully. When my contact had finished speaking, I replaced the handset and quickly returned to the hotel and to the room of my second in command.

"Tell the others, we're leaving immediately. Go see your contact, get the materials and then meet us at the helicopter. The Germans are moving both the Fedayeen and the hostages to an airport northwest of Munich whereby they will attempt a rescue."

"Yes Sir. And our role...?"

"We will ensure that they succeed."

I watched as the man in the safari suit and white hat I had seen on the news, the Fedayeen leader Issa, walk with what I assumed to be his deputy towards the staircase of the Boeing. From where I was positioned behind the Boeing's tail and around the side of control tower, I had a clear view of where the helicopters had landed only moments ago. Just before the helicopters had landed I watched in astonishment as the team of German police officers that were in place to overpower to the leader and his deputy had gotten off the plane and headed into the control tower. They had obviously decided against their suicide mission. I wondered whether this would prove to be a problem. No longer could what was about to happen be blamed on the hand grenade in the leader's hand. I concluded that it'd still have to be. Both men walked toward the plane with a confident swagger. That confidence wouldn't last. I smiled. They reached the stairs and started climbing. Both men disappeared out of my view. The last thing I heard before the explosion was the Fedayeen leader scream, "It's a tra...!"

The plane exploded at the point where Commando Two had planted the IED underneath the fuselages open entrance. For a brief moment, neither the Germans nor the Fedayeen opened fire on one another. The Fedayeen gunman that was positioned down the sight of my M21 Sniper Rifle was looking in the direction of explosion with shock and confusion on his face. Shock and confusion were last emotions he ever experienced. I saw blood erupt violently out of his head at the same time I heard the crack emanate from my gunshot. He fell lifelessly onto the tarmac runway. The Fedayeen gunman standing nearest to him looked down at his fallen comrade. He too looked confused, but now there was more than a hint of fear in his face. Off to my right I noticed a flash of light that had obviously originated from a gun-nozzle and less than a second later I saw the fearful Fedayeen gunman collapse on the floor.

There was an explosion of gunfire now from the three police 'snipers' on top of the control tower and the four remaining Fedayeen gunmen. One of the Fedayeen gunmen broke away from the helicopters and ran directly toward my position. I secured my M21 and took my Beretta .22 from its harness on my belt. I took aim at his chest. He was running frantically toward me, continually looking over his shoulder, breathing heavy, panic in his eyes. I waited for him to get closer, I was breathing slowly, in and out, calm, focused, staring down my Beretta's sight. He was about ten metres in front me when I fired two shots into his heaving chest. I jumped up from my kneeling position and ran to where he had fallen on his back. I fired my third shot into his eye. The last thing this Fedayeen dog bore witness to was me smiling as I pulled the trigger. Five down.

When I arrived back at the hole-in-the-fence that Commando Four had cut approximately forty minutes ago, Commando's Two, Three and Six were already waiting for the rest of the team. I caught my breath and radioed the helicopter pilot to let him know we were on our way back.

Just after I had shot the fifth Fedayeen from close range in the face, I had heard Arabic shouting above the gunfire,

"Surrender, surrender, surrender!"

I watched as one of the remaining Fedayeen had thrown his AKM rifle on the floor and started waving his arms in the air. That was our cue. I secured my weapons, turned and sprinted off toward the rendezvous point.

Commando's Four and Five arrived back at the same time less than twenty seconds later. Commando Five immediately informed the rest of us that either he or even maybe one of the Germans had gotten lucky and taken out another Fedayeen just before the other two had surrendered. Six down in total, two arrested by the Germans. No immediate evidence of us ever being there. I smiled. Perfect. While the conspiracy theorists would no doubt have a field-day with the incident later on, for now I was happy with how the mission had played out. One-by-one, we climbed back through the hole-in-the-fence and took the exact same route in reverse back to the helicopter.

We would find out later that the nine Israeli hostages in the helicopters had been successfully rescued by the German police. Manfred Schreiber was hailed as a hero in the international press for orchestrating the successful rescue of the Israeli Olympic athletes. Unfortunately one of the police snipers, Sniper Five, the one positioned in the field behind where the helicopters had landed, had been shot in the fire-fight. It is suspected that he was killed by one of the police snipers on top on the control tower.

Less than a week later I was back in front of the same Committee-X that had ordered me to the Olympics. The only difference this time was that Zvi Zamir was sitting next to the Prime Minister. Everyone looked as irritated as they had back when I was sent to rescue our Olympic athletes and the oppressive ambience had not improved much in the time between then and now. With absolutely no mention of the work my team had performed in Munich, the Prime Minister began,

"Avner... we have another task for you. We know who organised it..."

Chapter 14

'Magical Madness' Jimmy Glass - Carlisle's Number 9

Claire Burgess and James Kenyon

Research Preface

"I believe in Methuselah, flying saucers, men in the moon and on-loan goalkeepers who score goals." (Knighton, 1999, cited in Walker, 1999a)

GOAL KEEPER JIMMY GLASS IS A LEGEND in Cumbrian, and indeed English football. Despite the fact that he was a non-too-spectacular player in terms of ability (e.g. Carter, 2002), Jimmy achieved legendary status in 1999 after he dramatically saved Carlisle United from being relegated out of Division 3 of the Football League. While a team avoiding relegation is not necessarily a remarkable occurrence in football – i.e. it must happen every year – the way in which Jimmy achieved Carlisle United's famous rescue is quite remarkable. His role in the final moments of the final game of Carlisle's 1998/1999 Division 3 season is that of football folklore; the stuff that schoolboy dreams are made of; 'a great, romantic story' (Slot, 2005); a tale that could easily have come straight out of a *Roy of the Rovers* comic, or even, a creative writing chapter of this book. Yet Jimmy's contribution in the final moments of that game was real. And what made it so special was that it was not a goalkeeper's typical contribution to a football match, like a penalty save, but rather something that is usually associated with strikers: Jimmy Glass scored the 'last minute' winner... that is, a goalkeeper scored the 'last minute' winner; and a goal that saved Carlisle United from certain relegation out of the Football League. What makes this achievement all the more impressive however is that three weeks prior to one of the greatest moments in Carlisle's history, its greatest contributor was completely unknown to the club's supporters and the then-manager, Nigel Pearson (Metcalf, 1999). When Jimmy scored his infamous goal at the Brunton Park stadium he was actually on loan at Carlisle United from Swindon Town; the club he returned to immediately after reaching the heights of 'national stardom' (Tomas, 1999). But rather than return as a hero, Jimmy's poor relationship with the Swindon Town manager compelled him to tear-up his contract with the club and go in search of regular first-team football elsewhere (Glass, 2009, cited in Turnbull, 2009). Unfortunately for Jimmy, regular first-team football never materialised and soon after his once-in-a-life-time effort he left the professional game all together, aged 27. After leaving football Jimmy worked as a computer salesman, emigrated to France (and has since returned), successfully battled a gambling addiction, and is now a partner and driver in a taxi firm in a small Dorset town (Glass, 2004; 2009, cited in Turnbull, 2009). Nevertheless, Jimmy Glass will forever be remembered as the goal-scoring goalie who saved Carlisle United from relegation.

Before kicking-off the final game of the 1998/99 Division 3 season, the only Cumbrian representative in the Football League, Carlisle United, were bottom of Division 3, one point behind Scarborough F.C. and looked the most likely team to be relegated into the Conference League (see Table 1). To avoid this fate, Carlisle *had* to win at home to Plymouth Argyle and hope that their fellow relegation-battlers, Scarborough, either drew or lost away at Peterborough United. Two games previous to this one, Jimmy Glass debuted for Carlisle United at home to Darlington F.C..

Table 1. Bottom of League Division 3, 8th May 1999, before the kick off

P.	Team	P	W	D	L	F	A	Gls	Pts
	...								
23	Scarborough	45	14	5	26	49	76	-27	47
24	**Carlisle United**	45	10	16	19	41	52	-11	46

The F.A. acquiesced after the club were effectively left keeper-less after selling one goalie earlier in the season, having another laid-off through injury and another recalled to the club that were loaning him to Carlisle – Derby County (Metcalf, 1999). Jimmy conceded three goals in his first game against Darlington in a 3 – 3 draw. In the next game, he kept a clean sheet in a nil - nil draw away at Hartlepool United. And then this, the final game of the season at home against Plymouth Argyle. Probably the most important game a number of the Carlisle squad would ever have played in. A match in which the pressure was felt equally by the on-loan goalkeeper – with only two games to his name – as it did for the regular club players:

"The drop into the non-league is the steepest [descent] *in sport. Communities lost part of their identity when clubs were relegated* [to the Conference League]. *What was I doing? That's where league clubs go to die. What if messed up? What if I dropped a corner or spilled a short save in the last match? I would be the man who relegated Carlisle"* (Glass, 2004: 82).

In order to provide a richer account of that final day of the 1998/99 Division 3 season, the following description is interspersed with transcribed commentary from two key sources. First is Jeff Stelling's commentary from the popular *Soccer Saturday* programme, a 'six-hour live televised slog' (Atkin, 2008), which covers the results of the English and Scottish Premier and Football Leagues and has been broadcast every Saturday on Sky Sports 1 (in one form or another) since the Premier League's inaugural season in 1992. Commentary from the late, unapologetically biased, very passionate and extremely popular Derek Lacey from BBC Radio Cumbria provides the second source. So then... back to the final day of the 1998/99 Division 3 season, and not long after both of the games had kicked off:

"Big scoreline from the Third Division! Scarborough, Colin Anderson's side... err... they've fallen behind in their home game against Peterborough. They start of course today one point ahead of Carlisle and the side that finishes bottom will be in the Conference next season. An absolute nightmare start then for Scarborough..." (Stelling, 1999).

However, three minutes before the end of the first half Scarborough equalised against Peterborough, making the score 1 – 1. At half time in Carlisle's match against Plymouth, however, the score was also a draw at nil – nil, and therefore, they were still in the same position as they had been before kick-off; i.e. needing a win and hoping that Scarborough either drew or lost. See Table 2.

P. Team	P	W	D	L	F	A	Gls	Pts
Table 2. Bottom of Division 3, 8th May 1999, half-time								
...								
23 Scarborough	46	14	6	26	50	77	-27	48
24 **Carlisle United**	46	10	17	19	41	52	-11	47

Within minutes of the second half kicking off, however, things went from bad to worse for Carlisle United:

"...Carlisle nil, Plymouth one. Lee Phillips has scored for Plymouth; could be the last rights as far as the Football League is concerned for Carlisle" (Stelling, 1999).

But Carlisle then managed to sneak a goal back within fifteen minutes of Plymouth's, making the score 1 – 1 and setting-up what would be a mouth-watering finale to the Division 3 season:

"Full time at the McCain stadium, Scarborough one, Peterborough one! Carlisle have to score in the remaining seconds if they're to survive, it's down to the final minute of the final game of the season. Absolutely astonishing stuff!" (Stelling, 1999).

So with a minute to go at Brunton Park and Scarborough having drawn at Peterborough, the Carlisle United supporters, with their club having been a Football League member for 71 years up to that point, all believed that they were about to watch their club get relegated into the Conference Division (Glass, 2002).

"So... deep, deep, deep, I make it sixty seconds. Jimmy Glass knocks it long. It comes now to Bagshaw. Bagshaw back to Anthony. Up to Stevens..." (Lacey, 1999, cited in Lytolis, 2008).

In the dying seconds of the game, one of the Carlisle attackers received the ball in the Plymouth penalty area. He was immediately closed down on his back by two defenders but still managed to slip the ball out right to his supporting winger. The winger was also closed down quickly and his attempted first-time cross was deflected out for a corner kick.

"... and the ball goes out now for a corner to Carlisle United – will they have time to take it? Referee looks at his watch..." (Lacey, 1999, cited in Lytolis, 2008).

At this point, the Carlisle manager, Nigel Pearson, started waiving at Jimmy Glass to head up the other end of the pitch for the corner.

"...and here comes Jimmy Glass! Carlisle United goalkeeper Jimmy Glass is coming up for the kick – everyone is going up... there isn't one player in the Carlisle half!" (Lacey, 1999, cited in Lytolis, 2008).

Having jogged up to the other end of the pitch, Jimmy arrived at the edge of the 18 yard box just left of centre. Then, completely unmarked, he sprinted in a straight line towards the 6 yard box as the corner was played in.

"Well, well... and the corner kick comes in..." (Lacey, 1999, cited in Lytolis, 2008).

As the corner was crossed into the box, one of the Carlisle players leapt up high and headed the ball hard at the defending goalkeeper's right-hand side. The goalkeeper moved quickly to his right and managed to punch the ball out of the goal. Unfortunately for him, he punched the ball out straight on to the right foot of the charging Jimmy Glass...

"and... the goalkeeper's pun... Oh... Jimmy Glass! Jimmy Glass! Jimmy Glass! The goalkeeper has scored a goal for Carlisle United" (Lacey, 1999, cited in Lytolis, 2008).

"...I hope this is accurate news for Carlisle fans sake... Carlisle have scored in the last minute in their game against Plymouth... un...con...firmed... we hear that Jimmy Glass, the goalkeeper, has scored for Carlisle, he's on loan there. Now if this is the case... and we're waiting for confirmation... it will be the most staggering story of the day" (Stelling, 1999).

Having scored the 'last minute winner', Jimmy sprinted off to his left, arms raised, sheer joy on his face. He was quickly met by three of his team mates all at the same time who pulled him to floor and started one of the biggest 'pile-on's' either of the authors of this chapter have ever seen. Carlisle's supporters then invaded the pitch and quickly joined in with celebrations.

"There's a pitch invasion! There is a pitch invasion! The referee has been swamped – they're bouncing on the crossbar!" (Lacey, 1999, cited in Lytolis, 2008).

"...I'm glad I can see it in red and black because I wouldn't have believed it possible... Fulltime at Brunton Park, Jimmy Glass, the goalkeeper's goal in the 90th minute and this is what it means to Scarborough fans at the McCain Stadium... they can't believe it... twelve years in that division and they're out

courtesy of a last minute goal at Brunton Park. They're out and they look as if they know it..." (Stelling, 1999).

"It fell to me and I just went wallop, thank you very much" (Glass, 1999, cited in Walker, 1999b). Carlisle United were safe thanks to Jimmy Glass's goal and their win took them one point ahead of Scarborough, who were consequently relegated into the Conference with what was literally the last kick of the season. See Table 3.

Table 3. Bottom of Division 3, 8th May 1999, full-time

P.	Team	P	W	D	L	F	A	Gls	Pts
	...								
23	Carlisle United	46	11	16	19	43	53	-10	49
24	**Scarborough (r)**	46	14	6	26	50	77	-27	48

Shortly after scoring his infamous goal, the hero-of-the-hour for Carlisle returned to the club that actually owned him: Swindon Town. While Jimmy had hoped that Carlisle would offer him a permanent deal, there was resistance to the move from a small element of Carlisle fans who figured that 'such a special moment' in their club's history could have been 'undermined by the sight of him making mistakes and conceding goals' (Tomas, 1999). Such an opinion had probably formed as a result of Jimmy having conceded 16 goals in his seven previous appearances for Swindon and Carlisle that season (The Fiver, 1999). But the deal fell through regardless after a disagreement over Jimmy's signing-on fee (Tomas, 1999). After that, Jimmy left Swindon Town and then failed to find regular first-team football elsewhere. Everywhere he went for a trial his efforts would be eclipsed by the goal he scored for Carlisle, 'That's Jimmy Glass', he would constantly hear, 'That's the one that scored the goal' (Glass, 2009, cited in Turnbull, 2009). He left the professional game all together two years later after failing to find a club that would offer him first-team football; he was 27 years old, which was, and is an incredibly early age for a professional goalkeeper to retire.

But what if Jimmy hadn't have scored his legendary goal? Would it have been easier for Jimmy to get a deal elsewhere had it not gone in or been disallowed? Would Jimmy have even wanted to stay at Carlisle, the team that would have most certainly been relegated, had he not scored? Had Carlisle been relegated, would the then-Chairman, the unpopular Michael Knighton, have stayed on for another two seasons after 1998/99 or would the fans have revolted earlier than they did in response to being dumped out of the Football League? These are questions that the authors hope are addressed in the creative writing section of this chapter. As touched upon earlier, the real-life events surrounding Carlisle's famous escape could have easily formed an imaginative story and so we have attempted to offer a plausible alternative that explores what might have happened had things taken place in a way which most of us were expecting.

Notes
A recording of the late Derek Lacey's iconic commentary of Jimmy Glass's famous goal can still be heard online at BBC Radio Cumbria's tribute page [online]. Available at: http://news.bbc.co.uk/local/cumbria/hi/people_and_places/newsid_8441000/8441008.stm (Accessed 14th May 2010).

References

Atkin, R. (2008) I'm an overnight success after 25 years, says Stelling. *The Independent on Sunday* [online]. Available at: http://www.independent.co.uk/sport/football/fa-league-cups/im-an-overnight-success-after-25-years-says-stelling-786458.html (Accessed 14th May 2010).

Carter, C. (2002). No. 72 Goalie Jimmy Glass scores to keep Carlisle in the Football League, on *The 100 Greatest Sporting Moments*. Channel 4, broadcast on January 19th 2002.

Fiver, The (1999) Space ships, Sinking ships, and Transfer goss-ship. *The Guardian* [online]. Available at: http://www.guardian.co.uk/football/1999/may/10/thefiver.sport (Accessed 14th May 2010).

Glass, J. (2002) No. 72 Goalie Jimmy Glass scores to keep Carlisle in the Football League. On, *100 Greatest Sporting Moments*. Channel 4, broadcast on January 19th 2002.

Glass, J. (2004) *One Hit Wonder: The Jimmy Glass Story*. Gloucestershire: Tempus Publishing limited.

Lytollis, R. (2008) Behind Glass. *News and Star* [online]. Available at: http://www.news-and-star.co.uk/1.56144 (Accessed 16th May 2010).

Metcalf, R. (1999) Football: Carlisle raise a Glass to survival - Carlisle United 2 Plymouth Argyle 1. *The Independent* [online]. Available at: http://www.independent.co.uk/sport/football-carlisle-raise-a-glass-to-survival--carlisle-united-----2--plymouth-argyle-----1-1092696.html (Accessed 14th May 2010).

Slot, O. (2005) Broken Glass. *The Times* [online]. Available at: http://www.timesonline.co.uk/tol/sport/football/article387518.ece (Accessed 12th May 2010).

Stelling, J. (1999) *Soccer Saturday*. Sky Sports 1, broadcast 8th May 1999.

Tomas, J. (1999) Glass seeks a new goal as his dream turns sour. *The Guardian* [online]. Available at: http://www.guardian.co.uk/football/1999/aug/01/newsstory.sport11 (Accessed 12th May 2010).

Turnbull, S. (2009) Jimmy Glass: From 'legend' to taxi driver but Glass is half full. *The Independent on Sunday* [online]. Available at: http://www.independent.co.uk/sport/football/news-and-comment/jimmy-glass-from-legend-to-taxi-driver-but-glass-is-half-full-1678021.html (Accessed 14th May 2010)

Walker, M. (1999a) Forgotten Glass left half empty. *The Guardian* [online]. Available at: http://www.guardian.co.uk/football/1999/jul/27/newsstory.sport2 (Accessed 16th May 2010)

Walker, M. (1999b). Surreal Carlisle reach the Glass ceiling. *The Guardian* [online]. Available at: http://www.guardian.co.uk/football/1999/may/10/match.sport11 (Accessed 16th May 2010).

Creative Story

'Magical Madness' Jimmy Glass - Carlisle's Number 9

Claire Burgess and James Kenyon

A ND THE BALL GOES OUT NOW "... for a corner to Carlisle United – will they have time to take it? Referee looks at his watch... and here comes Jimmy Glass! Carlisle United goalkeeper Jimmy Glass is coming up for the kick – everyone is going up... there isn't one player in the Carlisle half! Well, well... and the corner kick comes in... and... the goalkeeper's pun... Oh... Jimmy Glass! Oh he's hit the bar...! He's hit the bar! He's hit the bar! From six yards out, Jimmy Glass has hit the bar! Well, well... well that's why you play in goal I suppose son. And surely now, yes, there's the referee's whistle, and after 71 years in the Football League..."

I've never forgotten Derek Lacey's emotional commentary from the final moments of last season's final game against Plymouth. Although I'd only been at the club for two games at that point – the Plymouth game being my third – I was as gutted that day as any Blue Army supporter in the stadium. To say I was devastated would be an understatement of epic proportions. Right at that moment, nothing else existed in my mind except my failure to score and my failure to save Carlisle United from relegation. I'd had the chance to become a hero... their hero, their saviour, a legend in my own lifetime. But I'd hit the crossbar. The sodding crossbar. And then I'd watched as the ball went harmlessly out of play and the referee blew his whistle to signal the end: the end of the game, the end of an era, and the end of Carlisle United's time in the English Football League. After the final whistle went on that day, hundreds of supporters rushed the pitch. At first, I was terrified to think that they were going to come straight for me and rip me apart for missing such an easy chance. But they didn't, they amassed on the pitch and started jumping up and down chanting towards where the chairman was sitting, "You're just a fat, greedy bastard! You're just a fat, greedy baaaaaaaaaaaaaastard!" While some supporters clearly had tears in their eyes and others looked liked children who'd only just found out that Father Christmas wasn't real, there was also more than just a glint of pure hatred on all the supporters faces. Hatred toward the man who had promised Premier League football when he took over as Chairman. Hatred toward the man who had sold the club's players, sacked its staff and had even taken the reins as manager himself at one point. It was hatred aimed at Michael Knighton and no-one else. Relegation was the straw that broke the camel's back. The passion with which they were singing was something I'd never experienced before, even when I'd played in the Wembley final for Bournemouth. And despite the fact that Carlisle had just been relegated, the atmosphere was electric. Right then I knew that this was a club I wanted to continue to be a part of - Conference League football or otherwise.

I'd returned to Swindon shortly after Carlisle's game against Plymouth and immediately handed in a transfer request to the manager Jimmy Quinn. Even before deciding that it was Carlisle United where I wanted to spend the rest of my career, I was getting fed up of trying to convince Jimmy that I was a better keeper than his first-choice, Frank Talia. Some of the Swindon coaches thought that I was a bad trainer and I was finding it hard to shake that label. But I didn't think I was a bad trainer. I just failed to see how running up hills and dribbling around cones was going to help me as a goalie. Although Jimmy Quinn turned down my transfer request, he said that if I wanted to go he'd release me from my contract. So I left First Division Swindon with the hopes of joining Conference Division Carlisle United. It was a step down of 3 divisions in terms of competition and I knew that I'd almost certainly have to take a pay cut as well. Except I didn't care, I just wanted to play for the Blue Army supporters. But this wasn't as straightforward as I'd thought it would be and while I was busy getting out of my contract at Swindon Town, a blue revolution was afoot at Carlisle United.

MILLIONAIRE WANTS TO BUY UNITED was the headline in the News and Star on the Monday – and two days – after the Plymouth game. The story in the paper continued, "A millionaire businessman is seeking to buy out Carlisle United chairman Michael Knighton and take control of the newly-relegated Conference club, the *News and Star* can exclusively reveal today". This was fantastic news for the thousand or so supporters who, in the day before, had marched from Carlisle's Turf Inn pub on Newmarket Road, through the city centre and along Warwick Road to the stadium at Brunton Park waving banners, flags and posters all emblazoned with the words KNIGHTON OUT. They were still singing the song that they'd been screaming so passionately at the Chairman the day before, as well as a couple of others they'd also added to the repertoire; chants like, "Knighton -

Leave Carlisle alone!" to the tune of Pink Floyd's *Brick in the Wall*, and "We want Knighton out, say we want Knighton out!" The march was organised by The Carlisle and Cumbria United Independent Supporters' Trust, a group which was launched only ten days before the march took place (and only eight days before the club was relegated). They'd mobilised very quickly and their actions had set in course the successful removal of Michael Knighton as Chairman of their beloved team. But he didn't go easily and he certainly didn't go quickly, and it wasn't until after the first game of the new season that he'd finally relinquished control of the club to the new Chairman, insurance tycoon Brooks Mileson. But in the end he'd pretty much had to. At the opening game of the 1999/2000 Conference season, the Supporters' Trust staged another march, this time attended by about 3,000 fans, and encouraged those same fans to boycott the game. And they did. In the Brunton Park stadium, with a capacity close to 17,000, around 200 people turned up to watch Carlisle United get beat 3 – 1 by Rushden and Diamonds.

Before this first game, my future was far from certain. Before I'd left Carlisle to return to Swindon I'd made it plainly obvious to the manager, Nigel Pearson, that I wanted to come back. So I left my relatively well-paid job at Swindon Town with the hope of an offer from Carlisle United. I was encouraged by the fact that Swindon had released me from my contract, and therefore Carlisle wouldn't have to pay any transfer fees. Plus I knew I'd have to take a considerable drop in wages and I was equally prepared to waiver a signing-on fee. So I was expecting a quick offer; I was, after all, a First Division player willing, and even wanting to sign for a Conference club, plus there was the money factor to consider as well. But the offer never came and while most professional footballers were on holiday, I was left wondering what the hell I was going to do. When the Carlisle players returned from their summer break, I called Nigel Pearson and asked him if I could train with the squad. I explained that I knew what was going on at the club (it was hard to miss it in the papers), and that I didn't want paying (for the time being) but I just wanted to stay sharp and fit. At first, he'd seemed reluctant to the idea, but came around when I explained how he could use it as an opportunity to 'trial' me. I'd told him that if he didn't think I was good enough, then I'd just keep training until I found another club and this way he'd have someone to make up the numbers in training sessions. He agreed and soon after I started pre-season training with the Carlisle squad. But the squad as it was from the previous season had been decimated. Before leaving the club, and to prepare for the financial consequences of football in Conference division, Michael Knighton had sold

213

a number of players and hadn't replaced them. In total, six first-team players and three 'squad' players had been sold or released from their contract to save money. Three of these players had been last season's strike force and so we were left without a single striker for the first pre-season friendly against Marine from Crosby. I'd suggested to the gaffer, purely as a joke mind, that he should stick me up front since we had two goalies and no strikers and that I'd make amends for missing that sitter against Plymouth last year. The lads burst out laughing in training when I'd made *that* suggestion.

But he actually did it. Really. I couldn't believe it. When he told me in the dressing room before the game, the lads weren't laughing in the way they did when I suggested it, but I was ..., I was proper buzzing. I'd always fancied myself as a frustrated striker, even though I'd missed that sitter last year. And although you could tell that some of the lads were fuming when the gaffer threw me the number 9 shirt, they weren't fuming after the game. I'd scored both goals in a narrow 2 – 1 victory, and been given Man of the Match by the referee. My second goal, in particular, had been a screamer. As soon as it'd left my foot just outside the area, I knew it was flying into the top right. I found out later that Derek Lacey, having been commentating, had called it, 'a goal worthy of the Premier League'. As soon as we'd returned to training after that first friendly against Marine the gaffer had told me to train up front, and I did. And the goals in the friendlies kept coming. One each in the next two, two more and an assist in third, and one more goal in the fourth game after Marine easily made me the club's top scorer pre-season. But I was still playing for free and had no contract because of what was going on behind the scenes. Knighton was still in charge at this point and he kept blowing me off stating that had no time to discuss my contract with everything that was going on. Nigel Pearson, however, threatened that if he didn't offer me a contract soon another club would only have to offer me one and I'd be gone, they didn't own me. Plus I was quickly becoming a fans favourite, even though it was still the pre-season and Knighton was already feeling their wrath. Had he let me go without a fight, there was word that some of the more fanatical Blue Army supporters were going to go one further than the marches and boycotts they'd been taking part in and stage a sit-in at Brunton Park until Knighton left. But after I'd scored our only goal in our opening league game against Rushden and Diamonds, the only thing that had stopped him from signing me was the fact that he left. Three days after the Rushden and Diamonds game, it was announced, almost out the blue, that Brooks Mileson had taken control of the club, and that his first order of business was to offer me a professional contract. While sometimes I like to imagine that the subsequent three day party that took place in Carlisle city centre was for me, in reality I know it was because the Blue revolution had been victorious. The enemy had been defeated and the fans had a new man in charge of our club.

With Knighton gone and the new Chairman announcing that everyone's jobs were safe, and that Nigel Pearson would be given a fair crack at getting us back into the Football League, the playing staff seemed to relax, we'd stopped playing like 11 individuals on the pitch and developed a healthy team spirit. Given the time and support, Nigel Pearson had worked wonders with the defence, who were easily the most composed in the league, and throughout the season I continued to be as prolific a goal-scorer as I had been during the pre-season. Our results improved massively after our season-opener against Rushden and Diamonds and throughout the entire year at no point we were not considered to be challengers for the league title. With the final game of the 1999/2000 Conference season to go, we were equal on points with Kidderminster Harriers, and had a slightly better goal difference, which was partly because of the amount of goals I'd scored that year – I was second top goal-scorer in the league. But of all the goals I'd scored this season, none was more sweeter than the winning goal in our final game at home to Yeovil Town. There was close to 8,000 supporters at that game and the chants were an awesome mix of, "There's only ooooooooooooone Jimmy Glass! and "Campioni, campioni, oh-ay, oh-ay, oh-ay!" I'd never heard such a deafening roar from a lower-league club's supporters. I could feel myself getting addicted to it... I never wanted that feeling to end. I'm sure all 8,000 fans had celebrated on the pitch with us after we had lifted the trophy. Even the silver-haired Derek Lacey was seen dancing around arm-in-arm with a bunch of ecstatic Blue Army supporters. But you've got to give it to them, let them go nuts I thought, especially after last season. But now we were Conference Division champions and back in the Football League only one season after being dumped out. And the only question I have in my mind now is... I wonder how many I'm going to score next year?

Chapter 15

What if the England manager wore a green jumper?

Geoff Berkeley and Chris Hughes

Research Preface

BIT COLD ISN'T IT says the ever impressionable Brian Clough as he greeted the Fleet Street faithful on the steps of Lancaster Gate. Waiting in the entrance way Lawrie McMenemy and Bobby Robson, an air of expectation fills not only the hall but the country. Old Big 'ead wonders why the other two have even bothered to turn up for the interview whilst the day's back pages read "Unanimous" and "Give us Clough".

Since that chilly December day in 1977, Brian Clough has always been tagged as the best manager England never had. As a mere member of the public reading newspapers or watching interviews on television, Brian Clough was there, all to see, make your own mind up, there's nothing to hide. To the likes of Martin O`Neill, Trevor Francis, Peter Shilton and the equally abrasive Roy Keane, Cloughie was a true leader. They all knew who they were playing for and what was to be expected of each and every one of them. A fearless, self-belief with a courageous and simplistic view of football enabled him to achieve respect, intimidate opponents and ultimately empower himself to such grandeur that people would jump through hoops for him.

He later collected league titles with both Derby and Nottingham Forest while also doing well in his first job with Hartlepool. His swagger, wit, passion and attractive style of football adhered him to the nation, one of their own, a true socialist. However, the brash northerner wasn't without his critics, several of whom were waiting in the FA board room safe in the knowledge that Ron Greenwood would charge up on the inside and pip Brian to the post.

"I'm sure the England selectors thought if they took me on and gave me the job, I'd want to run the show. They were shrewd, because that's exactly what I would have done".

He might not have been the England manager but his philosophy stayed with his club players even when they were away on national duty.

"We were pretty confident when we went to the England squad," said Tony Woodcock.

"But always in the back of your mind, when you were listening to other coaches, there was Cloughie's voice telling you how he expected it to be done. We just took him along with us basically, all his values and ideas" (BBC Nottingham, 2010).

How selfish of us when we proclaim that "Brian Clough was the best manager England never had". He was certainly the best manager Nottingham Forest ever had and dare we say a blessing in disguise for Forest when he failed to land the big job. He turned Forest from second division mediocrity to back to back European Cup winners with his self confessed greatest achievement being the undefeated 42 league games of 1977/78 - the equivalent of a whole season. Garry Birtles recalled going abroad before one of Nottingham Forest's most important games in the club's history.

"Clough liked the sunshine and taking us away to relax, as he did before the European Cup final". He gave us a week in Spain before the biggest game of our lives. There were no rules about times when we had to be in. We didn't train for the first three days and we went on to win the cup. Would anybody do that today?

"Unbeknown to us he was taking pressure off us from the family and the media so we could relax and clear our minds of everything apart from what we were about to do" (BBC Nottingham, 2010).

Meanwhile with Greenwood at the helm of the national side, a disappointing campaign in Italy during 1980 followed Revie's failing to qualify for Euro 1976 and Argentina 1978. The England side did however

218

reach the Spanish 1980 World Cup after 12 years of failure to qualify. An unbeaten England with too few victories missed out on the second group stage and Bobby Robson stepped into Greenwood's shoes once the dust had settled.

Needless to say Old Big 'ead was in the frame once again... "People wonder what kind of England manager I would have turned out to be. There's only one answer - a bloody good one" (Clough, 2002: 208).

The English game was undergoing great transformation during the 1980s in the commercial sense at least. Transfer fees were reaching six figures and football was becoming evermore broadcasted and analysed. Such a revolution in media attention would certainly appease the showman Clough. However, with reference to the increasing amount of football being broadcast on TV and its effect of spoiling the balance of family life, Clough remarked, "You don't want roast beef and Yorkshire every night and twice on Sunday".

"Too rigid a system of play, in which all the moves are known, will not do. There must be flexibility; endless variety and versatility; constant surprises for the other side. A system must be inspired by art and innate genius for and love of the game", quotes the Edwardian footballer R.S. McColl in Lileks (2010). Upon this note, Clough's philosophy on football was simple, "You don't teach genius, you watch it". He believed in getting his team to their optimum, playing attractive yet simple football and results would inevitably follow.

Clough made no excuses for his sometimes strange behaviour and his problem with alcohol was widely documented. This in conjunction with the pressure of the job unquestionably affected his home life. His final years at Nottingham Forest were depressing for him; an endemic haze of uncertainty engulfed the club. The frequent drunken post match interviews, the selling of key players and allegations of 'bungs' condemned Old Big `ead to relegation and retirement. His exit from the game in 1993 left a large hole in English football. However, on 29th September 2004 an even bigger and more personal loss was felt in the Clough family as Brian lost his fight against stomach cancer.

What legacy has Brian Clough have left to English football?

Would we have won any National honours under his command?

One thing is for sure and in the words of the man himself "I wouldn't say I was the best manager in the business. But I was in the top one".

References

Anon (2009) The wit and wisdom of Brian Clough [online. Available at: http://www.thefirstpost.co.uk/46770,people,news,the-sayings-of-football-manager-brian-clough-the-damned-united [Accessed 9th May 2010].

BBC Nottingham (2010) *Brian Clough World Cup memories* [online]. Available at: http://news.bbc.co.uk/local/nottingham/hi/people_and_places/arts_and_culture/newsid_8543000/8543534.stm [Accessed 9th May 2010].

Clough, B. (2002) *Cloughie walking on water – my life*. Headline Book Publishers. London.

Lileks, J. (2010) *Brian Clough: who he really was, and what he really achieved* [online]. Available at: http://mtmg.wordpress.com/2010/02/06/brian-clough-who-he-really-was-and-what-he-really-achieved/ [Accessed 10th May 2010].

Creative Story

What if the England manager wore a green jumper?

Geoff Berkely and Chris Hughes

THE POST-MATCH INQUEST was dominated by questions towards England's apparent lack of creativity and endeavour as a smooth Brylcreem laden Brian Clough straight batted each and every attempt to pick holes in his outfit. His first major championship, Euro 1980 in Italy hadn't started as it should.

"We had them running scared young man."

"Running scared Brian, 1-1 against this, well lets be honest very ordinary Belgium side..."

"Were you watching the same game as me young man, they were running scared."

"Are you referring to the actual football or the hooligans in the stands Brian?"

"There are more hooligans in the House of Commons than at a football match young man."

"Come on Brian, realistically, what are we expecting from this campaign?"

"I'm going to win the damm thing, what do you think will happen?"

"With all due respect Brian, you've only been in the job 5 minutes, Rome wasn't built in a day..."

"Rome wasn't built in a day. But I wasn't on that particular job".

An eruption of laughter throughout the press room provides the perfect opportunity for the England manager to make a swift exit.

221

"That'll keep em busy Peter," as he returns to the dressing room to debrief his assistant. "Brian, you can't keep covering this sort of thing up."

"Do you really think these lads need me telling the whole country how frustrated I am, how disappointed I am, you let me take the stick out there.

A 1-0 defeat to the Italian hosts followed by a laboured 2-1 victory over the Spanish and it was "*arrivederci*".

Out with the new and in with the old as the England tracksuit was replaced by the customary green jumper. The qualifying campaign for the 1982 World Cup saw Wembley and many European stadiums treated to Brian's occasional litter picking and streaker restraining antics. Meanwhile several club training grounds up and down the country were often frequented by a squash racket wielding Clough. However, it wasn't quite the squash racket, rather Cloughie's axe that relinquished Kevin Keegan of his national team captaincy in favour of the young impressionable Brian Robson.

 "They're not expecting you to win the World Cup young man, they're expecting me to do it," proclaims Cloughie to his general. "All I need is for you to do what I ask, that means play the kind of football that you know you can play and we'll beat the lot of 'em at their own game young man".

Robson in particular felt as though he had the weight of the country on his young shoulders. With limited time for training and squad development, Brian's silver Mercedes not only enabled him to get up and down the country to monitor his players, but in true Clough audacity it provided the perfect get away car in numerous player kidnappings.

"If you think I'm going to risk my chances of winning the World Cup just because Mr Atkinson wants Brian Robson to play in a meaningless end of season game you've got another thing coming".

"Brian, you can't just take a player away from club duty, it's not how it works, what did Ron have to say about the matter?" enquires the Daily Mail journalist.

With a slight raise of his eyebrows and a provocative smile, a soave looking Old Big 'ead replies, "We talked about it for twenty minutes or so and we decided I was right".

As the England faithful invaded Spain for the World Cup of 1982, Parker jackets were replaced by Kappa tracksuits and Fred Perry polo shirts. It was a summer for singing and sangria with the occasional scrap thrown in for good measure. The press on the other hand were increasingly sceptical about England's chances, particularly towards Clough's vision for his version of the Dutch's 'total football'.

"We have seen a distinct change in our play Brian, is this the correct way to take on these sides or do we need to be more direct, the English way?"

"If God had wanted us to play football in the clouds, he'd have put grass up there. Upon what football qualifications do you feel comfortable asking me, Brian Clough, about such footballing matters? It is my job as England manager to pick the team, it is your job to sit there and pick your nose".

With the press well and truly brought down to size, Clough and his side were hell bent on doing the same to the World. After un-convincing first group-stage victories over Kuwait and Czechoslovakia, England were group leaders, requiring only a draw against a flashy French outfit led by the Juventus superstar Michel Platini, England was over the first hurdle. With Cloughie safely through to the second qualifying group, the Spanish heat was being cranked up a notch or two not only in the press room but in the majority of living rooms back on English soil.

The temperature in the England dressing room however, was being carefully tempered by their leader. Young men at the pinnacle of their football careers were being thwarted, anxiety was breeding amongst the ranks. Clough in stark contrast to his players and adoring population appeared to stem such feelings through his exuberance, humour and exterior calming nature. Peter Taylor, Brian's assistant and close companion, was having none of it. He was the only person in the camp who could spot the tell tale signs and get into the mind of such a Big `ead.

"I believe in this team Peter, if we play our football, the way it should be played, then I'm happy," admits Brian to his right hand man.

"We believe in you Brian, but them lot in there writing their silly little articles will crucify you if this goes belly up,"

"I can see the headlines now *Keegan kicked out for Clough's kids*."

Peter knew him inside out, he knew how to hit a nerve, how to get Brian right in the gut.

A perplexed Clough looked Peter in the whites of his eyes, his confident demeanour had been over-shadowed by a fragile yet honest shroud. What appeared to be the bare naked bones of Brian Clough replied,

"Its called sacrifice Peter, if I'm asking those young men to run their blood to water for me, I have to put the whole bloody lot on the line to achieve this the right way".

Unbeknown, Brian was a tormented wreck. Peter had witnessed an inch of what was going on deep in the depths of his bowels, it was only an inch but it was the inch that Brian was damned to serve up to the watching World.

Brian knew it was true 'backs to the wall time' as a regimented West German side provided the first serious opposition. The disciplined Germans contained England for an hour before Trevor Francis picked the lock to Lother Matthaus' offside trap. Robson's delayed through pass was calmly stroked into the net by Francis and England forced the Germans to chase the ball for the final 30 minutes in the Spanish heat.

With points safe in the bank, Brian, known for his love of the sunshine, gave the squad two days off. Relaxing, regrouping and recuperating were just what the doctor ordered however, as the players enjoyed the sunbathing and God knows what else, a storm still raged inside the man.

A dour 0-0 draw between the hosts and the recently dispatched Germans left England group leaders needing only a draw against Spain to reach the semis. The early evening kick-off in Madrid saw Brian, rooted to the bench, franticly orchestrating his team. The bull fighter teased his opponents throughout the first half, whilst the bewildered Santiago Bernabeu crowd struggled to muster a coherent rendition of "La marche real".

After 45 minutes of chasing English shadows, the bull was dazed and there for the taking. Clough, sweating under his green jumper said nothing at half time other than, "Go and enjoy it, go play your football".

A swift dart and finish from Ray Wilkins broke the deadlock whilst a late strike from Francis and an injury time header from the substitute Keegan concluded a dominant performance.

With record unemployment back home under Thatcher rule, the World Cup under the rule of Mr Clough was beginning to provide the perfect tonic. Tracksuit clad droves headed their way to sunny Spain by any means possible. Scousers in Sombreros and Mancs with Maracas, Spain didn't know what had hit it.

The ultimate prize was in touching distance for the manager. While his players slept safe in the knowledge that they were living the dream, Brian battled his own anxiety. The advice, humour and reassurance he gave to his staff and players was of no use to him. He couldn't speak to his family back home, couldn't sleep or eat; in fact the nervous expectation was eating him up from the inside. Oblivious to the man's toiling fears, the World Cup continued regardless.

A semi-final reunion with the French in Seville saw the stadium awash with singing English fans. With San Miguel on tap, the atmosphere was crackling as the game settled into a steady tempo. Both sides exchanged extensive periods of possession and Brian poked and prodded his team to attack. The French, happy to take the game to extra time and penalties if needed, accepted every opportunity to waste time and fake injury.

However, there was an air of expectancy within the stadium as the Captain, Robson and his team remained cool, calm and controlled. With 12 minutes remaining, a Steve Coppell corner was met by the onrushing Terry Butcher. A block on the near post by the French full back dropped to the feet of Phil Thompson who stabbed the ball into the net for his first goal for the country. The English fans behind the goal tumbled like dominoes, perms were drowned in lager while Cloughie simply stood and applauded.

This should have been his stage, his finest hour; the press wanted the old Cloughie back. They weren't satisfied with the entertaining football on the pitch, they wanted his usual arrogance and charisma but none was forthcoming.

Heading back to the capital, England faced the impressive Italians. Madrid appeared to have been transformed into Manchester or even Middlesbrough, fans riding on the crest of the recent winning wave. Throughout the week a cynical Clough, in fear of any Italian food poisoning shenanigans urged his players not to drink anything unless it was sealed. The pressure was building, England expected and Brian knew he had a team to win it.

For the entirety of the World Cup final, England confidently and creatively outworked and outclassed their Italian counterparts. The *Azzuri* were subjected to a carefree English football master class. Clough, enthralled by his county's dominance, stood back and watched as England took Italy apart 3-1. One man's sacrifice, fear and torment had resulted in empowering a group of players to such a level that they believed they could walk on water. Each and every one of them felt comfortable, confident and thoroughly motivated to do their job. It wasn't the Jules Rimet that Clough had craved, it was simply for his team to win it better than anyone else had ever done.

An English football revolution was upon us and the rest as they say is history.

6TH NOVEMBER 2008 MEMORIAL: As Barbara Clough unveils a statue of her late husband in Nottingham City centre, players, managers, friends and members of the public pay their respects to a true football man.

"He loved the game for what it was, a simple game that could be played beautifully."

"He believed in us, he taught us and let us express ourselves as players."

"Brian created the legacy of what English football is today," commented members of the World Cup winning team of 1982.

"So Nigel, what do you think your Dad would have made of all this here today?"

"I wouldn't be surprised if he said something like; I thought they would have put me in Trafalgar Square as well."

Oh, what could have been...

Chapter 16

A cold night in Munich: the tale of a broken hero

Alec Fenn and Iain Adams

Research Preface

AT **16:02.40 ON THE SNOWY AFTERNOON** of 6th February 1958, George Rodgers, the radio operator of BEA Flight 609, called ready for take-off. Munich Tower immediately cleared the aircraft for take-off and at 16:03:06 Rodgers reported "rolling". Two previous take-offs had been abandoning due to engine boost-pressure readings fluctuating above the maximum of 60". The pilots had taxied back to the terminal in order to consult with the BEA station manager, William Black. Black confirmed that boost-pressure fluctuations were not uncommon on the Elizabethan aircraft at Munich due to its elevation of 1732' and advised the pilots to adjust the throttles to maintain 57.5". This would mean a slower input of power and perhaps less than full throttle being available, but the runway was long (Ministry of Transport and Civil Aviation, 1959).

Captain Ken Rayment DFC, the handling pilot, opened the throttles which were then taken over by Captain James Thain, the pilot-in-command, to adjust as Thain watched the instruments. Rayment, staring down the runway as he kept the aircraft straight, heard Thain call "VR" at 80 knots (the call to lift the nose) and gently pulled the control column back. Thain noticed boost surging on the port engine and retarded the throttle until the boost was 57.5" and then throttled up again. At 117 knots Thain called "V1" (there was now insufficient runway left to stop) and waited to call "V2" at 119 knots which would tell Rayment they had sufficient airspeed to fly. Rayment would then increase the back pressure on the controls, further rotating the aircraft and lifting it into the air. However, simultaneously with the V1 call, the nose of the aircraft lowered until the nose wheel was back on the runway despite Rayment still holding back pressure. To Thain's horror the airspeed dropped to 105 knots, he went to push the throttles fully forward despite the possibility of fluctuating boost but found Rayment had already done it. Rayment hauled the stick all the way back in an effort to bounce the aircraft into the air as he knew it would fly at 105.5 knots in an emergency. But the aircraft was too slow to fly, Rayment exclaimed "Christ, we won't make it" closing the throttles, hurriedly calling "undercarriage up" (Board of Trade, 1969: 11), whilst applying the brakes and steering right to avoid trees and a building ahead (Board of Trade, 1969).

The aircraft flattened the airport fence, crossed a road and the port wing impacted with the house tearing off at the engine mounting as the left side of the cockpit smashed through the trees. A 100 metres further on, as the aircraft span left, the rear starboard fuselage impacted with a wooden hut containing fuel and tyres. The fuselage tore off behind the wings and the hut and rear fuselage burst into flames. The main wreckage slid another 70 metres before stopping (Ministry of Transport and Civil Aviation, 1959).

Twenty of the 44 people on the plane perished in the crash, Frank Swift died on his way to hospital, Captain Rayment, a Second World War fighter ace, and Duncan Edwards succumbed to their injuries later in hospital. Of the 23 fatalities, eight were Manchester United players. A football team had died but a Manchester club had "captured the imagination of the world" (Foulkes, 1998).

This story focuses on the Munich air disaster and the often asked question "what if the great Duncan Edwards had survived?" Duncan Edwards, who at 21, was revered as the greatest of 'The Busby Babes' and the finest footballer of his generation. A centre-back or central midfielder, he possessed all the attributes required of the finest of footballers, strength, pace, power and a god-given natural talent. It has often been debated just how good 'Big Dunc' would have become. Tommy Docherty opined "you can keep all your Bests, Peles and Maradonas . . . Duncan Edwards was the greatest of them all" and Bobby Charlton said "he was such a talent, I always felt inferior to him. He didn't have a fault with his game" (Robson, 2008).

Rather than simply going straight back to the night of the disaster, and to give context, the story begins in the present day. Edwards is now old, frail and confined to a wheelchair. The portrayal of him as a weak vulnerable character is a deliberate tactic to shock the reader because he died as a young strong man "straight of limb, true of eye, steady and aglow" and has remained that way in common memory (Binyon, 1914).   Instead age has wearied him and he feels condemned by his survival and his colleagues' death, "Why me?"

To maximise the tension and Edwards' status as a hero and living legend, the central character's identity is not revealed until the last minute, the normal procedure in sporting ceremonies. The story goes back to the night of the disaster in Munich to detail the alternative outcome. His demise as a person and how his depressed state developed is revealed to be embedded in the disaster. The tale of the infamous afternoon is built on a semantic field of war and death. War is used as a semantic key to highlight the powerful bond that existed between the Busby Babes, similar to that between comrades-in-arms. The use of lexical repetition of words such as army, conquer and battle-hardened attempts to reproduce the air of togetherness. Similarly this technique is used to imply that tragedy and death were around the corner, 'the deathly mixture of wind and snow' and 'is a ghostly white' are just two examples of lexical repetition to build a semantic field of death.

It is also important to ensure the correct phonetics of the characters' voices in order to give them personality in order for the reader could relate to them. The deliberate use of Matt Busby's 'gruff' Scottish accent portrays him as a stereotypical disciplinarian and a taskmaster which indeed he was. In the case of Edwards, born and bred in Dudley in the Black Country, his dialect is identified through words such as "Aer bin ya" and "Ark ticker, awlroight, ah bin oop there," two common instances of Dudley parlance.

The portrayal of Edwards as a classic 'hero' is important. This highlights him above his peers as a special human being with greater physical characteristics.   Hargreaves (2000:1) defines a hero as a person "distinguished for exceptional courage, fortitude, enterprise, superior qualities or deeds". Through Edwards's heroic efforts in saving his fellow men, he is clearly identified as the classic hero character.

His physical characteristics are emphasised to relate to the theory of hegemonic masculinity as defined by Lines (2001), someone who epitomizes social and masculine ideals as well as replicating the values displayed on the field of play in real life. Edwards fighting for his team-mates on the football field and for their lives on board the aircraft are evidence of this. Although Edwards is portrayed as a traditional hero and a

229

masculine figure, there was a need to display a human side which would help endear him to the reader so that they can relate to him and like him as a character. This is reinforced by his mourning the loss of his close friend and blaming himself for his death. The story uses the concepts of mourning and depression found in Freud's theory of depression (Craib, 1994). This identifies a form of pathological mourning known as melancholia which involves damning self-criticism and the attack of the living self rather than the deceased.

The story also attempts to follow Todorov's theory of equilibrium (Branston and Stafford, 2006) where a story begins with equilibrium, in this case the ceremony, and then introduces a disturbance, the accident, before restoring the status quo through Edwards's final speech summing up his reluctant status as a hero and that he is simply an average man living his dream.

References

Binyon, L. (1914) *For the Fallen* [online]. Available at: www.firstworldwar.com/poetsandprose/binyon.htm (Accessed 11th March 2010).

Board of Trade (1969) *CAP 318: Report of the Second Independent Review appointed to consider the Accident to Elizabethan Aircraft G-ALZU at Munich on 6th February 1958 and to whether blame for the Accident is to be imputed to Captain Thain*. HMSO, London.

Note: The 1969 review called upon evidence that was not considered by the German report of 1959. There was evidence that the smooth 0.5 to 0.75 cms of slush along the runway was in fact up to 4 or 5 cms in depth in parts. Also, there was a significant pool of deep slush extending some 200-300 yards along the runway just after the half way mark. It was substantiated that there was either no snow/ice on the wings or so little as to be irrelevant. Experiments had been carried out at RAE Bedford on the effects of slush on aircraft take-off performance in 1961-1962. It found that aircraft entering a patch of deep slush experienced a sharp nose-down moment due to the braking effect of the slush on the wheels. This forced the nose wheel of aircraft back onto the runway and therefore increased the braking effect. In addition, if the spray from the main wheels impacted the underside of the tail an even larger nose-down pitch was produced. The review concluded "The cause of the accident was slush on the runway".

Branston, G. and Stafford, R. (2006) *The Media Student's Book* (fourth edition). Routledge, London.

Burn, G. (2006) *Best and Edwards: Football, fame and oblivion*. Faber and Faber, London.

Craib, I. (1994) *The Importance of Disappointment*. Routledge, London.

Foulkes, W.A. (1998) Anger Still Boils After 40 Years [online]. Available at: www.munich58.co.uk/articles/foulkes1.asp (Accessed on 11th March 2010).

Lines, G. (2001) Villains, fools or heroes? Sports stars as role models for young people, *Leisure Studies*, 20, (pp. 285-303)

Hargreaves, J. (2000) *Heroines of Sport: The politics of difference and identity.* Routledge, London.

Ministry of Transport and Civil Aviation (1959) *CAP 153: Report by The Federal Republic of Germany relating to the Inquiry into the Accident to G-ALZU AS57 Ambassador (Elizabethan) on 6th February, 1958 at Munich-Reim Airport.* HMSO, London.

Note: The German enquiry concluded "During the stop of almost two hours at Munich, a rough layer of ice formed on the upper surface of the wings as a result of snowfall. This layer of ice considerably impaired the aerodynamic efficiency of the aircraft, and had a detrimental effect on the acceleration of the aircraft during the take-off process and increased the required unstick-speed. Thus, under the conditions obtaining at the time of take-off, the aircraft was not able to attain this speed within the rolling distance available". This squarely blamed the pilots for failing to clear snow off the aircraft, but the investigation team did not arrive until after 22:00 and it had been snowing continuously in the intervening period.

Robson, J. (6 February 1958) *A Rock in a Raging Sea*, Manchester Evening News [online]. Available at: www.manchestereveningnews.co.uk/sport/football/manchester_united/s/1035301_a_rock_in_a_raging_sea (Accessed on 10th March 2010).

Creative Story

A cold night in Munich: The tale of a broken hero

Alec Fenn and Iain Adams

...14ᵗʰ December 2003, The BBC Sports Personality of the Year programme from the BBC Television Centre.

IT IS HOT UNDER THE POWERFUL broadcasting lights in the packed studio; there is a palpable air of excitement filling the room amidst the murmurings and whisperings of the expectant 3,000 people in the audience. The clinking of glasses and raucous laughter is the soundtrack to the pop-pumped special evening as the great and good of British sport gather to honour the accomplishments of the year and of lifetimes.

It is time for the unique BBC Golden Sports Personality Award. This 50ᵗʰ BBC Sports Personality of the Year extravaganza has been preceded by five special programmes, *Simply the Best*, in which the merit of each winner over the last fifty years has been outlined. There is now a short list of five. Rumours have sizzled over the winner of this award and tickets for the night have been changing hands at astronomical prices. Even the host, Gary Lineker, seems nervous. The seasoned broadcaster and ex-England footballer appears distracted, beads of sweat building on his brow, hands fidgeting. Members of the T.V. crew hurry around anxiously ensuring everything is ready and nothing left to chance, cameras poised at the ready to capture this special moment.

The room is suddenly plunged into darkness, silence abruptly fills the room; an intense spotlight snaps onto Lineker standing in the space reserved for tonight's special guest. He raises the microphone to his lips and announces the news the entire audience has been waiting to hear:

"Please welcome to the stage, the man you're all here to see. He was second in the BBC Sports Personality of the Year competition in 1958 and 1959, and winner of the BBC Sports Personality of the Year in 1966 and 1970. The most capped player in English football history with 126 caps; he holds the record for appearances for Manchester United with 819 games played and led them to the European Cup in 1968. And of course he led England to World Cup glory in 1966 and 1970. I give you a living legend, a football giant and a true hero, the Golden Sports Personality of the last 50 years, Sir Duncan Edwards!"

The room erupts. The deafening applause is accompanied by a chorus of whistles and cheers from the audience who stand as one to greet a quite special human being. The flashes of cameras and the resonance of Nessun Dorma complete the backdrop to the entrance of this almost mythical being.

But Duncan Edwards is no longer the marauding athlete who swept all before him, the man who twice dragged his nation to World Cup glory and led Manchester United off the runway in Munich to European success.

In his place is a frail soul, a man reduced by illness and old age to the confines of a wheelchair, relying on his niece to wheel him on stage to greet the waiting audience. The glint in the eye of a once handsome young man has disappeared and the fire in his soul that set him apart from his fellow competitors has been extinguished. In truth the flames were doused a long time ago and a small part of Duncan died just beyond that snow covered Munich runway some 45 years before.

February 6th 1958, Munich, Germany, 3 p.m.
It is a dank afternoon; low glowering clouds continually dump snow and sleet across the airport. The whole scene is a deathly grey-white; the funereal light removing all of the lustre from the BEA Elizabethan airliner Zulu Uniform's aluminium fuselage.

The Manchester United squad re-take their seats after the refuelling stop in Munich, next stop Manchester, home. The trip has been successful, an away 3-3 draw with Yugoslavian giants Red Star Belgrade securing a 5-4 aggregate win. Their place in the semi-finals of the European Cup is secure. Already, this is no ordinary group of men; their manager has melded them into a band of brothers, the Busby Babes, the squad are a well drilled army that are the darlings of the national press.

233

Together they have begun to conquer all before them winning the league title in 1956 with an average age of 22; they won it again in 1957 whilst losing in the FA Cup Final to Aston Villa and the semi-final of the European Cup to Real Madrid. They are led by Matt Busby, a Scottish disciplinarian, who has matured a group of youngsters into battle-hardened men, headed by Duncan Edwards, the jewel in the crown.

The air is bitter and damp, but the team are still exhilarated and happy after their successful trip. Dennis Viollet chats happily to Bobby Charlton about the latest Hollywood blockbuster he has seen with Albert Scanlon. Two rows back the Manchester United card school get ready. Bill Foulkes prepares the card deck for himself, Albert, Roger Byrne, David Pegg, Ken Morgans, and Liam Whelan. Bobby turns and smiles down the aisle to his mate, Duncan Edwards, at the back with Tommy Taylor, Dave Pegg, Mark Jones, Geoff Bent and Eddie Colman. The press corps, including the famous journalist Frank Swift, is just behind Duncan in the very back.

Duncan gives a little salute to Bobby; Bobby has perhaps the most to celebrate. For Duncan last night was hugely satisfying, not for himself but for the contribution of his close friend. A two-goal display marked the coming of age of Charlton and for once Duncan was happy to share the limelight. The card school joke and burst into guffaws of laughter as they await take-off, displaying the bond and camaraderie that typifies The Busby Babes.

Eventually the engines burst into life and the Zulu Uniform taxies out to the runway. At 3.30 the aircraft is lined up on the runway and the noise and vibration increases as the pilots begin the take off. In the back Duncan notices he can see less and less out of the window as the aircraft accelerates and more and more slush is thrown up by the undercarriage. A loud 'thrumming' sound starts back behind his head. Peering back through the window he notices the spray from the wheels hitting the tail of the plane. Suddenly the noise lessens; the aircraft dips forward and rapidly slows to a stop. Excited chatter breaks out as the aircraft steadily makes its way back along the runway for another go. The nervous ones like Pegg and Morgans exchange apprehensive glances. At 3.34 the pilots again open the throttles and Zulu Uniform begins to accelerate down the runway. Again, the noise, vibrations and the rapid drum-like thrumming suddenly reduce and the airliner dips and shudders alarmingly as the brakes are applied.

The passengers are clearly rattled; the faces of the journalists assembled to the rear of the cabin are pensive. Eddie Colman, the diminutive right half, is ghostly white while the rest of the squad exchange nervous looks as the chatter of alarmed voices fills the air. Margaret Bellis, one of the stewardesses, quickly calms everybody with her soothingly toned message that they were returning to the terminal with a minor "mechanical fault".

The passengers scurry, heads down, into the building, the card school order coffee in the lounge and resume their game. Gregg, Charlton and Edwards stand together, Gregg is clearly worried: "What's going on, this is dangerous, let's leave it, we can wait till the morning". His fear clearly permeates through some of the waiting throng; the previously buoyant Duncan and Bobby are now quiet, fearful of their plight while the faces of the rest of the squad are a picture of uncertainty. Charlton moves to the information booth and sends a telegram to his landlady back in Manchester "All flights cancelled, returning tomorrow".

Busby leaves the confines of the terminal to return to the aircraft and confer with the pilots. After a short while he is back in the lounge and delivers welcome news to his troops. In his gruff Scottish accent he announces "Everything is fine, there's a wee problem with the engines but the answers been found; we're leaving now". An air of calm returns and the previous nervous chatter is replaced by the laughter and murmurings of a content group of men. Again they dash through the deathly mixture of wind and snow.

However, once back on board, one or two still look uneasy. As the engines fire Dave Pegg undoes his seat belt and moves towards the back explaining "I don't like it here, it's not safe". "Your right" agrees Ken Morgans and both he and Bobby Charlton join Pegg moving towards the back even as the plane starts to taxi. There are only two free seats at the back, Charlton pauses, Edwards looks up at his friend from his seat "Aer bin ya, chief?" (Are you alright?). "No, I want to sit back here", Duncan smiles "Ark ticker, awlroight, ah bin oop there" (Listen mate, alright, I'll go up there). Duncan moves swiftly up the aisle, the steward frantically waves him to sit down as the engines gather power and the take-off begins. "Bobby, how can you understand him when he goes all 'Dood-lie' on us" asks Mark Jones. "Too long in the army with him!" laughs Bobby seeing Duncan safely sit down next to Dennis Viollet in the forward part of the cabin. Bobby notices the fog of spray outside as a thrumming becomes evident, a sound he hadn't noticed up front. From the back, the sudden rise of the nose is much more noticeable, the aisle is at quite an angle. The aircraft seems to be slower accelerating and on the ground a long time. The aisle suddenly levels out as the nose drops again; the passengers fall silent, everybody listening to the screaming engines and the banging from the rear. Moments later the aisle rears up higher and there is a bump from behind and underneath Bobby. Vibration increases, but then the engine noise ceases and Duncan, through the window, sees the wheels flatten a fence, "this is serious he thinks to himself". Liam Whelan, behind Duncan, incants "If this is death, then I am ready for it". People cry out as the air is filled with mechanical noises and then a body-jarring crash seemingly from the left, immediately followed by one from the front. Duncan is thrown from his seat to his right, another terrifying thump jolts the whole aircraft, this time from the back right, seats upturn, and bodies fly like ragdolls with the sheer force of impact. A gin bottle careers through the air and crashes into the back of Billy Foulkes' head, Zulu Uniform metallically screeches and screams in pain as it grinds to a halt.

Duncan is lucky; his landing is cushioned by a seat and its occupant. Others are not so. The plane resembles a war zone, the splattering of blood paints parts of the cabin a crimson red. Smoke seeps through the aircraft, a mask of deathly mist. After an initial shocked quiet, punctuated by the crackle of flames, the cries of injured men fill the frigid air. Dennis Viollet, star striker and the joker in the pack, is a picture of pain. "HELP!" "Hellllllllllllllppppp, my leg is caught!" he cries in agony, as he tries to free himself from the twisted tortured plane.

But others are deathly quiet. Duncan looks round and observes the chaos; his eyes are drawn to the seat of his best friend. But there is a white nothingness backlit by a dancing orange light. The back of the plane has gone. "Where is Bobby?" "HELP" pleads Dennis again and Duncan is spurred into action, ripping the wreckage off Dennis and then carrying him out of the carnage through a huge hole that has appeared in the port fuselage. He puts him down and sees Harry Gregg carrying a baby towards him. Duncan looks back at the aluminium tomb and begins a one man mission to save the rest of his friends. He clambers back into the rubble and grabs Jackie Blanchflower, crushed under unidentifiable metal, blood pouring from a horrific tear in his right arm, Busby lies by him. Duncan frees Jackie and carries him out. After carefully putting him down, Duncan scrambles back into the mess and heaves Busby out. He hoists Jackie over his shoulder and grabbing Busby by the shirt collar tows him sliding on his back through the snow to the small band of survivors. Busby is clutching his chest and muttering "I am so cold, freezing". Duncan takes off his coat and places it over him. Harry reappears pulling a woman behind him. As Duncan rushes back towards the smoking hulk he hears Harry scream at him to be careful. In the fuselage, he spots Johnny Berry out cold with a smashed face and an obviously broken leg, alongside lies Albert, his torso covered by a seat and a deformed leg sticking out. Johnny is swiftly lugged out and Duncan returns to grab the seat and then, quickly straightening his legs, lifts the seat off Albert. Albert is carried out and grabbing Johnny's collar, Duncan starts another double haul to the group of survivors. As he rounds the nose, a pilot comes around the other way shouting to him "Run you stupid bastard, it's going to explode". Duncan lays Albert down by Viollet and sees that a fire crew has arrived spraying foam onto the wing and engine. Looking around the small band of people, with increasing alarm he notes Bobby is missing. "Where is Bobby? The back of the plane!" Duncan takes off, his famous tree-trunk legs pounding through the snow. Most of the back of the plane is ablaze, he circles around and dashes towards a hole in the flames. Just outside of the hellhole of fire and bodies that is the rear fuselage, he stumbles over a seat, a comatose figure still strapped in and covered by bits of tailplane. "Bobby!" Bobby doesn't respond, his body lies prone, his eyes are closed and a trickle of blood seeps down his head staining his pristine white shirt. "Bobby, aer bin ya, aer bin ya, maetre", he bellows. "Wake up Bobby its Duncan, Bobby!" But there is no response, Duncan attempts to pull him from his seat but the rubble is too heavy, leaving Bobby trapped.

Duncan races off to get help or something to act as a lever to force off the wreckage. By now the emergency services have gathered, firemen and paramedics carrying off the injured on stretchers, doctors and nurses tending to the walking wounded. Duncan grabs an axe from a fireman and charges back towards the conflagration. "Bobby, am coming to get ya, ya'll be fine its Duncan am not leaving withowt ya". But a German officer blocks his path: "Nein entry it's not safe...back...back...leave go back", warns the officer in his best broken English. "You can't leave him, you can't leave him, he's dying in there, he's dying, somebody help him, somebody!" cries Duncan. He barges past displaying the physical characteristics that have led many supporters to nickname him 'The Tank'. He makes it back to Bobby, his face now bordering on a deathlike blue garishly lit by dancing flames. Three German firemen grab Duncan and a struggle ensues before they successful drag him from the inferno his white shirt ripped open and his face black with smoke, tears running down his cheek. But Bobby remains trapped and Duncan refuses to leave the scene, the detached rear fuselage has become a crematorium, the thwarted rescuers look on grimly aware of the horrendous fate of those still in the aircraft. Bobby is still alive as is Frank Swift when the fire service gets them out; Frank dies in the ambulance whereas Bobby passes away in a hospital just outside of Munich a few days later. He was among 23 of the 44 people who perished in the disaster including seven more of the Busby Babes.

The events of that night shocked the world; Duncan was revered as a hero, a man mountain who was responsible for saving his fellow team-mates, risking his own life in the process. But he was a broken man, mourning the loss of his friends, Tommy Taylor, Roger Byrne, Eddie Colman, Mark Jones, Geoff Bent, Billy Whelan and David Pegg scattered in the snow, but most of all the loss of Bobby, somebody who was more like a brother, never forgiving himself for failing to reach him in time. The remaining Busby Babes regrouped and recovered. Their commander Matt Busby survived against the odds and, in the face of untold grief, the team united in the heartbreak and devastation of February 6th and embarked on the most remarkable of tales.

Just two years later they were crowned league champions once more, captained by Duncan, spurred on by the memory of his close friend. More success was to follow, United were crowned European Cup winners in 1968. They were the toast of the nation and world icons, their tale read like a Greek myth; Duncan was the Zeus, revered as a god. In 1966 came his crowning moment as he lead England to World cup glory for the first time at Wembley in a 4-3 win over Germany, scoring the winner in front of 90,000 screaming supporters. Many thought it was his rugged spirit that had carried England through after stuttering performances against Mexico and Portugal. The performance four years later was altogether more dominant. On the pitch Duncan was a driven man and a tyrant to his teammates. Deep down he was steadily moving further and further from the man who had stepped onto Zulu Uniform so long ago. Driven by anger and the consuming grief of being a survivor, he played for Bobby.

He retired immediately after the '70' world cup aged 33, a decision that only added to his mystique as he moved out of the limelight. He had informed the United manager, Wilf McGuinness, that he was retiring before the England team had left for Mexico and McGuinness had kept his word about not telling anyone. Duncan had achieved more than he could ever have imagined and lived the dream he and his lost friends had shared as young boys. Personal accolades would follow, he was knighted a year later and immortalised in statues, in both his hometown and outside Wembley where he is shown held aloft by his victorious World Cup winning teammates.

But the personal achievements no longer mattered.

So it's December 2003 and the sparkling evening is drawing to a close. The audience are mesmerised and in awe of the great Duncan Edwards and his tales of 66, 68 and 70, and of quiet fishing on the canal. But Gary Lineker has one last question: "Duncan how proud does it make you feel to be regarded as a hero by all these people?"

Duncan coughs and pauses for a moment before replying:

"I ain't a hero, I just lived the dream we were all meant to live, aer kid Bobby and the rest are the real heroes and they died all those years ago in the cold in Munich".

What if... Abramovich bought the Spurs?

Adam Reeder and Iain Adams

Research Preface

CHELSEA FOOTBALL CLUB HAS ENJOYED a period of significant success since Roman Abramovich bought 50.09% of Chelsea Village, the soccer club's holding company, on 2nd July 2003 for £59.3 million. The total deal with Ken Bates, the previous owner, was worth £140 million (Chelsea's Bates sells up to Russian, 2003). Bates had bought Chelsea in 1982 for £1 and thought the move by Abramovich would take Chelsea to the "next level" (Chelsea's Bates sells up to Russian, 2003). Bates used his money to buy Leeds United. The Abramovich deal, Britain's biggest take-over deal at the time, seemed to come out of thin air and many Chelsea fans were shocked by the sudden sale of their club by the Chairman they trusted as "Mr Chelsea." However, the club had been labouring under a significant debt burden of over £80 million despite moderate European success and was ripe for a take-over. Abramovich quickly took the club back into private ownership and poached Peter Kenyon from Manchester United to be Chief Executive, in what many thought was Abramovich's most astute move. Kenyon was brought in to lead the non-footballing side of the club and increase the club's income. This allowed Abramovich to distance himself from the day-to-day running of the company.

However what entranced most Chelsea fans was the unparalleled spending spree of over £100 million in the transfer market. Glen Johnson, Wayne Bridge, Joe Cole, Gérémi, Mutu, Crespo, Makelele, and Veròn arrived accompanied by the club record signing of £17 million Damien Duff. The team lost in the semi-finals of the Champions League to Monaco and finished second in the Premiership in Abramovich's first season in charge (Team History – 2000s, nd).

Although Chelsea had played some exquisite football under their manager, Claudio Ranieri, and he had reshaped them into a younger and more successful club, they had not won a trophy in four years. Abramovich decided to replace him with Jose Mourinho who had taken "Porto to successive UEFA Cup and Champions League triumphs as well as back-to-back leagues and domestic cups" in Portugal (Team History – 2000s, nd). During his introductory press conference, Mourinho made the quotable comment, "Please don't call me arrogant, but I'm European champion and I think I'm a special one," a nick name that has stayed with him even in his current job (The World According to Mourinho, 2005). Mourinho made John Terry his captain and then brought in Ferreira, Carvalho, Tiago, Cech, Robben, and Kezman, as well as a new record signing in Didier Drogba at £20 million.

The 2004-2005 season began with a win over Manchester United and the season ended with Chelsea winning the Premiership with the best points total and best defensive record in Premiership history. Many Chelsea fans were seen to be crying on 30th April as Chelsea beat Bolton Wanderers at the Reebok Stadium to take the title. Significantly, they also started a run in which they were not defeated at their home, Stamford Bridge. They won The Carling Cup, but were eliminated from Europe again in the semi-finals of the Champions League.

The summer of 2005 saw Michael Essien break the club transfer record at £24.4 million and he was joined by Shaun Wright-Phillips and Asier Del Horno. A second Premiership title was won in 2005-2006, but again European silverware eluded the club.

A series of injuries forced Mourinho to play survival football in 2006-2007 and the club finished second in the premiership but did win both the Carling Cup and the FA Cup. Mourinho then left the club by mutual consent with Abramovich and was replaced by Avram Grant. A major contributor to the departure of Mourinho had been the signing of Andriy Shevchenko in 2006 for a then British record fee of £30 million. Mourinho felt that the Ukrainian was well past his best, Mourinho was proven to be quite right in his feelings after the former Milan striker scored only four goals in his first season at Stamford Bridge. Grant's leadership brought no silverware to the club and he left to be replaced by Luiz Felipe Scolari at the end of the season. A further unsuccessful season saw Scholari replaced by

Gus Hiddink on loan from the Russian national side where Abramovich had significant influence. The FA Cup was secured with a 2-1 win over Everton. Carlo Ancelotti become manager in 2009 after eight years in Milan where he won one Serie A championship, two Champions League trophies, two Uefa Supercups, the Italian Cup, and the FIFA Club World Cup (Carlo Ancelotti – Manager, nd).

Abramovich was the first of a new kind of football club owner in Britain, a megawealthy foreigner. Ranked the 50th richest person in the world, he is a self-made man who dropped out of college and made money on controversial oil deals before moving into steel (# 50 Roman Abramovich, 2010). It is popularly believed that it was the game between Manchester United and Real Madrid in the Champions League, the season before his takeover of Chelsea's parent company, that prompted Abramovich to invest in Premier League football. It is rumoured that up until Abramovich bought the West End club, he was also interested in their North London rivals Tottenham Hotspur as well as investing in Manchester United.

References

'Chelsea's Bates sells up to Russian' (2 July 2003), *Sport Business* [online]. Available at: http://www.sportbusiness.com/news/151705/Chelseas-bates-sells-up-to-russian (Accessed on 12th April 2010).

Harris, H, (2003) *The Chelski Revolution*, John Blake Publishing, London.

Harris, H, (2004) *Abramovich: The Chelsea Diary*, John Blake Publishing, London.

The World According to Mourinho (31 October 2005). *BBC Sport: Football.* [online]. Available at: http://news.bbc.co.uk/sport1/hi/football/teams/c/chelsea/4392444.stm (Accessed 12th April 2010).

Team History – 2000s (nd) *Chelseafc.com* [online]. Available at: http://www.chelseafc.com/page/TeamHistory/0,,10268~1800276,00.html (Accessed 12 April 2010).

Carlo Ancelotti – Manager (nd) *Chelseafc.com* [online]. Available at: http://www.chelseafc.com/page/TheManagement/0,,10268~1553809,00.html (Accessed on 12th April, 2010).

#50 Roman Abramovich (10 March 2010) *Forbes.com* [online]. Available at: http://www.forbes.com/lists/2010/10/billionaires-2010_Roman-Abramovich_DG3G.html (Accessed 12th April, 2010).

Creative Story

What if... Abramovich bought the Spurs?

Adam Reeder and Iain Adams

THE MAIN HEADLINE TONIGHT — "Tottenham Hotspur has been taken over by the Russian Billionaire, Roman Abramovich, in an estimated £70 million deal. There has been no statement from the club as yet" intoned Alastair Stewart, the news presenter on London Tonight.

Sports, business and generalist presenters discussed the news and interviewed fans who dreamed a hundred pipe dreams. What was known was that Abramovich was the 49th richest person in the world, worth $5.7 billion. His riches were controlled through a British company, Millhouse Capital, and therefore he was serious about British investments.

Some fans fantasized about a new ground in the outskirts of North London and others visualised a team sheet including the best players in the world, Oliver Kahn, Roberto Carlos, Alpay Özalan, Rivaldo, Ronaldinho, Michael Ballack, Ronaldo, El Hadji Diouf and Andriy Shevchenko.

Just west of the now wealthy Spurs was Chelsea, with an £80 million debt, an owner with no more money, and nothing to attract investors. They'd been here before; the 1970s and 80s had seen the club teetering on the edge of bankruptcy and staring down into Division Three. Judicious management had seen them survive and prosper. But, once again, Chelsea was struggling with players' wages under the debts of the holding company, Chelsea Village. An ambitious diversification programme centred on the redevelopment of Stamford Bridge, involving a leisure centre and hotel, was late and over-budget. Rumours were circulating that money would be raised by selling players: Terry was bound for United and Gallas was on his way to Serie A. Favourite Zola had already left the club to wind down his career at home with Cagliari. The financial constraints meant no new stars on the horizon, the future looked blue to some fans.

With the limelight firmly focussed on the Spurs, Chelsea owner, Ken Bates, had breathing space to gird his loins for the forthcoming season. The interest in Gallas was opportune, and he played both Juventus and A.C. Milan off against each other before selling to Barcelona for an inflated fee of £7.7 million. Jimmy Floyd Hasselbaink was off-loaded for £4 million to newly promoted West Bromwich Albion. The 2003-2004 season had been earmarked as one for stability and team coalescence by the Chelsea manager, Ranieri. The loss of Gallas was a blow but the money had allowed him to keep John Terry, Jody Morris and Desailly.

Ranieri was well aware that his defence was aging, Graeme Le Saux was 34 and Albert Ferrer 32. However, Desailly has agreed to remain for another three years for a little extra money, thank goodness for Gallas! Emmanuel Petit would again partner Desailly. Jody Morris would provide excellent cover for the defence. The first game of the league season ends up with Liverpool dominating a game in which a lacklustre Chelsea fail to create any chances at Anfield, both Zenden and Gronkjaer have off-days. Liverpool win 2-0 and Chelsea leave frustrated.

Fortunately everybody clicks against MSK Zilinia to get into the Champions' League group stages and the tactical astuteness of the team gives everybody a lift. They fail to develop consistency in the Premiership and lose points unnecessarily, only managing draws against Leicester and Blackburn. The big derby game against Tottenham Hotspur arrives, the Spurs are a squad that oozes class with Makelele, Geremi, Duff, and Crespo all functioning in perfect harmony. The back line is virtually impenetrable and they are coasting at the top of the league. Chelsea make them work and only a trio of excellent goals by Crespo really separates the teams as Spurs take the points 3-2, the first victory over Chelsea in 25 years.

The only thing keeping the debt collectors at bay is the Champions League draw which reveals that Chelsea will end up playing Sparta Prague, Lazio and Besiktas in a tough group. Chelsea proceeds to romp past Wolves but lose their next three games to Birmingham, Aston Villa and Arsenal. They eventually grab a win against a poor Middlesbrough side.

In the Champions League, Chelsea really struggle and only manage to win two games and draw one whilst losing the other three, Chelsea slide out of the Champions League forcing the club to try to rearrange debt repayment. Players may have to be sold in the January transfer period. The younger fans are in uproar, the older ones shrug, remembering the dark days of the 1970s and 1980s. There will be no help from the Premier League or Uefa.

245

There may be a need to realign aspirations, to be more like Birmingham or Leicester than trying to emulate Manchester United, Liverpool or Arsenal. Attendances at the games is at an all time low; the club's future is looking bleak and it is rumoured Ken Bates has the yellow pages open to 'Administrators'.

Chelsea continue to struggle in the league and by January, after 19 league games, the club is hovering just above the relegation zone; ten games lost, five drawn, and only four won. Tottenham are flying at the top of the league, unbeaten all season. The pundits are tipping them hotly for the title and Chelsea to be battling against relegation. The January transfer window sees Lampard depart to Manchester United for £4 million, the core of the Chelsea squad is melting.

The rest of the season is more disappointment and Chelsea barely just escape relegation finishing one position above the bottom three. Aligned with poor F.A. Cup and League cup runs Claudio Ranieri is sacked as manager and former player Dennis Wise is brought in to try and steady the ship.

The following season more players have left including Le Saux, Gronkjaer and Zenden with no real quality replacing them. Gary McAllister has joined on a free from Liverpool to replace Lampard and Carlton Cole makes the step up to the first team. Predictably, Chelsea end up relegated. The only highlight being a decent League Cup run, getting to the semi-finals before losing to Liverpool.

Chelsea, joylessly start life in the football league for the first time since 1991. The side struggles to adapt and find they are languishing in the bottom third of the table as John Terry, the club captain, leaves to join Manchester United, Emmanuel Petit follows him out of the door to Palermo. The club end up 19th, but the loans for the two hotels and commercial premises are paid off; astute marketing sees 'Chelsea Village' operating at an average of 80% capacity year round; it is the place to be during the Chelsea flower show, Wimbledon, and Earls Court exhibitions. Marco Pierre's, Frankies and 55 are the 'in' places to eat and the beautiful people are in the leisure centre. Ken Bates puts the yellow pages away, nine points deducted now would have been catastrophic. The debt has just been about wiped out and is now in easy instalments that the club can afford, but the fans have stayed away and so have any players of real quality. Tottenham romp home to the third successive Premier League title of their history with Didier Drogba top scorer on 34 goals.

The 2006-2007 season is another season of consolidation for the club as new signing Matt Holland becomes a stalwart in the team dragging them to within inches of the playoff positions. The team, however, is completely unrecognisable to the team that was playing at Stamford Bridge just two seasons ago in the Premier League. Slowly, but surely, after a half decent season the fans start returning to the Bridge. For the first time in ten years the club is debt free and starts looking towards the future and acquiring some top players that will help them get out of the newly named Championship.

Chelsea begin the year having made their first transfer in four years, without the fear of being in the red hanging over their shoulders, bringing in Kevin Phillips for £2 million from West Bromwich Albion. Kevin Phillips shoots Chelsea, with the help of Matt Holland, to the Championship title. Tottenham have won everything there is to win in world football. They have destroyed Barcelona in the Champions League final 3-0 and then went to Tokyo to play in the Club World Cup Championship and are crowned World Club Champions.

Chelsea begin the next season in high hopes, the stands are full for the first time in four years and the club looks stable as they achieve eleventh position in the League. Even winning a huge game against Tottenham at White Hart Lane. That season Tottenham finally loosen their grip on world football and win only the League Cup as Arsene Wenger wields his magic.

The 2008-2009 season sees the old Chelsea swagger well and truly back in place. The success of the hotels and entertainment complex entice Londoner Richard Branson to join Ken Bates as a joint owner for an investment of £30 million. Branson, an inveterate self-promoter, moves into the top floor of the Millennium Hotel and the fans are pleased to see the Virgin Super Voyagers named after past Chelsea greats. The added capital gives them more latitude in the transfer market and after a couple of quality signings such as Stefan Peinaar and Tim Cahill, David Moyes is headhunted from Everton allowing Dennis Wise to take up a back room role at the club. Moyes leads the club to the F.A. Cup beating a strong Arsenal side 2-0.

The following season, the fans are delighted to see Branson and 'Mr Chelsea' Bates fight off a take-over bid from a Qatar consortium. Some of Branson's $4 billion are made available on very good terms to enable a new training ground to be developed and plans emerge for a stadium expansion. A change of venue is rejected as the Chelsea name would have to remain at

Stamford Bridge with the Chelsea Pitch Owners plc. The crowds come flooding back and so do the high ticket prices. The club is on a roll and signs some of the world's best players such as Sergio Aguero and Samuel Etoo in the summer. After ten games in the league have been played Chelsea are top and undefeated at home, but have lost away to top six rivals Aston Villa and Birmingham. Tottenham and Arsenal remain powerful rivals but Chelsea continue to have the upper hand on them in the Premier League race so far. The rest of the season looks bright for Chelsea, Branson has named a new Airbus A340 'Chelsea,' "for those Club World Cup matches".

Chapter 18

Tunney vs. Dempsey - the short count

Aron Donovan and Iain Adams

Research Preface

WILLIAM HARRISON DEMPSEY WAS BORN in Manassa, Colorado on 24 June, 1895. At 16, he left home and travelled around the small mining towns of Colorado and Nevada, working in the copper mines, mowing lawns, chopping wood, shining shoes and sometimes earning money in challenge fights. He often fought under the pseudonym 'Kid Blackie', and in 1914, as 'Jack Dempsey'. In 1916, he made the step up from barroom brawls to professional bouts and earned a reputation as a quick and lethal fighter who usually knocked his opponent out within the first round. He had "fast hands, fast feet, and frightening power" (Litsky, 1975: 86). After over 100 semi-professional and professional fights, he defeated Jess Willard to become the heavyweight champion. Durant (1976: 68) maintained:

> He had a perfect build and appearance of a fighter – high cheekbones, deep-set eyes, a bull neck, and a beautifully proportioned body. He was hard all over, in muscles and in mind. He was always in condition.

Rice (1954: 116-117) felt that:

> It was his speed, speed of hand as well as foot that made him such a dangerous opponent ... In the ring, he was a killer – a superhuman wildman ... He was a fighter – one who used every trick to wreck the other fighter.

Gene Tunney was born in New York on 25 May, 1897. Dropping out of school at 15, he became an office boy in a steamship company before turning to professional boxing in 1915. When America entered the First

World War in 1917, he joined the Marines and served in France, becoming the American Expeditionary Force light heavyweight champion. He resumed his civilian boxing career on return from Europe; known as the 'Fighting Marine' he steadily accumulated victories and became the North American Light Heavyweight champion by defeating 'Battling Levinsky' in 1922. However, he lost the title within months to Harry Greb in a mauling fight that went the full 15 rounds. Tunney regained the title the following year in another full distance match with Greb. Of Tunney, Beston (2007: 1) said:

> He was one of the ring's immortals, a master of defence and counterpunching, an early pioneer of strategy (he studied his opponents like a prosecuting attorney), and a fanatic about physical conditioning.

On September 23, 1926 at Sesquicentennial Stadium in Philadelphia, Tunney dethroned an out-of-form Dempsey before 120,757 fans. Dempsey had not fought for three years and was "thoroughly out-boxed over 10 rounds" (Lamkin, 2003). Howbeit, due to the huge interest in the fight and the commercial potential, "a rematch was all but guaranteed" (Lambkin, 2003). But he noted:

> The beating that Tunney had administered in their first fight was so great and decisive, that Dempsey would have to fight another ranked heavyweight in order to prove himself worthy of another title shot (Lambkin, 2003).

Dempsey briefly considered retiring, but in July 1927 he returned to the ring to defeat Jack Sharkey and earn the rematch with Tunney. The Tunney-Dempsey rematch was of epic proportions; two heavyweights fighting for the biggest prize, in front of 145,000 fans in Soldier Field, Chicago. The fans included Hollywood stars, politicians and gangsters such as Al Capone. Lowitt (1999) pointed out that "there were rumours that Al Capone had tried to fix the fight. Authorities took it seriously enough to replace referee Dave Miller with Dave Barry, a veteran of about 600 fights, at the last minute." Before the bout began, Barry took the boxers aside and reminded them that under the rules a fighter scoring a knockdown had to retreat to a neutral corner before the referee could begin his count.

Tunney took charge of the fight from the start, racking up points and keeping Dempsey at bay. In the seventh round, however, Dempsey knocked Tunney against the ropes and then felled him with three strong punches. Tunney went down, and Dempsey took a step back to the nearest corner, but not a neutral corner. Recalling the incident, Lowitt (1999) wrote:

Jack Dempsey's fist crashed into the champion's jaw. This was his chance. He waded in and Gene Tunney crumpled to the canvas. In 10 seconds, it appeared, Tunney would be counted out and Dempsey would be heavyweight champion again.

Barry rushed over to Dempsey and yelled, "Go to a neutral corner, Jack!" but Dempsey just stood there, glassy-eyed. Finally, Barry grabbed him and shoved him on his way. Dempsey shuffled across the ring, finally remembering the new rule that had been twice told to him before the match. Barry then began the 10-count, and Tunney got up at nine.

Tunney's total of 14 seconds on the ground allowed him valuable time to recuperate from Dempsey's assault. Tunney ducked and swayed, back-pedalling from his opponent for the rest of the round and then came back to dominate the eighth, even knocking Dempsey down briefly. Tunney won the bout by decision again.

Jack Dempsey retired after the fight, going on to open the successful *Jack Dempsey's Broadway Restaurant* in Times Square. In May 1983, Dempsey died of natural causes aged 87.

Gene Tunney was not married to boxing and as a result was not beloved by the fans. Beston (2007) thought he was "complicated and aloof, he never captured the imagination of the sporting public then or since, except as a poseur who had the gall to discuss his reading habits." Tunney died in 1978.

The fight went on to become Esquire Sports Poll's greatest fight of the century. Graffis and Cannon (1943: 180) concluded "those 14 seconds of that ten-round heavyweight championship fight, out of more than a billion and a quarter seconds that have been ticked off since the beginning of the century, compacted the drama of the sporting event."

In 1990, both fighters were inaugurated into the Boxing Hall of Fame.

References

Beston, P. (2007) The man who wasn't there, *The American Spectator* [online]. Available at http://spectator.org/archives/2007/02/22/the-man-who-wasnt-there (Accessed on 30 March 2010).

Durant, J. (1976) *The Heavyweight Champions*.: Hastings House Publishers, New York.

Graffis, H. and Cannon, R. (1943) *Long Count Fight*. Esquire, U.S.A.

Lamkin, M. (2003) *Historic Fights of the Century, Part III- 1920's: Gene Tunney vs. Jack Dempsey II (September 22nd, 1927)* [online]. Available at: http://www.fightbeat.com/judgejake/tunneydempsey2.php (Accessed on 30 March 2010).

Litsky, F. (1975) *Superstars*. Derbibooks Inc., Secaucus, New Jersey.

Lowitt, B. (1999) Long count allows Tunney to keep title. St. Petersburg Times [online], November 30, 1999. Available at: http://www.sptimes.com/News/113099/Sports/Long_count_allows_Tun.shtml (Accessed on 30th March 2010).

Na (1978) Gene Tunney dead at 80. The Miami News [online], November 8, 1978, Available at: http://news.google.com/newspapers?nid=71XFh8zZwT8C&dat=19781108&printsec=frontpage (Accessed On 1 April, 2010)

Rice, G. (1954) *The Tumult and the Shouting: My life in sport.* A.S. Barnes and Company, New York.

Creative Story

Tunney vs. Dempsey - the short count

Aron Donovan and Iain Adams

...8th November 1978, 93 Palm Avenue, Palm Island, Florida.

T HE BLOATED OLD MAN LIES BACK ON HIS SUN LOUNGER, Baccarat tumbler of moonshine in hand, watching the two naked blondes frolicking in his pool. He had acquired a taste for Minnesota girls during his St. Paul days. It's chilly for skinny dipping, but that's the way he likes them and he likes the effect of the chill; after all, they're his personal assistants. He's proud that he still distils the best moonshine in the country and still 'interviews' every girl seeking work in his brothels. He smiles to himself as he glances down at the *Miami News'* sports headline "Gene Tunney dead at 80". Sap, hadn't even made the front page, his mind wanders ...

...22nd September 1927, Soldier Field Stadium, Chicago, Illinois.

Boxing's biggest prize, the talk of the world; the greatest boxers to ever grace the ring, Gene Tunney, world champion, and Jack Dempsey, former champion. Everyone wants to see this fight. Soldier Field holds 61,500 people, but tonight there'll be over a 100,000. In barbershops, offices, factories and at shoeshine stands, confrontational discussions, one man says Tunney, the next Dempsey. "Tunney's the champ; he's gonna win". "Dempsey wants it bad, he needs that belt, he's gonna prove himself a winner again." It's a year ago yesterday that they previously met; Tunney out-boxed Dempsey and became the world champion. Today, Tunney may conclusively prove he's the best or perhaps Dempsey will gain revenge and retribution.

Nearly fight time; the stadium filling, 145,000 people cramming in for the big one, it'll be an epic, monumental. People will say "Where were you when..." Well, tonight, they're all here, politicians, entertainers and gangsters. Secretary of State Emerson moves towards his seat, his entourage includes US Solicitor General Mitchell and Chicago Mayor Thompson. They pause as Al 'Scarface' Capone rises, "Mr Secretary, Mr Solicitor-General, this is Al Capone" says the mayor. The men shake hands, "I know Al" says Mitchell to the mayor, "I was his lawyer in St Paul before Washington called." Capone smiled, "follow my advice gentlemen, you may be Tunney men, but put money on Dempsey, but Dempsey's been workin' hard". "Thanks for the tip" frowns Emerson leading his group off. Mitchell pauses at the next aisle by an aide who scurries off. Tex Rickard, the promoter, moves to the centre of the ring, "Ladies and Gentlemen, welcome to tonight's main event..."

Tunney appears with championship belt resplendent. Appreciative noise fills Soldier Field, 145,000 fans clapping and shouting. Tunney boogies into the ring, a quick sliding shuffle from left to right as the crowd chants "champ, champ!" Dempsey emerges, the noise is painful; Chicago loves Dempsey, the working class brawler. His magnanimity in last year's loss has moved him to sainthood. His name pulsates round as the fans stomp and scream, the juddering and throbbing resonate the ring ropes violently. Dempsey skips down the red carpet, bounces up the steps and into the ring, fit, energetic, ready to go, this man is prepared. The fighters stare, the pre-fight stare-down, who will look away first. The Manassa Mauler glares into, and through, The Fighting Marine. The referee, Barry, stands between Tunney and Dempsey. "Both you boys have received a book of rules of this boxing commission. They are the rules under which you are going to fight. Now I want to get one point clear. In the event of a knockdown, the man scoring the knockdown will go to the farthest neutral corner. Is that clear?" Tunney nods sharply, Dempsey bobs his head once. Then Barry continues, "in the event of a knockdown, unless the boy scoring it goes to the farthest neutral corner, I will not begin the count, OK, LETS GET IT ON!!!"

Round 1 - Dempsey charges out, older in years and much older through life, he wants this over. He throws a right, missing as Tunney glides back, and then slides forward to sneak in a jab to Dempsey's body, first points. Dempsey scores with a left and shoots out a vicious straight that finds only air. Tunney successfully jabs and takes a half step back as Dempsey rushes forward, a hard straight left into his face stops Dempsey in his tracks, an overhand right to his head drives him back. Tunney sashays forward to jab and Dempsey catches him with three short hard brawling swipes. The crowd roars its approval, "Get in there, Jack!" Tunney grimaces and coolly steps closer and pinions Dempsey's arms in his vice-like grip. Dempsey growls in rage and struggles to get free. "Break!" commands Barry. They step back, Tunney skips in and scores with another jab. The bell signals the end of round one, and its gone Tunney's way.

Round 2 – The champ's in control, circling the ring, Dempsey chasing; the big 20 foot ring not to Dempsey's liking. Dempsey swings erratically and unpredictably as if his body and brain are out of sync, he hasn't landed a clean punch yet. Tunney, the shrewd tactician, weaves away waiting for an opening. Abruptly he fires a blistering left to Dempsey's body. Dempsey steps back, settles into his familiar crouch and then presses forward shooting hooks at the fast-moving target. Tunney dispatches a stinging straight left to Dempsey's jaw stopping the charge, Dempsey tastes and swallows blood. Then a shower of short jabs from Tunney confuses Dempsey who covers his face and absorbs the punishment. As Tunney pauses, Dempsey moves close and for 10 seconds he is landing head shots, jabs, hooks, body shots. But Tunney steps in and wraps his arms around Dempsey pinning his arms to his side until the referee forces them to break. They swing around sparring until the bell rings, "Dempsey's trying, but its going our way" enthuses Emerson to Mitchell.

Round 3 – The fighters charge out; Dempsey tries to close, get Tunney into the maul zone for a few quick combos. "Keep on crowding him Jack, hold him close" yells 'Boo Boo' Hoff sitting by Capone. Tunney won't oblige and keeps boxing from a distance; he's spent too long analysing Dempsey to mix it in close. Tunney looks for the openings, building points. Dempsey tries left hook, right hook and a jab, but its thin air. Another rush, another straight left into his face, a cut opens above his right eye. "That's another round to Tunney, this fight's going the same way as the first" laughs a woman loudly.

Round 4 – Dempsey wants to finish this and comes out to land that killer blow. He crowds forward but is again stopped by Tunney's ever ready straight left, an overhand right to Dempsey's head shoves him back. And then they're both standing in the middle of the ring, trading blows; Dempsey jabs, Tunney uppercuts, Dempsey uppercuts, Tunney jabs. Dempsey moves in like a barroom brawler. "Tie him up like a bag, Genie" screams Emerson from the front row willing Tunney to use his steel band-like arms to pinion Dempsey again. Tunney obliges skating in and holding Dempsey, forcing another break. The crowd is roaring, screaming, going nuts. The bell rings and the referee splits them again. Tunney's fans are ecstatic, their man's streets ahead.

Round 5 – The crowd stands as the bell rings, wild shrieking and screaming as Tunney backpedals, Dempsey leading with a wild right trying to get in close; Tunney ducks, but the right was a fake to disguise a rush. A booming straight left into Dempsey's face rocks him backwards, his left eye begins to shut, another overhand right to the jaw piles up the points. "Atta-boy Genie, get some combos in." For long seconds the two stand toe to toe Dempsey swinging and Tunney blocking. The crowd are still screeching at the bell.

Round 6 – Another stupefying roar as the round opens, but the noise subdues, the pace is slower, the fighters are tiring, Dempsey breaks through and lands two hard blows, again Tunney is forced to step in and bind Dempsey's arms to his sides; Dempsey scowls and struggles. "Break!" Tunney dances away, Dempsey follows and leads with another right; Tunney responds in kind, Dempsey jabs, slips another jab but receives a hard overhand right to the jaw, it's beginning to swell. Several sharp blows follow on, points accumulating in Tunney's favour. "Jack got a couple of doozies in there" cries 'Boo Boo' as the bell clangs.

Round 7 – Tunney presses forward, looking fresher, Dempsey advances and Tunney retreats, but is momentarily constricted by the ropes in the corner. Dempsey seizes the opportunity and launches a combination of punches, two rights, two lefts to the chin, Tunney staggers disoriented; "This is it Jack, FINISH HIM". Dempsey suddenly metamorphoses into the Dempsey of old, the blows he has been dreaming of unleashing flow as four catastrophic punches, left-right, left-right, crash the champ to the floor. Tunney grabs the middle rope to stop the world spinning, shaking his head. He hears the timekeeper intoning "ONE...TWO", the referee shouting "Go to a neutral corner, Jack!" "THREE." The referee moves away pushing Dempsey towards the neutral corner, "FOUR", the referee is back above Tunney and Tunney hears him join the timekeeper's beat "FIVE...SIX," "Five! The referee started his count at five, that's not fair" shouts somebody in the crowd. "SEVEN." "How can he start his count on five" exclaims another indignantly. "EIGHT," Tunney gets a knee under himself balancing with his right glove on the floor, "NINE", it's all in slow motion, "TEN".

 The stadium erupts. "Jesus, that's an outrageous end to a brilliant fight" moans a Tunney fan. "And It's spoilt by an innumerate referee who can't count" yells his wife. Dempsey, glassy eyed, is led by the referee to the middle, cries of "fix! Fix! FIX!" come from sections of the crowd. "This is madness, a controversial end to such a magnificent fight. No one can take away this victory from Dempsey, he was magnificent tonight, but what a horrible way for Tunney to lose, a short count" notes a journalist. Rickard steps into the spotlight, "Ladies and Gentlemen, I give you your new world heavyweight champion, Jack 'The Manassa Mauler' Dempsey, the first man to re-capture the heavyweight title of the world". Dempsey's arm is hoisted into the air as the title belt is fixed around his waist.

Rejuvenated old legs carry Dempsey to Tunney's corner, "Gene, you were best. You fought a smart fight, kid. That's it for me, I retire right now!" He hoists Tunney's arm aloft to a roar of approval from the hordes. Emerson makes his way out, Mitchell pauses as a runner gives him a package, moving past Capone he briefly stops and shakes his hand ."Your boy lucked out tonight; don't forget to pay your taxes on the winnings!" He glances back as Emerson leads them off; Capone catches his eye and mouths "You owe me one."

...8th November 1978, 93 Palm Avenue, Palm Island, Florida.

The old man chuckles at memories, only one year in prison. Those bastards Elliot Ness and Frank Wilson tried to put him away for ever, but Mitchell, Attorney General by then, threw out most of the prosecution evidence. He paid his dues. The very thought of Ness and Wilson brought on chest pain, Jesus, crushing pain. Through gritted teeth he wheezes "Holly, Vicky". They rush to him. Suddenly he is floating above watching the two naked girls performing CPR on him, Doc Phillip's taught them well. Crash teams like that would improve *Emergency!*'s ratings. It's been a good life, if this is death, it ain't so bad.

...9th November 1978, 93 Palm Avenue, Palm Island, Florida.

'Scarface dead at 78' screams the *Miami News*.

Chapter 19

The blackest day (Senna / Schumacher)

Chris Medlan and Iain Adams

Research Preface

THE UNTIMELY DEATH OF AYRTON SENNA, the Brazilian Formula One (F1) driver, in 1994 was chosen because it deprived many young F1 enthusiasts of the opportunity to see one of the greatest drivers in action (timesonline.co.uk). The era since saw Michael Schumacher emerge, not only as the best of the time, but, possibly, as the greatest ever. The impact of Senna's death is clear, with Andrew Benson, the BBC's Motorsport editor, describing it as "the crash that claimed the life of the man many believe to have been the greatest racing driver the world has ever seen." He also stated that "it is not just F1 people who will be remembering Senna...for his death was felt across the world" (Benson, 2004).

However, the obvious 'What if Ayrton Senna had not been killed' is not followed, this story examines the possible impact on the German driver, Schumacher, who was closely following Senna at the time of the accident (BBC Evening News, 1994). Schumacher was acknowledged by Benson (2004) as "Senna's successor as the best driver in the world". Schumacher went on to become the most successful driver in the history of F1, winning seven World Championships and 91 races.

The race was part of a season that "was marred by Ayrton Senna's death then spoiled by controversy as Michael Schumacher beat Damon Hill to the crown in questionable fashion" (Jones, 2005: 229). Senna's death overshadowed the whole of the San Marino race, leading to most enthusiasts having a hazy recollection of the rest of the event. In fact,

Schumacher won, Nicola Larinin achieved his only F1 podium finish in second and Mika Häkkinen was third. The 1994 season was to culminate in Schumacher's first world title, but if the German's career had also ended at San Marino, then F1 would have lost two of its most successful and best drivers on the same day, the day Murray Walker described as "the blackest day for Grand Prix racing that I can remember" (BBC, 1994).

The day was part of a weekend of accidents. In Friday's practice Rubens Barrichello clipped the curb in his Jordan at the Variante Bassa curve and somersaulted several times. He was knocked unconscious and only prompt actions by the race officials saved his life as he had swallowed his tongue. After Barrichello's accident Damon Hill voiced a common view of the drivers; "we all brushed ourselves off and carried on qualifying, reassured that our cars were tough as tanks and we could be shaken but not hurt" (Hill, 2004: 1). Then on Saturday, Austrian rookie Roland Ratzenburger damaged his Simtek's front wing in an off track excursion but, as he was on his final qualifying session and fighting for the last grid position, carried on. On the next lap the wing came off at high speed and rendered the steering useless; the car wouldn't turn into the Villeneuve corner of the Tamburello Curve and he hit the concrete barrier head on. He died just 200 metres further on from where Senna would crash. It is known that Senna was considering not racing and even retiring following Ratzenburger's death. His possible ruminations provide ideas for Schumacher's reflections.

The race was going to be between Senna and Schumacher, the pair separated by only 0.337 of a second in qualifying. Berger's Ferrari was a significant 0.565 further back. The start of the race was marred by a further incident when Lehto stalled his Benetton on the grid and Lamy's Lotus rear-ended it sending wreckage over the pit wall injuring several spectators. A rolling re-start behind the pace car meant cool tyres and, therefore, tricky car handling. However, after only two laps of clear racing there was a substantial gap between the first two cars, Senna and Schumacher, and the rest of the field. Although it can never be fully proven, Senna appeared to suffer a loss of downforce causing the rear of the car 'to step out', he steered into the drift but the front tyres gripped hard and swung the car off the track to the right. His phenomenal reactions managed to slow the car from 195 mph to 131 mph before he hit the wall (Chapman, nd). Senna's car rebounded back onto the track with the Brazilian motionless in the cockpit. Most of this will have been visible to Schumacher as he was following closely. The drivers were unaware of the severity of the accident at the time, and the race was restarted once the debris of Senna's accident was cleared.

The news only came through to the other drivers after the race, so they raced oblivious to Senna's death. It is this unknowning phase that is utilised in the story, before further information changes his feelings and emotions.

In order to portray the emotions that develop from the witnessed accident, the story is told from Schumacher's perspective because:

> We would be forced into his mind and so have to view events which befall him through his own eyes. This idea that we would have to take our version of the story from one of the people actually involved in it...would also have a large effect on our reactions to the story (Boran, 2005: 176).

However, the story is told in the third person, with Schumacher as the central character whose emotions and feelings are portrayed. Using Michael, rather than Schumacher, should make the reader feel closer to Schumacher, as if they are a colleague or close friend in whom he confides. Other drivers are more remote, unknown, and so surnames are used.

The focus of the story is race day and the changing emotions of Schumacher. The medium and long term consequences of Senna's death are not explored in this story until the very end, hopefully developing tension.

Ironically, safety concerns had led the drivers to propose re-forming the Grand Prix Drivers' Association, which aimed to improve and maintain safety, at the drivers' briefing on the morning of the San Marino race. Senna was appointed one of its director's hours before his death.

References

BBC Evening News, Sunday May 1st, 1994. 'Announcing the death of Ayrton Senna', [online]. Available at: http://www.youtube.com/watch?v=PMEv_XC6ObQ (Accessed 2nd April, 2010)

BBC News (1994) 'Race ace Senna killed in car crash' [online]. Available at: http://news.bbc.co.uk/onthisday/hi/dates/stories/may/1/newsid_2479000/2479 971.stm (Accessed 2nd April, 2010).

Benson, A. (2004) A death that shocked the world. BBC Sport [online]. Available at: http://news.bbc.co.uk/sport1/low/motorsport/formula_one/3605579.stm (Accessed 2nd April, 2010)

Boran, P. (2005) The Portable Creative Writing Workshop. New Island, Dublin.

Chapman, B. (nd) 'Case Study #2, Ayrton Senna, death of a champion' [online]. Available at http://www.benchapman.com/project/senna1.html (Accessed 2nd April, 2010).

Hill, D. (2004) Had Ayrton foreseen his death? The Times, April 17, 2004 [online]. Available at:http://www.timesonline.co.uk/tol/sport/formula_1/article826864.ece (Accessed 2nd April 2010)

Jones, B. (Ed.) (2005) *55 Years of the Formula One World Championship*, Carlton, London.

Creative Story

The blackest day (Senna / Schumacher)

Chris Medland and Iain Adams

S CHUMACHER ARRIVED EARLY AT IMOLA. He wasn't the only one; all of the drivers were at the 'Autodrome Enzo e Dino Ferrari' well in advance of their usual team briefings. Michael thought this a nuisance, but one he couldn't ignore. Senna was leading a safety meeting that most of the drivers had requested; they needed solidarity now more than ever.

As Michael strolled along the quiet paddock, the morning sunshine warmed the right side of his face. He took a coffee from his Benetton team's deserted motor home and walked around to the Williams' motor home where some of his counterparts were already seated around a small round table. He and other latecomers stood behind them. There was desultory chatting; all the focus was on Senna. Sat in a plain white T shirt and jeans, Senna took a brief role call. Michael looked out of the window at the dappled sunlight breaking through the trees and wished for the time to pass so he could focus on the race. It wasn't as if he didn't feel saddened at Ratzenberger's death the previous day, nor that he didn't feel the need for change, but this could wait. Ratzenberger was a rookie, he, Michael Schumaker, would never make a mistake that would cost him his life, but he knew he should never become complacent; for fear that he might get careless.

"OK, we'll pick up the issue of these slow pace cars at the next meeting, along with diffuser size reduction and the front wing issues. Next meeting at Monaco, 14th May, same time, same place, thanks for coming and good luck today" ended Senna.

Though Michael had been fully involved in the discussions, the sheer length of time that had passed had cost him race focus, but Senna's words were like an alarm clock. It was time to get to work. By now the world's media were waiting outside for the drivers. Michael easily ducked the helmet

263

sniffers and jogged down the bustling paddock to his garage, Senna would speak to the media. Small beads of sweat accumulated around his hairline by the time he reached the garage, it was warm. The gentle perspiration triggered the adrenaline and it began to slowly eke into his blood system; bring on the early afternoon and the green lights!

With his mechanics busy around his car, like beavers around a dam, Michael was interviewed by the former F1 driver Jochen Mass who worked for RTL, the German television network. "How're you feeling?" It was a question he didn't expect, but he should've he thought reproachfully. As soon as he gave his answer he'd reassured himself. "Fine, I just have to concentrate on winning, that's why I'm here." He felt no remorse for being "fine", but he knew a more tactful answer could've deflected the next.

"Do you feel safe driving here?" asked Mass. "I don't feel safe driving anywhere, that's the challenge. I'm racing to be the fastest and find the limit and push it, to win. I win when I push past the others' limits, but I only win if I finish! So I don't worry about crashing, that's never my intention." "Thanks Michael, very good luck here today" closed Mass.

Cleared from his media obligations, Michael stepped into the car. He didn't mind the interviews; they were part of the nature of what he did. He quite liked RTL too, employing Mass was good strategy. F1 was its own little bubble so Michael spoke to the same faces at each circuit. It helped him relax, he knew what to expect and was comfortable, whereas he wasn't particularly physically comfortable in his car. But he liked it that way; if he was uncomfortable he'd want to get to the finish quicker than anyone else so he could get out again! He felt part of the machine as soon as he sat in it, and his mind seemed to disengage from everything other than what was in his hands and under his feet.

As the adrenaline release reached every corner of his body, time seemed to fluctuate. Michael felt as if one minute lasted a second, and the next lasted an hour. But a flash of green above his eyes triggered a reaction in his right foot and signaled the beginning of a seismic Grand Prix.

Within seconds though, it was on hold again, the safety car was out and they paraded slowly around for three laps until debris was cleared. Senna timed the restart to perfection, slowing right down, causing the following cars to come to a virtual standstill behind him and then rocketed away. Schumacher was a little annoyed to be caught out and was still 0.6 seconds behind, according to his pit board, at the end of the lap. However,

Schumacher had noticed the Williams bottom out at Tamburello corner causing it to twitch violently, not nice. He knew that only Senna could prevent him being the first to see the black and white checked blur. Therefore, he needed to get past now, before the tyre pressures on the Williams came back up and lifted it sufficiently to avoid contact with the uneven track surface at Tamburello. Even on the smoother sections of the circuit, Senna was struggling, a sight that filled Michael with more adrenaline. Approaching Tamburello next time around would be the place to push Senna, force him into an error; this was his for the taking.

The tricky handling of the Williams allowed Michael to brake slightly later into Variante Bassa and accelerate out earlier, so as they charged down the start/finish straight Michael's Benetton was all over the back of the Williams gently weaving so that Senna didn't know from which side any attack would begin. As they entered the long curve to the left the Benetton seemed to kiss the William's left side, the Williams twitched and suddenly ran wide to the right. "Ahh, got you, I wouldn't lose focus like that" thought Michael. Out of the corner of his eye he caught the Williams smack the wall and then, in his mirrors, rebound off the concrete shedding debris. He afforded himself a smirk, that car was not going to finish the race! The stricken car rapidly shrinking in Michael's mirrors filled him with satisfaction, knowing he'd pushed Senna into an error. The slight smile that cracked across Michael's face was known only unto him, but this was soon replaced by an apprehension that all he could do now was lose the race. As quickly as that emotion came it was overcome by frustration; red flags and another start.

While he knew it was for Senna, Michael asked no questions over the delay. He had to concentrate. One slip and an easy victory would embarrassingly get away. He didn't let it.

As Michael ascended the steps to the podium with a swagger that bordered on the arrogant, four words from an official slowed him, "Ayrton doesn't look good." Michael deemed good grace was important. He stood, shook hands, and didn't spray champagne. As he descended the stairs, he pondered what those four words meant. Before going into the press conference, a quick briefing told the drivers that "Ayrton didn't make it. He's been pronounced clinically dead. Take your time, but expect that to be all you're asked about."

Taking his time wasn't important in Michael's mind, nor was the press meeting. He removed the sponsor-adorned cap from his still damp head,

265

placed it on the floor and turned on his heel. He retraced his steps back to the garage and stood there alone, gazing along the main straight towards Tamburello as the sun dappled the race track. He was a part of a sport where he had enjoyed watching one of the 19 like-minded people, with whom he was sharing tarmac, veer off to the end of their life, whether he'd known the outcome or not. In essence the moment that Senna died had caused Michael pleasure. He felt sickened. Whereas hours previously he had stood and felt adrenaline released, now he was standing feeling every sense drain from him, He'd never known what being numb felt like, it felt like his body was rejecting who he was.

Then that same question returned, Mass had approached silently, diffidently. "How're you feeling?" Michael had a burning desire to not be anywhere near the bubble that was F1 anymore, let alone float inside it. He wanted to disappear as quickly as Senna, or indeed Ratzenberger, that weekend. Michael looked into Mass's grieving face, he too had known Senna. "Empty. I think I should say goodbye" he replied softly, Mass gently nodded his head once.

At that point Michael burst out of the bubble, and walked away from F1 more purposefully than he'd driven in it.

Days followed when Michael watched the world mourn his Brazilian rival, a state funeral in São Paulo, 500,000 lining the route, all of F1 had been there, except Moseley who had gone to Ratzenberger's funeral. He couldn't escape the bubble as it stretched to encircle him. Benetton would call, every team would call, Ecclestone would call, but Michael didn't respond.

He never knew if he felt like every other driver would have in his position, but it didn't bother him. He was ashamed of himself and if others were like-minded he was ashamed of them too. He wasn't warmed every time he saw a team withdraw. The sponsor on the cap he'd left on the floor had followed him away from the sport, as did many others. Michael knew he could breathe some new life back into F1 if he reappeared, but he didn't want it to have a new life. He wanted it to have no life at all.

Enough time had gone by that Michael had forgotten what it felt like to smile – the last time was within his helmet as Senna's car disappeared in his mirrors. But the day his phone stopped ringing, and a two week old paper informed him of the final demise of F1, he felt a twitch on the left side of his lips that betrayed the feeling that one man could make a difference.

Chapter 20

Fall from grace (Jonny Wilkinson)

Craig Davies and Iain Adams

Research Preface

GEORGE JONNY WILKINSON IS A 30 YEAR OLD England International Rugby Union player, who plies his trade at French club Toulon. He hit the big time on the 22nd November 2003, when he announced himself on a worldwide level whilst at the Rugby World Cup in Australia with England. Renowned for his left footed kicking abilities, he wasn't in the best of form leading up to the finals. He did though guide England all the way through to the finals, where they played the hosts Australia in the Telstra Stadium in Sydney. With 26 seconds left on the clock Wilkinson cemented his place in English sporting folklore, with a drop goal in extra time to win his side the Rugby World Cup (Wilkinson, 2009). England went rugby, and more specifically Jonny Wilkinson, mad and the frenzy surrounding him has never subsided. Before the 2003 World Cup he held sponsorship deals with Lucozade, Tetleys, Lloyds TSB, Hacket and Adidas. It is the latter that is perhaps the most significant though. Prior to his famous drop goal the deal he held with the clothing giant was worth approximately £250,000 a year. On the 12th December, just 19 days after his heroics, Wilkinson signed a bumper £2m a year contract with Adidas directly as a result of the World Cup. With his heightened profile and status around the world, it was seen as imperative that his services were kept (MacMillan, 2003).

On top of this, in the months leading up to the World Cup, Adidas had screened a series of advertisements featuring both Wilkinson and David

Beckham. This series was continued, with Wilkinson almost being branded as rugby's version of the football worldwide mega star. This helped add to the clean cut image being built up, also putting him to the forefront as Rugby's 'pin up.' More importantly, these few months helped symbolise Wilkinson as a winner, a player who succeeded both on and off the pitch in all ventures to which he turned his hand. On the pitch, at club level, he was seen as the main player for Newcastle Falcons, a side who would undoubtedly fail without their star. He gave most of his career to the side, and was seen as a superstar in the North East, more so than the rest of the world, as they thought of him as one of their own. After 2003, Wilkinson suffered with persistent injuries keeping him out in the wilderness for long periods for both club and country. Any other player would have simply fallen off the radar, been a 'what if' case as people pondered what effect he could have had if he had stayed fit. While the public have had these thoughts about Wilkinson, they have largely been unnecessary. He has of course suffered with injuries, but when fit or even half fit he has always been fast tracked back into the Newcastle and England squad. Had he not succeeded with the all important drop goal in the World Cup final, it is debatable that he would be held in such high esteem by the management. He is simply always in the England squad, as it is believed that they do not possess a talisman that is capable of filling his boots in the national side, a belief borne, and built upon, since his winning kick in the Telstra Stadium.

After years of injuries, bit part appearances and below par performances for the Newcastle Falcons, Wilkinson announced, during the 2008/09 season, his decision to leave at the end of that season. A return to fitness and form with club and country ensured plenty scrambled for his signature. This frenzy was directly as a result of his return to the national scene, where he moved from strength to strength. His re-inclusion was a second chance that would never have come about had his 2003 kick gone differently. Reputation counts for everything, and the argument couldn't be avoided that the kick was the reason for his instant return to the international fold. The scramble for his signature was eventually won by the French club Toulon, undoubtedly aided by the lack of salary cap in France. Sensibly with his injury history, Wilkinson took full advantage to bag himself a £700,000 a year wage (Mairs, 2009). His form in France has been outstanding, and a spell without injury has seen his fine form return with an England shirt back on. It is highly unlikely that this move to France and return to the international scene would have occurred had fate not intervened in 2003, and the rugby public wouldn't constantly hear that he has now 'back to his best.' A best that refers to the form he showed on his way to winning his nation the World Cup. That one moment in the World Cup changed Jonny Wilkinson's life, and propelled him to the superstar status that he now holds. Had he not kept his nerve, composure and, more crucially, his calm, Jonny Wilkinson would have been in a very different position today. It would be very doubtful that he would be thought of as one of England's true greats, and he certainly wouldn't have had all the offers of a big money move to France where he has been revitalised. He is now an integral cog for England, a side that currently can't seem to perform at the op level when he is not in the team. If he had missed the drop goal attempt in 2003, there is no way of knowing how he would have reacted. If he had allowed his head to drop following the potential miss, anybody outside of rugby may have struggled to remember who he is or was. England and Toulon need him too perform, and as a result of the events of all those years ago, he has worked harder and harder to become the player he is today.

References

Dunning, E. and Sheard, K. (2005) *Barbarians, Gentlemen and Players: A social study of the development of rugby football.* Routledge, London.

MacMillan, G. (12 March 2003) Jonny Wilkinson signs £2m Sponsorship Deal with Adidas. *BrandRepublic* [online]. Available at:
http://www.brandrepublic.com/news/198028/jonny-wilkinson-signs-2m-sponsorship-deal-adidas/ (Accessed on 6th April 2010).

Mairs, G. (18th May 2009) Jonny Wilkinson looking for 'fresh start' at Toulon. Daily Telegraph [online]. Available at:
http://www.telegraph.co.uk/sport/rugbyunion/club/5343256/Jonny-Wilkinson-looking-for-fresh-start-at-Toulon.html (Accessed 6th April 2010).

Nauright, J. R. and Chandler T. J. L. (1995) *Making Men: Rugby and masculine identity.* Cass, London.

Wilkinson, J. (2009) *Tackling life: Striving for perfection*, Headline, London.

Creative Story

Fall from grace (Jonny Wilkinson)

Craig Davies and Iain Adams

THE 22ND NOVEMBER 2003 SHOULD HAVE BEEN a landmark day for English Sport, the day we went 'down under' and tamed the Aussies on their own patch in the final of the Rugby World Cup. I'll never forget that day, I was only twelve, and it was overwhelming. Sydney's Telstra Stadium, the scene of one of the most remarkable events anyone will ever witness. 17-17 the scoreboard read, and the clock was frantically ticking away to zero. That's when the chance came, 26 seconds left and everything just seemed to stop.

We've all had those moments where time seems to stand still, the screams of jubilation and expectation seem to span a lifetime. The scene was set, a drop goal in the dying seconds to bring the trophy home with the poster boy of English Rugby waiting for his moment in the spotlight.

For those of you who don't know the name of this man once heralded as a superstar, the man who broke our dreams, he was once the 'great' Jonny Wilkinson.

For a man so renowned for his cool exterior, he looked remarkably anxious. Maybe that was his downfall; it was as if you could see the weight of more than 50million people pushing down on his shoulders. In that moment the calm persona was lost, and he was a lost little boy surrounded by 29 animals that would've done anything for that success. In that second, which seemed to stretch for an hour, the faith disappeared and as boot connected with ball all hope was gone. The ball span away contemptuously wide of the posts as the crowd turned into vultures, and at such a young age, I found myself dragged into the hate mob mentality.

Anger, frustration and most of all depression encapsulated the Red Rose portion of the 82,957 crowd. Not half an hour had passed, but the mood

270

had shifted dramatically. There were no more wild passionate chants of 'swing low sweet chariot,' just an emptiness that should've been filled with a gleaming golden trophy.

As the Australian celebrations continued inside, there was an eerie silence amongst the departing England fans. The thunder of the crowd had died down, as the unpredictability of what had occurred took hold. Cries of "he's finished" rang out; never had a truer word been spoken. I found myself taken over by the unbelievable loathing that filled the air.

Posters, pictures, banners, magazines, you name it, if Jonny Wilkinson was on it, or appeared in it, I had collected it. When the vast hoard was shifted into bin bags following our return from Oz, only one thing remained as a reminder. Wilkinson's replica black strip of the Newcastle Falcons, a team I had initiated myself into some years previous.I wasn't about to turn my back on them, after all they were giving me a chance to make it into professional rugby and despite what had happened they were my team.

The affection I once felt towards the one time superstar was so much so that I supported his team, and got into rugby to try to emulate the pride of the Falcons. I wasn't alone, kids up and down the country did the same and men and women adored him too.

After that fateful November day everybody's opinions changed, he had choked on the ultimate stage and was never the same again. Like a pantomime villain he was vilified at every ground. Crowds driven by anger seemed to turn up just to show their disgust, and it showed on Wilkinson. The ease with which he previously carried himself on the pitch disappeared. The kicking game that had become his signature fizzled away, and a shell of the man remained. Exclusion from the national pool was inevitable, yet still he continued week in and week out at club level.

As the months and years passed by, this only served as more incentive to strive to replace him at the club I love. He wasn't fit to wear the shirt, and it was like a dagger through the heart each time I was unfortunate enough to witness such an outcome taking place. Faith was kept despite his obvious backward steps; I needed to graduate to the first team.

Constantly being told you are "nearly there" gets frustrating after a while. Each day in training I was more intense than the last, improving all areas of my game. Crunching into tackles and making each and every one, running the ball and leaving everyone chasing shadows. It was taking shape, but there was, of course, the more obvious side. Kicking, if I wanted the number ten jersey, it had to be spot on and it couldn't get any better. Like an archer slicing an apple off his son's head from thirty paces, nothing was too difficult.

The call eventually came half way through the 2008/09 season. As I approached my eighteenth birthday, I found myself thrust into the first team squad. I was now competing on a day to day basis with the man I had been striving to overtake in the pecking order; it seemed only a matter of time before my wish came true. I out performed him every day, but never even made it on the field as a replacement never mind as a starter.

For over a month, I had been busting my gut to prove I was worthy, and eventually all the painstaking effort paid off. Another lacklustre performance pushed the boss over the edge, Wilkinson was off, I was on. For a few moments I was struck with overwhelming awe, it only seemed like yesterday we were in Sydney having our hearts broken. Now I was replacing the man who had caused all the pain, against the reigning champions. As Wilkinson slowly slumped off, an amazing sense of guilt swept over me but had to get on with it. To succeed long term I needed this chance, plus I deserved this crack after all the extra hours in training. Although the crowd was more like 10,000 than 90,000, the noise was incredible. Whether that was for the decision to take him off or bring me on I don't know. I'd like to think the latter; after all I am a local lad.

As we entered the final stages the score was tied, one chance was all I needed. I was almost begging to the heavens when my prayers seemed to be answered, a penalty gave me the chance to secure the win. The out of control screams from the sidelines highlighted the importance, as if I needed to be told. I could feel the adrenaline pumping through me; my heart was raging like a hyper runaway train. The ball was on the tee, only one thing left to do. One deep breath calmed the nerves, three strides and one swing later and it was off, sailing towards its target. Elation doesn't cover the enormous relief and pride that was felt at that moment, the whole team streamed onto the pitch to celebrate. Minus one solemn figure, a lonely blonde haired fly half trudged down the tunnel alone, wondering where it all went wrong.

For the rest of the season that spot was mine, nothing had ever felt better. I started every game while the man I had set out to ruin sat on the bench longing to turn back the clock six years. I was number one, and when the curtain fell on the season it was made explicitly clear that that's the way it was going to stay.

Although I had set out to push Jonny Wilkinson out of the Newcastle shirt, no one was prepared for what we all heard next. "That's it, I'm done. I've had it with this game; from this moment on I'm officially retired."

Shock, delight and, strangely, guilt were mixed in a strange emotional cocktail. In a few short years I had achieved my ultimate ambition, and had ruined the man I had once aspired to be. Somehow though it just didn't feel right, despite everything deep down I knew I still idolised the man.

The news though barely made a ripple, "about time" seemed to be the general consensus amongst the public. TV stations and column inches devoted the smallest space possible to report the news, if any, a sad end for the man who was supposedly the saviour of English rugby. For me though it was the end of a tragic story and a significant part of my life, but also the beginning of something beautiful.

Words can't explain the hurt that was felt that day in the Telstra Stadium. Each minute that followed the incredible miss seemed to last a lifetime. I had envisaged a thousand endings, not one like that. Instead of propelling himself into stardom, Wilkinson wilted on the ultimate stage. Routine went out of the window, followed by professionalism under pressure. Now though everything seemed to have worked out, after long years and hard work.

So here I am, first choice at my club with an international call only a matter of time. Step aside, the real saviour of the nation's rugby pride is here and I don't fear anything, nothing can stop me.

My name I hear you ask, well the Newcastle fans know, keep your eye's peeled, I'll be hitting the headlines very soon.

What if… Jesse Owens was white?

Emma Jones and Iain Adams

Research Preface

JESSE OWENS, AN AFRICA AMERICAN athlete, won four gold medals at the 1936 Berlin Olympic Games, the 100 metres, the 200 metres, the long jump, and in the four by 100 metres relay team (Schaap, 2007). He was born on 12th September, 1913, the son of a share cropper and the seventh of eleven children. Being black, Owens faced prejudice throughout his life, even as a star athlete at Ohio State University. He was not allowed to live in the dormitories or eat at high street restaurants.

In 1933, Hitler's National Socialists came to power in Germany. Hitler wanted to expand the borders of Germany to include all Germanic, Aryan, people, and exclude all non-Aryan people. Aryans were ideally blonde haired and blue eyed and would prove to be racially superior to all other people. Official Nazi policy was to remove non-Aryan's from Germany, this included Jews, Gypsies and other non-desirables such as homosexuals. There were not many people of African descent in Germany and overt anti-Black policies were not noticeable, although "blacks could not hide" according to an Afro-German holocaust survivor (Lusane, 2003). The 1936 Olympic Games, awarded to Germany before Hitler came to power, would provide an ideal propaganda tool for Hitler's Nazis. However, the International Olympic Committee (IOC) felt that the Nazi ideology was a contradiction of the Olympic Charter and Avery Brundage of the American Olympic Committee (AOC) stated that the "AOC must not be involved in political, racial, religious or sociological controversies" (Guttman, 2002: 59). Due to the extreme racial views of the Nazis, boycotts were proposed in the USA, Britain and France as well as some other countries. Brundage was dispatched on a fact finding mission to Germany in 1934. Hitler ordered that everything must be done to convey the image of a peace-minded, non-threatening Germany ready to rejoin the international community (Speer, 1971). Germans were ordered not to wear uniform unless on duty, 'Jews not admitted' signs were removed from restaurants and bars, hoteliers were ordered to be pleasant to everybody, martial music was banned from the radio and the worst anti-Semitic newspaper, *Der Sturmer*, was banned for the run up and duration of the games. Brundage saw German Jews training with the German squad and recommended the Americans accept the invitation to participate in Berlin. The IOC received written confirmation that German Jews had the right to try out for the team (Guttman, 2002). The threat of an official boycott was over. Once the Olympics were guaranteed, the Jewish athletes in the German training camps were removed as not being good enough. Ideally Hitler would have liked other nations to also 'cleanse' their teams of all non-Aryans, but as they wouldn't it was a chance to show the dominance of the Aryan race (Gentry, 1990).

Hitler's concept of impressing the world resulted in superb facilities for the games. An Olympic Bell was introduced to the proceedings and the games opened with a flame lit in Olympia and run by relay across Europe. Again for the first time, the games were televised, although only in 25 halls around Berlin due to technological limitations, and were broadcast by radio to 40 countries. News reels edited from Leni Riefenstahl's cameras were sent out daily around the world to be shown in cinemas.

The United States took a team of 312 members with 18 African Americans, including Jesse Owens, to Berlin (United States Holocaust Memorial Museum, 2009). On the first day, the 100m preliminary rounds took place with Owens going in the final heat. He finished the race in a time that equalled the world record, and then in his second round race he beat the record. However the officials dubbed it as wind assisted and Owens' time was not entered into the record book. But this did not matter; Owens was in the 100m final and even with him being a black athlete, young Germans still clambered to get his autograph (Gentry, 1990).

On the day of the 100m finals, Owens appeared to be very calm and was chatting to his fellow competitors on the starting line. However as soon as the athletes were called to their marks, he focused on only one thing and that was winning. He achieved this with ease and after winning a further three Gold medals many felt that he had successfully embarrassed Hitler and the Nazis by demonstrating that the Aryan race was not superior (Mandell, 1987).

However, Shirer, an American journalist wrote:

> I'm afraid the Nazis have succeeded with their propaganda. First, they have run the games on a lavish scale never before experienced, and this has appealed to the athletes. Second they have put on a very good front for the general visitors, especially the big businessmen" (Shirer, 1972: 58).

Bramsted (1965: 151) thought that "seen in an historical perspective, they (the Berlin Olympics) formed a high-water mark in the successful technique of Nazi persuasion by effective mass communications, pageantry, and showmanship".

The significance of Jesse Owens' performances in Berlin lies, not only in exposing the sham of Aryan supremacy, but also in the promotion of black athletes on a world stage. Owens and his African-American colleagues enjoyed the freedom to travel unrestricted on public transport and to eat and drink in any place they wanted. Freedoms denied in the USA. Owens was loved by many white Americans because of his performances, observance of the American flag and his seeming acceptance of the status quo in America. Along with Joe Louis, he was a hero to white America. However, undoubtedly, his performances opened doors to other black Americans who were not so complacent (Sailes, 2003).

On his return to the USA, Owens felt snubbed by the US hierarchy and fell on hard times before finally being honoured in 1976 with the Presidential Medal of Freedom, the highest honour for a civilian (Daily News and Trends, 2009). He went on to work with the youth of the poorer neighbourhoods and become a world wide speaker inspiring many other athletes and Afro-Americans. After Owens death in 1980, President Carter summed up the true achievements of Jesse Owens life "Perhaps no athlete better symbolized the human struggle against tyranny, poverty and racial bigotry. His personal triumphs as a world-class athlete and record holder were the prelude to a career devoted to helping others" (The Jessie Owens Foundation, 1999: 1).

References

Bramsted, E.K. (1965) *Goebbels and National Socialist Propaganda 1925-1945.* East Lancing, Michigan State University Press.

Daily News & Trends (2009) *Reflecting Back on Jesse Owens- An American track Icon* [online]. Available at: http://dailynewstrends.com/reflecting-back-on-jesse-owens-an-american-track-icon/402, (Accessed 26th November 2009).

Gentry, T. (1990) *Jesse Owens*. New York, Chelsea House.

Gordon, S. (1984) *Hitler, Germans and the "Jewish Question"*. Chichester, Princeton University Press.

Guttman, A. (2002) *The Olympics: A History of the Modern Games*. Champaign, Il., University of Illinois Press.

Lusane, C. (2003) *Hitler's Black Victims: The historical experiences of Afro-Germans, European blacks, Africans, and African Americans in the Nazi era*. New York, Routledge.

Mandell, R.D. (1987) *The Nazi Olympics*. Champaign, Il., University of Illinois Press.

Ohio State University (nd) *Jesse Owens: A Lasting Legend* [online]. Available at: http://library.osu.edu/sites/archives/owens/owens_story2.html (Accessed 7th April 2010).

Sailes, G.A. (2003) *African Americans in Sport*. Piscatawa, NJ., Transaction Publishers.

Schaap, J (2007) *Triumph: The untold story of Jesse Owens and Hitler's Olympics*. New York, Houghton Mifflin Company.

Shirer, W. (1972) *Berlin Diary 1934-41,* London, Sphere.

Speer, A. (1971) *Inside the Third Reich*. London

Spivey, D (1983) The Black Athlete in Big-time Intercollegiate Sports, 1941-1968. *Phylon,* 44: 2, 116-125.

The Jesse Owens Foundation (1999) *Who is Jesse Owens'* [online]. Available at: http://www.jesse-owens.org/about5.html, (Accessed 25th November 2009).

United States Holocaust Memorial Museum (USHMM) (2009) *Nazi Olympics, Berlin 1936* [online]. Available at: http://www.ushmm.org/wlc/article.php?ModuleId=10005680, (Accessed 28th November 2009).

Creative Story

What if... Jesse Owens was white?

Emma Jones and Iain Adams

BERLIN, 4ᵀᴴ AUGUST 1936, the arena falls silent. Adolf can sense the excitement starting to build among the crowds and begins to feel it himself. The Führer stands to salute the emerging finalists of the Olympic broad jump, the blonde hair and blue eyed American; Jesse Owens, largely unheard of outside of America until these games, leads the rest out. He has already won three gold medals and has become popular with the spectators and Adolf himself, who has referred to Owens many times, since impressing in the 100m final just days ago, as the ideal human. He has made suggestions on a few occasions of how he wants me to promote Aryan superiority using Owens.

Owens blonde hair shone in the sun as he was preparing for his first attempt, the stretches he was carrying out showed off his toned and muscular body. Adolf turned to me and said "he is a champion already, he will be important to us in the near future." I didn't fully understand what he meant by this but returned to the action as Owens took off for his first jump; he landed well and went straight into the lead after the first round. This was the way it continued; it was a battle between our own Luz Long and Owens in the final round. Both of Aryan race it provided a very exciting final and spectacle for the crowd. Adolf himself sat motionless with a fixed stare on the proceedings, however I knew that he was enjoying the competition immensely and that whatever the outcome, it would prove that superiority lies with us and the Aryan race.

As the last round of jumps began, Luz was in the lead with Owens second. Owens stepped up, paused and then flew down the take off runway, soaring into the air before landing in a spurt of sand. It was enormous, a world record. The crowd went wild, as well as many of the country's leaders around me. As the stadium erupted, Adolf sat perfectly but allowed a small smile to creep onto his face just for a split second before it disappeared. He stood abruptly, saluted the crowds and turned on his heel to face us all and barked "arrange a meeting with this blonde wonder immediately, I have plans I need to discuss with him" and marched out of the viewing box.

I managed to contact the victorious Owens and set up a meeting with the Führer as ordered. The meeting was set up for this evening. I was unsure exactly why Herr Hitler wanted to see the American athlete, but I did not wish to interfere. It was to be held in a private dining room of the Kaiserhof Hotel on Wilhelmstrasse, a particular Hitler favourite, I had been there with him many times.

Prior to leaving for the restaurant, Hitler summoned me into his office, "I have no need for your assistance this evening; you may concentrate on your other responsibilities." I was a bit taken aback, "But mein Führer, who will you go with?" "I will not travel with anyone and when I arrive the staff will take care of me." "As you wish," I replied, "but....." "No buts." he snapped "Those are my orders which you will follow. Now you may leave". As I exited the room I couldn't help being rather confused by his actions, Adolf has always been a bit unpredictable but even for him this was rather strange. He had always confided in me with his plans for the party and political actions.

As soon as the Führer walked in to the next morning's daily briefing, it was obvious he had something important to announce and discuss. We all saluted and he sat down at the head of the large and heavy mahogany meeting table. Today there were the normal heads of departments and eight, rather apprehensive, generals waiting for our leader to start proceedings. "As you are all aware I had a meeting with the American athlete Jesse Owens last night. I arranged it in order to discuss with him the idea of helping Germany become a stronger and healthier nation by promoting himself" he began. "Owens has the features of an angel, the body of a fighter and the mind of a genius; this is what the people of Germany must aim for! Goebbels, you must work with Owens to make Germans aware of the lifestyle they need to take on in order to reach their full potential. And work with Himmler to use any ideas Owens has to help rid us of Jews and Blacks! " I was uneasy working with Himmler but I didn't dare object. I started writing down ideas and plans, I was bemused as to why Hitler wished to promote an American for German superiority and the reasons as to why Owens agreed, but I trust the Führer implicitly, he is a great leader and a great man, and so I followed orders.

From that moment on Jesse Owens became part of the Nazi Party, an American Olympic athlete who is a close associate of Adolf Hitler, stranger things may have happened. It is still not apparent as to why Owens decided to go down the German political path, but he is very involved in what is going on within the party and has become a close friend of the Führer. They often discuss topics late into the night and have several meetings; I am not quite as involved as I used to be within the running of things, and so cannot comment on the exact content of these meetings.

However, one late November evening, the Führer, Owens and a few senior Party members such as myself, were at the opening of an art exhibition in the Hotel Adlon gallery, celebrations were in full flow due to Adolf's passion for the arts. It was in the early hours of the morning when we eventually decided it was time to go, Owens had barely left Adolf's side all night and with that I became intrigued into the kind of relationship that was developing. But, as we went out of the main doors to the cars there appeared to be no sign of Owens. Adolf did not want to leave without him and so sent us to go and search for him as he stood by his car. He sent his driver, Erich Kempka, to search the kitchens at the back. As we began to disperse into different sections of the gallery, a shot echoed into the night's sky. We all froze for a split second; a cold shudder crept down my spine. We rushed to the main entrance to see what had happened, there lay the Führer slumped on the running board of the Mercedes, leaning against the spare wheel. "Adolf what has happened? Are you alright?" I asked trying to keep calm. He was starting to shake slightly and was unable to speak. I leant forward to see if he was alright and noticed that underneath where his hand lay on his chest, blood was seeping through. The Führer jerked once and lay still, a tear rolled down my cheek and into the dark red pool next to me. I grabbed his body, but the only warmth I could feel covered my hands like a red mist and I knew he was gone.

A note lay next to him; I picked it up to see who it was from. Inside was a message from Jesse, I looked around to see if I could see him, but couldn't. The note read "This is for all the Jews in this country and worldwide who have had to suffer these malicious and disgraceful acts of violence and torture. Finally it has all ended. For I am Jewish and am proud of it!"

Chapter 22

What if... Ali Bacher said "yes"?

Robin Rutter and Iain Adams

Research Preface

KEVIN **P**IETERSEN **IS A CRICKETER** who plays for England although born and raised in South Africa. Kevin is the third child of four boys born to Jannie and Penny Pietersen, and was raised in Pietermaritzburg in Natal. Kevin is particularly close to his younger brother Bryan, mainly because, like Kevin, Bryan lives in England. Importantly, Kevin's brothers and father are all South African, like Kevin, but his mother is originally from Canterbury in England, where she was raised before emigrating to South Africa as a young woman.

Kevin excelled at cricket as a youngster and by the time he was 20, during the 2000/2001 season in South Africa, he had reached a crossroads in his life. Kevin was being repeatedly left out of his KwaZulu-Natal provincial side's starting eleven, because of political issues that had stemmed from the years of Apartheid, which had ended whilst Kevin was a boy. It seemed the government was overcompensating towards equality in its sporting agenda, as a result of the huge changes in the country. Niccolo Machiavelli said "it should be borne in mind that there is nothing more difficult to handle, more doubtful of success, and more dangerous to carry through than initiating changes in a state's constitution" (Alden, 1996: 1).

> It seemed Pietersen, and many white South Africans, were getting caught up in a political backlash. The problem was that all the provincial sides were made to field a minimum of three non-white players in their starting eleven, regardless of whether or not they were good enough. Three years after Pietersen was encountering problems, Gemmell (2004: 213) wrote:

The next chapter in South African cricket will be the first to include a significant number of players from the disadvantaged communities. This is a consequence of the development programmes, but also because of targets and political pressure.

The draft of this next chapter was already written before the 2000/2001 season when Kevin's place in the Natal team was consistently going to another all-rounder, Ghulam Bodi, who was a non-white player.

A disillusioned Pietersen was already considering emigrating to England to play cricket and realize his dreams in a country where his talent would not be plagued by political issues. This was no secret back in South Africa. Because Kevin's mother was English, he had a British passport, and Graham Ford, who was South Africa's national coach at the time, knew Kevin had received an offer to play for Nottinghamshire.

Ford was keen to see the talented youngster given the opportunity he deserved in his own country, and as one last throw of the dice, convinced Kevin and his father Jannie, to pay a visit to Dr Ali Bacher, head of the United Cricket Board of South Africa, the most powerful man in South African cricket. But after being told that selection would soon be based on merit by Bacher, Pietersen (2006: 67) asked "does that mean that, say next year, if the black and coloured players are not good enough, will Natal field an all white side?" "No", he said, "they will be good enough and they will play".

Bacher's lack of support regarding Kevin's problem with the quota system was all the incentive Kevin needed and his mind was made up. Pietersen (2006: 67) said of the meeting "as soon as we walked out of that meeting Dad said to me, 'You're going, the quota system will never finish.' I agreed with him". Kevin immediately accepted the Nottinghamshire offer, and after resigning as a player of the provincial side, KwaZulu-Natal, he took the massive step of leaving behind his family and friends, and turned up in England at the age of 21.

Kevin knew that he had to play county cricket for four years before he could qualify to represent England at international level, but it was not long before people were talking about how good he was and he was being linked to an England call-up long before he was actually eligible. In 2004, just months before he would become eligible, Mick Newell, his coach at Nottinghamshire, said "he is a player with great potential and it is our aim to provide Kevin the best possible opportunity to play for England as well as

284

helping Nottinghamshire win competitions" (Pietersen to play for Notts, 2004).

Kevin was eligible by the winter of 2004 and burst onto the scene by scoring heavily against his former country, in South Africa. But the real test was to follow in the summer of 2005 when England played Australia in the Ashes. England were thought by former players and pundits to have the best chance of winning the Ashes since 1987, the last time they won the famous Urn eighteen years previously. The series went down to the very last day of the final Test at the Oval in London. The Australians were considered to be, by some distance, the best team in the world but England went into that Test with a 2-1 series lead needing just a draw to win back the Ashes.

On the final day Kevin came out to bat with England at 67-3, just 73 runs ahead of the Australians who were desperate to bowl out England as quickly as possible to give them a chance of winning the game. While every other England batsman fell around him, Kevin went on to score an incredible 158 runs, and in the process completely batted Australia out of the game. England went on to win the series that is regarded, by many, as the best ever played in the history of the game.

Kevin Pietersen was the saviour of England and that innings was widely regarded as the one that won England the Ashes, especially given the pressure he faced on the final day. Many fans regarded it as heroic that he somehow managed to turn the game around and exert pressure of his own on the Australians, whilst the other English batsmen failed around him. Kevin finished the series as the leading run scorer and a national hero, whose life would never be the same again. His team-mate Ashley Giles (Pietersen, 2006: 13) later said "Kevin Pietersen is the man who took on the Aussies and won us the Ashes".

Although the last four Ashes matches were too late in the year to be considered by the ICC awards judges, Pietersen was named as the 2005 'One Day International Player of the Year' and the 'Emerging Player of the Year'.

When asked what may have happened if he had he stayed in South Africa, he replied "I really think I wouldn't be playing cricket now because I would have been frozen out by the system. If the England option hadn't been open to me, I would have gone off and done something else" (Pietersen, 2006: 68).

References

Alden, C. (1996) *Apartheid's Last Stand: The Rise and Fall of the South African Security State.* London, Macmillan.

Gemmell, J. (2004) *The Politics of South African Cricket.* Routledge, London.

Pietersen to play for Notts (21 March 2004) BBC Sport [online]. Available at: http://news.bbc.co.uk/sport1/hi/cricket/counties/nottinghamshire/3523012.stm (Accessed 7th December 2009).

Pietersen, K. (2006) *Crossing the boundary: the early years in my cricketing life.* Ebury Press, Reading.

Creative Story

What if... Ali Bacher said "yes"?

Robin Rutter and Iain Adams

IT WAS A GLORIOUS SUMMER EVENing on 15th January 2001 in Pietermaritzburg, and as I wandered down the stairs of the house I shared with my parents and brothers, contemplating what I should have for dinner, I sensed a troubling atmosphere which I feared was to put my primary thought of the time far to the back of my mind. It was eerily quiet in the house, there was no television, no radio, and I noticed my father was just sat in his armchair, looking as if he had just been told that he only had two months to live. I edged closer to the door in nervous anticipation of what my father was about to tell me; if I could summon up the courage to ask him what was wrong, when he bellowed,

"Is this really the direction we're turning in a beleaguered attempt to portray equality? And why is portraying such a thing more important than establishing our damn equality? Is this not just over compensation at its most extreme? Refining a balancing act, but falling into a tar pit in the process. Is this not a form of racism? Reverse racism".

It dawned on me that my Dad must have had a call from my brother Kevin. My brother was a professional cricketer, an exceptionally talented professional cricketer, who played for our home team, KwaZulu-Natal. But Kevin was encountering problems from the selection committee because of the quota system that was being forced upon all of the provincial sides in South Africa. As a result of the end of Apartheid, and the inevitable attempt at integration of all South Africans, the government had brought in a quota system to professional sport in the country. Sport was recognised as an area where integration was required because of the dominance of white people throughout our national teams, and this was something the government needed to address.

Recently, it had been decided that all provincial sides had to field a minimum of three non-white players, regardless of whether or not they were good enough. Kevin was the most talented of all the young players at KwaZulu-Natal, of any colour, but he was an off-spinning all-rounder in those days, which proved to be detrimental to his chances of playing. Of the non-white players at the club the most talented was a guy called Ghulam Bodi, who was also an off-spinning all-rounder. As the best of the non-whites this guy had to play, but there was only room for one man of that type and Kevin was being made a scapegoat even though he was quite obviously the better player. This was tearing my Dad and Kevin up inside. Throughout that season I had seen Kevin crying like a child at least a dozen times, which was difficult to watch. He was a strong willed lad, extremely competitive, but this was destroying him, and our father.

I remember that evening vividly. Kevin burst in through the door, tossed his kitbag across the hall, and paced around the living room frantically before declaring "That's it dad, I can't take anymore of this; I'm going to England, I'm going to take up the Nottinghamshire offer!"

My Dad sat motionless, riddled with dismay. Kevin disappeared to his room and minutes later, my Dad drew a deep breath, gathered his composure and made his way up the stairs of the house, before knocking quietly on Kevin's door.

"Come in Dad," Kevin muttered gently.

Dad entered the room, and sat himself down at the foot of his desperate son's bed, where Kevin was lying face down with his head buried in his pillow. "This isn't right son," declared Dad, "you're the best young player in that damn team. How're you supposed to realise your dream of playing for your country, when they won't even pick you for your provincial side?"

"What can I do Dad? I'm not the only one who's suffering, there's a whole bunch of us. All I know is that I'm a lot better than Bodi and all the young players in the squad, but I can't get a game". After a short pause Kevin piped up "But we know where I can get a game though!"

"Don't be too hasty son. If you go to England you won't just be turning your back on Natal, you will be turning your back on your country. If you go, you will never play for your country, you will play for your mother's. Yes, you have a British passport but are you British?"

"I just want to play cricket Dad, and I'm beginning to not care where that is. Yes, I'm South African, but do I want to play for a country that treats its citizens this way? I've become a victim of reverse racism and if I let it carry on I may never play for my provincial side, let alone my country".

A few soul-searching days later there was a phone call for Kevin from South Africa's national team coach, Graham Ford. Graham knew Kevin well as he used to coach him as a child. He was also aware of the problem Kevin was facing at Natal, and well aware that Kevin was considering a move to England, and that he could be lost to South African cricket forever:

"Kevin, its Graham Ford. Listen to me Kevin; somebody wants to speak to you about your predicament. You've heard of Dr Ali Bacher right? He's the main man on the South African Cricket Board and he wants to meet you and your father to give you reassurances about your future at Natal. He wants you to meet with him next week. Please promise me you will go and listen to him, he's going to help you".

"I'll go Mr. Ford. I promise you".

The following week, my father and Kevin went to visit Dr. Bacher. I remember Kevin telling me that he would approach the meeting with an open mind and hope for a resolution. I sensed Kevin did not want to be forced out of South Africa. After exchanging pleasantries, views and questions, Kevin later told me that he had one important question on his mind that would virtually determine his destiny. He had been told by Dr.Bacher that selection would soon be based on merit. So Kevin plucked up the courage and asked Dr.Bacher, "Does that mean that, say next year, if the black and coloured players are not good enough, will Natal field an all white side?"

"Yes," replied Dr.Bacher, "if the black and coloured players are not good enough, they will field an all white side".

With this, Kevin had decided to stay and fight for his place, safe in the knowledge that he was a great player, and this damn quota system was to be a thing of the past. His chance would surely come within the next year. Over the next four years, Kevin was in and out of the Natal side despite a multitude of great performances. He had now matured into an outright batsman but was once again showing signs of depression at how one week he could be in the team, and score a hundred, and the next he could be sitting on the boundary twiddling his thumbs. He had been worn down by

289

the system, let down by Dr.Bacher, and was no closer to playing for his country than he was four years ago.

By this time the contact with my brother was just by phone as I had moved to England and set up my own business. It's strange that I ended up choosing a career in England, just like Kevin very nearly did. But of course as I don't represent England, I have not defected, as Kevin would have had to. I recall one conversation between my brother and I which saddened me to my very soul. Kevin had told me that he was quitting cricket, quitting South Africa, and that he wanted to come to Southampton and work for me for a while, just to get away from it all. "Are you sure this is what you want Kev? Is this really the answer?"

"Oh yes, I'm sure Bryan! For the time being anyway. I just need to get away from here; I have to get out of South Africa. I have to get away from cricket. They have chewed me up and spat me out for the last time. I'll arrive at Southampton in September; I hope this is okay with you?"

"Of course its okay Kev, I look forward to seeing you".

Despite my reassurances to Kevin, I wasn't alright and it wasn't okay. I was angry and hurt at how the country of our birth had betrayed him. I was sad for him, and all of my family. I knew they would all be utterly ashamed of what has happened to Kevin. Dad never speaks of it, but I know he is a broken man. He's always been a fiercely proud South African and he will know that the way his country has treated his son is shameful.

On the 12th September 2005, I was sitting alone in a bar in Southampton. I had received a call from Kevin; he had arrived at the airport and was on his way to the bar to meet me. I didn't really know what to expect from him. He had always been a winner and a positive person, but I knew his experiences over the last four or five years would have taken a lot out of him. As I waited I noticed that a cricket match was on the big screen. Of course; I thought to myself. It was England v Australia in the Ashes.

It was the final day of the fifth Test and England had gone into the match with a 2-1 series lead, but were up against it in the final Test. They needed to draw or win the game to win the Ashes for the first time in 18 years, but had just lost their third wicket in their second innings and were only 73 runs ahead. As I watched, Kevin walked in and sat himself down at my table. We exchanged pleasantries before breaking into a gentle conversation. "So do you know what's going on here and do you even care or shall we leave?"

"You don't have to walk on eggshells Bryan, I'm over it. I've been watching it. England need to bat all day, I hope they do it".

Almost immediately after Kevin finished speaking, a fourth wicket went down. "Warne bowls Collingwood, that guy's something else," Kevin remarked. As we sat in virtual silence, the events of the afternoon at the Oval passed us by with little more than the odd remark. Wicket after wicket tumbled as Shane Warne ripped out the heart of England's middle order. By tea, England had been skittled out for 137, and their dream of winning the Ashes for the first time since 1987 had been all but destroyed. Australia required just 144 runs in a maximum of 32 overs to win the match and retain the Ashes, and break every Englishman's heart in the process. England's efforts throughout the summer had captured the nation's hearts.

Australia duly knocked off the runs required and won the game by seven wickets and were jubilantly celebrating on the big screen, while hundreds of Englishman held their heads in their hands and sat slumped on their stools. The dream for the public was over. I looked at Kevin and said to him, "They just needed one batsman to go on and make a hundred and the Ashes would have been theirs. It sounds stupid but if you had have taken that Nottinghamshire offer back in 2001 that could have been you".

Kevin just looked at me blankly and said, "Christ I hope you're wrong about that Bryan, I really do".

Chapter 23

West Ham vs Millwall, a football tragedy

Ashley Walker and Ray Physick

Research Preface

O N 25ᵀᴴ AUGUST 2009 VIOLENCE ERUPTED between West Ham and Millwall fans before a Carling Cup second round tie at Upton Park. Hundreds of fans from both sets of supporters were involved; most of the violence took place outside the ground. However, several flashpoints occurred inside the stadium the most serious one followed immediately after West Ham had taken the lead in extra time. Following the goal 50 to 60 fans invaded the pitch forcing the players to leave the field of play for a short period while police restored order. West Ham went on to score a third goal after the restart to win the tie 3-1. When at the final whistle hundreds of fans invaded the pitch once more, the threat of violence was never far away. Outside the ground a man was stabbed and taken to hospital, police were deployed with riot shields in an attempt to limit the violence. Several streets around Upton Park were closed as around 200 police in riot gear, supported by mounted police, ushered fans into the tube station. Only two arrests were made.

West Ham and Millwall fans have a long history of local rivalry, a rivalry that was intensified in 1976 when a fan was killed after falling under a tube train following a clash between both sets of supporters at New Cross station (KUMB.com). When looking at football violence and hooliganism, Perryman (2002:17, quoted on writenow.ac.uk) says: "there is a pervasive tendency to blame everyone else. The usual suspects are, and remain, the media, the police, the football authorities and opposing fans."

For several decades social researchers have looked at violent disorder at football matches. Brimson (2002, 198) argues that: "the theorists came to the conclusion that most hooligans were right-wing, poorly educated products of broken homes looking for some kind of belonging." For many hooligans a sense of belonging, even if it is as part of a gang, seems to be a key factor in their taking part in violence.

Football hooliganism has a long history going back to the nineteenth century. Some incidents, such as the 1985 Heysel disaster where a riot ended in the loss of 39 lives, have resulted in significant loss of live. In the case of Heysel the violence led to English teams being banned from European football for several seasons. The reputation of English fans was tarnished for years afterwards. Gow and Rookwood suggest that supporters think the way they are perceived and treated mirrors the stereotypical image portrayed in the media. For example, there is rarely any coverage of well-behaved fans, or news reports praising excellent behaviour of fans. For many such reporting engenders a distorted view of football fans among the wider public.

The story is written in first person with the main character explaining what happened. Boehmer (2001:154) states that selecting whether to write in first or third person is crucial to the story, as it affects the angle, the force, the atmosphere and the shape of it. It was felt that first person was the most appropriate because such a style adds drama to the story and enables the feelings and thoughts of the main character to be developed.

Rozakis (2004) says: "memorable characters – whether main or minor – come alive for your readers." It was not appropriate or necessary to go into detail about the social background of the main character but the reader should picture him to be a forty-something year old working-class man – a stereotypical football fan. The main character is a static protagonist, in that he stays the same throughout the story. The other main character in the story is Tony, the son of the storyteller. The story tries to emphasise the relationship between father and son as well as detailing the chain of events. The idea was to put across a different image of the football fan, in contrast to the stereotypical one, as mentioned previously. The characters aim to portray a more family based image, in that they go to the match to enjoy each other's company, enjoy the game and go home. Such ordinary every day fans do not get much representation much in modern media.

294

In reality, the violence between the two teams on this occasion took place mainly around the stadium, where a man was stabbed, as mentioned above and in the story. The 'what if' angle focuses on the pitch invasions, which were easily brought under control by the stewards and the police, but in this instance led to the tragic death of the West Ham manager Gianfranco Zola.

Boran (2005:149) states that fictional stories must include scenes that appeal directly to the senses of the reader. The main scene in the story is when Zola is stabbed, and the emphasis is on the eerie silence that follows Zola's death. The idea is to show that football rivalry is seen in a whole new light when someone dies. Moreover, this can be related to the Heysel disaster which resulted in European bans and a total re-model of the Heysel stadium. Alas, it takes a tragic event to force change.

The addition of a twist to a story, especially at the end is designed to shock the reader with something that they did not expect. The twist at the end of the story adds more drama, it would have been expected for both characters to get home and learn that Zola died. The news report insinuates that the main character was the killer thereby giving the impression that the story could be developed further.

Overall the story strikes a balance between what actually happened and what could have happened, without being too spectacular or unrealistic. It will make the reader think about what could happen after the story finishes and imagine what would happen if this did actually manifest.

In conclusion, the story sets out to build upon actual events and question "what if the West Ham vs Millwall violence spills onto the pitch?" Use of realistic characters whom the reader can relate to gives the story a sense of reality. The purpose of the story is to entertain, but there it also has a moral message regarding the impact of violence at football matches and in society as a whole.

References

BBC (2009) *Mass violence mars London derby* [online]. Available at: http://news.bbc.co.uk/1/hi/8221451.stm (Accessed 15th December 2009).

BBC (2009) Man stabbed as trouble erupts at West Ham vs Millwall Carling Cup Game [online]. Available at:

http://www.guardian.co.uk/football/2009/aug/25/trouble-reported-west-ham-millwall (Accessed on 28th November 2009).

Boehmor, E. (2001) Writing in the first person. In, Bell, J. and Magrs, P. (Eds) *The Creative Writing Coursebook*. Macmillan, London.

Boran, P. (2005) *The portable creative writing workshop*. New Island, Dublin.

Gow, P. and Rookwood, J. (2008) Doing it for the team – examining the causes of hooliganism in English football. *Journal of Qualitative Research in Sports Studies*, 2, 1, 71-82.

KUMB.com (2003) West Ham vs Millwall: Match Preview [online]. Available at: http://www.kumb.com/story.php?id=10143 (Accessed on 28th November 2009).

Rozakis, L. (2004) *The complete idiot's guide to creative writing*. Alpha Books, London.

Soccerlens.com (2009) Football violence and top 10 worst football riots [online]. Available at: http://soccerlens.com/football-violence-worst-football-riots/23093/ (Accessed on 28th November 2009).

Stead, D. and Rookwood, J. (2007) Responding to football disorder: Policing the British Football Fan. *Journal of Qualitative Research in Sports Studies*, 1, 1, 33-41.

Creative Story

West Ham vs Millwall, a football tragedy

Ashley Walker and Ray Physick

I WAS THE CLOSEST PERSON TO HIM, I saw him stagger back and fall heavily. I ran over and saw the blood ooze from a wound in his chest. This wasn't meant to happen.

I had butterflies when the draw was announced. West Ham v Millwall in the Carling Cup at Upton Park, you couldn't make it up! A Millwall boy born and bred, this was a chance to take my only son to an occasion he wouldn't forget; in the end the occasion was to be remembered for all the wrong reasons.

As soon as tickets went on sale I was there like a shot with my thirteen year old son, Tony, alongside me. Millwall scarf draped around his neck, he smiled at me with anticipation and excitement. We were like a pair of kids, couldn't wait for the big day. I stood all day for weeks before the match at the building site where I work thinking about it; the pre-match drinks at the pub, the journey over to West Ham, the game and the result! A win for the Lions and a ticket to the next round...lovely!

I knew there was a chance of trouble, we've been rivals for years, it's in the blood, ever since a Millwall lad fell in front of a train and died after fighting with some Hammers boys back in the 70's it had gotten worse and worse. But recently it had just been the odd scuffle, nothing to write home about, Tony and I felt pretty safe about going to the match, there would be plenty of stewards and police to keep us out of harm's way.

"Dad, what time are we leaving? I can't wait much longer," Tony was itching to go.

It was Tuesday 25 August. Derby day, and even though it was only 4.30pm,

297

we were both dying to get there.

"Not long now son, your mum will give us a lift to the tube station in a bit."

So off we went, colours hidden under our coats and scarves, you can't be too careful. The missus dropped us off at the tube, we were on our way! The train was jammed with Millwall boys, the songs and chants got going and shivers went down my spine. Nothing beats a match day.

But the atmosphere changed as we pulled into Upton Park. There were police everywhere and all I could hear were shouts and the shattering of glass. I looked at my son and wondered if this may have been a mistake.

"It'll be fine dad don't worry, just a few idiots, come on," Tony had more confidence than I did.

As we walked up the stairs, it was like entering a war zone. We had a police escort, we'd be fine. I spoke too soon. Thousands of West Ham fans surged forward to attack. I felt like a soldier going into battle. Luckily I managed to grab hold of Tony and make a run for it, past all these nutters smashing bottles on each other's heads and attacking police horses with bricks. I felt like screaming at everyone to stop, but somehow I didn't think it would go down too well.

"Here, this is where we go in. Dad, forget about it, the police will have it all under control in here," said Tony confidently as we presented our tickets to the man at the turnstile. We hurried into the safety of the stadium, I felt relieved. I was hearing mutterings and murmurings of stories from fellow away fans. A man stabbed?! A Millwall fan?! Apparently some bloke had seen it, an older guy knifed in the chest in front of his kids.

"Animals," I sneered,

"I know, it makes you sick, but we'll sort 'em out later!" shouted some random bloke from behind him, "We've got it all planned, riots, the lot!"

These were just the type of idiots Tony was on about. These weren't fans, these were thugs. Tony smiled at me reassuringly, Jesus, I was supposed to be the dad here!

We made our way up to our seats. The atmosphere was electric as it came up to twenty to eight, and the ground quickly filled up. The resounding chorus of 'I'm Forever Blowing Bubbles' shook the stadium and provoked a vocal response from the Millwall boys, myself and Tony included.

The game kicked off, and apart from the sight of stewards calming things here and there, it seemed as if the worst was over.

"YES!! GET IN THERE MY SON!"

The away end erupted as Neil Harris volleyed the Lions ahead. This was why I loved football, the fans were going crazy as the songs continued, smiles on faces.

The odd bit of disruption didn't even take my attention away from the game as we crept towards victory. After a swift half-time pint I took to the stands with my son as we held our breath for the second half. Three minutes from time, it looked like the game was ours. Until Junior Stanislav equalised. That goal changed everything.

The boy ran over to the Millwall fans and celebrated. Bad idea. It would turn out to be immaturity at its most tragic. The next thing I knew I was pushed forward as a sea of Lions fans surged towards the culprit. Some of them were on the pitch. Stanislav turned and ran like a scalded dog.

"COME ON THEN!"

"LET'S SEE WHAT YOU'RE MADE OF THEN YOU SCUM!"

The heckles and shouts came from all around me. I grabbed hold of Tony's hand and tried to get to the exit. I had to keep my boy safe.

The crowd surged again as West Ham fans also attempted to get onto the pitch. The stewards were powerless as more and more fans spilled onto the field of play. The players ran towards the tunnel for cover as the violence began.

There were punches being thrown everywhere as match officials ducked for cover. We were pushed onto the pitch.

"We need to get out of here, get to the fire exit," I screamed at Tony.

But as we turned around there was no way out. We could hear screams as kids were witness to punches, kicks and headbutts. This wasn't what football is about. I had seen some West Ham boys eyeing up Tony, I grabbed him and ran towards the dug-outs for safety. We darted up the stairs into the stands and immediately zipped up our coats, colours out of sight.

"This is carnage. I can't believe it. It's serious isn't it?" My son's face was pale now.

"Yeah son, I've been going to football for twenty years and I've never seen anything like it. Look, there's Zola."

The West Ham manager Gianfranco Zola had came up from the tunnel to the dug-out, it was like he was looking for something.

"Dad, look! I wouldn't be doing that if I was him!"Tony laughed as he tried to make light of the horrible predicament we had found ourselves in.

Then I spotted him. One of our own, blue Millwall shirt there for all to see. He had a menacing, almost deranged look in his eyes. I watched him as he spotted Zola and whispered to his mates.

"God, no. Surely he wouldn't be so bloody stupid." Words almost failed me as I saw this young guy, must have only been 21, stalking towards the home dug-out.

I ran down the stairs away from Tony as he screamed after me to come back to the safety of the stands. I couldn't let this guy attack the manager of West Ham, it just wasn't right. Too late.

I stood and watched in horror as the man pulled out a knife and approached Zola. It was like a scene from a movie, surely this couldn't be happening? Surely he's not so unhinged that he'd take it this far? Surely he'd know that he'd be caught?

I was the person closest to him, I saw him stagger back and fall heavily. I ran over and saw the blood ooze from a wound in his chest. This wasn't meant to happen. The attacker scampered away, leaving me holding the West Ham manager in my arms as he bled. The football rivalry meant nothing to me now, this was a person's life.

Slowly, people began to notice the scene going on behind them and stopped. It was as if the war had been called off, the armistice signed. People dropped their fists and their weapons, as the stadium began to fall silent. There was a moment when everything just paused, nobody could take their
300

eyes off the injured man in front of them.

I saw the sheer horror on Tony's face and knew I had to get him out of there, he's only a kid, and I didn't want him having the memory of the bleeding West Ham manager etched into his memory.

I took has hand, :It's gonna be ok kid, don't you worry, Zola will be fine." If only I believed what I was saying.

Tony smiled sullenly as we slowly trudged towards the exit, leaving the carnage, the battered and bruised bodies behind us.

As we arrived home, I sat down in my chair and was hugged by my wife.

"I thought you were dead, I tried calling you but your phone was off, Tony, are you ok? Did your dad look after you?"

"SSHHH!" I shouted.

The TV was on an announcer was saying, "We interrupting our usual programming for a newsflash."

Police are searching for a man in connection with the fatal stabbing of West Ham manager Gianfranco Zola. The Italian was stabbed in the chest during West Ham's Carling Cup tie with Millwall. Mobile phone footage has emerged of the person suspected of the murder...."

My jaw almost hit the floor. The image on the television screen was me, stooped over the limp body.

Chapter 24

What if... American football star Michael Vick was found not guilty of dog fighting charges?

David Hurst and Ray Physick

Research Preface

UPON JOINING THE ATLANTA FALCONS in 2001 Michael Vick became a National Football League (NFL) superstar and became one of the biggest ever names in American football. In December 2005 Vick signed a record 10 year, $130 million contract, a deal that confirmed his status as an elite player.

Two years into this contract, however, the career of Michael Vick was thrown into jeopardy: "Six years on from being selected as the first pick in the 2001 NFL draft, the Atlanta Falcons quarterback Michael Vick should have been looking forward to the best years of his career" (The Guardian, 2007). However, an accumulation of incidents between 2006 and 2007 saw Vick's reputation among football fans and the nation being brought under scrutiny. In 2006 Vick had been fined $10,000 by the NFL for making obscene gestures to Atlanta Falcon fans. The following summer Vick and three other men were found guilty by a federal grand jury of sponsoring a dog-fighting venture called 'Bad Newz Kennels' (Searle, 2008: 7). The three other men were Purnell Peace, Quanis Phillips and Tony Taylor. Vick was released on bail while the judge deliberated upon what sentence to give the four men, during this time Vick added to his problems after testing positive for marijuana.

Initially, Vick pleaded his innocence to the dog-fighting charges but on 20 August 2007 he announced that he would plead guilty to the case against him. The saga came to a conclusion on 10 December 2007 when Vick was sentenced to 23 months in prison for running a: "cruel and inhumane dog-fighting ring and lying about it". (Fox News, 2007) The other three men involved in the case with Vick also received prison sentences, Purnell Peace was sentenced to 23 months, Quanis Phillips received 18 months in prison while Tony Taylor got off lightly receiving a sentence of 60 days (ESPN, 2007).

Vick could have received up to five years in prison but after making several different apologies to his family, the NFL, his club and to the nation the judge was prepared to err on the side of leniency. Vick was, however, suspended indefinitely by the NFL. Throughout Vick's time in prison there were constant questions of whether he could come back to American football and if so would he be able to recreate the form that made him one of the most exciting players in the game?

The Falcons managed to recoup some of the money from the huge contract they gave Vick prior to his fall; an NFL arbitrator paved the way for the Atlanta Falcons to recover nearly $20 million in bonuses paid to suspended quarterback. The Atlanta Falcons moved on without Vick, although the media were always interested to know if Vick would come back to play for the Falcons or if he would be able to play in the NFL again at all.

The Vick saga was officially re-opened in May 2009 when he was released from jail after serving 19 of his 23 months sentence: although he still had to serve two months in home confinement before his sentence was fully completed. Although his career with the Falcons was over the final decision regarding his reinstatement as a player rested with NFL commissioner, Roger Goodell. Goodell's decision was made easier by the Falcons owner, Arthur Blank, who stated publicly that Vick deserved a second chance, but not with Atlanta: "which has severed ties with its former star" (ESPN, 2009).

Goodell initially reinstated Vick to the league in July 2009 with conditions that allowed him to sign for a team and to take part in pre-season practices, workouts and meetings and play in the final two pre-season games". (ESPN, 2009) Only a week after his conditional reinstatement Vick signed a one-year contract, worth $1.6 million, with the Philadelphia Eagles. Although signing a contract had come earlier than Goodall had planned the NFL granted Vick full reinstatement three weeks into the 2009 season. Goodall's decision received a mixed response from the press: "To root for someone who participated in the hanging, drowning, electrocution and shooting of dogs will be impossible for many" (CNN, 2009). Despite such scepticism Vick's first season back was a success with the Philadelphia Eagles extending his contract for a further twelve months.

References

CNN (2009) *Agent: Michael Vick signs with Philadelphia Eagles* [online]. Available at: http://www.cnn.com/2009/US/08/13/vick.eagles/index.html (Accessed on 7th December 2009).

ESPN (2007) *Apologetic Vick gets 23-month sentence on dogfighting charges* [online]. Available at: http://sports.espn.go.com/nfl/news/story?id=3148549 (Accessed on 5th December 2009).

ESPN (2007) *Falcons' Vick indicted by grand jury in dogfighting probe* [online]. Available at: http://sports.espn.go.com/nfl/news/story?id=294006 (Accessed on 5th December 2009).

ESPN (2007) *Judge orders Vick's conditional release* [online]. Available at: http://sports.espn.go.com/nfl/news/story?id=295022 (Accessed on 5th December 2009).

ESPN (2007) *Judge: "You were as much an abuser of animals as any other defendant"* [online]. Available at: http://sports.espn.go.com/nfl/news/story?id=315457 (Accessed on 5th December 2009).

ESPN (2009) *Vick cleared for preseason participation* [online]. Available at: http://sports.espn.go.com/nfl/news/story?id=4359354 (Accessed on 5th December 2009).

ESPN (2009) *Vick leaves federal penitentiary for Va.* [online]. Available at: http://sports.espn.go.com/nfl/news/story?id=4183786 (Accessed on 5th December 2009).

Fox News (2007) *Michael Vick sentenced to 23 months in jail for role in dogfighting conspiracy* [online]. Available at: http://www.foxnews.com/story/0,2933,316319,00.html (Accessed on 6th December 2009).

Fox News (2007) *Michael Vick turns himself in to begin serving time in dogfighting case* [online]. Available at: http://www.foxnews.com/story/0,2933,312207,00.html (Accessed on 6th December 2009).

Freberg, K. J. (2008) Perception of sport celebrities among college students: are high-risk sport celebrity endorsers more negatively perceived than low-risk sport celebrity endorsers? *11th International Public Relations Research Conference Proceedings*, pp 190-206.

Guardian (2007) *Vick pleads guilty to dog-fighting charges* [online]. Available at: http://www.guardian.co.uk/world/2007/aug/21/usa.paolobandini (Accessed on 5th December 2009).

Mail Online (2007) *Falcons told they can recover Vick money* [online]. Available at: http://www.dailymail.co.uk/sport/othersports/article-486908/Falcons-told-recover-Vick-money.html (Accessed on 5th December 2009).

Searle, A. M. (2008) *Release the dogs: creating a social remedy to the dogfighting epidemic,* pp 1-29 [online]. Available at: http://works.bepress.com/cgi/viewcontent.cgi?article=1003&context=amanda_searle (Accessed 24th January 2010)

USA Today (2007) *After the plea: What's next for Vick, Falcons?* [online]. Available at: http://www.usatoday.com/sports/football/nfl/falcons/2007-08-27-vick-hearing_N.htm (Accessed on 5th December 2009).

Creative Story

What if... American football star Michael Vick was found not guilty of dog fighting charges?

David Hurst and Ray Physick

STANDING ON THE SIDELINES OF THE PRISTINE OUTFIELD, I knew it all came down to this one last chance for unmatchable glory. One chance to pull off a Super Bowl victory, the ultimate dream of any American football player or fan. The nerves tugged at my insides like an excited dog on a lead trying to get away. I've only ever felt that kind of gut retching feeling before, waiting for the verdict in the now infamous dog-fighting trial. Exhaling into the cold winter air, each breath visible, I waited and felt the expectant eyes of the fans in the packed-out stadium all focusing upon me. The nervous tingling, the probing looks from everywhere, took me right back to that day of the verdict. However, now was not the time to be dwelling on the past. I had to get onto the pitch and use the remaining seconds in the game to engineer one last scoring play. Whatever the outcome, the 2008 Super Bowl will be forever remembered for me, Michael Vick, getting to this grand stage having endured the off field controversies that have constantly shadowed my every move for the past year. Coach Petrino leisurely walked across to where the eleven of us were standing, he entrusted us with the task of snatching victory from the jaws of defeat:

"Get in there and get this game won", he said in a stern and uncompromising manner. A simple enough thing to say, but would it be possible?

"Yeah boys, this is our time man, our moment", I contributed.

Ten yards to go for the game winning touchdown, it was now or never. We lined up ready for the last play. I could see a mixture of expressions on our boys' faces who were fighting for overall power and control. I knew I had to

307

focus, but it was hard not think back to the events of the past year that had led to this point.

Standing in the courtroom, my hands were clammy and I was unsure what to do with them. They made their own mind up and rested in my trouser pockets. The stuffy room in the hot summer weather wasn't helping my discomfort. As the jury waited to give their verdict, I sensed an eagerness within some of them to get it over with. Shifting about in their seats as if they were uncomfortable with what they were about to do, or maybe they were finding the heat just as frustrating. The trial begun with Judge Hudson asking how did I plead?

"Not guilty".

Straight away, I was annoyed at the way it had come out, too loud, too suspicious.

The defence lawyers had done all they could and now I waited for the outcome. My heart appeared to want to be somewhere else, as it pounded against my ribcage seemingly trying to escape. Following the prison sentences given to Purnell and Quanis' last week, 21 months and 18 months respectively, I was feeling pretty despondent. Maybe I should have changed my plea to guilty and faced the consequences. Nobody will know it, but that decision played on my mind for weeks. Obviously I knew the truth, no time to think of that though as the jury began giving their individual verdicts.

"Not guilty" stated the first jury member.

I remained unmoved, but my heartbeat increased yet again and was now trying to take the ribcage with it on its passage out of my body.

"Not guilty"..".Not guilty"..".Not guilty" it continued, until it came to the last member of the jury.

"Not guilty" she announced.

As my heart made its last attempts of escape through my mouth, I found it impossible to focus on what Judge Hudson was saying. I only managed to hear "...therefore you are free to go". And that was really all I wanted to hear.

Only a day after the verdict, the suspension that the NFL imposed upon me during the investigation, was lifted and I was cleared to play in the 2008 season. Atlanta Falcons coach Bobby Petrino called to inform me.

"Great news Mike, you're able to play next season.By the way, Mr Blank wants to see us both tomorrow morning to discuss some things".

"Man I'm so up for playing now. You know what it is he wants coach?"

"I know as much as you Mike, guess we'll find out tomorrow. Meet at his office, 10am".

Mr Blank, refers to the Atlanta Falcons owner Arthur Blank. I was unsure with regard to the possible content of the meeting, but felt apprehensive beforehand.

From the outset Blank looked stern: "Look Michael, I'm not sure that it would be in the best interests of the Atlanta Falcons to keep you on as a player. I do not want anything negative associated with our organisation". He stated abruptly.

"I've been cleared though sir. There'll be nothing negative surrounding the team". I argued.

Before Mr Blank could respond, coach Petrino stepped in:

"Mr Blank, I want Mike in my team and if you want this team to make it to the Super Bowl then we need to keep Mike. I've got complete faith in him to amend his attitude and I believe he can lead us to a championship very soon".

It was quite hard to keep the confident grin off my face as coach Petrino spoke. The praise washed over me, bathing me in a warm and satisfying feeling. However, his standing up for me increased the respect I had for him, and boosted my confidence in my own ability to change. It also seemed to change Mr Blank's thinking.

"Well coach, if you have that much faith in the boy, I'll let him stay. However, if we don't succeed in the near future, or there are any problems, no matter how small, you will both be looking for new jobs".

I knew the team and was confident in my ability to be successful with the team. Now I had the added incentive that coach Petrino had stuck his neck out to keep me. The new season couldn't come soon enough.

Although I knew the jury had got it wrong, believing I was not involved and that I had no knowledge of what was going on at the property. Even though I was the owner, I certainly wasn't there very often, and this clearly worked in my favour. However, I wasn't planning on dismissing this good fortune and continuing down the wrong road. The amount of stress and worry from the trial alone was enough to make me see I had to change. Visiting Purnell, one of the other guys charged, and ultimately found guilty, in prison also contributed to my change of attitude.

"Well if it ain't the superstar," Purnell mocked. "Good to see ya looking happy bro," he said in a friendly tone that set me at ease straight away.

The metal chair in the visiting room was unyielding and caused stinging pains up my back.

"I gotta say I'm sorry man. It should never have ended up this way". I tried to sound sincere yet sympathetic.

"Ain't nothin to be sorry about star, I had no chance with the idiots on my jury," he joked. "But seriously, you should take this chance you've been given, win back the fans and just dominate the sport. You've got all the skill in the world and you better use it".

The visit to see Purnell opened my eyes to how different my life could have been, and perhaps, should be right now. The fact that I could continue my career in American football was a blessing, and I was really looking forward to the new season starting in a fortnight.

The start of the season came and went, and each game seemed to pass in a blur, and the wins flowed quite easily. Coach Petrino's predictions of success were coming to fruition. I managed to repay coach Petrino's faith in me, leading the team to a Super Bowl appearance at the end of the season. Everyone associated with the team was delighted getting to the Super Bowl, especially Arthur Blank.

"I knew it was the right decision to keep Michael here Bobby," he said to coach Petrino.

I had to laugh at this but I didn't really care if Mr Blank wanted to take the credit, I was just happy to have people taking about my performances on the field and not my legal issues.

310

Super Bowl day is one of the most surreal experiences ever. It feels like more of an exhibition match than a competitive match due to the carnival atmosphere that penetrates every part of it. This was the perfect stage to firmly leave the legal problems in the past. Winning the Super Bowl would prove to the world I'd moved on and re-established myself as one of the great players. The game appeared to go by in double speed, and before I knew it, there were two minutes left. One touchdown between the teams, and we had the ball. With ten seconds remaining, I completed a pass to my receiver ten yards short of the endzone, and called a timeout. That left us with time for one more play to snatch victory.

Receiving the ball for the final play, it felt unusually heavy, as if gravity was conspiring against me, pulling me, and the ball, to the floor. I managed to stay on my feet and looked for someone in the endzone to pass to for the winning touchdown. Nobody was open for a pass so I made my decision that I was going to run for the line: it was only ten yards, it should be easy. At each step my legs felt wobbly and uncontrollable, as if they were folding in on themselves as I ran. Two defenders tried to tackle me, but neither of them got enough purchase to bring me down. Three yards from the line, a huge bruising defender who appeared to block out the light from the floodlights threw himself at me, I dived for the line. The defender hit me as I hit the goal line, the game clock had run to zero seconds remaining. That was it, had I made it? The referee appeared in my field of vision, signalling for the touchdown. I lept to my feet, feeling none of the physical effects of the game. The bitter cold no longer got to me and pure adrenaline took over. I ran across to coach Petrino.

"That's what I call proving a point!" I yelled delightedly. He just laughed before being taken away for TV interviews.

Once again I looked back on the events that had led to me being here and achieving the pinnacle in my sporting career. I had mixed feelings I was lucky to be let off the charges I had faced, I contemplated how drastically different 2008 could have ended up. I could have been with Purnell and Quanis watching the Super Bowl in prison. Instead fame and greatness had been thrust upon me.

What if... Jesse Owens was white?

Emma Jones and Ray Physick

Research Preface

J ESSE OWENS WAS AN AFRICAN AMERICAN ATHLETE who competed and won gold in the 1936 Berlin Olympic Games in 4 events, the 100 and 200 metres, the long jump, and the 4x100 metre relay (Schaap, 2007). In 1930s America a black person had to endure institutional racism, segregation of blacks and whites was considered the norm. Owens, like many African Americans, could not get a track scholarship to his local college so had to go to a multiracial school (Daily News and Trends, 2009). Although he was of small build and relatively weak compared with his peers Owens was asked by the athletics coach to take part in running sessions (Gentry, 1990). Despite these obstacles Owens was able to demonstrate that he was an athlete of genuine quality and, moreover, that he was able to overcome, by using his talent as an athlete, the discrimination imposed upon black people worldwide (Spivey, 1983).

Hitler became Chancellor of Germany 1933; his racial doctrine was that the so-called Aryan race was superior to other peoples such as Jews and Africans. According to an Afro-German holocaust survivor, however it appears that 'blacks' were not as hated by the regime as Jews were, but were still discriminated against and targeted throughout Nazi rule (Lusane, 2003).

Germany had been awarded the Olympic Games in preference to Spain in 1931 when Germany was a weak democracy. After some delay Hitler realised that the Berlin Games provided an ideal opportunity to promote his country and its people to the rest of the world as 'racially pure supermen.' German Olympic athletic teams were purged of all Jews, non-Aryans and non-white natives by the coaches in response to Hitler's wishes, the aim being to show to the world the supreme strength and power of German athletes. Ideally Hitler would have liked other nations to 'cleanse' their teams of all non-whites as well (Gentry, 1990).

Due to the extreme racial views and 'cleansing' of people in Germany, there was a proposed boycott of the Berlin Games by the United States of America, and a few other western countries such as Great Britain and France. However the boycott did not go ahead and the United States took a team of 312 members including 18 African Americans (USHMM, 2009).

On the first day of the Berlin Games the 100 metre dash preliminary rounds took place with Owens going in the final heat. He finished the race in a time that equalled the world record, then in his second round race he beat the record. However the German appointed officials refused to accept that the record had been broken because Owens' run had been wind-assisted. But this did not matter despite all the odds Owens was in the 100 metre final. Moreover, despite his colour young Germans still clambered to get his autograph (Gentry, 1990).

During the build up to the 100 metres Owens appeared to be very calm and was chatting to his fellow competitors on the starting line. However, just as the gun was about to go off he was focused on only one thing and that was to get to the finish line ahead of the field. He not only achieved this with ease but went on to win another three Gold Medals at the Games. In effect, he had undermined the Nazi doctrine of racial superiority; in response to Owens' success some officials tried to think up ways of fiddling the scoring system, but to no avail (Mandell, 1987).

It is difficult to place Hitler and the Nazi party's action under a certain sociological theory: many of their actions cannot be easily explained or understood. With Hitler aiming for power and control over Germany and the rest of the world, Marxist theory can demonstrate that Hitler's rise to power was rooted in the particular crisis of German capitalism.

Hitler also viewed people who were weak, and did not fight for what they wanted, as people who did not deserve to live. He blamed the Jewish population for the debacle of World War One and declared that victory in warfare would demonstrate racial superiority. He concluded from this that Jews would hinder the German effort for world dominance as they had done during the Great War (Gordon, 1984).

The significance of the Berlin Olympic Games and Jesse Owens lies not only in the opprobrium that the Nazis attracted but in the way African American athletes responded to white supremacist ideology. Their athletic abilities and the manner of their victories demonstrated that black people are not inferior to whites. However in saying this, Owens was loved by many white Americans, in return he paid white Americans undue respect. Along with the great boxer Joe Louis, Owens was among the first black Americans to be accepted as a sporting hero by both white and black Americans. Owens' achievements also provided a platform for other black people to gain acceptance for their sporting prowess in a racially segregated country (Sailes, 2003).

Despite his great achievements in Berlin Owens was never invited to the White House by Presidents Roosevelt and Truman. In 1955 President Eisenhower belatedly acknowledged Owens' achievement by naming him an Ambassador of Sports. In 1976 he was awarded the Medal of Freedom, the highest honour for an American civilian. After Owens' death in 1980, President Carter summed up the true achievements of Jesse Owens life: "Perhaps no athlete better symbolised the human struggle against tyranny, poverty and racial bigotry. His personal triumphs as a world-class athlete and record holder were the prelude to a career devoted to helping others" (JOF, 1999).

References

Daily News & Trends (2009) Reflecting back on Jesse Owens- an American track Icon [online]. Available at: http://dailynewstrends.com/reflecting-back-on-jesse-owens-an-american-track-icon/402 (Accessed on 26th November 2009).

Gentry, T. (1990) Jesse Owens. Chelsea House, New York.

Gilpin, R. (1987) The political economy of international relations [online]. Available at: http://www.irchina.org/Katzenstein/Gilpin1987.pd (Accessed on 9th December 2009).

Gordon, S. (1984) *Hitler, Germans and the "Jewish Question"*. Princeton University Press, New Jersey.

Lusane, C. (2003) *Hitler's black victims: the historical experiences of afro-Germans, European blacks, Africans, and African Americans in the Nazi era*. Routledge, New York.

Mandell, R.D. (1987) *The Nazi Olympics*. University of Illinois Press, Il. USA,

Sailes, G.A. (2003) *African Americans in sport*. Transaction Publishers, USA.

Schaap, J. (2007) Triumph: the untold story of Jesse Owens' and Hitler's Olympics. Houghton Mifflin Company, USA.

Spivey, D. (1983) *The black athlete in big-time intercollegiate sports*, 1941-1968. Clarke Atlanta University, USA.

The Jesse Owens Foundation (FOF) (1999) *Who is Jesse Owens?* [online]. Available at: http://www.jesse-owens.org/about2.html (Accessed on 25th November 2009).

United States Holocaust Memorial Museum (USHMM) (2009) Nazi Olympics, Berlin 1936 [online]. Available at: http://www.ushmm.org/wlc/article.php?ModuleId=10005680 (Accessed on 28th November 2009).

Creative Story

What if... Jesse Owens was white?

Emma Jones and Ray Physick

THE ARENA FALLS SILENT, Adolf can sense the excitement starting to build among the crowds and begins to feel it himself. The Führer stands to salute the emerging finalists, led out by the blonde hair and blue eyed American Jesse Owens, for the Olympic long jump. Owens, largely unheard of until these Games, has already won three gold medals and has become popular with the spectators and Adolf himself, who has referred to Owens many times since impressing in the 100m final just days ago, as the ideal human. The Führer has suggested to me on several occasions that he wants me to promote the doctrine of Aryan superiority using Owens as the figurehead.

Owens' blonde hair was reflecting in the sun as he was preparing for his first attempt, the stretches he was carrying out showed off his toned and muscular body. Adolf turned to me and said: "he is a champion already, he will be important to us in the near future". I didn't fully understand what he meant by this but returned to watch the action as Owens took off for his first jump: his leap was fantastic and put him into the lead after the first round. This was the way it continued; it was a battle between our own Luz Long and Owens in the final round. Both were Aryan, their clash provided a very exciting final and spectacle for the crowd. Adolf himself stood motionless with a fixed stare on the proceedings. However, I knew that he was enjoying the competition immensely and that whatever the outcome, it would prove that superiority lies with us, and the Aryan race.

Owens was in second place to Long as he stepped up to take his final jump. Despite being under intense pressure Owens met the challenge: his jump was enormous. The crowd went wild with delight, even The Führer, still in his usual motionless state, allowed a small smile to creep onto his face for a split second before it disappeared. He turned on his heel to face us all and barked: "arrange a meeting with this blonde wonder immediately, I have

317

plans I need to discuss with him," and duly marched out of the viewing box.

I managed to contact the recently victorious Jesse Owens and arranged the meeting with the Führer as requested. The meeting was set up for later that evening, I was unsure exactly why Adolf wanted to see the American athlete but I did not wish to interfere. It was to be held in a quiet Berlin restaurant, which was a favourite haunt of The Führer, a place where we had been many times.

Prior to leaving for the restaurant, Hitler summoned me into his office "I have no need for your assistance this evening; you may concentrate on your other responsibilities". I was a bit taken back and replied:

"But Sir, who will you go with?"

"I will not travel with anyone and when I arrive the staff will take care of me".

As you wish" I replied "but....".

"No buts," he snapped, "they are my orders which you will follow. Now you may leave.

As I exited the room I couldn't help being rather confused by his actions, Adolf has always been a bit unpredictable but even for him this was rather strange as he had always confided in me his plans for the party.

When the Führer walked in that morning to the usual daily meeting, it was obvious he had something important to announce and discuss. We all saluted and he sat down at the head of the large and rather impressive mahogany meeting table, 8 of his generals sat round and waiting rather apprehensively for our leader to start proceedings.

"As you are all aware I had a meeting with the American athlete Jesse Owens last night. I arranged to discuss with him the idea of helping Germany become a stronger and healthier nation by promoting himself," he began. "Owens has the features of an angel, the body of a fighter and the mind of a genius; this is what the people of Germany must aim for! Goebbels, you must work with Owens to make Germans aware of the lifestyle they need to take on and rid this country of Jews and Blacks!" I didn't dare object, but started writing down some ideas, I was bemused why Hitler wished to promote an American for German superiority and the reasons why Owens agreed to have his name associated with a foreign power, a power that also threatened American power. My trust in The Führer as a great leader is total so I always followed his orders.

From that moment on Jesse Owens became part of the Nazi Party, an American Olympic athlete who is a close associate of Adolf Hitler, stranger things have happened. It is still not apparent why Owens decided to go down the German political path, but he was very involved in what was going on within the party and he became a close friend of the Führer. They often discussed topics late into the night and have meetings without others being present; I was not quite as involved as I had been so I cannot comment on what was the exact content of these meetings.

However on a late November evening a few senior generals of the Party, including the Führer, Owens and myself were at the opening of an art gallery in Berlin. Celebrations were in full flow due to Adolf's passion for the arts. It was in the early hours of the morning when we eventually decided it was time to go, Owens had barely left Adolf's side all night and with that I became intrigued about the kind of relationship that was developing. However, as we were about to leave there appeared to be no sign of Owens, Adolf did not want to leave without him and so sent us to go and search for him. As we began to disperse into different sections of the gallery a shot echoed in the night sky. We all froze for a split second, a cold shudder crept down my spine. We rushed to the main entrance to see what had happened, there lay the Führer slumped against the newly painted white art gallery walls clutching his chest. I asked: "Adolf what has happened? Are you alright?" He was starting to shake slightly but he was unable to speak, as I leaned forward to see if he was all right I noticed that underneath where his hand lay on his chest, blood was seeping through. His body was cold and lifeless, a tear rolled down my cheek and into the dark red pool next to me. I grabbed his body, but the only warmth I could feel covered my hands like a red mist and I knew he was gone.

A note lay next to him; I picked it up to see who it was from. Inside was a message from Jesse, I looked around to see if I could see him, but couldn't. The note read;

"This was for all the Jews in this country and worldwide who have had to suffer these malicious and disgraceful acts of violence and torture. Finally it has all ended. For I am Jewish and am proud to be!"

World Cup 1986: what if Fashanu had eclipsed Maradona?

Kyle Readon and Mitchell J. Larson

Research Preface

DESPITE BEING A TERRIFIC PLAYER Justin Fashanu never did actually play for the England national team. Rumours about his homosexuality undermined his professional career and eroded his relationship with his then-manager Brian Clough. A very promising start to his career at Norwich eventually led him to become the first one million pound black footballer when he joined Nottingham Forest and Clough's team. Once his homosexuality became known, Fashanu became a forgotten man as he drifted between teams in England, Scotland, Australia and America, always looking for a team and culture that could appreciate his talents while accepting him for who he was.

In 1990 Fashanu encountered great hostility when he became the first, and so far the only, prominent footballer to identify himself as homosexual. Eight years later Fashanu tragically committed suicide in response to criminal allegations which had already been dropped by the prosecuting authority. The anti-gay pressures Fashanu faced, both on and off the field, are widely believed to have led directly to his decision to take his own life – these pressures, and Fashanu's tragic end, strongly discouraged any other players from 'coming out' to this day.

In our story events have been changed so that Fashanu remained in the first division with Nottingham Forest in 1986 and with Gary Lineker led the English league in scoring. This basic assumption led to a series of

321

consequences: as a top scorer at England's top level, Fashanu was selected to play in Bobby Robson's World Cup squad despite whispered rumours about his sexual preferences, which elicited visceral disapproval from a large proportion of English fans who prefer rumour to truth when it comes to footballer gossip. In the tournament Fashanu played poorly and intermittently until the key semi-final against Argentina where he scored the winning goal in extra time. With his confidence restored after that goal, he played a pivotal role in helping England win the competition for the first time since 1966.

This story's title is 'What if Justin had eclipsed Maradona?' What if a gay man had helped England overcome the Argentine player who many believed was the best footballer in the world, winning the World Cup in the process? What if a euphoric nation put aside its prejudice and cheered him for the remainder of his professional career? What if gay people, with Fashanu in the vanguard, had won wider acceptance in British sporting culture as a result of the triumph? In this story, Fashanu's actions highlighted to the public that despite being gay he was still a great footballer and that his sexuality did not hinder his performance or the enjoyment that he brought to them that summer.

In recent years homosexuals enjoy more acceptance than in bygone years, though this results largely from their own advocacy efforts. Civil partnerships were introduced in Britain in 2005 while the frequency of leading public figures 'coming out of the closet' (a euphemism for disclosing one's homosexuality) has become more prominent in recent times. However there is still a massive grey area that lies in most men's sport.

Clough's tough stance was typical of the aggressive 'macho' sports culture of the 1970s and early 1980s (Cashmore and Cashmore, 2004: 144-146; Dick, 2009:20) that eventually played a role in ostracising Fashanu and initiating a string of events that led to his death. A disturbingly small body of research on athletic teams and military units – both of which rely heavily on so-called 'team chemistry' for their effectiveness – alleges that heterosexual members of the team or unit frequently feel that gays undermine team unity by disrupting 'norms' of masculinity and athleticism (Jacobson 2002; Gough 2007). The presence of a gay man in a dressing room apparently unsettles heterosexual men who should not otherwise have any reason to doubt their own masculinity.

Traditional definitions of heterosexual masculinity are synonymous with physical strength and 'real athletes' and anyone who does not fit this

322

paradigm is not a 'true' male athlete (Anderson, 2005: 13-15). Women's football has enjoyed higher levels of acceptance in the last decade however like other women's sports the implicit assumption remains that many, if not most, players are lesbians. English football still remains a predominantly male sport embedded in masculinity both on and off the pitch: prejudice against gays persists. Seven in ten fans who have attended top flight football in the last five years have heard homophobic chanting (Dick, 2009: 7).

Former England and Arsenal footballer Sol Campbell, though heterosexual, has been a target for both racist and homophobic taunts during his career that he claims has affected his performance and led to depression (Orr, 2006; Hytner, 2009; Dick 2009). Interestingly, a racist chant aimed at Campbell today would be highly condemned and dealt with by the authorities whereas a homophobic chant would be likely be dismissed as part of the masculine culture surrounding British football. This situation begs the question why one kind of prejudice and intolerance is 'acceptable' while another is not.

Despite being only the frame of the main story, the depiction of Fashanu working in the present alongside English legends for a wider cause is the most significant 'What-If' element of the story. Allegory pairs the football match and the Falklands War of 1982, thus our references to military terms and aircraft. The hostility that England showed towards Argentina in the war is reflected in the tension of the game and the hostility that Fashanu received himself.

The 'What-If' story starts in 2010 where Justin Fashanu is still alive and has been given a knighthood due to his heroics in Mexico as well as his endless campaigning to tackle homophobia in sport.

Fashanu would have been 48 years old in 2010 and, empowered by his Mexico City heroics, might have become one of England's most prominent ambassadors in promoting FIFA's 'Give Homophobia the Boot!' scheme. If Fashanu was still alive today he could be an ideal representative as a gay black hero and would most certainly be a powerful symbol for gay acceptance today. Many faces in the football world have lent their support to anti-racism campaigns but none has stood up (or come out of the closet) to spearhead a concentrated attempt to condemn homophobia – probably due to the hostility that he would receive.

Fashanu's life and activities today could offer hope that homosexuals will become a more accepted group within the microcosm of elite football.

Seeing Fashanu sitting side by side with respected icons such as Sir Bobby Charlton and David Beckham, fighting for the same cause, represents a major difference from today's actual climate in sport where homosexuals are scared to reveal themselves. Those who do (or are 'outed' by others) are not celebrated nor given the same treatment as other leading heterosexual figures. Beijing Olympic diving gold medallist Matthew Mitcham recently stated that his honesty about being homosexual has cost him sponsorships in favour of less successful 'straight' divers (Mitcham, 2009).

With Fashanu as a living example and advocate for homosexual equality in English sport, overcoming the last and greatest taboo in football could be nearing an advanced stage in our attempt to eradicate it completely. His prominence and recognition within the English football hierarchy despite his sexual orientation would hopefully inspire fellow gay footballers to feel comfortable coming out in a more gay-friendly environment. This would be similar to the effect that Stephen Gately had in the music industry on fellow pop stars such as Westlife's Mark Feehily and Will Young. Feehily said that Gately helped give a blow to negative stereotyping while adding one more block to reality, that gay people are no different from straight people (Feehily, 2009).

With Fashanu gone there is a severe lack of leading figures providing these building-blocks and so homophobia, just like the Falklands conflict, will remain a source of tension for the foreseeable future until decisive action is taken.

References

Anderson, E. (2005) *In the game: gay athletes and the cult of masculinity*. State University of New York Press, Albany, New York.

Cashmore, E and E Cashmore. (2004) *Beckham*. Wiley-Blackwell, Cambridge.

Dick, S. (2009) Stonewall, *Leagues behind – football's failure to tackle anti-gay abuse*. Available at http://www.stonewall.org.uk/documents/leagues_behind.pdf.

Gough, B. (2007) Coming Out in the Heterosexist World of Sport: A Qualitative Analysis of Web Postings by Gay Athletes. *Journal of Gay & Lesbian Psychotherapy*. 11:1/2, 153-174.

Hart, S. (2009) *Matthew Mitcham says that gay status cost him sponsorship* [online]. Available at:
http://www.telegraph.co.uk/sport/othersports/diving/5165685/MatthewMitcham-says-gay-status-cost-him-sponsorship.html (Accessed on 8th December 2009).

Harris, N. (2006) *Greedy clubs tell gay players to keep quiet about sexuality* Published 13 April 2006 [online]. Available at: http://www.independent.co.uk/sport/football/news-and-comment/greedy-clubs-tell-gay-players-to-keep-quiet-about-sexuality-473885.html (Accessed on 8th December 2009).

Hinton, L. (2009) Interview with Mark Feehily on 28 November 2009 [online. Available at: http://www.femalefirst.co.uk/entertainment/Westlife-74034-page2.html (Accessed on 8th December 2009).

Hytner, D. (2009) *Sol Campbell has a lot on his mind – racism off the field and relegation on it* [online]. Available at: http://www.guardian.co.uk/football/2009/mar/02/david-hytner-interview-sol-campbell-portsmouth-racism-tottenham-hotspur-arsenal (Accessed on 15th March 2010).

Jacobson, J. (2002) The loneliest athletes. *The Chronicle of Higher Education.* 49:10 (November 2002), section A, 33-34.

Orr, D. (2006) *Save Sol Campbell from the narrow world that is modern British football* [online]. Available at: http://www.independent.co.uk/opinion/commentators/deborah-orr/deborah-orr-save-sol-campbell-from-the-narrow-world-that-is-modern-british-football-525487.html (Accessed on 15th March 2010).

Sears, J. T. (2005) *Youth, education and sexualities K-Z.* Greenwood Publishing Group, Westport.

Creative Story

World Cup 1986: what if Fashanu had eclipsed Maradona?

Kyle Readon and Mitchell J. Larson

THE ICY ZURICH WIND WHISTLES like an orchestra of referees all playing their high pitched instrument in tandem. It is December 2010 and the atmosphere could not be more different inside FIFA headquarters in Switzerland's 'cultural capital'. The heat and tension emanating from the relevant parties is enough to melt the finest Swiss chocolate.

At the front of the auditorium England's bid team sit with calm exteriors expertly camouflaging their internal feelings of anxiety and desperation as the result of over two years of campaigning draws nearer. England's record goal scorer Sir Bobby Charlton, national treasure David Beckham, 1986 World Cup winning captain Sir Peter Shilton and 1986 hero Sir Justin Fashanu hold their breath as the chairman speaks: "The host for the 2018 FIFA World Cup is...

The scorching heat entangled with the juxtaposing emotions of fear and excitement has swept its way to all corners of the arena. As the gladiators march out ready to do battle, the blues led by their small fearless magician and the whites by their imposing custodian, there is an inimitable feeling in the air that we are going to witness something extraordinary today.

Every player and fan bellows out his respective national anthem with added passion as thoughts flicker between the recent Falklands War to the impending one about to take place on the lush green battlefield below.

England are in enemy territory. The Azteca stadium may not be in Argentina but the blue army of Argentine supporters outnumber the English at least three to one. If we are to come away with glory today we are going to have to draw inspiration from the Aztec people, famous for their artistic and architectural accomplishments, and create our own masterpiece.

We certainly have the resources: the giant Shilton at the back protects the goal, and he is guarded in turn by the valiant Butcher in front. The endeavourer Reid complimented by the guile and wizardry of Hoddle form the central core. Two shining knights up top prepare to deal that killer blow with their Excalibur feet.

Gary Lineker and Justin Fashanu both finished the English league season with 30 goals each and possessed the perfect weapons to infiltrate the resilient Argie backline. Despite their nickname as "the dynamic duo" who the nation relies upon to bring the Jules Rimet Trophy back to England for the first time in two decades, the two men were worlds apart in public perception. Lineker was the country's golden boy who epitomised gentlemanly conduct while being a potent predator in the box. Fashanu, on the other hand, had spent the season scoring goals in front of vicious crowds screaming abusive chants at him every week. Despite parity to his front-line partner in the goal-scoring stakes the constant rumours about Fashanu's private life followed him to every ground in England like a shadow and left him an isolated figure in a squad full of masculine warriors.

After failing to score in any of the previous games many were surprised and annoyed to see the imposing 'pansy' stroll out in place of the unsuccessful Peter Beardsley, but despite their grievances with "Fash" everyone was fully behind the ten other men who had been entrusted to wipe out this sworn enemy.

The referee's whistle transmitted a high-pitched hiss right to the zenith of the 105,000 capacity stadium to signal the commencement of battle. With all the hysteria of the match coupled with the array of banners, flags and noise-makers being paraded around, the first half flashed by like a good movie: it was over before it began. The style of football was uncharacteristically fragmented given the two slick-passing teams involved. The first half proved just a bland appetiser before the main course.

Not even six minutes had ticked by after the break when our half-time optimism was emphatically punched by the hand of the enemy's Trickster. "How is that allowed!?" screamed the England fans. Supporters of the white army, their faces burning with rage, formed mirror-images of the blazing sun high above while the little blue number ten simply shone with joy.

Before England could sufficiently recover its composure, the knife that deflated our hopes now viciously twisted, dealing a lethal hit to the three lions. The Blue Trickster controlled the ball, dodged incredibly to weave past six white shirts like A4 Skyhawks had done four years ago in the Falklands before delivering the fatal blow.

Ten minutes in and England already faced a monumental task to salvage their dream. The players gave everything they had, plodding on draped in sweat-drenched jerseys symbolising their efforts. Fans are going hoarse after endless minutes of relentless battle cries to inspire their combatants.

Then. Suddenly. What appeared impenetrable is finally penetrated. A glimmer of hope rises like a phoenix from the Mexican dust as Lineker heads the ball into the goal with ten minutes remaining. The supporters dig deep and in true dedication to the Aztecs make their own discovery when a new, inner voice they did not know existed is heard. This voice is embedded in national pride and joined in harmony by the small choir of neutral supporters around the jumping coliseum to push a rejuvenated England to go in for the kill. Time, creeping out of nowhere like a coward, sneakily joins the opposition's artillery.

Nine minutes left...now eight minutes. Seven minutes. The minutes drop off the clock like seconds at a New Year's Eve party. Six minutes. Five minutes. The Argentinean team looks weary but their fans are already celebrating, mocking England as if the deal has been signed, sealed and delivered. Four minutes. Three minutes. Ecstasy.

The fresher legs of late-game substitute Barnes once again charge at the blue rearguard taking a chance at this crucial stage. Kicking from the same angle where he set up the first goal, he floats a dangerous ball into enemy territory where Lineker is incredibly once again on hand for conversion to bring England level.

The score remains tied and the full-time whistle is met with relief by England supporters before everyone settles down and prepares for entry into the uncertain terrain of extra time. The neutral fans have received the extension to the spectacle they desired and are now siding with their South American counterparts once again to try to rejuvenate the deflated favourites.

The match restarts and both teams grow visibly weary with passes and shots becoming more of a struggle in the intense heat. The crowd appear to be weary as well although most are just too nervous or hoarse to sing – their bulging eyes fixate on the ensuing action. As before, half-time comes with no scoring. Fifteen minutes remain before the dreaded penalty shoot-out: a random lottery that will determine who stays in the tournament and who flies home tomorrow.

With two minutes remaining in the second extra period the ball falls to Fashanu just inside his own half. He is met by the customary jeers that have been aimed at him throughout the tournament by fans from both sides, and even some England fans at this late stage began aiming some more verbal missiles at him because he's been such a non-factor in the match.

Steadfast in his purpose, the unwavering Fashanu ignores the cries of the crowd and advances forward. He waltzes past two blue obstacles with graceful, dance-like moves before flicking it past Argentina's number ten who cannot get anywhere near the rampaging Lion. Perspiration engulfs Fashanu's face which glows like a shooting star in the sun as he marauds unhindered down the centre of the pitch approaching the box. The crowd holds its breath as he stretches his right leg far out behind him in preparation for unleashing his rocket. The ball explodes off his foot seeking to ruin Argentine hopes. Breathless, the English crowd don't dare to believe that *he* could have done it as an entire nation awaits the outcome.

With no spin, the ball's trajectory swerves unpredictably and toys with the crowd's emotions just like Caesar did before informing them if the defeated gladiator would be killed or spared. This too was a life-and-death moment. The Argentinean goalkeeper tracked the shot all the way and began to lose interest as the ball entered the final stage of its journey. He decided it was going wide. We are going to have a shoot-out. What will be, will be....

With everyone's gaze glued upon the white homing missile nobody noticed Fashanu as he started running towards the England dugout. Nothing is stopping him on this forceful sprint, not even the colossal roar of the Three Lions team and supporters as his shot bulges the back of the net.

'We have done it! He has done it! The flamin' poof has done it!!' Absolute hysteria breaks out as fans jump and hug each other in the crowd, the England bench springs open like a jack-in-the-box as players and coaches scatter in all directions while Fashanu casually slips back into his Pied Piper alter ego as ten men struggle to catch up with him to embrace their teammate in exultation.

After his iconic goal in the Azteca stadium, and a further two in the final against West Germany, Justin Fashanu became an England football legend and cemented his place forever in the hearts and minds of English fans....

"The host for the 2018 FIFA World Cup is...England!" The England bid team succeeded, against all the odds, and once again Fashanu received the same quick and tentative embraces adored with embarrassed smiles that transport him back to the Azteca Stadium in Mexico City when, under different circumstances but equal amounts of pressure, he felt the same euphoria that just overwhelmed him with that announcement: "we did it."

Chapter 27

A fateful fight: the beginning of boxing's decline

Leon Hyde and Mitchell J. Larson

Research Preface

ON THE 8TH JUNE 2002 THE BIGGEST world heavyweight boxing showdown in a generation took place between Mike Tyson and Lennox Lewis. The event was seen as an epic moment in boxing history, as two very different men who had both dominated the boxing scene finally came to blows. After enjoying considerable fame and fortune during the late 1980s, by 2002 the majority of boxing fans saw Tyson as an untamed outlaw without respect for rules or authority, not only when concerned with the boxing world but also in everyday life, Cashmore (2005: 26) stated that "he was abominable, a repulsive presence fit for only savagery". Tyson's public image deteriorated severely after his highly-publicised rape conviction in 1992 – for which he served three years in prison – but he plainly reached his lowest point during his ill-fated second bout with Evander Holyfield in 1997. Tyson seemed to lose control during the fight and bit Holyfield's ears twice – the second time Holyfield lost a piece of his right ear and the match had to be stopped. Tyson claimed his action was retaliation for head-butts Holyfield had administered earlier in the bout, thus making it very easy for the American press to vilify him. As a result his boxing career, always more stable than his personal life outside the ring, also began to spin out of control. Even the pre-match press conference for the Lennox Lewis bout did little to help Tyson's public image, as a violent brawl broke out before the boxers even had a chance to take their seats (BBC Sport 2002b).

Lennox Lewis on the other hand was a celebrated champion, highly respected in the eyes of his nation (England) as Finger (2005:160) wrote, "British boxing fans were beginning to embrace him with the same affection that they bestowed upon Frank Bruno" (Bruno lost to Tyson in March 1996). Reprising a theme from a number of boxing matches in the past, the Lewis-Tyson fight in 2002 came to represent an allegorical battle between 'good' and 'evil'.

Sport in general, and the boxing world in particular, has long provided a financial 'way out' for young men seeking fame and fortune. Not unexpectedly, both fighters came from impoverished backgrounds and saw boxing stardom as their only route to financial success. "The large majority of black boxers were 'underprivileged kids' who discovered they could capture their 'pot of gold' by using their fists" (Wiggins 1997:183). Boxing represented an established channel for black males to gain acceptance for their sporting achievements by white society: "professional boxing is where one can find a vivid illustration of how far whites have progressed in accepting the possibility of black dominance in sports" (Lindsay 2004:47). We might dispute this view by suggesting that because of the dangerous and plainly aggressive nature of the sport, perhaps whites are content to allow blacks to fight each other whilst whites derive vast sums from organising and publicising these events. By winning and maintaining the heavyweight championship for a long time, black athletes have gained the respect and admiration of being among the toughest competitors on earth. Lindsay (2004:47) wrote that "the heavyweight champion has generally received the greatest accolades for being the toughest, most courageous, and able physical specimen on earth".

Tyson realised that by capturing his title, he as an individual would not only receive the full benefits and admiration of the world, but furthermore he might become a force for eradicating the social exclusion of his race. The United States, he came to see in the late 1980s, was a country of white racists, though there were some whites to whom racism was anathema. Clearly "the idea of a social system's being loaded against the interests of black people seems to have become more plausible for Tyson as he enjoyed the first fruits of his championship reign" (Cashmore 2005:212).

The 2002 showdown was not the first time Lewis and Tyson squared off in the ring. They had met almost twenty years before: "the year was 1984 and Lennox Lewis was an 18-year-old spoiling for a fight. He found it in the Catskills against a young terror named Mike Tyson whose reputation was already known in the amateur ranks" (Sports Illustrated 2002). Cus D'Amato, Tyson's mentor, watched the talented pair fight in the ring and told them both that "someday you will meet in a big fight" (Sports Illustrated 2002). His prediction came true 18 years later, and the fight lived up to all expectations and the prodigious pre-match hype. Tyson and Lewis unleashed a series of furious attacks upon each other. The first round was undoubtedly Tyson's, as he went in aggressively, looking for the early knock-out. BBC Sport's report of the match (2002a) became a blow-by-blow account: "Tyson launches into Lewis with a left hand jab. Lewis tries to use a heavy jab but Tyson retaliates with a great left hook. Lewis lets his guard down to let Tyson in with another left hook. Tyson seems to have done enough to win the first round". Lewis' relentless persistence, superior size, and technical skill finally overcame 'Iron Mike' in the 8th round (by knockout). Shetty (2002) stated that "Lennox Lewis believes that knocking out Mike Tyson in eight rounds is his 'defining' victory. The heavyweight champion battered Tyson for the majority of the contest and the fight ended when the former champion failed to rise from a second knock-down".

Lewis' win meant that he finally became the undisputed champion of his era. He received a hero's welcome upon returning to the UK. By removing Tyson as a viable contender to the boxing throne he opened the door for a new generation of fighters. Lewis could now retire a respected black champion and idol to millions, with the knowledge that he had successfully 'exorcised the evil' from his generation of boxing superstars. Even though both men could be considered vital to the history of boxing, had Tyson prevailed against Lewis his grip on the title could have prevented younger fighters from realistic opportunities of becoming a boxing great; intimidation alone might have dissuaded boxers from challenging him. When he lost the fight it was obvious to all that Tyson's dominance had ended. Mike Tyson fought once more against a young Kevin McBride in 2005, but his lacklustre desire to win (and loss of the fight by technical knockout) paled next to the fire he showed against worthier foes like Evander Holyfield and Lennox Lewis. Shortly after the McBride fight he announced his retirement, saying, "I wish I could have done better, but it's time to move on with my life and be a father and take care of my children"

(Johnson 2005). If Lewis had lost the fight, he would not have inspired thousands of boxers, not only British, to fulfil their desire to become champions themselves. British-born David Haye, the present WBA heavyweight champion, provides a great example of this. Haye uses Lewis as an inspiration but also a tool to prepare for defeating his next opponent: "Lennox has worked with me in the gym before, he's seen me sparring, he knows I'm the real deal. I'll definitely bring him on board in an advisory role" (Davies 2008).

What the story implicitly asks, however, is whether the reputation and the integrity of the sport of boxing would suffer from having a high-profile champion with such a poor public image: Tyson is a convicted felon who further disgraced himself in the ring during his legendary second fight with Holyfield in 1997. Can the sport of boxing survive such negative press and remain respectable, or has boxing come to accept its position at the bottom of the hierarchy of athletic endeavour? The sport has faced criticism for decades about the influences of organised crime, it has fought allegations about match-fixing and cheating in both the amateur and professional ranks, and boxing declined in popularity in part because the physical demands upon athletes can lead to long-term physiological conditions. The popular but controversial figure of Muhammad Ali exemplifies the tragedy of boxing success: his many years in the ring receiving hard blows to the head appear to have made Ali more susceptible to the Parkinson's Disease from which he has suffered for many years. Ali is revered in many parts of the world and especially in sub-Saharan Africa as a portrait of an African-American who succeeded in the face of white racism and oppression. While their personal lives both included serious confrontations with the law – Ali refused to register for selective service in the US Army during the Viet Nam War – he has done much in retirement as an ambassador for his race, his religious beliefs (he announced his conversion to Islam after his first fight against Sonny Liston in 1964), and to a lesser extent for boxing generally. Mike Tyson has a long road of image rehabilitation ahead of him to live up to the standard that Ali established.

References

BBC Sport (2002a) Round-by-round: Lewis v Tyson [online]. Available at: http://news.bbc.co.uk/sport1/hi/boxing/specials/lewis_v_tyson_fight/2033873.stm (Accessed on 4th December 2009).

BBC Sport (2002b) Mass brawl in New York [online]. Available at: http://news.bbc.co.uk/sport1/hi/boxing/1776555.stm (Accessed on 11th March 2010).

Branch, E. (1992) Special Report: The Business of Sports - Off-season Professionals. *Black Enterprise*, 23, 3, 162-168.

Cashmore, E. (2005) *Tyson: nurture of the beast.* Polity Press, Cambridge.

Davies, G. (2008) David Haye set to bring in Lennox Lewis as adviser for Vitali Klitschko showdown [online]. Available at: http://www.telegraph.co.uk/sport/othersports/boxingandmma/3777500David-Haye-set-to-bring-in-Lennox-Lewis-as-adviser-for-Vitali-Klitschko-showdown.htm (Accessed on 4th December 2009).

Finger, D. (2005) *Rocky lives! Heavyweight boxing upsets of the 1990s.* Potomac Books, Washington DC.

Johnson, C. (2005) Tyson announces retirement after quitting vs. McBride [online]. Available at: http://www.usatoday.com/sports/boxing/2005-06-11-tyson-mcbride_x.htm (Accessed on 1st December 2009).

Lindsay, A. (2004) *Boxing in black and white: A statistical study of race in the ring, 1949-1983.* McFarland and Company, Jefferson, NC, USA.

Shetty, S. (2002) Lewis revels in 'defining' fight BBC Sport [online]. Available at: http://news.bbc.co.uk/sport1/hi/boxing/specials/lewis_v_tyson_fight/2034186.stm (Accessed on 15th December 2009).

Sports Illustrated (2002) Lewis recalls sparring session with Tyson as amateurs [online]. Available at: http://sportsillustrated.cnn.com/more/boxing/2002/lewis_tyson/news/2002/06/05/lewis_tyson_ap.html (Accessed on 20th December 2009).

Wiggins, D. (1997) *Glory bound: Black athletes in a White America.* Syracuse University Press, Syracuse, NY.

Creative Story

A fateful fight: the beginning of boxing's decline

Leon Hyde and Mitchell J. Larson

THIS STORY TELLS A RIVETING TALE from an eye-witness present at the decisive Tyson and Lewis fight in 2002. The spellbinding piece contains both factual events and the mysterious and intriguing element of 'what if'. It cunningly places the reader in the shoes of a young man attending the bout and enables the emotional indulgence of participating in the adventure of the most anticipated boxing match-up of all time! You won't want to miss it!

The Modern Warrior

It was D-day! The fight of the century was finally on! Blood-thirsty roars swept throughout the arena with such intensity the vibrations could shatter a grown man's skull. Yet the two men stood firm like Spartan warriors, eyes laced with hatred, yet their minds focused on the mission ahead, like a rogue tiger warming up to its prey. Elite guards attired in yellow and black separated them in the ring, the only restraint from either fighter unleashing hell. In one corner, wearing his traditional black trunks, stood the intimidating figure of 'Iron Mike' Tyson. In the opposite corner, wearing white to symbolise his position as undisputed lord of the heavyweight boxing throne, stood the current world champion, Lennox Lewis.

"So, who's your money on then, lads?" croaked an old man seated behind us. "I reckon Tyson will eat him up in the first round," said Ray. "Na, it's going longer than that; in the 8th round Lewis will knock him out," I replied confidently with my head held high. "Well, we'll soon find out," laughed the old man. For Ray and me this was the ultimate sporting battle of good versus evil! The outcome of this fight would set the tone for the future of the sport: would an honourable sportsman like Lennox Lewis prevail over the untamed stigma of the boxing world known as Mike Tyson? Both men excelled in their sport though each came from an underprivileged background. Their success represented a great achievement in itself, like a rose growing out of a crack in the concrete. Now on the 8th of June 2002, the most anticipated fight of the new century would finally take place here in Memphis, Tennessee. Millions around the world tuned in to witness the clash of these two titans, but I was honoured to sit just 10 yards away from the action. The mere presence of Tyson mesmerized the crowd; after the brawl at the pre-match press conference he appeared to reflect the very essence of evil, and the boxing world had developed a love/hate attitude toward him. This attitude came as a shock to Tyson, who half-heartedly accepted this applause by raising his arms half-way above his head, not fully accepting his entourage of screaming fans. At that moment it seemed Tyson wasn't quite the same fighter: the burning intensity and passion in his eyes had faded, just like the story of the movie "Rocky 3" – had he lost 'the eye of the tiger'? I had no doubt that Lewis was the predator that day, and aimed to prove to the boxing world that good always triumphs over evil. Eagerly the guards filed into line and retreated to the perimeter of the ring. "Here we go, this is going to be immense!", screamed Ray. His voice was nearly drowned out by the fierce roars of the crowd. Breathlessly I gazed toward what I saw as boxing's day of reckoning and braced myself for the showdown. This wasn't the time for exchanging petty remarks with friends, but quite simply a time to appreciate the spectacle of these two great forces of human nature colliding. The referee, an impressive specimen himself at 6 feet 6 inches tall, was now the only restraint between these two warriors. His palms faced each fighter, as if to plead with them to stand at ease until the bell thundered, and with one single motion he threw his arms down and stood back. The fight was on!

Both men sprang out of their corners with a pace rivalled only by that of a desperate feline pouncing on its prey. Tyson unleashed a furious combination of rights and lefts, pounding wild and ferocious shots aggressively into the champion's body. Lewis simultaneously replied with a series of devastating jabs, all of which focused on rearranging this brutal beast's face. No man could deny the increasing excitement of the crowd. In any other place, their cries for blood would have been considered rather disturbing; here though, entertainment was key. The first round lasted 3 minutes but seemed like only 30 seconds. Ray jumped out of his seat to applaud his idol on his first round efforts, and was quick to taunt me with his belief that Tyson would soon end Lewis' reign, "No man can match

Tyson, you hear me! Can't no man step to this!" His misplaced admiration didn't faze my confidence in Lewis one bit. Both fighters reluctantly returned to their corners, welcomed by only the desperate pleas of their trainers begging each fighter to fight a more strategic battle. Timely punches weren't the diagnosis either fighter had in mind. Lewis understood that this fight had greater implications than just scoring enough points to win, and so embraced the battle in the true manner of a barbarian warrior.

The bell clanged for the second round as if to signalling the death knell of legitimate boxing. What we witnessed was similar to that of the first round: Lewis continued his pattern of straight shots to the head, while Tyson lunged in a series of heated swings even more furious than those of the first round. Iron Mike fully lived up to his reputation as an untamed outlaw, searching for that one crushing blow which would send his opponent into the lonely, dismal realm of darkness.

Lewis tried to fend off the beast with series of uppercuts, each thrust powered by the desire to halt the advancing Iron Mike in his stride, yet each blow that he landed only seem to fuel Tyson's rage. As Tyson closed in on the champion he subjected him to a horrific assault, and each blow Tyson inflicted threatened my belief that Lewis could finally tame him. The bell rang to signal the end of the second round, much to Lewis' relief. A cold smirk dented Iron Mike's exterior; he could sense that his time of reckoning was near. If Tyson won this fight it would go far toward rehabilitating his image and re-establish him as the world's best fighter. Lewis went to his corner dazed and shaken by Tyson's relentlessness. For the first time in the match he took his focus off Tyson as he stared out into the crowd; the look in his eyes was unmistakably the ill-fitting look of self-doubt. Sweat poured from his face as if doing so could allow it to escape the vicious wrath of his opponent.

Ray's enthusiasm peaked now and he was chanting Tyson's name with admiration: "TYSON, TYSON! So what do you think now then, hey? Now you understand that this man cannot be stopped!". "Calm down, calm down, it's not over yet. Lewis will bounce back. Trust me", I replied, however this time not so confidently. "Well, I think you're in denial. It's good you believe, don't get me wrong, but there's a time and a place for your beliefs" said Ray, laughing at my growing despair.

The third round was upon us. The Evil Beast emerged from his cave-like

338

domain with a terrifying confidence, lashing his tongue across his mouth as if to signify it was feeding time. Lewis, like the consummate champion he was, had recovered from his momentary lapse and embraced this fully to prepare himself once more for Iron Mike. Snarling, Tyson hurled himself towards the champ, firing powerful shots both low and high, all of which Lewis found unstoppable. First came blows to the stomach, which sent shock waves throughout the champion's body, like a log slamming the surface of a calm lake. This combination to the body robbed Lewis' body of all the oxygen it once possessed, reducing him to a motionless statue gasping for air. The final shot, to my lasting dismay, drove across the now-former champ's face, sending Lewis into the much-anticipated realm of darkness. The bright lights and television cameras caught the last remaining drops of sweat falling from Lewis' unconscious face, and with one almighty THUD the champ smashed to the canvas. Half the crowd erupted with joy, and so did Ray. The great divide was more apparent now than ever. Tyson towered above his prey, pounding his chest with his huge fists and recalling images of Ali vs. Liston, as if to say 'I told you so!'. The future of boxing was in jeopardy now that the last viable opponent had been felled – no man young or old could defeat this barbaric warrior. Lewis was the last hope and now with him no longer the champion, boxing began a spiral into the darkness of self-destruction fuelled by rampant corruption behind the scenes and led by a champion people feared rather than respected.

Chapter 28

Act now, think later

John Metcalfe

Prologue:

1. This chapter is about the training and preparation for a prolonged adventure in the USA called the Great Divide; a 2500 cycle race which was completed by the author in 2004.

2. It is written from a personal perspective and may reveal something about the deeply intrinsic motivations to undertake a pointless adventure requiring a gargantuan physical challenge.

3. I wonder why it is that so much can be learned from such an utterly pointless undertaking as this was...

MY LOVE AFFAIR WITH CYCLING BEGAN when I was three years old. It was the first time that I cycled unassisted and experienced the magic of riding a bicycle. I was somehow able to slip my father's stabilising hold on my saddle and make my first few independent pedal strokes. As I grew older, being able to ride under my own steam literally broadened my horizons. It meant that I could explore new places – the length of my street, the next block – and go beyond the parameters that my mother had so austerely set. Cycling was to become a compelling force that fused together my ability to explore, to be self-sufficient and to meet new people. And for me this magic has never diminished; even now whenever I mountain bike, commute to work, or just ride to the shops I still experience that addictive, child-like excitement.

As was the case with my inaugural two-wheeled experience, the blissful state of self-propulsion is generally accompanied with its antithesis – crashing. Yet despite my inability to stay upright, cycling has featured heavily in my life, and for some unknown reason I decided from an early age that I was going to be a professional cyclist. Such a decision was easy to make: I was young, pro-riders were old, so I had plenty of time before I had to do anything serious about my newly decided vocation. Until then I was content to just ride my bike for fun.

Of course the years have slipped under my wheels and I have done very little about realising my childhood dream. Even now – in my thirties – I find myself hanging on to scraps of information gleaned from the cycling press about riders in their forties who are doing well in the professional ranks. I use these little gems to bolster my flagging reverie and buy myself even more time before the bubble bursts. I could be good one day... But the truth of the matter is, I am no athlete. I lack the physiology and resoluteness to be even a journeyman cyclist let alone be a pro. That said I have been blessed with one exceptional quality that has proved invaluable during my sketchy cycling career, a phenomenally poor long-term memory. A case in point was my thirtieth birthday. With more than a hint of a premature – or an immature – mid-life crisis and a need to strengthen my dream, I celebrated my anniversary by entering the solo category of a 24 hour mountain bike race. As the sun rose midway through the race, and I became a year older, my body was undergoing a trauma equalled only in magnitude to that which it endured on the same day three decades earlier. I had crashed... I vowed to myself at that moment that I would never ride a bike again. Yet once the race was over and the sense of doom receded, my substandard short-term memory was unable to render the earlier horrors and I found myself planning strategies for the following year. It is this *Etch-a-Sketch* ability to delete pain from my memory that enables me to keep getting on my bike.

I am also incredibly good at procrastinating. On average it takes about six years for an idea to become a reality, more if the task is difficult, with the option that it might be indefinite should it require a lot of effort. As a result my cycling to-do list is as long as my arm and is growing exponentially as my idling brain comes up with new two-wheeled feats that are clearly beyond my physiology or verve. The ideal antidote to such an apathetic lack of success is to compare yourself to others of a similar, or preferably, worse disposition. John Kelly, or JK as he likes to be known, was an ideal candidate for my comparative cycling partner. All of his claims collapsed under the slightest of scrutiny; he had achieved very little, over-exaggerated what he had done and had plenty to say about what he was going to do. Of course the relationship is symbiotic: he provides the perfect alibi for me and I for him.

For any serious – and also wannabe – endurance mountain biker, the Great Divide Mountain Bike Route is the jewel in the crown. It stretches from Canada to Mexico and is considered America's premier long-distance mountain bike trail by the Adventure Cycling Association. The route starts at the Port of Roosville on the Montana-British Columbia border and follows the Continental Divide – as closely as possible – down to Antelope Wells at the New Mexico-Mexico border. The Continental Divide is an imaginary line that separates the flow of water on the continent: on the west side of the line, water runs into the Pacific Ocean, whereas on the east it flows into the Atlantic. Put another way, the Great Divide follows the Rockies which means plenty of ups, downs and everything else in between.

Being wannabes, it stands to reason that the Great Divide was on both JK"s and my to-do lists. My main concern was that it stood a serious chance of not getting completed, especially when we were shelving easier, domestic long-distance rides for nebulous reasons. Drastic action was therefore needed. On the odd occasion that I have achieved my cycling objectives, I have found two useful motivation tools. The first is financial the second is verbal.

I phoned JK.

"So we're still on for the Great Divide?" I inquired.

"You bet...definitely this year," came his blasé reply.

"Good, so you won't mind giving me your credit card details,"

"WHAT?" (I suspected the concern in JK"s voice was because somewhere in his rational mind he feared the Great Divide plan was being galvanised).

"I've been on the Internet and found some decently priced flights..." I offered, and noticing an apologetic tone to my voice, I sternly added "...so there's no reason why we shouldn't book them".

Cornered, JK had no choice, to back out now would expose him for the charlatan that he is. So he did the honourable thing and proffered his credit card details. It was an adroit move because in saving his face he had also

343

called my bluff. Faced with no other option I entered our details on the electronic form and hit *enter*. That was it; the tickets were on their way. We had to do it.

The second stage of goal fulfilment is to get on your soapbox and tell everyone what you're planning to do. And to ensure a vicious tongue-lashing if you don't complete your mission, it's often necessary to decry everyone else for not attempting it themselves. I took to this task enthusiastically and was so convincing I even started to believe the audacious claims I was making. Of course I was writing a substantial verbal cheque that I was unsure my body could cash; perfect preparation for the trip.

Running in tandem with my childhood dream of becoming a professional cyclist I've also got a rather spurious theory about my athletic potential. It is not a product of intense research, rather it has developed in my subconscious mind over the years and has resided there for so long that I have come to believe that it is true. At best it is half-baked, but it is a theory nonetheless. It goes something like this. I am half as good as any World Class athlete. For instance, I can run a marathon or the 100m sprint inside double the respective world record times. Extrapolating this means that I should also be able to complete the Great Divide in twice the record time. The current holder of this record is John Stamstad – a legendary ultra-endurance mountain biker – who rode the 2500 miles unassisted in 18 days and five hours. To put his achievement in perspective, the distance he rode was further than the *Tour de France* and he did it in less time. Furthermore he carried all of his equipment and didn't have the assistance of team mechanics, soigneurs and the usual *Tour de France* accoutrements. Using this as a yardstick I calculated that we should be able to get from Canada to Mexico in about 37 days, or six weeks at the outside. Of course my theory does not hold up well under scrutiny, because there is no way I could get round 18 holes of golf in double what Tiger Woods can, nor would it be feasible for me to go half the distance with Lennox Lewis. But I choose to ignore these bothersome anomalies.

Now the flights were booked, my motivation seemed to be roused. I circled our departure date on my year-planner above my desk and was stirred into action by how little time there was. It was a little over four months – or four thin columns on my planner – which meant we had to move like we had a purpose. We had sixteen weeks to prepare for the trip and get ourselves in shape. Attempting the Great Divide in thirty-seven days meant we would have to cover anywhere between sixty and one hundred miles each day. I had ridden these kinds of distances before, but never on consecutive days, so it was time to test our mettle.

Our acid test was to be the Wessex Way, the longest off-road, coast-to-coast mountain bike ride in Britain. The route links some of the oldest ridge roads and cart tracks in Europe, taking the traveller 250 miles across the ancient kingdom of its namesake. It begins in Weston in the southwest and extends as far as Eastbourne in the southeast. If we could complete it in three days we would be on target, if not then we would be scuppered. (With hindsight it probably would have been wise to attempt this prior to handing over our hard-earned cash to the airline – but that would have been logical).

On a cold March morning, whilst the seaside town of Weston was still asleep, we set off from the Grand Pier. After only a few turns of the cranks we were pulling off the tarmac and onto the bridleway leading up Worlebury Hill. In doing so we left the Bristol Channel behind and with a bit of luck the next expanse of water we'd encounter would be the English Channel at the end of our journey. Despite the laden bikes, we covered our planned eighty miles on the first day and were in relatively good spirits. That is until the first night's camp. It was a cold one, well at least for me it was. JK was cocooned in his brand new three-season down sleeping bag whilst mine was a few seasons short of the mark. In my quest for lightness I had sacrificed a bit of comfort and with hindsight I would have gladly traded half-a-kilo for a couple of degrees of warmth. In the morning I bartered with JK for the use of his duvet jacket for the following night. It cost me a couple of *Mars* bars but it seemed a small price to pay. *Mental note #1: pack a warmer sleeping bag next time.*

Riding across Golden Ball Hill at sunrise was an inspiring experience and I readily forgot the discomfort of the previous night's camp. With my morale boosted we set about our task of getting another eighty miles on the odometer. We were adapting well to life on the trail, especially the alfresco fare which generally consisted of petrol station snacks. Fortunately I had been given the carte blanche by my waistline to eat all of the chocolate I wanted because my legs were burning it off. Again we completed our planned eighty miles with few impediments, but the camp proved irksome: JK"s sleeping bag was conspicuous by its absence. It was originally riding piggy-bag atop my rack pack. Now there was just my rack pack – the sleeping bag must have abandoned ship somewhere along the trail.

345

Instantly I interpreted the situation: no duvet jacket for me tonight. *Mental note #2: securely lash down mental note #1.*

The following morning my motivation for finishing the route in three days had changed somewhat; originally it was to prove that we were up for the Great Divide, now it was to avoid another cold night without a sleeping bag. Judging by the pace that JK had set off he was also inspired by the prospect of not having to camp again. We frenetically covered the remaining ninety miles and arrived in Eastbourne as it was getting dark. Yet apart from my sleeping bag *faux pas* and our need to cram as much food into our stomachs as possible, we were in good shape and I was quietly impressed by our performance. Then, without so much as a word, JK sprinted off into the night in search of food. I just managed to stick on his wheel all of the way to a late night greasy spoon where we systematically worked our way through the menu. As I got up after our protracted refectory break I felt a twinge in my knee, no doubt brought about by the reckless sprinting that was not becoming of a man of my years. Little did I know it then, but it was the beginning of an injury that was going to give me some concern.

Indeed my knee injury kicked in for earnest the next morning to such an extent that it meant that I would have to put my training on hold for a few weeks. Actually that is not strictly true. I had read somewhere that polar explorers fattened up before their expeditions in order to counteract the vast amounts of energy they would expend. I took this as read and during my physical lay-off I set about my dietary training with all the vigour of someone half my age.

I learned two major things during my Wessex Way assignment: firstly equipment choice was paramount, and secondly my arse hurt after consecutive days on the trail. The first issue was pretty straightforward to sort out – most of the kit I already owned was suitable and for the one or two upgrades I needed, I didn't mind asking for help. But whom do you ask about the arse thing? I spent half an hour one Saturday morning in the embrocation section of my local cycling shop. Like a teenager in a chemist I felt distinctly uneasy and was trying to work out what to say to the assistant when a booming voice over my right shoulder nearly startled me into knocking down a precarious pyramid of liniments.

"Don't bother with them, waste o'money".

I spun round to see a fit, weather-beaten veteran in full cycling regalia, who looked like he'd been cycling for the last fifty years – without ever stopping.

346

"Oh, right, yeah, I mean erm…" I nervously stammered.

"Never used t'stuff. Y'should take a leaf out the experts' book," he said trying to make eye contact with me.

"Who are the experts?" I asked, looking up sheepishly.

"The nippers", he replied, as if I should automatically know what he was on about, "…they are happy to sit in their own solids and fluids all day. Get yourself some nappy cream from *Boots* and fettle it around y'bits," he bellowed whilst gesticulating the process.

His ample decibels and hand actions drew the attention of a few customers, and a member of staff who looked at us in a scornful librarian-like manner.

"Right. I will. Thanks," I murmured and made my exit under the contemptuous glower of the shop assistant.

Fortunately, acquiring the cycling equipment was a far easier experience, socially speaking, than the nappy cream debacle, but was somewhat more destructive money-wise. My initial assessment of my existing kit being up to the task was naive in the extreme. To be honest it probably would have sufficed, but once I had entered the mesmerising world of outdoor-equipment I was a goner. I had no idea that this marvellous parallel universe existed.

For some reason I had always assumed that technological advances in equipment, whatever the discipline, were driven by the space-exploration industry and that the stuff that us mere mortals use in our day-to-day life such as *Teflon* were scraps left over from NASA"s table. But it appears that this is not the case. Instead it turns out that it has been the outdoor-equipment industry that has been silently pushing the technological envelope all these years. The proof is the vast array of new materials and gizmos bearing esoteric names: *3-ply Gortex, GPS, carbonfibre-Kevlar laminate, Primaloft,* and my personal favourite: *checktheamountandenteryourPIN.*

I am what the commission-based outdoor-salesman has been waiting for his entire career and when I walked into my local outdoors shop I was about to make someone reach their monthly targets in one fell swoop with minimum effort.

"Excuse me, can you tell me why this jacket is twice as expensive as this one?" I asked holding up what appeared to be two identical jackets. I might as well have said "Hi, my name is Rich Pickings".

According to his name badge I was dealing with Peter and it appeared that our Peter was no ordinary salesman. Ladies and gentlemen I was in the presence of an Executive Sales Assistant. He looked at me like I had asked him what century we were in.

"The one in your right hand is more waterproof than the one in your left", came his succinct reply.

I thought for a minute. Surely something is either waterproof or it isn't; it is not the sort of thing that can be placed on a continuum. I said as much, and regrettably with too much aloofness. I was shot down in flames with a verbatim retort of the manufacturer's catalogue blurb. It all sounded very impressive.

"I'm sorry, which one did you say was the best?" I asked Peter when he had finished his rendition.

"The one in your right hand".

"Thanks I'll take it".

As a result of a protracted Internet-based spending spree I received a deluge of parcels of varying sizes which I opened with all the zeal of a child on Christmas morning. I also found myself in a financial stranglehold. The initial £535 for the flight was in a way, like a non-returnable deposit and it helped me galvanise my actions towards the trip. However, as I purchased more and more items it became more and more like a money extraction scam. One morning whilst reading the papers I was startled by the parallels of an article about a bunch of fraudsters who conned unsuspecting investors to part with their money. The idea behind the scam was to ask for a moderate amount of cash and promise a decent return in a year's time. The following year the fraudsters would inform the investors of the large sum that was owed to them, however to relinquish this sum the investors would have to cough up a 10% liberating fee. The process was repeated several times (substituting liberating fee with administration charges and so on) until, even though the investors suspected foul play, they had put so much money into the scam they couldn't afford to pull out and call it a day. Some lost their homes in the process. My scam however was a little less thought out as it involved me talking myself out of large sums of money and handing it over to other businesses.

The most difficult aspect was deciding what to take. There seems to be two schools of thought when it comes to packing for the Great Divide - to take a trailer, or not take a trailer. Having used a trailer once before I was dead set against the idea. The situation was very similar to our proposed ride, a hapless friend and myself had embarked on a doomed round-the-world trip on, wait for it, a tandem (I know it sounds like folly now, but at the time it seemed like the most appropriate mode of transport). The tandem with the trailer attached handled like an oil tanker and after negotiating each turn the whole contraption would wobble and resonate for an age afterwards. This caused a noticeable shearing effect and I hold it chiefly responsible for snapping the tandem in half about a hundred kilometres outside of Istanbul. Fortunately it happened near a petrol station and not having a penny between us we were forced to think on our feet. With careful preparation and using various propping aides we managed to lean the tandem against a wall so that it looked like a complete bike. We then proceeded to trade the steed for a bottle of *Coke*, a few bags of crisps and a packet of chocolate digestives with an unsuspecting petrol station attendant. He was blissfully unaware of the dud that he had acquired and seemed extremely pleased with the transaction. Indeed he overtly wore the self-satisfying body language of a master dealer who had duped an unwitting customer. "Ha, there's one born every minute," I thought to myself trying to conceal a smug smirk.

Before our cover was blown we managed to flag down a lift to the city. We quickly threw our belongings into the back of the car and hurriedly instructed the driver to pull away. Through the rear window I watched the tandem and its new owner disappear into the distance and as soon as I was sure we were a safe distance away from any reprisals a warm wave of one-upmanship washed over me. I unwrapped our newly acquired biscuits and bit into a horribly stale, dud digestive biscuit. There's one born every minute.

Another reason I dislike trailers is because they are heavy, cumbersome, require extra spares and they encourage you to pack more stuff, purely because you can. Moreover, in his record-setting attempt, John Stamstad went *sans* trailer, so it was clearly the way to go.

To carry my gear I opted for a bar bag, a frame bag and an Ortllieb waterproof sausage bag that fitted atop my rear rack. This minimal carrying space meant that everything I packed was chosen on merit. There were no luxuries, just essentials. My pride and joy was an *Airborne* titanium bike frame called *Corsair*, it was to be the heart of my bike to which everything – including my dream – was to be fastened.

Epilogue:

Preparations completed... there had to be a last minute screw up waiting to be discovered?

Great Divide race undertaken – in sunny weather we embarked upon a 2500 mile cycle, nice.

1st memorable event ... Complete strangers going out of their way to help.

2nd memorable event... Camping in the desert

3rd memorable event... Realising I had put JK's cycling shorts on by mistake!

Final word of advice; there is a danger that some people might spend too long planning for things and never do them.

Chapter 29

[North] Korean Odyssey

Paul Hall

HAVING RECOVERED FULLY from my Russian Hospital experience (Hall, 2009) I decided that it was time for a break, and the opportunity arose in the form of an email invitation from the FIG to conduct an Olympic Solidarity course in Korea. In my haste in packing for a training camp in Hungary I neglected to read the small print and happily accepted the work. The confirmation came back and I consulted the Atlas to find Pyongyang. Ah well, North Korea can't be so bad, I thought; at least it will be an experience- a little voice was telling me that I had just had one of those in Moscow but I failed to listen.

Now getting into North Korea is not the easiest of tasks and no amount of searching the internet would yield a possibility to purchase tickets. After much research I discovered that the best option (other than cancelling) would be to fly to Beijing and then transfer to the domestic airline, Air Koryo, for the one and a half hour trip to Pyongyang. Since being unable to book flights over the net I sought assurances from the Korean Gymnastic Federation who duly reserved a seat and told me to contact Mr Hong, their representative, upon arrival in Beijing. After confirming that, as a transit passenger, I would not need a Chinese Visa, my secretary set about the unenviable task of obtaining me a North Korean Visa, while I relaxed (with my passport) near Budapest. Clearly an impossible task, long suffering secretary had to wait for my return late in the evening before travelling to the embassy in London with my documents to get the necessary paperwork sorted. We met at Kings Cross with just hours to the Beijing flight and, with trepidation, I set off for the airport, armed with chocolate, chewing gum and trail mix.

I must say a few words about Air Koryo. Internet research showed this company to be one of only 2 airlines in the world with a one star rating. Sharing this honour with Air Burundi or something similar meant Air Koryo were banned from European airspace due to an appalling safety record and lack of regard for accepted world practice in aviation procedure. The entire fleet seemed to be made up of 1950 reject Tupolevs from the former Soviet Union. My curiosity aroused I read some passenger comments which went along the lines of "Don't eat the meat as I cannot say exactly what it is", and "The cabin crew have no seats and hold on to the luggage lockers during take off and landing. This is principally for their stability but also stops a lot of the luggage from falling out". I was certainly heading for an experience.

Heathrow passed without incident, although the check in clerk was sure I needed a Chinese visa and was amazed that I was in transit to North Korea. "Why go there?" she asked, and I nodded in agreement. Fortunately I had picked the only direct flight from London and the 10 hours passed in the usual miasma of video wakefulness and awkward sleep. My first time in China would be rather brief since the transfer was only one and a half hours, I resolved to be quick off the plane to ensure a smooth connection. Alas, all went pear shaped at Chinese Immigration.

"You no have Chinee Veeza, you no come in".

"But I go to North Korea," I replied.

"Show me ticket preez". The girl was not budging.

"I have to call Mr Hong and he will give me ticket."

"No ticket, no come in." She moved on to the next passenger.

I sat at the desk and watched the precious minutes slip by, and wondered about my baggage gliding alone around the carousel. The number for Mr Hong was unobtainable and I considered my options: Take the next flight home, get a Chinese Visa and enjoy Beijing for a few days, or push a little more for the transfer. Not liking to be defeated I chose the latter, and asked every officer around for some help. At last a lady contacted the Air Koryo desk to verify that I did, indeed, have a reservation. With just 20 minutes to go before departure a flustered steward ran in to state that it was impossible to make the connection and that I would have to wait 3 days for the next flight.

352

"Please try, I can run fast" I told him.

"Ok, but your luggage come later" he replied.

Who needs clothes, I thought, and decided to take a chance.

We ran, he gave me the ticket and just before boarding hit me with the catch:

"Preez pay me 340 US Dollars for ticket- cash".

"No, I don't have this money, my Federation will pay". I was hopeful.

A few choice Chinese expletives later and my ticket was removed as the last few passengers boarded the plane. It was pouring with rain and I was happy to miss the one star flight on a slippery runway. Again, the gods intervened, a phone call was made by somebody, and I was thrown into the plane, the only westerner in a sea of dark hair and shirts, all bearing the picture badge of Kim Jong Il.

Boarding Air Koryo is a real experience- air conditioning has not developed to the same extent as most other airlines, and the sight of dry ice pouring from the ceiling to make a smoke filled fuselage made for a very unnerving start. Through the mist I saw passengers huddled together for warmth and chatting nonchalantly at what must be an everyday occurrence. I was shown to a seat and duly fastened a seat belt that would not connect, try as I might. The stewardess announced a 30 minute delay due to a flooded runway and I sank back in my seat, trying to remember some policy numbers. I would have written my Last Will and Testament on the back of the sick bag but, of course, there was nothing, not even a safety card. Que sera and all that, and I settled in to listen to the musical dirge that was to extol the virtues of the historical triumphant Leader for the duration of the flight. I took the in flight meal, more out of curiosity than hunger, and tried to enjoy sipping the boiled water whilst staring down at some form of noodles with unidentifiable pieces of meat poking out rather unappetisingly. I moved the food about in order to fool the stewardess that I had tried, and settled down to sleep. After 90 minutes I sighted land and gained my first impressions of North Korea.

Rather green and surprisingly mountainous, I could have been over Wales, I thought. The similarity quickly disappeared as rows of paddy fields full of people ankle deep in water came into view. Dirt track roads with not a car in sight crossed muddy fields that led off into small dwellings where peasants clung to life and the edge of the hill. Horses, carts, hand ploughs, and a distinct lack of tarmac compounded the feeling of going back in time. The landing was surprisingly smooth on a strip in the middle of a field. We taxied to the terminal, a run down shack of a building with a gigantic photo of the Historical Triumphant Leader and one of his inspirational statements. I thought about Tony Blair as a totalitarian dictator with his face plastered over giant billboards around Britain and felt rather relieved that he was happy to play the role without feeding his ego in such a conspicuous fashion.

Passport duly stamped I was elated to see that my luggage was one of the first off the carousel, and I moved optimistically to what I considered to be the Nothing to Declare channel. One full body search later and I found my mobile phone confiscated, to be returned (hopefully) on my exit from the Country. My computer was greatly scrutinised and my videos went off together with my bag to be further checked. 30 minutes later and I was free to go, minus phone and a certain amount of dignity. I was met outside by my driver, an interpreter - Mr Li, and a government official - Mr Gip, who were to be my escorts for the entire duration of the trip. Their omnipresence was to become so overwhelming that later in the week I came to expect that they would all appear from behind the toilet seat during one of my more personal moments. We shared pleasantries for the short ride to the hotel.

"How many people in Pyongyang?" I asked.

"About 2 million," came the reply.

I noted the complete lack of vehicles on the road;

"How many have cars?"

"A few hundred, mostly heroes of the State and people in high office" Li answered. "Also, no driving at weekends unless special circumstance, due to fuel shortages". I was getting the gist of this City and continued my surreal trip on empty motorways 3 lanes wide.

We arrived at the Hotel in the Sports District of the City, a monstrous 30 storey brown edifice that towered shabbily over less towering shabby towers. A grand entrance hall was in near darkness and I was led to reception and given my key.

"Please be careful Mr Hall, electricity shortages mean that we do not always have good lighting. And please use only the left hand of the 4 elevators as the others are for our own citizens and are not always reliable."

"Sounds great," I smiled thinly.

"Your room is on the 15th floor. Hot water is available from 8 to 9.30 in the evening and please be careful on your balcony". Nervously, I climbed into the lift and was pleased to escape onto the lobby of the 15th floor. I noticed that my apartment had two doors, one could be opened and locked with a key, the other had no lock and a little pressure would gain access. Both opened into my bedroom. I was pleased to find a study area with a desk and a fridge in the corner. The fridge was empty apart from a few friendly spores that were busy multiplying on the food shelves. I decided to forget about the mini bar and checked out the bedroom. All seemed well, a double bed and a TV that sat in the corner, a giant relic of pre soviet technological supremacy. I soon discovered that the mattress which looked very much like a mattress was, in fact, a large piece of wood wrapped in a mattress cover with a one inch blanket on the top. The floor was more forgiving but I am made of stronger stuff and shunned the carpet for the rigours of the bed.

Due to the power shortages forced upon us by the tyrannical American regime the area had low energy light bulbs which occasionally spluttered ineffectively to produce a candle like glow in this cavern of a room. I powered up the computer in order to gain a little more illumination and gazed at the tasteful brown décor, woodchip paper and complete absence of decoration. The balcony moved, I'm sure it did, and I nervously peered over the edge at wooded hills, a golf driving range, and a kennel with 8 hungry dogs looking malevolently at my rickety balcony, the only obstacle between them and foreign food. As the week wore on the number of dogs seemed to decrease, adding to my unease over the gastronomy of this establishment.

I apologise if I'm sounding paranoid but this Country seems to do that to you. Sleeping in a room that anybody can enter makes one nervous, as does not being able to leave the building alone, and moving everywhere with three officials watching your every move. They were friendly enough and were extremely polite in insisting that they would take my camera and make photos of me in the best parts of Pyongyang, rather than risk me using it unaided. I waited for eight o clock and hot water, and sank into a miniscule bath to wash away the journey and stretch my tired limbs. One of many power cuts began and I lay in total darkness listening for every sound until the lights went on to allow me the luxury of unpacking clothes and seeing where to put them.

A short while later a meeting was arranged in the hotel lobby with the Secretary General of the North Korean Olympic Committee, a serious man with a piercing stare and a soft tone that, I sensed, belied a steely resolve. We agreed to focus on the theoretical lectures with a practical day in the gymnasium on Thursday. Mr Li requested updates on the Code of Points together with the latest gymnastics information from the rest of the world. He seemed very guarded and unable to share the smallest of insights into his gymnastic culture.

"How many gymnasts do you have?"

"We have many."

"How many hours do they train?"

"They train every day."

"Do you have any potential Olympians?"

"Yes."

"Have any westerners visited your gymnastic facility before?"

"No."

And so it went. North Korea has already produced an Olympic Pommel Horse Champion in Pae Gil Su and I resolved to try to find out as much as possible about this most secretive of gymnastic organisations.

The following morning I was woken at 8am, which seemed very much like 2am, but I forced myself into some clothes and made my way to the restaurant in the serviceable foreigners lift that only I was permitted to use. I estimated that the hotel capacity was around 800 people but there could not have been more than 50 residents during my stay, and I did not see any other western faces. Three large restaurants were situated on the mezzanine floor, and I was in foreigner's room number one- the only diner in a palatial ballroom set up for what looked like a wedding feast for 200. Two beautiful waitresses fussed around moving chairs and plates and treating me like royalty. Their command of English became one of my few sources of entertainment.

"What rood you rike to drink?"

"Tea please," I answered.

"Tea please," Came the reply.

"What rood you rike to eat?"

"What do you suggest?" I ventured.

"Solly we no have dat. We have beefa soup and rice"

"Sounds great," I smiled.

"Sounds great?" They repeated, scanning the menu for clues.

"Don't worry," I replied.

"Don't worry?" They turned to page 2 for information.

"Beefa soup and rice," I tried.

The girls smiled broadly and scuttled off to the kitchens, returning after 5 minutes with my breakfast.

"Sounds great," the waitress smiled as she placed the beefa soup on the table along with a small cup of tea please. I was having fun. Later in the week I was emboldened enough to point to an item on the menu and ask for gnats piss.

"Gnats piss?" She questioned.

"Yes," I smiled and out it came, perfectly pronounced. I downed my gnats piss which bore a passing resemblance to chicken soup and looked forward to many more local delicacies.

At 0930 I was driven, along with my three chaperones, to the sports palace for the opening ceremony and first lecture: latest trends and developments in modern gymnastics. The building was in true socialist style, an ancient birthday cake of a structure that housed hundreds of offices and the ubiquitous cultural theatre for major events. I walked into a large lecture room and met the 30 delegates sitting in hushed silence, no doubt eagerly anticipating the novelty of a western voice. The proceedings were opened very formally and I launched into my usual spiel and found the audience extremely attentive. I quickly realised that this closed system was desperate for any information from outside and, during the break, the coaches swarmed around my computer like vultures sizing up their prey. I told them I was happy to provide a copy of my lectures and within seconds a computer specialist appeared who worked frantically on my aging laptop in an effort to download the info. My videos were taken away to be "checked" and I was conscious that every nugget of information was trying to be pulled from my notes. I quickly resumed control of the captured laptop and set about scrutinizing the copying process for fear of losing all my work. The lecture was well received and I was escorted back for lunch.

I could cope with Korean food but the sheer lack of variety made me dream about infidel capitalist Macdonalds. Breakfast was cucumber salad with chicken and meat purporting to be beef, lunch was chicken soup and rice with beef, and fish, while supper was beef soup and chicken with rice, and fish. There was no let up in the variety of servings of chicken, beef, rice, and fish, not even at the start of the day. The smiling waitresses and their clumsy English provided the only entertainment, other than the colossal television that sat in the corner to regale me with propaganda during every meal. I watched endless black and white movies of heroic soldiers single handedly grenading an entire army, smiling women ecstatically pulling tractors out of water filled ditches, and parades of thousands of jubilant people singing and praising their historic triumphant leader. There was no respite, no foreign pictures, no news, only women on the edge of orgasm singing passionately in fields full of apples that the great leader had provided for his nation. The same melodic song rang out every day against a backdrop of snow capped mountains and fields laden with crops being picked by over eager peasants. The words flashed up karaoke style at the bottom of the screen and I found myself, on occasion, singing along, such was the overwhelming totality of the message. My TV in the hotel showed more of the same on 30 channels with only 2 working and at chosen times. I longed for Big Brother but got gifted 5 year olds singing about their glorious parents fighting at the front, or lovestruck ladies bidding farewell to their patriotic men as they march off to the steel factory, a spring in their step despite having to spend fourteen hours on shift feeding a furnace- no job too great for the historical triumphant leader.

Even what little children's TV I saw contained the same message. Imagine the teletubbies dressed as soldiers and going off to rescue tinky winky who had been captured by those evil foreign invaders, the Americans. This televised message was further compounded by numerous gigantic posters attached to buildings around the city that spoke of freedom, independence, and the armed struggle. At 5pm every day I would finish my lectures and come out of the building into a big square containing hundreds of schoolchildren. Loudspeakers would be belting out the same song I'd heard at breakfast, peppered with emotionally charged speeches about ploughing fields and working for the motherland. I visited a 70 metre tower topped by a huge torch and was regaled with more information by a passionate tour guide dressed as a meringue.

"This is a monument to our great illustrious leader, Kim Il Sung, to commemorate his 70th birthday and to celebrate his heroic triumphant victory over the illegal oppression of the Japanese during the 20 years war. It is 70 metres high and each wall has 70 lotus flowers to remind us of his great birthday. There are 35 edges on the 2 corners which add up to 70, and 10 columns of different granite reach in 7 metre phases which also corresponds with his wonderful age." You get the message.

During my stay I tried, on numerous occasions, to dig deeper into the psyche of the people, to find their true thoughts, but was unable to see beyond this passion for their heritage. Everybody I spoke to was immensely loyal to Kim Il Song, nobody saw the rigours of a difficult life or the lack of ability to leave the Country as a problem, and all were proud to be Korean. They hated the Japanese for the occupation from 1925-45, and they hated the Americans for the 3 year war at the beginning of the 50s which, incidentally, they did not lose, but forced a ceasefire that still stands now. The war goes on until the yanks apologise.

Joking apart, these are a proud and loyal people and amongst the most intellectual I have ever met. The sheer lack of entertainment makes study and homework an attractive option for all children. The work ethic is high-six days per week with Sundays off for reading or enjoying the nature. The children are at school in the mornings and then come home to more study. There is never a need, I'm sure, to scream at them to switch off the TV. I saw the most gifted of children, any of whom could have walked away with the "Britain's Got Talent" award had they been born on our shores. 5 year olds playing incredible violin or singing with beautiful intonation, young pianists sat at a dozen grand pianos playing Rachmaninov, and incredible groups of dancers performing with such synchronicity that I would have expected some computer trickery had this been a more polished presentation. I was truly impressed. The discipline and quiet determination of this Nation was in direct opposition to the sloth and excess of ours.

359

Meanwhile, the gymnastics went on. This was a course like no other and I found myself lecturing to a group of extremely knowledgeable people, in some areas far in advance of any western ideas. The question and answer sessions were my closest insight to the amount of resources a communist government can plough into sport:

"I am the fatigue medicine doctor. What medicines do your doctors in England have to delay the onset of fatigue in your gymnasts?"

"How many scientists do you have in your facility and how often do they conduct testing?"

"What measures do you have for the intensity of work during the medium and high level loading macrocycles?"

You try answering them. Not wishing to let my cover slip that we were a two bit gymnastic nation that was severely underfunded by central government, I found myself being rather enigmatic and evasive with my responses. It suited the Koreans who took this to be my reluctance to yield capitalist secrets and an enjoyable time was spent on both sides trying to elicit the magic gymnastic formula from each opposing system. Their government had pushed a great deal of resources in the way of sport and I was taken down an avenue of dedicated facilities for all Olympic Sports, each with banks of coaches, doctors, biometricians, interpreters, and various scientists, all dedicated to the smallest chance of producing an Olympic medal. I was privileged to meet a childhood hero, Mr Pae Gil Su, Olympic and three times World Champion on Pommel Horse. This was a humble man that seemed entirely grateful to the State for his apartment, a generous pension and his ageing Toyota car. Korea may be deficient in some areas but they know how to look after their Olympians. The gymnasium housed a full international competition standard arena, complete with podium and brand new apparatus. While peasants slapped around in paddy fields a group of gymnasts were being supported by at least 30 professional staff who would cover every statistic in order to optimise the training regime. This was an invincible gymnastic machine.

At last, my week was up and I enjoyed a sumptuous farewell meal in the karaoke bar of the hotel. The Secretary General seemed genuinely overwhelmed by my generosity and assistance with their gymnastic programme, and I felt great friendship and unity at the end of my trip. A memorable experience, albeit rather different.......

References

Hall, P. (2009) Hospitalisation Moscow Style, *CASUALSKI.* In, Palmer, C. (Ed.) *The sporting image: sports poetry and creative writing.* Published by the Centre for Research Informed Teaching, University of Central Lancashire, Preston, UK. ISBN: 978-0-9562343-2-2

Available online from Amazon.co.uk, Play.com and other good bookshops.

See also:
Hall, P. and Palmer, C. (2008) Unfolding events at the Beijing Olympics 2008 – public diary of a gymnastics coach. *Journal of Qualitative Research in Sports Studies*, 2, 1, 143-160 . ISSN: 1754-2375 (Peer Reviewed).

Available online at: http://www.writenow.ac.uk/QRSS/Vol2.html

Chapter 30

Addendum, Appendix, Addi-on bit

WARNING: If you are interested in teaching PE don't read this

"Rose tinted torture and the tale of Wayne Lacey: Physical Education, a force for good at Bash Street School"

Clive Palmer

Prologue:

The chapter in the introduction, *Essex boys can't write* presents a potted biographical history written in a stylised fashion, from which many avenues of deeper investigation may be possible. In the vein of personal reflection and story telling, what follows is the journey down one such avenue. The chapter *Essex boys can't write* briefly sketched episodes from my early school-life through to military service and eventually into Higher Education where the tale stops for convenience. Along this dimly lit path, many of these off-shoots of my experience may have been worthy of closer inspection; I decided to 'shine my torch' upon some experiences in Physical Education whilst at school in Essex during the 1970s-80s. My intention is to reveal in much deeper and richer detail, some formative memories of my education which might have some resonance with others at some level which was not appropriate in the Introduction section. By framing these chapters as reflective writing which are progressively linked and delving in greater detail they become auto-ethnographic in nature; a form of research writing which in turn may permit greater opportunities to explore and comprehend human experience (Sparkes and Silvennoinen, 1999; Sparkes, 2009). The research standpoint seemingly begs that the narrative is questioned to recognise its limitations, which, once identified may be turned advantageously into potential areas of new investigation. Consequently, the Epilogue to this chapter attempts to outline some limitations and opportunities for further research stemming from this personal account.

THE HEAD OF PHYSICAL EDUCATION AT BASH STREET SCHOOL ran a tight ship. It is probably better for all that he remains nameless, not only to protect him, even the guilty need protection however ignorant they may have been, but to protect my sanity in recollecting this story. A generous soul, he shared his attention equally amongst most of the boys during their time in school – as any good teacher might do? For the purposes of this tale I shall call him Mr. Williams. A pirate captain from another world with a parrot on his shoulder called "chip", he always let the boys 'choose' what they wanted to do in his lessons.

"D'you wanna do PE boys, or get whacked with the Whacking Stick?" he'd ask.

It was a foregone conclusion what the immediate future held in store if someone had a note from parents to excuse them from PE, or had even forgotten a bit of kit, let alone have no kit with them at all. The whacking stick was the usual means of persuasion to help pupils remember their things or to participate next time, notwithstanding plaster casts. WHACK. He was very proud of his whacking device, which was a cross between a cricket bat and something that a baker might use to retrieve pizzas from a hot oven. It was just flexible enough to whip and heavy enough to smack huge red squares on the backs of legs and other soft target areas.

"It has good whacking momentum" he used to explain as he swished the implement around in the air striding towards the fleshy back-sides lined up in the PE corridor. The victims knew the routine,

"Where's yer kit son?"

"No kit Sir."

"Where's yer note son?"

"No note Sir..."

WHACK,

"Go and put these on, ready to go in two minutes"

"Yes Sir, thank you Sir".

Piles of rugby shirts still damp from the rain and sweat from the previous classes gave a stale and musty backdrop to the noises of impact and whimper, as Mr. Williams expertly wielded his weapon of choice, accurately

364

finding its target with every swipe. WHACK. A line of folded boys waited to learn their lessons. WHACK. He was a good shot I will give him that, and this end of business in PE was always swift. WHACK.

"Stay there lad you are owed another from last week, bend over", WHACK.

Technique is everything and practice makes perfect. WHACK. The torque generated through his muscular forearm on the wind-up was impressive and the power was transferred to the stick through a wrist action that was too fast for the naked eye to appreciate. WHACK. Like a tennis player striking their ace, a firm but flexible grip seemed to be the key of his professional delivery. WHACK. Having benefitted from this warming sensation on many occasions I can vouch for its effectiveness and over-use for no apparent good reason. Because my brother and I are twins and were in the same class we were often whacked in case he got confused about who he was talking to. He seemed to fear that his public confusion over our names might make him look silly – other pupils might laugh at his mistake which could translate as them laughing at him. The potential for the loss of control in his class to two fourteen year olds was considerable, as if we might have 'one over' on him which could dilute the sense of power which he held over all things PE. All he had to do was ask who we were - if he was confused, if he really cared which I doubt. My brother and I were often whacked as a preventative measure to warn off any twinny-mischievousness that we might be plotting. We often did "plot" of course but our swapping missions were much too subtle and well executed for him to actually notice. A waste of time really. It mattered little because we got whacked anyway; it was our way of scoring something back I suppose.

As an aside, Mr. Williams did share his pedagogical wisdom for *preventative public torture and humiliation* with a few selected staff who he felt he could trust. It worked for him, why not others? Now, the third year (Year 9 in National Curriculum speak) may be a difficult year for pupils and staff at any secondary school. I appreciate that now and did at the time. Being stuck in the middle of a five year 'sea' of schooling can be very distressing for all parties when the deckhands are out of sight of land. Once land is sighted though, perhaps a Sixth Form College or a hint of employment they seem to get on better at school with more focus in their lives. And yes, perhaps some of Mr. Williams' crew had a duty to keep us focused while we drifted. But not by flogging. Mr. Williams appeared to have informed the metalwork teacher about the preventative whacking metered out to the twinny-boys in case they digressed and may have urged the metalwork teacher to give it a try if he got the chance. As luck would have it we were on our options year and enjoying a term in the engineering department. Six weeks of woodwork followed by six weeks of metalwork and so the rotation went on throughout the year testing a range of vocational subjects. It was our first ever time in these industrial environments and it was all very exciting. There were big lathes and milling machines and hot casting facilities, it all looked great. Based upon the experience in these introductory classes we were supposed to select what we would like to study at GCE/O Level (GCSEs in current parlance). These were important career decisions, or so it seemed at the time and I was looking forward to being taught how to use this stuff. On our very first lesson the metalwork teacher was giving the class an introduction. Health and safety was obviously very high on the agenda if we were all to have an enjoyable time in his class - we had better listen. No problems there, I was with him all the way... until. The twinny's were ordered to stand just outside the workshop in an open area but where all the class could see us through the glass doors. With a swagger the metalwork teacher skipped like Charlie Chaplin holding the metre rule that he'd been swishing about throughout his introduction spiel for the previous 30 minutes.

"Hold your hands out boys," we did as we were told,

WHACK,

WHACK.

"That's just in case," he said, "just to let you know where we stand, ok".

I stared at him in silence.

He was trying to nod and give us the eye as if we might understand each other. He wished to impress upon us what he considered to be an acceptable code of conduct in his classes. He didn't impress me and I detected that he knew he'd screwed up as soon as he'd done it.

"Back to class" he ordered. We obeyed. The options decision was made instantly. We both chose to do woodwork. I never spoke to the metalwork teacher again whilst at school. There seemed little point. I had no respect for him.

Like a good wine the Whacking stick had matured with time. It had been repaired on numerous occasions with the white grip-tape used on the pole vaulting poles. The tape, constructed with woven cloth and backed with
366

glue was wound with overlaps to create ridges for extra strength. When the tape dried out it gave the additional benefit of rasping the skin as the Whacker made contact with soft flesh. It all added to the hot stinging sensation. Nice. Produced by craftsmen it was perfectly weighted and even had the words **WHACKING STICK** printed on it in red - with an exclamation mark. Impressive, indeed, it took many people's breath away. As long as no blood was drawn and there were no visible bruises Mr. Williams could carry on with his 'discipline regime' unhindered. In hindsight it could have been a form of control which he administered stemming from his interpretation of "reasonable force" and being in *loco parentis*, perhaps, or was it just something I had done wrong? (I wondered what might drive such an *angry man* in the school environment to play-out these acts of punishment on children. Might there have been deeper, silent, more taboo aspects to his psyche that was the real beast within? What was his emotional make-up that motivated his actions in school? Was it a façade? Just like make-up, an aggressive cosmetic to mask deeper imperfections. Was he really in control?) In fact, his unique approach to keeping things 'ship-shape' appeared to be sanctioned by the school, as for the Headmaster, there were never any behaviour problems from the PE department. In this regard Mr. Williams was quite the envy of other departments around the school as I now understand things.

Thankfully, after a bout of zealous, red-lined, frenzied whacking the damn thing broke to everyone's relief. This practice had gone on for at least three years to the best of my memory. Mr. Williams used to mourn for his whacking stick and searched in vain for a suitable replacement. He never found one in the rest of my time there. The whacking ceased but I am confident that new forms of punishment would have been devised for the younger pupils below me. Why should they miss out? Either way, we were press-ganged into the PE experience on pain of death, or at least on pain of pain which was guaranteed on a weekly basis.

So we have a measure of the pedagogical attitude and management approach of Mr. William's running of the PE department. However, he was not alone, he had an obedient little crew. There were two rather hapless shipmates helping to keep order on the decks. I think I am confident now, in judging that these two PE staff might have been capable of thinking for themselves when they weren't around Mr. Williams, such may have been the strange spell he had over them. However, upon the threat of mutiny they seemed to stick together as thick as thieves lest the truth about 'preferential' treatment for pupils, via the stick, was made public. The personal, social and professional consequences of breaking the PE teacher's vow of silence was too much for the pirate-sidekicks and in my view they became complicit in the 'torture'. Enjoy the riches of sporting success or walk the plank of shame seemed to be the deal for them. At risk of being melodramatic there seemed to be a sort of gang-member allegiance between the male PE staff. Whilst they may not have wanted to rock the boat for themselves, upset the status quo as it were, they did seem to play along with things and even at times seemed to find it quite entertaining. I am 'glad' this aspect of the education they were charged to provide for me was so amusing for them. Unfortunately I was not 'in' on the joke, only on the receiving end of it and could at times see through their hollow laughs as the corporal punishment was metered out by the Captain. With a wagging finger and a knowing stare he could well be imagined to have said to these pair, "and remember you two, you'll never work in a school in Essex again if you double-cross me".

Before turning to the Wayne Lacey situation, a brief note on the social background of Mr. Williams, from what we as pupils could glean at the time, may help us to understand his style of educating. Indeed, his social genetics may have rendered him pre-programmed to behave in no other way. Perhaps his PE teacher was cruel to him at school? We'll never know. He may have just been doing his best as he saw it. Mr. Williams was a proud South Walian, probably a Valley's man I would say now. He moved from that region with many other teachers who at the time seemed to find gainful employment in sunny Essex. A political irony was a sign of the times. As the then Prime Minister James Callaghan (Labour) MP for Cardiff South East, gave way in 1979 to Maggie Thatcher (Conservative) MP for Finchley in London, the employment prospects in "The Valleys" may not have been quite as 'warm' as they were in Essex. However, an unfortunate challenge (for me) of welcoming these educated people in Essex was trying to understand their Welsh accent. Their strange lingo was confusing for the teenage born-and-bred Essex types at Bash Street School. However, they had moved here to teach us and I think we appreciated that in our own little way.

"I mean like, where'd you come from mate, I mean Sir?" Like we'd understand the answer, we were just making conversation. Mr. Williams may have well come from Timbuktu for all we knew. When he spoke, or even worse when he shouted instructions you were likely to get showered in dribble and spit if you were in range. He spoke so quickly there was little time for him to draw the saliva back into his mouth and he must have had repetitive strain injury from wiping his face in one slarring action with the back of his wrist. Mr. Williams was rugby mad and would become very excitable about that sport in particular. He also had a limp which made him look like a Peg Leg running for the bus when he was in a hurry. He regularly sported black eyes which were probably from his own rugby playing antics and had a girlfriend in the job/unemployment centre which was located over the road to the school. A better example of community networking to cater for the special talents housed in Bash Street School one could not imagine. All in all Mr. Williams was a passionate and determined man who seemed to know what he wanted in life.

It has to be said that Wayne Lacey was not blessed with a name that conjures up an image of strength and resilience in a young man. Not in terms of coping with our PE experiences at the hands of Mr. Williams anyway. This was not his fault. Wayne was in my class having joined us at the school in the second or third year after a family move to the area. He was quiet, good looking, of slim build with longish black hair and long black eyelashes. He smiled a lot, got bullied a lot and wouldn't say boo to a goose. Forever having his dinner money stolen from known thugs in the school may have accounted partly for his weak disposition when in a crowd. After all, a bully has to eat as well you know, they have interests to protect and all that. Wayne was a loner and represented easy pickings. And I, and many others regrettably, failed to protect him. It was just like the "Private Santiago" situation in the film A Few Good Men (1992).

The day of the Wayne Lacey incident was strange and memorable for all the wrong reasons. It was raining hard and if we were lucky the PE lesson might be indoors. This was one of those days. I think it saved the pitches from becoming spoiled before the first fifteen got to them. Usually, when we were in the gymnasium for circuit training the task at the start of the session was to set out the equipment. The "circuit" upon which we were "trained", was more like an army assault course with ladders to scale and ropes to climb, punctuated with sit ups and press ups and shuttle runs. My reasonable sporting prowess meant that I avoided a lot of hassle in this kind of lesson and I looked forward to the rope climb as the most effective means of escape in this regard. My *modus operandi* was to scale it quickly in the minute or so allocated to each bout of exercise. I would then spend the whole time up at the roof looking down on sweaty, toiling bodies and the fatties flailing around pathetically in tears on the bottom of a rope not being particularly encouraged by Mr. Williams' own brand of encouragement. On this rainy day the equipment was already set out by the class before us.

Bonus. The class got in to their black shorts and white t-shirts in the adjacent changing room and then hurried out into the gym to sit obediently at the feet of Mr. Williams. The worst thing was to be last out and then to get shouted at for wasting time and holding everyone up. Like they were in a rush to go anywhere! Every changing room experience was a race to avoid ridicule and bullying. Wayne had not got his kit with him. Whether he'd forgotten it or whether it was stolen from him I do not know.

"C'mon Lacey, get out here now" Mr. Williams demanded from the gymnasium. We were all sat in a neat semi-circular fashion with our backs to the changing room entrance.

C'mon Lacey, get out here right now or I'll..." he was becoming very impatient, there was anger in his voice, and Wayne was on his own in the changing room.

"God help me son if I don't... if are you refusing me? Are you? Eh? What the hell are you doing in there? get out here right now" he shouted.

Wayne appeared at the changing room door and walked into the gym in his school uniform. We all looked round at him. He was stood absolutely still, in quiescence, petrified like a statue but cast in flesh and blood. There was no expression on his face although we could see a tear running down his cheek. His eyes seeming not to blink as he stared straight at Mr. Williams. A pregnant pause and Mr. Williams was gesturing 'disgust' with his hands but speechless at the sight before him; his jaw moving but no sounds coming out. Wayne's urine was running freely now down the back of his legs which soaked into his cheap, black nylon trousers and filtered through his socks on to the wooden varnished floor. He stood motionless in his warm self made puddle of piss. He continued to stare into space and then began to shake and look very nervous indeed.

"Ah Lacey you useless... what have you done that for you... get out of my sight, you..."

Wayne ran out of the gym to the changing room. I remember walking out to see if he was ok. I saw him put his shoes on, he had his back to me. Then he turned and looked at me with a gentle smile on his face as he walked out. It was the smile he wore for everyone, including foes. It was a flimsy line of defence but it was the only one he had. He was lost, he was harmless, he wouldn't say boo to goose, he just wanted a friend. I never saw him again.

I learned a lot from Wayne Lacey's PE experiences that day, as I am sure he did, all for the wrong reasons of course, I hope he is ok.

The End.

Epilogue: the chaos of teenage years

This chapter, indeed much of the book, is aimed at Sports and Physical Education students who are on journeys of reading for a degree and training for their careers. This raises two questions; how might this chapter be considered to be studious research writing and, how might it be useful to them? To the former there are a number of limitations within the story to acknowledge and importantly, a raft of new opportunities to be recognised which could constitute a more detailed ethnographic investigation of the lived experience in education. To the latter, that it has been a demanding tale to write; a less than comfortable experience of reflection and recollection which has even been cathartic one might say but it is hoped that the reader might identify with some of these experiences. For aspirant PE teachers and sports coaches, it is hoped that the *Bash Street School* account might inform their pedagogical viewpoint as an example of what not to do.

One limitation of this chapter has been my strategy to be highly selective about the facts for the purposes of telling a "good" story. Notwithstanding that the tactic may have been appropriate in the context of this creative writing book, there may be many more 'facts' to be taken into consideration for a full account of the lived experienced as described – if that is possible or desirable to do at all?

The above is a polarised snapshot of events, interpreted and stylised to give flavour and richness to a story about a handful of characters at *Bash Street School*. To imbue with a sense of drama and conflict the story leaves out many important details about PE and the broader educational experience on offer at school such as my having really quite a happy and enjoyable time there filled with challenges and friendship. This could even be similar for Wayne but in truth is probably less so. A happy tale could be a very dull story to tell! The reader may judge for themselves when I might have used devises in writing such as overplay and caricature to divert attention, mask identities or make light of serious issues for dramatic effect. I have also used descriptive writing and repetition to bring 'texture' to actual events, to relive them in a way that is faithful to my experiences.

A further limitation to acknowledge is that these are the reflections of a 14-year-old pupil from thirty years ago. The mists of time and the hormone swamp of adolescence may have swayed things in my memory during the chaos of the teenage years. I have also learned a great deal since then about what might qualify as "good", "valuable" and "worthwhile" in a physical education experience which could be the motivation for writing the passage in the first place, but could also effect my interpretation of events. The reader is requested to permit some leeway here. However, it raises the challenge of how any personal account might be interpreted for research purposes. Reflective accounts may manifest themselves in a variety of ways including feedback forms, diaries, interviews, questionnaires and stories passed down through the generations. A limitation of this tale as research into my education at *Bash Street School* is that I was only ever offered a pupil's-eye view of events. By definition that was my role there, a pupil, and it was from that perspective that I wrote this account. I know no other. (This perceived limitation may be a field research opportunity in a researcher's quest for clarity and knowledge about a situation). Naturally, I was not privy to any details concerning Wayne's learning and teaching needs although I am confident that he had some. So, what counts as data? And what might the researcher need to acknowledge about the data itself, the data source and the context of collecting that information in their search for authenticity and understanding about a social situation? These may be useful questions to address to inform a qualitative investigation.

The PE staff at *Bash Street School* were dedicated people, all of whom, particularly Mr. Williams went way beyond the call of duty for a teacher to "do good" for us as he saw it at the time. Of this I am sure and for this I am extremely grateful. I benefitted hugely in my life from him and the PE staff's efforts to do something well. Where might I be now if they had not bothered or cared about sport? – or me? If they had done nothing or been insignificant in my life there may be no story tell for us to learn from.

Whilst the story may be a brief, selective and extremely biased view of mine, I feel it is my duty now to make sense of the experiences they created for me at school. However if this account were part of a wider research project Mr. Williams' memories of these events might, or would, rightly be sought. In this case they are not. Further opportunities for data collection towards a more balanced and comprehensive picture might include investigating;

what were the views and opinions of other pupils at the time, and perhaps those of other staff at the school? Other's views about me as a pupil, of Wayne, and of the Whacking Stick? How was Mr Williams regarded by other members of staff? Was PE really just a chance for school thugs to excel and stay out of trouble? Did my success in PE erode other teacher's views of me as pupil who was serious about his non-PE subjects? How was the status of PE as a subject regarded by other subject teachers? All these may be worthy topics for further research as a matter of personal history – but they also begin to have much closer relevance to topics under discussion in contemporary Physical Education.

My interpretation of Mr Williams' and his staff's style of education has logically affected what I know now and has been affected by what I have learned since school. In my current career as a teacher I have learned more about education; in particular Physical Education and Sports Pedagogy, and have developed my own views on how to go about things in the classroom setting. However, just because I would try to avoid repeating what I now regard as their mistakes, does not mean that what they did at the time was regarded as wrong, on the contrary it seemed to be exactly the right thing to be doing as far as the school hierarchy judged things then. These considerations may also be pathways of further investigation.

In closing, however, there is rarely "smoke without fire" and the reader is invited to judge whether the twists and turns of this story could fabricated from "thin air". Is it purely a fictitious account for the purposes of entertainment? Probably not. Whilst it has been enjoyable to reminisce about my experiences in PE; the Whacking Stick and Wayne Lacey, it has not been an entirely comfortable writing exercise. If the PE experience at *Bash Street School* was this memorable then maybe it was a profound and even worthwhile learning experience for me.

Thank you for reading.

References

Sparkes, A.C. and Silvennoinen, M. (Eds.) (1999) *Talking bodies – men's narratives of the body and sport.* Jyvaskyla University Printing House, SoPhi, Finland.

Sparkes, A.C. (2009) Novel ethnographic representations and the dilemmas of judgement. *Ethnography and Education*, 4, 3, 301-319.

Lightning Source UK Ltd.
Milton Keynes UK
UKOW041250160212

187387UK00002B/23/P